STATELESS

Also by Elizabeth Wein

The Enigma Game

Code Name Verity

Rose Under Fire

The Pearl Thief

Black Dove, White Raven

STATELESS

ELIZABETH WEIN

LITTLE, BROWN AND COMPANY
New York   Boston

Little, Brown and Company
Hachette Book Group
1290 Avenue of the Americas, New York, NY 10104
Visit us at LBYR.com

Simultaneously published in 2023 by Bloomsbury Publishing in the UK and Penguin Random House Canada
First US Edition: March 2023

Little, Brown and Company is a division of Hachette Book Group, Inc. The Little, Brown name and logo are trademarks of Hachette Book Group, Inc.

The publisher is not responsible for websites (or their content) that are not owned by the publisher.

Library of Congress Cataloging-in-Publication Data TK

ISBNs: 978-0-316-59124-9 (hardcover), 978-0-316-59125-6 (ebook)

Printed in the United States of America

CW

10 9 8 7 6 5 4 3 2 1

For Elizabeth,
still writing at the other
end of the table

Spread Map TK

No man is an island, entire of itself; every man is a piece of the continent, a part of the main; if a clod be washed away by the sea, Europe is the less, as well as if a promontory were, as well as if a manor of thy friends or of thine own were; any man's death diminishes me, because I am involved in mankind; and therefore never send to know for whom the bell tolls; it tolls for thee.

—*JOHN DONNE*

CIRCUIT OF NATIONS OLYMPICS OF THE AIR

—◇—

~ EUROPE'S FIRST YOUTH AIR RACE ~

22–30 August 1937

Promoting Peace Through Sport
Among Our Young People Today

THE RACE CONTESTANTS, BY NATION:

KINGDOM OF BELGIUM:
> Master Gaby Dupont, age 17, flying a Tipsy B

CZECHOSLOVAK REPUBLIC (CZECHOSLOVAKIA):
> Master Jiri Jindra, age 17, flying a Beneš-Mráz Bibi

FRENCH REPUBLIC (FRANCE):
> Master Antoine Robert, age 19, flying a Hanriot 436

GERMAN REICH (GERMANY):
> Second Lieutenant Sebastian Rainer, age 19, flying a
> Bücker Bü-131 Jungmann

KINGDOM OF GREECE:
> Master Philippos Gekas, age 20, flying an Avro Tutor

KINGDOM OF ITALY:
> Master Vittorio Pavesi, age 18, flying a Breda Ba-25

KINGDOM OF THE NETHERLANDS:
> Master Willem van Leer, age 16, flying a Koolhoven FK-46

KINGDOM OF NORWAY:
> Master Erlend Pettersen, age 20, flying a Breda Ba-25

REPUBLIC OF POLAND:
> Sub-Lieutenant Stefan Chudek, age 19, flying an RWD-8

KINGDOM OF SWEDEN:
> Master Torsten Stromberg, age 20, flying a Raab-Katzenstein
> RK-26 Tigerschwalbe (Tigerswallow)

SWISS CONFEDERATION (SWITZERLAND):
Master Theodor Vogt, age 18, flying a Bücker
Bü-131 Jungmann

UNITED KINGDOM OF GREAT BRITAIN AND
NORTHERN IRELAND:
Miss Stella North, age 17, flying an Avro Cadet

THE CHAPERONES:

DIANA STEPNEY-MILTON, LADY FRITH
The United Kingdom, flying a de Havilland Dragon Rapide

MAJOR FLORIAN ROSENGART
Germany, flying an Albatros L-75 Ace

CAPITANO ERNESTO RANZA
Italy, flying a Breda Ba-33

CAPITAINE MARCEL BAZILLE
France, flying a Hanriot 436

THE RACE DESTINATIONS, STARTING FROM SALISBURY, ENGLAND (OLD SARUM AIRFIELD):

BRUSSELS, BELGIUM (MONT DES BERGERS AIRFIELD, CHARLEROI)

GENEVA, SWITZERLAND (COINTRIN AIRPORT)

VENICE, ITALY (NICELLI AERODROME, LIDO)

PRAGUE, CZECHOSLOVAKIA (RUZYNĚ AERODROME)

HAMBURG, GERMANY (HAMBURG AIRPORT)

AMSTERDAM, THE NETHERLANDS (SCHIPHOL AERODROME)

PARIS, FRANCE (LE BOURGET AIRPORT)

PART ONE

WASHED AWAY
BY THE SEA

Saturday, 21 August–
Monday, 23 August, 1937

PART ONE

No Parachute
Salisbury, England

I didn't realize those vultures were going to see me as fresh meat until it was too late.

I pulled up to park at the end of the line of visiting aircraft, brought my aeroplane to a stop, and cut the engine. I couldn't start it again without someone swinging the propeller for me.

"It's Stella North! I say, chaps, it's Britain's own 'North Star,' here at last!"

"The Flying English Rose!"

One of the reporters was hatless and without a jacket, his shirtsleeves rolled up, informal and swaggering. "May we call you Northie, like your flight instructor?"

The moment I took off my goggles and leather flying helmet, the man leaped up onto the lower wing of my borrowed Avro Cadet bi-plane and leaned into the open cockpit. He grabbed my hand.

"Welcome to Old Sarum Airfield! You're the eighth to arrive! We know you're committed to an exclusive interview with the *Daily Comet*, but would you mind answering just a few informal questions about Europe's first-ever youth air race? How do you feel about being the only girl in the competition? Didn't your guardian give an interview objecting to your participation?"

I pulled my hand away with a vicious tug and unclipped my parachute without saying anything.

The hatless reporter laughed. "Some kid! Are you sure you're the right person to represent Britain in an international competition?"

I pressed my lips together tightly.

I wasn't at all sure.

By sending my application to the flashy and formidable race organizer, Lady Frith, I'd deliberately disobeyed my adoptive parents. Aunt Marie was tearful and melodramatic: *It would break your dead mother's heart, dirtying your hands and face with engine oil, sleeping in rented rooms with a dozen strange young men all over Europe!* Uncle Max played the proud exiled aristocrat: *You owe no loyalty to the King of England. As soon as the Bolsheviks are out of power we will go back to Petrograd.*

As if he hadn't been saying the same thing for nearly fifteen years! Even I could see that the Soviet Union was never going to let them come back.

England was my home. It meant the world to me that I was representing Britain in this race—"uniting nations through aviation," as Lady Frith put it. But I dreaded the press finding out that their "Flying English Rose" left Russia as a refugee at the age of three and wasn't technically a subject of the King.

Other reporters were pelting me with questions now. I wondered how I was going to escape this crowd.

"Don't you wish there was another girl besides yourself flying in the Circuit of Nations Olympics of the Air? How do you feel about the participation of pilots from Nazi Germany? Will the stop in Hamburg be your first visit to the German Reich?"

It would, and I was burning to prove myself a better pilot than the young German Luftwaffe air force officer I'd be racing against. But I dared not say anything so ambitious in public.

"Lady Frith's planned your route through seven major European cities, so why isn't she starting the race from London? D'you think you're meeting here at Old Sarum to impress the Germans with the strength of Britain's Royal Air Force?"

I protested through clenched teeth. "I really couldn't say."

Two men in gray fedora hats climbed up on the lower wing on my other side, supporting themselves by hanging on to the upper wing struts like trapeze artists. I felt the jerk as the plane took their unexpected weight. The swaggering hatless man who'd shaken my hand waved a notebook at me. "Just quickly, Northie, are you going to perform in the air show in Paris after the awards ceremony?"

A fourth journalist jumped up alongside him. "Have you met any of the other racers yet? They're a handsome bunch, aren't they? Aren't you worried about unwanted advances? What about you being one of the youngest contestants? Or at seventeen do you feel you have more flight experi—"

"*Get off my wings!*" I bellowed at them all.

I scrambled to stand on my parachute on the seat. "Get off! *Get off!* The wings aren't strong enough to hold all of you! *GET OFF! You'll break my wings and I won't be able to race!*"

I hit out at the notebook in the swaggering journalist's hand and sent it flying. He gave a grunt of angry surprise and jumped to the ground to retrieve it.

I could feel my face getting hot. *Hell's bells*, what would he write about me now? *The Flying English Rose has got nasty thorns—*

But I had to protect my plane, at any cost.

"*GET OFF!*" I yelled wildly.

They climbed down from the wings, but I was trapped in my cockpit like a finch in a cage surrounded by cats. Two dozen reporters crowded against the sides of the plane, jarring it, all shouting for my attention at once.

"Tell us, Northie, have you conquered your fear of crossing the Alps?"

"Don't you think it's unfair that the Belgian contestant is being allowed to fly a specially modified machine?"

"How do you feel about the Swedish racer breaking his fiancée's nose?"

My mouth dropped open and snapped shut again. I hadn't known that. Was it true, or were they trying to frighten me? Or both?

The hatless journalist in shirtsleeves lowered his voice, suddenly coaxing, "Would you say something inspiring for our women readers who'd like to learn to fly? It's so unnatural for a young girl to put herself in danger. Most women haven't the strength nor the endurance nor the knowledge of a man when it comes to flying an aeroplane. Aren't you worried that someone will try to sabotage your machine, as happened to some of the planes in the 1929 Women's Air Derby in America? Wing wires corroded with acid—fire in the baggage compartment?"

Now I was sure he was trying to scare me.

But I was beginning to feel ridiculous about being so tight-lipped. I tucked my stopwatch and its chain into my jacket pocket and folded my map into my flight bag, trying to appear collected and unruffled. Then I looked up and met the man's eyes. I raised one hand to hush them, and they went expectantly quiet.

"I've fulfilled exactly the same requirements as all the other contestants," I said coldly. "And you probably know that Louise Thaden and Blanche Noyes competed against men and *won*, almost exactly one year ago, in the American speed race. So women *can* fly and be good at it."

They all bent their heads, scribbling in silence, until someone piped up earnestly: "Oh, *thank you*, Northie, and can you also tell us what you'll be wearing to the Valedictory Banquet tonight?"

Now they'd managed to make me self-conscious about what I looked like, in addition to being desperately worried about my plane and trying not to let distrust of my fellow contestants go galloping away with me. Blast it, did they really want to know about my *clothes*? I gasped in annoyance at the silly question and pushed untidy hair out of my eyes with one hand. The ribbon that was supposed to tie back my hair had pulled loose when I'd taken off my flying helmet.

I wished I was back in the air.

Standing on my parachute in the Cadet's open cockpit, holding on to the upper wing for balance, I was above this rabble, but the moment I climbed out of the plane and set my feet on the ground, it would be like opening the finch's cage and letting the cats do their worst.

Why were these scavengers even allowed near the landing aircraft? There ought to be guards about, or at least policemen, someone associated with the army communication school that operated here. Where were the chaperones who were supposed to be looking out for me and the other eleven young pilots flying in that afternoon? Where was the race organizer and patron, Lady Frith, the leading lady in this pantomime?

The aggressive reporter who'd asked the menacing question about sabotage thought he had my attention now. He said smoothly, "Northie, is it true you don't hold a British passport?"

"I have a passport!" I snapped in wild alarm. "I am *English* and I have a passport."

Cameras whirred and clicked and there I was, captured on film with my guard down, my hair flying every which way like the mane of a shaggy Shetland pony, my mouth open and my eyes wide with guilt, caught. An impostor.

I had to escape them somehow. I absolutely had to get away from them.

It seemed like there was an entire ocean of worn grass separating me from the sanctuary of the Old Sarum hangars and offices. There were dozens more people over there; I could see one or two in flight gear, probably my competition. I glanced over at the plane parked next to me. It was another bi-plane with upper and lower wings painted exactly the same color as mine, a fresh forest green. But the F on its tail showed it was from France.

A tall man in a coverall flight suit was standing by the plane's nose, carefully winding the propeller. His skin was dark and his hair was just beginning to be dusted with silver, though his face was still youthfully unlined. There weren't many Black people in southern England, and I knew from photographs that this must be the French chaperone, Capitaine Marcel Bazille.

The race chaperones, who would escort the racers in their own aircraft along the same course, were experienced pilots, aviation heroes. Apart from Lady Frith, the first woman to fly solo from Portugal to the Azores, all of them were flying aces of the Great War. Capitaine Bazille was also a doctor of veterinary medicine and the mayor of his town. No doubt the reporters had been hounding this extraordinary man too, just before I pulled up. He'd had to wait until the crowd moved back before he could start the other plane's engine, so the propeller didn't kill anybody when it suddenly leaped to life.

I could just see another head in the pilot's cockpit of the French plane, his face hidden beneath a leather flying helmet and goggles like mine. He was leaning out around his windscreen to watch the chaperone.

That must be the French race contestant—one of my competitors.

As I watched, Capitaine Bazille cried out, "*Contact!*"

The reporters around me all swiveled their heads to look, as if they were watching a tennis match.

"*Contact!*" the pilot in the plane yelled back.

Capitaine Bazille swung the propeller and jumped aside. Then, as the engine roared, no one could hear anything else. The reporters all backed away, clutching their hats and notebooks in the sudden wind of the whirling propeller.

There was an acre of grass airfield between me and Old Sarum's military buildings. But there were only a couple of paces between my own wingtips and those of the French plane, and the startled reporters had now left me a gap to get between them.

Hanging on to my helmet and goggles, I snatched up my flight bag and swung down from my cockpit. As the French plane began to roll forward, I hurled myself across to it, leaped onto the wing, and scrambled into the empty passenger seat in front of the French pilot.

———◇———

The pilot leaned forward over his windscreen, right behind me, and shook me roughly by the shoulder.

"Get out of my plane!" he yelled in my ear, in English.

The plane was veering sideways over the grass because he'd had to take his feet off the rudder and brake pedals to be able to reach me. There were controls in the front cockpit, too, and I straightened the plane with my own feet. He sat back down and his voice seemed farther away, over the sound of the engine.

"This is a test flight! Get out!"

I gave him a thumbs-up, pretending I couldn't hear. I pulled on my helmet and goggles and strapped myself into the safety harness. The pilot behind me idled the engine so that I couldn't help but hear him yelling at the back of my head.

"Get out of my plane! What in tarnation do you think you're doing? Sizing up the competition?"

He didn't sound the least bit French. His fluent English had a twangy drawl that reminded me of Hollywood. American— that was it.

"I'm getting away from those blasted reporters!" I yelled back. "You owe me a favor! You couldn't have got your engine

8

started if they hadn't left your chaperone alone to go after me. Go ahead with your flight! I won't touch anything!"

"The heck you'll touch anything," he growled. "You'll regret it if you do. And I don't owe you a wooden nickel."

I glanced back over my shoulder. Capitaine Bazille had his hand on one of the reporter's arms, holding him back. The French pilot must have seen it too, because he agreed irritably, "I want to get out of here and I'm not gonna waste time arguing. Those skunks aren't my friends either."

He thumbed his nose at the reporters waving their hats and notebooks at us, then increased the engine's power. That was the end of our conversation—we couldn't say anything to each other over the noise.

But the French pilot told me a lot about himself just by the way he handled his aircraft.

I could hardly believe how fast he taxied, bumping over the grass field as if he were making a getaway from a bank robbery. It wasn't reckless: it was hard, controlled speed. On the ground the plane's nose pointed at the sky, so the French pilot had to zigzag to taxi because he couldn't see straight ahead of him; his sharp turns threw me roughly from side to side. He was going so fast that the very second he turned into the wind I felt the wings lift.

Around us, disturbed skylarks soared out of the long grass at the edge of the airfield, and we soared with them into a blue and gold late-summer afternoon sky, almost straight into the air, effortless. I had the impression that the plane was flying itself—that the French pilot didn't have to think about the takeoff any more than the skylarks did.

This was my competition. My heart sank. If all the other

racers flew like this, I was going to be completely out of my depth.

As I pulled the unfamiliar harness tighter and made sure my flight bag was secure, I realized in alarm that I'd left my parachute in my own plane.

I gripped the sides of my seat so I wouldn't be tempted to touch the flight controls. I wondered what his "test flight" would include.

We climbed only to about five hundred feet, not very high, and passed over Old Sarum's fleet of Fighter Command Hector bi-planes. For the past few years the Royal Air Force had been grimly expanding bases that could protect England if the Nazi government in Germany tried to get aggressive. Alongside these military machines, the racing aircraft stood out boldly, all different types, small and gaudy.

We left the airfield. The ancient green mound at Old Sarum, crowned by its ruined castle, dropped below us. We reached the river Avon, and then the pilot turned so steeply that it took my breath away. For a moment I was afraid we'd dive into the thousand-year-old ruins. But he leveled out smoothly and began to follow the river.

Within five minutes we were over Stonehenge.

It was obviously what he'd been aiming for. It was incredible to look down on from five hundred feet overhead. The late afternoon sunlight cast long shadows behind the old stones, their heavy arches painted in strokes of light and dark against the green summer grass, the wide ring of markers around them making the whole landscape look like a giant ancient sundial.

I wished I'd flown here by myself, on my way over from my

home airfield at White Waltham. It would have been an easy detour. But I'd been so focused on the race I hadn't thought for a moment about touring.

The French pilot circled around the great stone circle in the golden light for longer than it had taken to fly there, holding his plane in a steep turn so steady and perfect that he caught up with his own slipstream and it buffeted the wings as we came around. The view was breathtaking.

Then suddenly he broke out of the turn and began to climb. The roar of the engine was deafening. We rose steadily higher and higher, two thousand, three thousand, four thousand feet above the ground. And then he pushed the nose down and we were diving, plunging so fast it felt like my insides were being rearranged. The wind sliced at my cheeks as we plummeted toward the stones and the earth below and—he *knew* I didn't have a parachute.

With another jolt to my guts he pulled the nose up. Now his plane was thundering aloft again with the engine roaring, and I realized he was going to loop. As far as he knew I might not have even strapped myself in.

He was reckless and arrogant and oh, I *hated him*.

I wasn't scared and I was damned if I'd let him think that I was, especially if he was *trying* to scare me. He was obviously a better flier than I was, and there wasn't anything I could do about his showing off—I wasn't an aerobatic pilot and it would have been suicide to try to control the plane myself. So I just gave him a fierce thumbs-up, so he'd know I realized what he was doing, and let him get on with it.

Then we were upside down and for a split second

Stonehenge was above me, and a moment later it vanished beneath the edge of the upper wing. The engine cut and we swooped dizzyingly earthward in silence. Instead of finishing the loop, he let the wing spin—now we were spinning down toward the stone circle, and then suddenly we weren't, and he leveled the wings.

He gave a whoop. *"Fantastic!"*

It was beautiful. It was *magnificent.*

The engine roared back to life and he began to climb again, and I realized he wasn't thinking about me at *all.* He didn't care in the slightest whether I was scared by his showing off, or even impressed.

He was flying because he loved it, soaring in long, exuberant loops through a golden August sky over Stonehenge.

A Man of Many Nations

Twenty minutes later, the reckless French pilot slipped his plane in steeply to land back at Old Sarum. Dazzled by the exuberance of his aerobatics, stomach swooping again at the plunging rate of his descent, I had to sit on my hands to prevent them from trying to grab the flight controls. It had been a long time since I'd been a passenger in someone else's plane.

But he landed with scarcely a bump, as lightly as he'd taken off. His flight skills were simply breathtaking.

I braced myself for another battle with the reporters. But, thank heaven, they were no longer swarming around the racing planes. They'd been herded to a roped-off area by the hangars, like sheep rounded up for shearing, with a couple of uniformed men directing them like Border collies. Only one man waited by my Cadet, just at its wingtip, shading his eyes against the sun as he watched us approach over the grass.

It wasn't Capitaine Bazille. This was a white man about the same age as Bazille, with thick, short, gray hair that gleamed like silver. He frowned critically as he watched the French pilot edging his plane back into the space next to my Cadet. When we were only a few paces away from him, I could see that the frowning man's eyes were the same intense blue as the large, clear gem he wore in the lapel of his blazer, and I realized that I knew who he was. This was the Blue Topaz, another legendary flying ace of the Great War—Major Florian Rosengart, the German chaperone.

I couldn't tell if he was looking at me or the French pilot. But he was surely wondering what I was doing in the other racer's plane.

I didn't think I'd violated any of the competition rules, but I wasn't sure. As the French pilot shut down his engine, I managed to scramble out of my seat ahead of him. I jumped from the lower wing of the French plane onto the short grass, dropped my gear at my feet, and pushed the loose hair back from my face. Then I held out my hand to the German chaperone.

"Major Rosengart, I'm Stella North."

Good form forced him to accept the handshake of an unfamiliar young lady without showing disapproval. The frown vanished smoothly, and his thin, bony hand was warm and firm as it gripped mine.

"Miss Stella North!" He greeted me in accented English, with a smile of welcome. "But this is a French aircraft you are flying? I am confused."

14

"That's my plane behind you," I explained quickly. "I've just been along with the French racer on a test flight. I joined him to get away from the reporters—there were so many of them, and I panicked."

The French boy tossed his own gear out onto the lower wing of his plane and began climbing out himself. "And she better not have touched anything in the front cockpit," he growled.

Major Rosengart looked past me, at him, and let go of my hand.

"You know this man?" he asked.

"Not at all!" I shook my head. "There wasn't any other way to escape from that mob, and I just jumped into the nearest plane. It was a very silly thing to do." Ugh, I hadn't thought about how the press might report my joyride with the French pilot. *Northie Gets Cozy with the Competition!* I didn't want to think about it. "I hope I haven't broken any rules," I said soberly.

"I don't believe you have," Major Rosengart answered. "But perhaps it was not wise." Then he turned all his attention on the French pilot. He spoke with careful precision, as if he were thinking hard about choosing his words in English. "And so—" said Major Rosengart. "So you are Antoine Robert."

This was the first time I was actually able to take a look at Monsieur Antoine Robert.

He was stockily built, with hair the brown-gold of old honey. His hair was a little too long to be quite respectable, and after our wild ride it now stood in a dozen different tufty directions. His old-fashioned French flight jacket came down to his hips and was belted at the waist like a tunic; the leather

15

was so worn it looked like something had been gnawing at it. He had thick, square brows over clear, gray-green eyes.

He said gruffly, "Yes, I'm Antoine Robert, but I go by Tony Roberts. My mother is American; she calls me Tony."

"I am pleased to meet you," said Major Rosengart. He stood still another moment, then took a step forward with his hand out. "Yes, I am pleased."

His bright blue eyes met Tony's, and they held each other's gaze the whole time they were solemnly shaking hands, as if they were sealing an unspoken challenge.

"You fly for France," said Major Rosengart. "You are an instructor at a French flight school. Nevertheless I believe we are countrymen? You were raised in Germany?"

"*Ja, mein Major,*" Tony said, with a little polite bow of his head, never lowering his eyes. "But I learned to fly in America and Spain."

"*Spain!*" The word came out almost as an explosion, as if he hated the place. "Yes, so I understand. You learned to fly before the war began there, and now that there is war, you have fled to France. Remarkable." Major Rosengart nodded. "You see, Miss North, your opponent is a man of many nations."

"*I didn't flee—*" Tony began, then shut himself up with an audible click of his teeth. He looked away, breathing hard, and pulled himself together. He tossed his head back to get the hair out of his eyes and said defiantly, "Yes, well, it wasn't fun when the Fascists started bombing Madrid last year, and there's no sign of the siege letting up, so here I am."

"Tony Roberts." Major Rosengart repeated the name carefully. "Lady Frith says you introduced yourself this way when you landed here earlier this afternoon. Why did you take off again?"

Tony became the first to look away. He sounded suddenly childish as he admitted sheepishly, "I wanted to see Stonehenge."

Major Rosengart turned back to me with another swift, pleasant smile and said in apology, "Forgive me, Miss North, I am impolite not to give my attention to you as well. But I am not pleased about this excursion. When the race is underway, there will be no unauthorized flights."

He faced Tony once more, and accused, "You left Miss North's aircraft here unattended amid a crowd who might have damaged it, which could well be to your advantage when the race begins tomorrow morning. I trust you intend no harm to another racer or to another racer's aircraft."

"I left my own aircraft unattended!" I protested.

"I didn't ask *Miss North* to come along," Tony agreed. "Probably she's the one wondering how to damage *my* plane. *Jehoshaphat!*"

There was a terrible, embarrassing moment of silence. The German chaperone was right about leaving my plane alone with the reporters. That nasty character who'd talked about sabotage could have put a heel through one of my wings the second I left, or done something more sinister that I might not find right away.

Then Major Rosengart scolded Tony coolly, "That is indefensible incivility this early in your competition. You young people can have no reason to wish ill to one another, in a race for peace and sport."

"None but the prize money," said Tony with equal cool.

"Apologize to Miss North."

Tony turned to me and uttered obediently, "I don't wish

17

you the least bit ill." It felt less like an apology than that he was poking gentle fun at Major Rosengart's careful English. "If you'll excuse me, *Miss North*, I'm just going to take a look in the front cockpit and make sure you haven't disconnected anything."

He scrambled back up onto his plane as if he meant business.

Like Tony, now I wanted to check the Cadet inch by inch to make sure nothing was broken.

"I'd better take a look at my plane too," I said to Major Rosengart.

"I will do that for you," he replied, and climbed up lightly on the wing of my Cadet. He lifted out my parachute and handed it out to me, then seated himself in the pilot's cockpit.

I bit my lip in frustration, annoyed. No doubt Major Rosengart felt he was being gallant, but I was just as capable as Tony of checking for damage myself. There wasn't room for both of us up there, so I walked around the outside of the Cadet, running my hands over its fabric wings and body. I couldn't see anything wrong.

But Major Rosengart was thorough. Sitting in the cockpit, he adjusted the seat so it was further back and pushed on the pedals to make the rudder move to and fro. Then he pulled the seat forward and did it again. The ailerons at the edges of the wings fluttered as he made sure they, too, were moving freely.

It wasn't the first time a man had taken a job like this away from me. I stood politely seething in the shadow of my own wings, unable to check the controls myself as long as he was sitting there.

"Miss North, you do not need to wait here," Major

Rosengart called down to me. "Please go meet with Lady Frith in the operations building. She is anxiously awaiting you. There are still four young men yet to arrive, and the Italian contestant is now an hour overdue. It is beginning to be a matter of concern." He gazed for a moment at the sky, as if he expected the missing racer to appear at any second. "It will put Lady Frith's mind at ease to know you have arrived safely."

I didn't doubt him. Lady Frith had promised to take personal responsibility for both my safety and my conduct during the race. She'd done her best to woo Uncle Max and Aunt Marie, inviting them to have tea in her Salisbury manor house, introducing herself as Diana Stepney-Milton rather than using her title, encouraging Aunt Marie to call her Diana. If I did anything out of line it would quickly get back to my aunt and uncle, and I wanted to keep Lady Frith on my side.

"Mr. Roberts, this is an opportunity for you to demonstrate more gentlemanly behavior," Major Rosengart added. Then he went back to his work in the cockpit of my Cadet.

The insolent French boy with the American-sounding name and accent climbed down from his own plane. He glanced at Major Rosengart balefully for a moment, then rolled his eyes and beckoned me with a jerk of his head.

"C'mon," he said gruffly. "I promised *Voici Paris* an interview, and I bet you've got something scheduled with the *Comet*, before we all head over to Lady Frith's fancy dinner. Safety in numbers, right? Let's face the music together."

Tony turned abruptly toward the aerodrome's administration buildings, his flight gear slung over his shoulder.

I took a deep breath, picked up my gear, and headed after him.

"Did you find anything suspicious in your front cockpit?" I asked resentfully.

"Nope."

"I didn't think you would."

"I'm not taking any chances," he said.

"I wouldn't either, if I burned fuel like you do," I told him.

He shrugged. "I'd say Stonehenge was worth it." Suddenly he asked casually, "Is it true what the *Comet* said about you and birds? 'Our English Rose is batty for anything with wings. She learned to fly because she wants wings of her own'! Or did they make that up to warm folks' hearts?"

I swallowed my pride and confessed through gritted teeth, "I did say that about wanting to have wings of my own. I work for the Natural History Museum in London, and I'm a member of the Royal Society for the Protection of Birds. I spent a month last year on a nature reserve in Cheshire, sitting in the rain with field glasses in a hide built of sticks, counting migrating birds. Flying a plane is more challenging and not as wet."

"So you're in this race for the birds?" he asked.

Was he serious?

Lady Frith had promised the triumphant pilot a brand-new Miles Falcon aeroplane, such as won the King's Cup air race in 1935, and *five thousand pounds*. That amount on its own was enough to live on comfortably for at least ten years—if I won, I could go anywhere I wanted, study anything, live in the Galapagos Islands for a year, follow migrating geese around the world—*anything*!

But that wasn't *all* I was in it for. I wanted to prove myself in the sky and on the ground. I wanted men like Major Florian Rosengart to hold me responsible for my *own* actions

20

and to respect me for them. I wanted to prove that an English woman is as good as a German man, or a French man, or any man. I wanted to prove that groundbreaking female fliers like Lady Frith and Amy Johnson weren't just once-in-a-lifetime exceptions.

I wasn't going to tell Tony Roberts any of that.

"Of course I'd like to win," I said deliberately. "Surely we'd all like to win. But I want to win fairly. What's the point, otherwise? We're supposed to be racing in the name of peace."

"Peace!" Tony gave a low, expressive whistle. "*Phew!* The Blue Topaz! I'll bet he has some combat stories, if he's not too starchy to tell them. The Germans and Italians aren't in it for peace. They just want to show off their fancy new planes."

"Well, Lady Frith is doing exactly the same thing," I said. "She's showing off the Royal Air Force's strength in Britain by starting here at Old Sarum."

Tony waved a hand toward the Hector bi-planes. "These dinosaurs!" His casual tone suddenly became sober. "Trust me, Major Florian Rosengart is laughing at them. Germany's new fighters are about a hundred and fifty miles an hour faster than these."

I wasn't sure if he was exaggerating or not.

"Anyway, what are *you* in it for?" I demanded in irritation. "For France?"

"I just feel lucky someone else is paying for me to spend two weeks in the air," he said candidly. "Sure, I could use the money. But I'm in it for the flying."

He turned to look at me for a moment. "Just like you."

I set my face and walked a little faster, not returning his look. I *was* in it for the flying.

But I didn't think I was just like him.

I wondered if the ten other competitors were going to be as self-assured and opinionated as Tony Roberts, or Antoine Robert, or whatever his name was. I wondered if we were *all* going to be as wary of one another, and all as anxious about sabotage.

Civil War

"*Masz ogień? Du feu?* A light?"

The Polish pilot, Stefan Chudek, waved an unlit cigarette at me and the other racers.

We stood on the low steps in front of Salisbury Cathedral, wrathfully eyeing the press photographers who were waiting to snap a formal portrait of us in our evening clothes for the Valedictory Banquet. We'd been told that Vittorio Pavesi, the Italian contestant who was late arriving at Old Sarum, had flown into the airfield at Winchester by mistake, twenty miles to the east. He was still getting dressed while the rest of us left Lady Frith's Elizabethan manor house, Maison-des-Étapes, and crossed the green square to have our picture taken in the gilded light of sunset.

The young men were all sweating in their black woolen jackets and white ties, but I was cold in my first really grown-up evening gown, mallard-blue silk with a plunging neckline and gauzy swinging cap sleeves that left my neck and arms bare. The professional photographers had already set up their equipment and stood nervously checking their watches, glancing in anguish over their shoulders every now and then at the rapidly sinking sun.

Stefan, the Polish pilot, was also an air force officer in his own country. He was thin and full of energy, and such an addicted smoker that the tips of his fingers were permanently stained yellow. His clothes and breath reeked heavily of tobacco; even his white tie and black tailcoat smelled of stale smoke.

Those who were close enough to hear Stefan's request for a light and understand it began to hunt politely for matches in the unfamiliar folds of their evening clothes. With the flair of a magician, the German pilot beat the others to it.

I'd seen his photograph in the newspapers, but in the flesh and wearing formal evening clothes, he made me do a double take: he looked so much like Tony Roberts. They were of a similar stocky build and medium height, both square-jawed. After the first shock of confusion, I saw that this boy was neater and stood straighter, his expression more neutral. He gave a flourish of one hand, and a silver cigarette lighter suddenly flashed between his fingers. I didn't even see him reach into his pocket.

He flicked the lighter with his thumb, and a thin flame appeared in the low evening sunlight warming the cathedral square. He held out the light toward Stefan.

"Thank you," said the Polish pilot, and added in French, *"Merci."*

"I am not French," the other boy corrected seriously.

Then, as if he were asserting his own identity, he said, "I am Sebastian Rainer. I race for the German Reich."

"Oh, you fly the Bücker Jungmann aircraft?" Stefan asked. "I saw you land."

Sebastian nodded. "Yes, and the Swiss contestant flies one like it. It is a good training aircraft, but not the fastest in the competition. What are you flying?"

"Also a trainer, a Polish design, we call it RWD-8. A monoplane, parasol, high wings and open cockpit—"

The rest of us cautiously eavesdropped. This was something we were all interested in—who had the swiftest aircraft, and consequently who was going to be the stiffest competition. Our planes were ordinary tourers and trainers, not specially designed for speed, but some of the machines were sleek new models or had efficient modern engines.

"The Jungmann is powerful, but not as fast as the Breda 25," said Sebastian coolly, glancing over at Erlend Pettersen, the Norwegian.

Then everyone listening eyed him up too. Erlend was unmistakably Scandinavian, with a sunburned, round, fair-skinned face and fluffy untidy hair like a ruffled canary. His Breda 25 could cruise more than twenty miles an hour faster than my Cadet.

"The Italian contestant also flies a Breda 25," Erlend said defensively. "And he is late."

A few of the other pilots snickered.

"What's that plane you fly?" I asked Tony Roberts. It didn't seem particularly flashy or powerful—no more than mine, anyway—but he was obviously a flashy pilot, and I wondered why he'd chosen it.

"It's a Hanriot 436," he said, sounding just as defensive as Erlend. "The French chaperone is flying one just like it. It's a French plane but they fly 'em in Spain; my Spanish flight instructor suggested it."

The German pilot was listening, and now his heavy eyebrows went up. "In Spain!" Sebastian exclaimed, almost exactly as Major Rosengart had done. "Now, while there is a civil war raging? They fly these slow machines in combat?"

Tony gazed at him with contempt. "No, of course not in combat," he said scornfully. "As reconnaissance aircraft. Not dropping bombs on civilians like your Condor Legion planes did at Guernica."

"But what was this bombing at Guernica?" Sebastian asked. "We do not drop bombs on civilians."

Everybody stared at him.

Surely all of Europe, if not the world, knew what had happened at Guernica in Spain last spring.

If Sebastian was trying to start a fight with the other racers, it worked. I forgot about keeping my mouth shut in front of the reporters.

"The bombing was in *April*! Only four months ago!" I cried. "The whole community was burnt! Buildings crushed! Old people and young mothers and horses and dogs—children—*babies*!"

I wasn't the only one who was outraged.

"How have you not heard of *Guernica*?" Erlend, the Norwegian, exclaimed. "It was mostly German pilots who did it, their Condor Legion—the worst headlines of all the war in Spain have been about Guernica!"

Sebastian was silent for a moment. Then, as if his spinal cord were made of ice, he said levelly, "It is not a name I have heard."

I stared at him for another second or two in disbelief. Slowly it dawned on me that Sebastian honestly didn't know. The German newspapers must have told a different story to those of Britain and France and Norway and most of the rest of the world.

Tony Roberts lowered his voice, jerking his head toward the reporters to remind us all how easily anything we uttered could be turned into international gossip. He said to Sebastian, "That's some propaganda machine Mr. Hitler's got going for you in Germany. I guess it's easier to teach air force pilots to fly if you keep 'em in the dark about what they're going to be doing."

Sebastian raised his chin a little in defiant pride. Then he admitted in a low voice, "It is true we see things differently in Germany."

The pressmen couldn't hear what we were saying, but they could see we were snarling at one another. They swarmed closer, hampered by the photographers, and started peppering us with shouted questions.

"D'you think the Italian pilot might be late on purpose? Perhaps he's looking for attention? Do you think it could give him some kind of advantage? Say—has he missed any briefings? Is he—"

"What's it like flying for the air force?" one of the reporters asked Tony Roberts. "Would you say the German Luftwaffe is the best in the world?"

Tony stared at the man blankly.

"Ever try out one of those new Messerschmitt fighter planes?"

Tony took a step back, clenching his fists, a look of wild confusion in his frown.

Sebastian Rainer suddenly stepped forward and gave a little bow. "None of us is a test pilot, so no," he answered gravely. "The Luftwaffe does not entrust its most valuable new machines to mere second lieutenants. But I believe you mistake this man for myself; it is I who race for the German Reich in the Circuit of Nations Olympics of the Air."

There was a collective gasp of understanding and laughter, and cameras clicked. It was a justifiable mistake. Anyone who only knew Sebastian and Tony from their pictures in the papers might easily confuse them.

Now the press pounced on them both.

"Oh, so *you're* Antoine Robert, flying for France! But didn't you live in Spain all through your teens—didn't you take your license at the Aero Popular Flying School in Madrid? What d'you think about the war there? Were you in Madrid when the siege began? What was that like?"

Tony gaped, speechless, at the man who was delivering this barrage.

"Can you tell us anything about those new planes, Leutnant Rainer? The Messerschmitt fighters? How long will it be before you'll be flying them? D'you think you'll have to fly them in combat against the Spanish Republicans?"

"I do not know the answers to those questions," Sebastian responded in his cool, level way. Tony just rolled his eyes ungraciously and shrugged.

"Can we get a photograph of you together? The French and German pilots who look alike, both racing for peace?"

Tony and Sebastian threw each other assessing glances. I remembered that Tony had been raised in Germany; *I believe we are countrymen,* Rosengart had said.

Tony gave a curt nod. Sebastian moved to stand next to him on the wide entry step in front of the cathedral door.

"Please turn to each other—share a look—"

They faced each other grimly, their eyes locked with knowing purpose, as if they were about to fight a duel to the death. The photographers jockeyed for position with one another.

"And have you two met before? Have any of you met before?"

Erlend Pettersen, the tall Norwegian pilot, tossed a few polite, humorous words to the reporters. "The only thing we have done since leaving the aerodrome is to shave and get dressed."

They swarmed around Erlend now. Tony and Sebastian briskly turned away from each other.

"How are you feeling about tomorrow's flight?"

"It is a beautiful evening," said Erlend evasively. "Perhaps the fair weather will last."

"What about the competition?" The questioner glanced over at Torsten Stromberg. Like Erlend, Torsten was a pale-haired Scandinavian, but slender and shortsighted, wearing steel-rimmed spectacles. "Say—" The reporter suddenly pounced on him. "You're the Swedish pilot who broke his fiancée's nose—weren't you going to be disqualified?"

They were terrifyingly accurate at finding our weak spots. I had to bite my lips to keep from sneering.

But their last missile hit home.

Torsten pushed his way past Erlend. Calmly, he snatched the reporter's felt hat from his head and dropped it on the wide stone step. Without a word, he crushed the hat beneath one shining black dress shoe.

Then he turned and kicked the battered hat sharply toward the rest of us. It bounced off the Swiss pilot's chest and landed at the Polish pilot's feet.

Everyone fell silent for a moment. The Swiss pilot abruptly dusted off his dinner jacket.

A rattling symphony of camera shutters erupted around the Swedish pilot. Torsten whipped off his glasses and coolly began to clean them with his handkerchief. The rest of us edged away, out of line and uncooperative; when my back bumped against the cool, rough stone of the cathedral, harsh through the thin silk of my dress, I realized I'd cornered myself.

Capitaine Marcel Bazille took Torsten by the shoulder and led him aside. Major Florian Rosengart was there too, physically placing himself between Torsten and the journalists. I was sure the whole affair was going to get uglier in a moment.

And then the missing Vittorio Pavesi appeared, trotting across the green lawn in front of the cathedral to join us.

Ghoulish Numbers

The reporters turned their attention on Vittorio Pavesi like buzzards, meeting him halfway across the lawn.

Unlike the rest of us, he adored the attention.

He was almost intolerably excited about the race. Gallant in white tie and tails, black hair slicked down with Brylcreem, and sporting a desperate effort at a dashing black mustache on a very childish face, Vittorio threw answers at the newspapermen like a prince scattering gold coins as he came to join us on the cathedral steps.

"No, I am not in the air force yet. Yes, it is true that I am a friend of Bruno Mussolini. Yes, the very one, the son of the dictator! In fact, we have the same birthday, though he is a year older than me—he has already flown in combat in Ethiopia and Spain. The plane I am flying is a gift from Bruno and his father! Of course Mussolini's Fascism has improved Italy!

He is rescuing our economy, and he is an international hero, outlawing enslavement in Ethiopia, providing a model government for Germany and Spain—"

I wanted to slap him across the mouth to shut him up.

I did not know how he could stand there spouting propaganda about trains arriving on time and sunny fields of ripe wheat when his friend Bruno Mussolini was killing barefoot children with explosives. I knew that the Italian Air Force had gassed civilians in Ethiopia last year, and that their bombers had helped the German Luftwaffe destroy Guernica four months ago. I'd seen the newsreels: the Ethiopian emperor begging the League of Nations for help, Spanish refugee children sheltering in tents in English fields, women digging through rubble in the fallen town.

The other boys kept quiet too, hanging back while Vittorio collaborated with our mutual enemy, the tabloid press. I wondered how many of the racers felt the same way I did.

Thank heaven, though, now that Vittorio was here, we were able to line up at last for the group portrait. The photographers shouted directions and the chaperones abruptly arranged us with me in the middle of the front row, right between the look-alike French and German pilots. I bristled at having to get so close to them. But the photographers crowded Tony and Sebastian in on either side of me, making me stand a little at an angle to them, no doubt to outline my shape in the silk gown.

"I say, Northie, would you mind taking off those long gloves for the photograph? It will better show off that ravishing frock if your arms are bare—"

Ugh, why should my ravishing frock and bare skin matter in the least?

But I obediently pulled off my gloves, and Major Rosengart reached out to hold them for me. I couldn't wait to get a little warmer. I hoped vainly that the gooseflesh on my arms wouldn't show up in whatever photograph they printed.

At that moment Lady Frith herself came sailing across the lawn, resplendent in a cloth of gold evening gown.

"Don't move an inch—we must have a photograph with the chaperones as well!" she cried. "What rabble you are—" That was aimed contemptuously at the press. "I did tell you to wait for me!"

Everyone gaped. The race organizer's gown was blinding in the low sun, and attached to her shoulders was an iridescent gauze cape split up the back, so that as she strode hastily toward us it billowed behind her like wings.

"At last, all the Olympics of the Air pilots together in one place!" she cried. "Hurry up now, the Valedictory Banquet is waiting to begin—*no, I am not giving another interview this evening.*" She clapped her hands sharply to command quiet from the pressmen. "One more photograph with myself and the chaperones, and then you've got five minutes to pack up. After that the High Street Gate will be locked and you won't be able to leave the cathedral grounds. Any of you not taking pictures had best clear off now, if you don't want to spend the night on the lawn!"

"That's the stuff," Tony commented under his breath. "You tell 'em, Frith."

A couple of the other racers snickered in appreciation.

We lined up again quickly. The twelve Circuit of Nations Olympics of the Air pilots were captured glaring into the evening sun, standing stiff and elegant for the world to look at, uneasy representatives for peace in Europe.

The men armed only with notebooks tipped their hats to Lady Frith and began to slink away. The cameras snapped one last time, and the photographers hurriedly dismantled their equipment.

Then the rest of us trooped back across the cathedral lawn and into Maison-des-Étapes, where, thank heaven, the press weren't able to come with us.

---◇---

Maison-des-Étapes was a big house but it wasn't a palace. That night Lady Frith hosted all the race contestants in bedrooms on the same floor, two or three boys to a room as if it were a boarding school. I had a room to myself, of course; but we all had to queue in the passage to share a single bathroom.

It was like being behind the scenes at a play, with the young men stripped down to their undershirts. I was in my dressing gown, which I kept firmly tied over my pajamas, trying to be inconspicuous. As the only girl, I was *told* to bring a dressing gown, but none of the others had one; in fact none of them even bothered with slippers, trying to keep the weight of their baggage down for flying. They were mostly in stocking feet or barefoot, except for Tony Roberts, who rather ridiculously still had on his black dress shoes beneath pajama trousers. Sebastian Rainer, the German racer, stood very straight with his leather washbag held under one arm, nervously spinning his toothbrush back and forth between his fingers.

I needn't have worried about anybody looking at me. Every one of us had our eyes on the twirling toothbrush. And in any case, now the boys were talking with bloodthirsty enthusiasm about the chaperones. Peace did not come into it.

"The French flier—Capitaine Bazille—how many aircraft did he cripple in flight in the Great War?" asked Theodor Vogt, the lanky Swiss pilot, whose face was painfully pockmarked by acne. "I think Bazille damaged more than thirty—"

"Ah, but Capitano Ranza, our Italian chaperone, crippled thirty-three," interrupted Vittorio Pavesi with relish.

"*Thirty-three! Phew!*" Tony gave a low whistle, as he'd done earlier, and I remembered that he'd been curious about combat stories. "What about Major Rosengart, the German? The Blue Topaz?"

Vittorio was right there with an answer. "Oh, *Der Blaue Topas*—twenty-six kills. The Allied pilots said Rosengart's eyes were so keen he could fly alongside you and shoot you with his pistol. No enemy in his sight ever escaped."

"He is not as famous as Bazille or Ranza." The Dutch racer, Willem van Leer, spoke suddenly with a fierce intensity that felt somehow defensive, as if he expected everyone to disagree with him. He was a slim, tightly-wound boy with silky black hair. "But Rosengart was in the news again last March, and I think that is why Lady Frith invited him as a chaperone."

"I remember," said Vittorio Pavesi. "It was to do with the civil war in Spain. He worked on the Rocketman Affair!"

"'*Rocketman?*'" Theodor repeated in bafflement. "Oh—you mean *L'Homme de Bombes*."

The Dutch racer said, "I think it is the same. Do you remember what happened? There was a German pilot shot down and captured by the Spanish Republican forces, and they took him to one of their field hospitals—"

He paused to take a breath, and Vittorio picked up the story eagerly: "He was out of his senses after a blow to the head, and he raved about his secret work on jet and rocket development back in Germany. It was other wounded men who called him Rocketman, Spaniards and Russians who hated him because he was fighting against them. He became enraged by their mocking, and he stole a scalpel—"

Tony Roberts gave a derisive snort, and with the heel of one dress shoe he kicked the wall we were all standing against. The baseboard gave off a hollow thud as if he'd hit it with a cricket bat. Everybody jumped. In the silence that followed came a sudden light clatter as Sebastian Rainer's nervous fingers fell still and he dropped his toothbrush. He bent to pick it up again.

Tony muttered suddenly, "Aw, I borrowed cuff buttons from Lady Frith's butler for tonight and forgot to give 'em back."

Abruptly he gave up his place in the queue and thumped back down the stairs at the end of the passage.

I thought he was astonishingly rude. The Rocketman Affair was a vile story that I didn't particularly want to hear again either, but Tony needn't have interrupted and then *left*, however breathlessly annoying Vittorio Pavesi might be.

It didn't take Vittorio long to plunge back in, though, exactly where he'd left off. "—Stole a scalpel and killed them all. And a doctor and a nurse and two nuns! Then he leaped out a window and escaped."

Everybody nodded. The story had been a tabloid sensation

for a while, not actually of international importance but with fascinating public appeal because it had been so horrific. Of course, when the hellish bombing of Guernica happened in April, everyone forgot about the so-called Rocketman going berserk in a hospital ward.

The youthful, high-strung Dutch pilot looked annoyed, no doubt because he himself hadn't been able to get a word in. "What had Major Rosengart to do with it?" he asked irritably.

"The International Criminal Police Commission was called in to investigate," Theodor remembered. "Major Rosengart was one of the detectives."

Sebastian Rainer began twirling his toothbrush again. As we all turned to look at him, he spoke for the first time since we'd left the dinner table.

"They called in Major Rosengart as a flight expert," he corrected coolly. "He was defending the Luftwaffe in a diplomatic role, not investigating the killings."

"He is a policeman, though, is he not?" asked Theodor.

"Yes, he is a policeman," Vittorio confirmed enthusiastically. "It was considered a murder, or I should say several murders, not a war crime. Fourteen dead!"

Thirty-three crippled aircraft, twenty-six kills, fourteen dead—I could not understand why anyone would want to commit these ghoulish numbers to memory. I wished I didn't need to be so cautious about good form, or that I had an excuse to storm off down the stairs after Tony Roberts.

I couldn't wait to be far away from Vittorio Pavesi.

A Dead Straight Line
The English Channel

I was tenth in the departure lineup on the first morning. I got to watch Erlend Pettersen and Vittorio Pavesi set the pace in their Breda 25 bi-planes. They were the fastest machines in the competition and I couldn't believe how much Vittorio's plane looked like mine—same size, same racy forest green, wings the same shape—and yet it was so much *faster*. My heart twisted with envy as the Italian pilot took off.

But as we watched, he turned and began soaring swiftly to the south, flying in a completely different direction than the Norwegian pilot had headed fifteen minutes before him.

The Belgian racer was already in his plane, waiting for the mechanics to start his engine. Capitano Ernesto Ranza, the Italian chaperone, swore softly in his own language. Then he shouted at the Belgian racer.

"*Altolà!* Stop!"

Capitano Ranza gestured to the mechanics. "The Belgian

must wait. Bring the starter over here! I will go next—I will go now. I must follow Vittorio." He ran for his own plane.

"That noisy Italian kid's gone off in the wrong direction again," Tony Roberts commented drily. "I bet he's planned his course the wrong way round."

Nobody laughed. There was a stiff breeze and high clouds, and we knew there was a weather front coming from the west, with rain predicted to arrive later that day. I was anxious to get off the ground while it was still fair, and I thought everybody else probably felt the same way. We all stood watching Vittorio's plane appear to grow smaller, then become a dot, then vanish against the gray sky.

Capitano Ranza leaped into his plane, and the engine roared as the mechanics got it running. He started taxiing out across the airfield ahead of his scheduled departure time, ahead of the Belgian contestant who was supposed to take off next, rushing to get into the air to try to herd Vittorio Pavesi back on course before the hapless Italian race contestant accidentally flew to Paris.

"Gentlemen! Miss North!" Lady Frith gave one of her sharp handclaps to get our attention. "Stop standing there staring at the sky. You have maps and aircraft to check, don't you?" She was again dazzling to look at, wearing a flight suit constructed of quilted silver lamé, cinched at the waist and tight in the chest, cunningly designed to exaggerate her figure and to shine in newspaper photographs. Her waved hair, cut very short in a shingled bob, fit her head like a golden cap. "You may be inexperienced fliers but every one of you is a licensed pilot," she reminded us. "Not a single one of you should be focused on anything but your own departure just now."

The burly Czech pilot, who would be the next to take off after the Belgian, jogged out to his aircraft without saying anything.

But the Swiss pilot with the acne-ravaged skin, Theodor Vogt, turned to Lady Frith and said in a bold rush, "I want to take off before the German."

Each of our takeoff and landing times was to be noted by airport officials, with an extra few minutes figured in as a handicap to the faster planes. Our departures were arranged so that the fastest planes were timed to go first, for safety, to avoid those of us in slower aircraft getting in their way. But here we were, the first morning of the race with only two of twelve contestants in the air, and already the schedule was falling apart.

"The German racer should not depart ahead of me," Theodor insisted. "I am likely to be faster. I am a champion of aerobatics in Switzerland, and Leutnant Rainer is a new pilot trained on gliders without power. I do not want to have to overtake him in the sky if it can be avoided."

"You and Leutnant Rainer are flying exactly the same type of aircraft," Lady Frith responded crisply. "There is a full quarter of an hour between your takeoff times. It is very unlikely you will catch him in the air."

"Perhaps I may discuss it with Major Rosengart?" Theodor asked politely.

Sebastian Rainer agreed in his neutral way, "And I would like to discuss it also."

Now I was getting angry, and I wasn't the only one. This should have happened *yesterday*, or earlier that morning at any rate. If their argument caused a delay, it threatened to affect everybody who went after them. Looking around, I noticed the Greek and Polish pilots muttering to each other in annoyance. None of us wanted to be late leaving and risk getting caught over the English Channel in wind and rain.

The reporters, like crows gathering, also knew that something was up. They'd been banished to the roped-off area by the hangars, and now they seemed to be having a heated argument of their own. I watched the crowd for a minute, wondering what was going on, and saw that someone, a woman, was trying to break away from the rest of them. An airfield official held her back.

She waved wildly and shouted when she saw me.

"Northie! Stella—*Stella!*"

It wasn't a reporter at all. It was Jean Pemberton, the pilot who'd taught me to fly—the woman who'd helped me find my sponsors, who'd drummed up a new plane for me to borrow, and who'd supported my race entry behind the backs of my aunt and uncle, including giving me a new place to live.

"*Jean!*"

I broke away from the other racers and ran. The moment I reached her, the guards let her through the barricade. It was wonderful to feel Jean's wiry arms hugging me.

We walked back to the knot of racers and chaperones together, and Lady Frith came forward to kiss Jean on both cheeks and make her welcome.

"I knew your aunt and uncle weren't going to come say goodbye to you," Jean told me breathlessly, "so I came myself. I thought you needed someone proudly waving the Union Jack as you set out!"

She unrolled a paper sack she was carrying and pulled out a British flag—just a little one, the kind children wave at

41

parades. "This one's for you. I've two more for me, one for each hand. You must fly it from your cockpit in every place you land! I'm determined to see you off, but I have to be back in Maidenhead to give a flight lesson at noon, and the drive takes about an hour and a half. They wouldn't let me fly in, so I had to come by car. And then I got swarmed by those reporters the moment they saw me!"

"They're awful," I confessed. "If I'd known what they'd be like, I might not have sent in my race application."

"Pooh," said Jean airily. "Imagine if Amy Johnson had been put off by reporters! She'd never have made it to Australia." She lowered her voice and added warmly, "Remember your first solo flight, Northie?"

"Gosh, yes. How could I ever forget?"

A lark had flown into my propeller and stopped my engine. I had to make an emergency landing in a farmer's field, the very first time I flew alone.

"Anytime you start to feel angry or envious or uncertain, just remember your first solo," Jean said. "Don't worry about the press. They can't hurt you. And don't worry about all these boys, either—" She swept one of the little flags around her in a dismissive gesture at the other racers. "You're just as good as they are."

"*Thank you*, Jean," I said.

"All the other challenges—crossing the English Channel for the first time, and the Alps—well, those are *exciting*! You'll *love* flying over the world's empty places, the sea and the mountains."

"Jean, you always say exactly the right thing," I exclaimed. "It was just the reporters frustrating me, and the boys counting

42

shot-down aircraft...Never mind, you've reminded me what I'm here for."

Jean laughed, and pressed the flag into my hand. I zipped it inside my flight jacket where I'd be able to keep it secure and still reach it easily.

I started my Avro Cadet's engine for the Circuit of Nations Olympics of the Air at precisely 10:15 a.m. British Summer Time on Sunday, the twenty-second of August, 1937. Skylarks rose all around me from the long grass at the edge of the airfield as I began to taxi, and I waved my British flag defiantly at the clicking cameras.

Then I was safe in the air again at last, alone with the larks and the wind, over the English countryside and out to sea, on my way to France and Belgium.

———◆———

Jean was right. My heart soared as I crossed the coast of Kent and struck out over the open sea for the first time in my flight experience. I could just see France on the horizon, the cliffs like a smear of white paint, growing steadily closer all the time. Alone in the sky, with a whole continent waiting to be explored—it was *wonderful*.

I'd been in the air for just over an hour and a half, and was most of the way across the English Channel, when I saw a winged shadow ahead of me.

At first I thought it was the silhouette of my own plane cast against the sky. But in a moment I realized there were two silhouettes, and they weren't shadows. They were aeroplanes, sharply outlined against ominous, steel-blue clouds. In the distance I could see the white of France's chalk cliffs, the green of fields beyond, and the sprawl of the port at Calais.

The aircraft ahead of me were both bi-planes like my Cadet, their double wings making distinctive and black parallel lines against the clouds. They were too far away for me to see any other color or detail.

I had a few ideas about whose planes they might be. After their argument, Theodor Vogt and Sebastian Rainer had ended up taking off *together*, parallel to each other on the big military airfield, to allow one of them to naturally pull ahead of the other. They might well still be close enough to see each other. And the German chaperone and Tony Roberts, who'd taken off just ahead of me, might be right behind them.

I glanced down at the instrument panel of my own plane. Yes, I was still on course. This first leg of the race was the most straightforward, a dead straight line between Old Sarum Airfield near Salisbury and Mont des Bergers airfield just outside Brussels. In another few minutes I would have flown across the English Channel for the first time *on my own*, like an aviation pioneer, like a swift or swallow or cuckoo on its way south.

I stretched up to glance over the side of the open cockpit and gasped as the wind hit my face. Seen through the glass of my goggles, the sea below me was a sheet of steel-gray silk, polka-dotted with the foamy curls of whitecaps. There wasn't anything wrong with my eyes. But when I ducked back behind the windscreen, I could still see the two planes silhouetted in the sky ahead. One was heading northward just off the coast of France, and the other was descending toward it from above.

Chillingly, they seemed to be flying straight toward each

other, the way I imagined those battle-grim aces coming together in combat in the Great War.

For the first time since I'd taken my license, I forgot to pay attention to my compass heading. I flew straight toward the other planes, using them as navigation points, unable to look away from them.

They were on a collision course. The higher plane seemed to be diving at the lower one on purpose.

It *could* be the Swiss and German pilots, flying their matching Bücker Jungmann training aircraft. In another few seconds they'd smash together—

I shouted into the wind, *"Look out! Look out!"*

The noise was whipped into nothingness, ringing only in my own ears and impossible for anyone else in the world to hear.

The silhouettes merged closer.

It happened in silence—or, not exactly in silence, because my ears were roaring with the sound of the steady, reliable engine of my own plane. But I couldn't hear the other planes, any more than they could hear my pointless shout of warning. They hovered side by side for a second or two, one a little higher than the other.

I watched in horror and disbelief as the lower plane suddenly pitched forward, banking steeply as if to make a sharp turn. But the pilot never straightened the wings. In another moment the plane was plummeting toward the sea in a spiral dive, gathering speed with every corkscrew, violently out of control.

It folded into pieces like matchsticks and paper as it struck the sea.

The other plane flew steadily up and away, straight ahead of me, and vanished over France.

———◆———

My mind tried to make sense of what I'd just seen.

The planes hadn't touched each other. I had no idea why one of them would suddenly fall out of control.

Perhaps it had been a couple of pilots practicing for an air circus, or air force pilots practicing flying in formation, and one of them miscalculated a stall or that last steep turn or just—perhaps it was just a completely tragic coincidence, two aircraft crossing paths all unaware of each other, and one pilot was too startled to react quickly enough. Perhaps they hadn't been part of the race. *Oh please,* I prayed, *please let them not have been other racers, PLEASE NOT.*

I swallowed and ground my teeth together. My mouth was dry and my eyes stung, but I flew as low as I dared over the rolling waves of the English Channel. I angled the Cadet so I could see the surface of the water without having to lean up and out of the cockpit.

I was lower than the white chalk cliffs of the French coast. From two hundred feet, the sea looked as if it were full of litter from an abandoned picnic. The torn pieces of wing and fuselage of the wrecked plane were indistinguishable; I couldn't even tell what color they'd been painted. The aircraft couldn't have been more thoroughly destroyed if it had gone crashing at a hundred miles an hour into a brick wall.

I circled over the debris, staring and staring at the water below me, looking for a trace of the fallen pilot among the bobbing bits of splintered wood and soaked fabric. I knew he couldn't possibly have survived the crash.

The relentless circling began to make me feel faintly sick.

Anyway, there was nothing. I couldn't even see anything that might have been part of the cockpit. Already it could well have been dragged beneath the surface of the water by the weight of the engine, taking the strapped-in pilot along with it.

I felt more and more queasy. It probably wasn't just the circling. A quarter of an hour had passed before I suddenly realized with a shudder that if I stayed here any longer I wouldn't have enough fuel to make it all the way to Brussels. There were gulls above me now, wheeling and hovering, their flight effortless. I didn't want to hit another bird, here over open water, with no place to land, and the wreckage of the destroyed plane floating all about me.

So I took a deep breath and began to climb back to a safer height.

And as I climbed, I saw a third plane. This one was far above me, passing overhead on its way to the French coast. I'd stayed so long in the same place that another racer had had time to catch up to me and pass me. It was probably the bespectacled Swedish law student, the violent Torsten Stromberg, who'd taken off fifteen minutes after me in an ex-military trainer he'd called a Tigerswallow.

But the other pilot didn't seem to see me, or the drifting wreckage far below him; and by the time I'd regained my height, I was alone in the sky again.

I had time, during this climb, to do the work of a competent pilot: to think about resetting my course, to make sure

I was safely on the right heading for Brussels and Mont des Bergers airfield, to reset my stopwatch and mark off the Calais checkpoint. I wasn't lost, I wasn't in danger—

My hands didn't shake, but my heart pounded. Behind the lenses of my protective goggles, my dry eyes stung. I was staring so hard into the sky ahead of me, still *looking* for I didn't know what anymore, that I forgot to blink.

Those fatal few seconds kept playing through my mind over and over, like a Pathé newsreel waiting for the feature to begin, over and over, miniature as a vision in a crystal ball or at the wrong end of a spyglass, perfectly outlined: the silhouettes of two aeroplanes, one crossing directly ahead of me, and the other descending from the north, closing in on each other as I watched.

None of our small planes involved in the race were equipped with radios. I wouldn't be able to tell anyone what I'd witnessed until I reached my destination.

It wasn't a dream.

I knew I'd seen one pilot somehow forcing another pilot to his death.

Turbulence
Brussels, Belgium

Y
ou can't stop paying attention to your flight controls, or your flight path, just because you've witnessed someone being killed. You have to keep flying or you'll die, too.

For the next hour I focused almost all my being into finishing the first leg of the race and getting to Brussels safely.

But in the back of my mind I couldn't help thinking about the other race contestants, all eleven of them, the whole masculine pack of ambitious, oil-smeared representatives of Europe's fledgling pilots, confident in their national pride, belonging to their home countries in a way that made me feel like an impostor. Which one was dead now, and which one was coldhearted enough to have killed him, and had the coldhearted one *known* whom he was killing, or had he just seized on a golden opportunity to put another pilot out of the race? It was the only leg out of seven days' flying where we would be crossing a significant stretch of water in the middle of our flight, and an accident at sea wouldn't be easy to trace.

The fields and forest below my Cadet's green wings seemed ordinary, almost familiar, as I made my way across France and into Belgium. None of it was very different from what I was used to flying over in England. But the weather was strangely unsettling, as if the sky itself had been shocked into turbulence. The wind picked up and began veering, so that I had constantly to correct my track. And I kept gaining height, lifting close to dark clouds that I didn't dare fly through; or losing height and suddenly finding myself dangerously close to the treetops.

The ominous sky didn't scare me. But there was a feeling of dread in the pit of my stomach that wouldn't go away.

I bit my lip and held my course and flew stubbornly onward until Mont des Bergers airfield turned up, just south of Brussels where I expected it to be, a sprawl of concrete and modern hangars.

The dread leaped from my stomach into my throat. Now I'd have to face those unknown, dangerous young men I'd been trying not to think about while I flew.

Mont des Bergers was the site of Fairey Aviation's Belgian aircraft factory, with an enormous paved runway. With my mind galloping ahead to the menace of meeting the other racers, I tried to touch down much too high as I came in to land. The Cadet plummeted, its wheels slamming onto the concrete. The plane didn't bounce, but it gave a bunny hop, front wheels and tail wheel. It thumped forward again on the front wheels, jarring my teeth, and—

"Hell's bells!"

I swore out loud and pulled back hard on the control column.

Then, thank heaven, I was securely on the ground. I tore off my goggles and flying helmet and gave a gasp of relief as cool air from the propeller's slipstream fanned my hot face. I breathed deep, trying to swallow the dread.

What would Jean tell you, Northie? I asked myself severely, and answered, *Do your after-landing checks and find a place to shut down the engine.*

I turned to taxi toward the other racing aircraft. I didn't know them well enough yet to be able to tell if anyone in particular was missing. The only one I recognized was Lady Frith's large Dragon Rapide, at the end of the lineup of the racers' small planes, like a mother duck with a brood of mismatched ducklings. The planes were parked in front of the Mont des Bergers flying school, cheerfully decked with bunting in the colors of the Belgian flag.

The little Union Jack that Jean had given me was still zipped inside my flight jacket. I'd forgotten about it.

I didn't feel like waving it now. I couldn't even look at the excited group of people with cameras and notebooks, standing behind a barricade of rickety wooden tables on a well-trodden handkerchief of grass. I didn't know how in the world I'd be able to give my interview to the *Daily Comet*.

Three men in overalls directed me to pull up next to a familiar green bi-plane. It was the French aircraft flown by Tony Roberts, who had taken off fifteen minutes ahead of me. Tony was still sitting in his cockpit as I slotted the Cadet alongside his plane. He must have landed just before I did.

I took a long, deep breath. If he was a murderer, I couldn't let him know I'd seen anything.

Well, I'd spent my whole life role-playing the perfect

51

English schoolgirl, not letting my classmates know anything about my family or my past, nodding at teachers and using a clear, clipped accent to avoid trouble. I knew how to hide behind a neutral mask and a polite answer.

I climbed slowly out of the Cadet and hopped down from the lower wing, steeling myself for the storm that was about to break.

At the same time, Tony suddenly struggled out of his own cockpit. Like me, he'd already torn off his leather helmet and flying goggles. He tossed them out onto the concrete; then he climbed out of his plane and stood rooting around in his pockets, like someone searching desperately for a lost wallet or passport.

I didn't think I'd ever seen anyone look so grimly bad-tempered after a successful flight.

As my glance went from Tony's fallen flight gear to his face, he met my eyes with so much fury and hatred in his glare that I took a step backward and held one arm up in instinctive defense, as if he were a vicious attack dog crouching to leap at my throat.

The flight school manager stepped forward to greet us in French.

"Congratulations on completing the first race in the young people's Olympics of the Air! You are Antoine Robert and Stella North of France and the United Kingdom, isn't that so? You have both made excellent time. Welcome to Belgium, and to Mont des Bergers aerodrome!"

I turned away from the furious Tony. My mouth felt too dry to speak for a moment, and I swallowed. My French is as fluent as my English, because French is the language of the

Russian aristocracy, and Aunt Marie and Uncle Max used it every day of my life. I swallowed again. "Good afternoon, and thank you, sir," I said.

Now Tony, too, turned to the official and gave a sharp, neat trace of a bow, just a slight inclination of the waist and head. Flushing faintly, and speaking the worst French I had ever heard, he growled, "Thank you. Excuse me the bad language, but my parents lived lots of years in Hamburg speaking German."

His accent in French wasn't German—it sounded like he was trying to speak Spanish. The angry French pilot spoke terrible French with a Spanish accent, and seemed brazen about it, too, as if stumbling with an unfamiliar language didn't embarrass him.

He was breathing heavily, struggling to keep some emotion under control. Apart from that first furious glance, he didn't look at me. It's true we hadn't made a good impression on each other the day before, but now it felt like he thought he had a reason to hate me.

"I speak German well, French not so well," he added, speaking through clenched teeth. "I have Spanish too, living in Spain many years. Now I am French Antoine Robert again, I am a teacher in the air, I teach to fly near Paris."

"Ah, yes, since the Great War we have both German and French speakers here in Belgium, too," said the flight club manager pleasantly. "Come with me; we will record your times before you make your press interviews. The Italian contestant has not yet arrived, nor the Italian chaperone; the reporters may ask you about them, and it would be best if you do not speculate about why they are late."

Of course Vittorio Pavesi hadn't arrived yet; he'd flown off in the wrong direction.

Then I realized what that might mean.

"The others—" I swallowed again. "Everyone else has made good time?"

"Yes, the wind is behind you! The Swiss and German pilots arrived together. The Swedish pilot is expected next."

If Vittorio Pavesi was the only one of us who was missing, then—

I could scarcely bring myself to finish the thought. Perhaps he was still on his way to Paris. Perhaps the accident I'd seen hadn't involved any of the other racers after all.

I glanced around at the parked planes, trying to tally them, but I wasn't sure whose was whose.

Tony Roberts exclaimed, "I want now—" He hesitated. "I want—"

Suddenly he turned to me and said coldly in English, "Your French seems pretty good. Tell this guy I gotta talk to the chaperones. I gotta talk to the chaperones before I talk to the damned newspapers, and I sure as hell am not talking to *you*."

Something about the French pilot's flight must have shaken him as badly as mine had.

Tony leaned over to gather up his things, strewn across the ground between us. He folded at the waist in one swoop without bending his knees, like an athlete warming up with toe touches. "*Jehoshaphat*," he muttered to himself, and came up with a toss of his head to shake the hair out of his eyes.

"You're not at all French," I accused.

It came out sounding like I was calling him a traitor.

"I live in France and I fly a French plane and I teach

French kids to fly at a French aero club," he fired back. "And I'm flying for France in this race. So lay off, sister."

And I *understood him.*

A small, shocked part of my heart jumped in sympathy beneath the brave little Union Jack zipped into my flight jacket. Except for the drawling, overly familiar American slang, it was almost exactly what I would have said if someone had accused me of not being British. *I live in England and I fly an English plane and I do cataloging work for the Natural History Museum in London.* Defensive and false and afraid of being found out.

I pressed my lips together and didn't answer. I had something I wanted to report, too. I asked the flight school manager to take us straight to the chaperones.

Unnecessary Loose Objects

Tony Roberts stormed along beside the airport official as we crossed the concrete. He didn't look at me, but I watched him suspiciously. He moved with an odd, uneven gait, not exactly limping, but as if sitting in a cramped cockpit for nearly three hours had made his legs fall asleep and they hadn't woken up yet. He clutched his flight gear against his chest with his right hand; the left hand was a clenched fist.

I had no idea why he seemed so venomously angry with *me*. But—perhaps he'd seen the accident too. Perhaps he even thought I'd caused it.

Or perhaps he'd caused it himself. Perhaps he'd thought it was my plane that had gone down, and now he was simply shocked to find I'd landed safely.

I wondered what he was going to say to the chaperones.

Capitano Ranza was still chasing down Vittorio. The

French chaperone, Capitaine Bazille, had taken off last and wasn't scheduled to arrive for another hour and a half. But Lady Frith and Major Rosengart were sitting at one of the rough wooden tables in front of the clubhouse, their heads bent together over a notebook filled with columns of numbers.

Major Rosengart looked up as Tony and I approached. He quietly closed the notebook. Lady Frith leaped to her feet and threw herself at me in an engulfing clasp of welcome.

"Northie, my dear, I am relieved to see you," she exclaimed. Like the press, she'd picked up my flight school nickname from Jean Pemberton. "I was nearly worried," she scolded, giving my shoulder a little shake. "Monsieur Robert landed ahead of you! He had to make a refueling stop, and you didn't—you should have been here a good five minutes before him. Do you know you are a full quarter of an hour behind your scheduled arrival?"

"I do know!" The words came bursting out of me in a passionate low voice. I forgot the dryness in my mouth now. "Another plane crashed into the sea, just off the coast south of Calais—"

"You saw *a crash?*" Lady Frith exclaimed.

"Yes, I—"

Suddenly I was reluctant to admit that I'd seen an *attack*.

I already suspected Tony Roberts because he'd taken off right ahead of me. But now a terrible new thought struck me: Lady Frith might have been the attacker. I knew that she'd planned to fly higher than the racers in her takeoff group because her plane was so much more powerful than any of theirs; she was scheduled to overtake them all and land ahead of them in Brussels. It wasn't impossible that the eccentric and

57

highly strung race organizer might try to nudge Britain into a better chance of winning the race by intimidating another racer, or trying to throw him off course.

Perhaps she'd only meant to frighten the other pilot, not startle him into a spiral that knocked him plummeting out of the sky.

If it *had* been Lady Frith, I didn't dare let on to her that I'd seen what had happened.

And if it had been any of the others, if it had been this angry French pilot standing next to me, I couldn't possibly let him know I'd seen his attack—especially when I had no proof.

"*Yes, I saw a crash*," I insisted, unfolding my map rapidly on the table as I spoke. "I saw it happen and flew down to try to look for the pilot in the water. But he—or she, I suppose, I don't know if it was one of ours—no one could possibly have survived."

I snatched up a pencil to mark on the map the place where it had happened.

"It was here—maybe someone else will be able to..."

I scribbled down my times and the coordinates I'd been flying on.

Tony Roberts stood braced and still next to me, listening. Lady Frith and Major Rosengart were silent too, both staring at me.

"Maybe someone else will be able to search the area," I finished bluntly. "But there wasn't much left of the plane. That's why I was late."

Major Rosengart sank his face in his hands for a moment. Lady Frith was left speechless. She stepped back, and the Belgian flight school manager jumped behind the table to hold her chair for her. She flopped back down into it like a giant silver fish gasping for air.

Rosengart looked up. His far-seeing eyes rested for a long moment first on Tony, and then on me. Serious and unsmiling, he addressed me in his formal but fluent English.

"Miss North, I hope this is not a hysterical reaction to a trying flight."

"A hysterical reaction!" I exclaimed, infuriated. "Do you think I've been hallucinating? I—"

"Now, now," Lady Frith interrupted. "Why, *Northie*, of course it is a trying day for all the contestants; the first leg of a distance race is always nerve-racking." Lady Frith leaped from her chair again and laid calming hands on my shoulders.

I clenched my fists and very purposefully tried to level out my breathing. Major Florian Rosengart was a Great War flying ace and I was a seventeen-year-old girl pushing herself into a world of men: being hysterical on the first day of an air race was probably just what he expected of me.

I didn't know how to go on. If the chaperones weren't going to take me seriously, I was completely on my own.

Into the awkward silence, Tony Roberts stepped right up to the table and gave his surprisingly formal little sketch of a bow.

"I've got something to report too," he said grimly.

He slammed down on the table a small, flat silver object that he must have been holding in his closed fist the whole time.

"This was stuck between my rudder cables. I didn't know it when I took off this morning. I noticed something wrong after I was already in the sky."

He turned briefly, for just a second, and shot me a cold,

dagger-filled look through narrowed eyes, as if he expected me to know exactly what he was talking about.

Major Rosengart's gaze rested on the shining object Tony had placed on the table. I also stared, realizing that this was the thing Tony had been hunting for when he'd stood there in the shadow of his plane's wings turning out his pockets. It was an ordinary silver cigarette lighter, unfussy and elegant, with square edges and a black enamel rim. In a rectangle engraved in the middle was a monogram: A.R.

Major Rosengart was almost as dismissive of Tony as he was of me. He said, "It is careless to have unnecessary loose objects about you in flight."

"I didn't have," Tony said stonily. "*It isn't mine.*"

Suddenly he spun on one heel and turned on me.

"*You* were so keen to sit in my plane yesterday. You were flying with me for half an hour. You had plenty of time to shove this down between the rudder cables to jam things up—"

"You were doing aerobatics!" I exclaimed, pushing Lady Frith's calming hands off my shoulders. "I'd have killed us both if I'd done that!"

"You could have dropped it there before you got out!"

"Why would I carry around an expensive silver cigarette lighter just in case I happened to pull up next to you as you headed out to do some showing off? They aren't even my initials, they're your own! You could be making up this story to get me in trouble! *I don't even smoke!*"

"*Neither do I!*"

Then he added, with the artless candor of a five-year-old, "At least, I don't smoke *much*. Not enough to have fancy equipment for it!"

Rosengart picked up the lighter and looked at the mono-gram. The silver flashed in his hands.

After a moment he flipped the cap open and slid his thumb down over the flint wheel. A flame snapped into life, pale in the daylight. He lifted his thumb, closed the silver cap, and the flame vanished. He held the lighter out to Tony.

"Does it not belong to you?" he asked. "It is engraved with your initials."

"Do I look like I'd waste money on a monogrammed silver cigarette lighter?" Tony said contemptuously.

He really didn't. His leather flying jacket was as scuffed and cracked as if he'd been buffing it with sandpaper.

"They must be somebody else's initials too, because *no*, it doesn't belong to me."

There was ice in his voice, but Tony was holding himself together with the cold-blooded calm of an experienced pilot under pressure.

Lady Frith pulled the notebook out from beneath Rosen-gart's pen, and opened it. She flipped pages, scanning names she surely knew by heart, confirming that none of the other racers had the same initials as Antoine Robert.

"Oh sure, I'm careless," Tony burst out, defending himself angrily, his words tumbling over one another in a torrent of outrage. "I overlook *stuff*. I forgot to give back those cuff but-tons I borrowed last night. I lost my stopwatch before we even took off this morning—it's a Swiss Hanhart, with my dad's name scratched on the casing with a pin, if anyone finds it! I had it in the air yesterday, tied to my belt loop with a piece of string, and I must have lost it after I landed. So yes, I guess I'm careless about *things*. But I'm *not careless about flying*. I checked my plane this morning, looking for my stopwatch, and I didn't see a lighter. Which means someone must have put *that* in right before I took off."

"It obviously wasn't me yesterday, then!" I snapped.

"How did you find it?" Rosengart asked quietly.

Tony glanced at me, then shook his head and turned back to the chaperones. "I was just coming to the English coast today when the rudder jammed," he stormed on. "When I kicked at the pedals to try to make it work, it got stuck hard right. I didn't want to fly out over the Channel with a jammed rudder, and I wasn't going to get to Brussels without refueling anyway, so I thought I'd do that at Lympne before I left England."

He paused, and I could hear the way his breath shook before he continued.

"I went into a spin as I turned to land. I couldn't do a damn thing to stop it. The only reason I'm still *alive* is because the rudder came unstuck at about a hundred feet."

When he paused to collect himself again, no one said anything. After a moment he went on, "I was so disoriented I didn't even have time to check the wind or make sure I was still over the airfield. I landed with a real thump about two meters away from a Hawker bomber, and it's only blind luck I didn't land on top of it."

He took another shaking breath and added bluntly, "And then I got out and was sick."

Tony rubbed his eyes, leaving a smear of damp dust across his grubby cheekbone.

"If you don't believe me you can darn well call up Lympne and ask them. I got an earful from the airport manager, and they nearly didn't let me take off again—I thought I was going to have to drop out of the race before I'd even finished the first day! And then I found this blasted lighter on the floor beneath the rudder cables. From where I'm standing, it looks like sabotage, and *it stinks*."

It took a moment for all of Tony's words to sink in.

Then Lady Frith cried out with passionate disappointment, "Sabotage! One of you bright, young talented people? Oh, surely not!"

"There was all kinds of sabotage in the Women's Air Derby in America in 1929," I reminded her furiously, something she must have known perfectly well. "There was a fuel tank that got mysteriously drained, and magnetos that stopped working— someone's luggage caught fire in midair—loads of things! And someone was killed very early in the race, too. They thought it was carbon monoxide poisoning from a faulty air system."

Tony took a step back and folded his arms. He didn't say anything else. I hadn't meant to defend him; I didn't even trust him.

"What about the accident I saw?" I cried out. "What if that plane was sabotaged, too? What if it was one of us? *What if it was Vittorio Pavesi?*"

Lady Frith bit her lip. She stared at the list of names in her notebook, her face twisted with anxiety. "We'll get the French coast guard to investigate. We'll give them this map, with the coordinates you've marked."

Major Rosengart wrapped the small silver cigarette lighter in a handkerchief and tucked it into the breast pocket of his jacket.

"And this must not happen to anyone else," he said quietly.

Navigation Errors

L ike a force of nature, Lady Frith pushed me ahead of her past the reporters and into the flight school clubhouse. She didn't want me to talk to the *Daily Comet* that afternoon after all; she didn't trust me to keep my mouth shut about what I'd seen. My mouth was clamped shut already, more than she knew, but I'd been dreading the next press interview. I gave a long sigh of relief as I waited for her to take a telephone call from Capitano Ranza.

I listened with a thumping heart to her half of the conversation, desperately hoping that he would tell her he'd caught up with Vittorio Pavesi and that they were both now on their way to Brussels to join the rest of us.

"What—you've been all the way to Paris and you've found *no trace* of him?" Lady Frith exclaimed into the receiver. "He must have realized his mistake before he got there and adjusted his course. If so, it's likely he'll arrive here any minute. You ought to make your way to Brussels as well, but there's bad weather coming, so perhaps you had better wait until tomorrow morning."

I found myself clenching my jaw so hard, as I listened, that it began to ache. Lady Frith didn't seem to want to connect the missing racer with the accident I'd seen. Again I wondered uneasily if she'd had something to do with it.

The racers were supposed to go on a bus tour of the city that afternoon. Lady Frith canceled it. Even after the slower racing aircraft landed, we all had to wait anxiously at Mont des Bergers airfield, hoping that Vittorio Pavesi might turn up before dark.

I seemed to be the only one who felt sure he wasn't going to. Well—I and one cutthroat and secretive other.

But I didn't know who that was.

By half past five, sheets of rain were flooding from the sky, so torrentially that water began to pool ankle-deep in places on the concrete airfield. It was obvious no one else was going to land there that evening.

But Lady Frith refused to cancel the gala dinner scheduled for us in Brussels. The head of the Belgian Air Force, the mayor, and Queen Elisabeth of Belgium were all expected to attend; so was the Belgian contestant's father, Capitaine Dupont, a Great War flying ace who had lost both legs in the war. It would be awkward not to go ahead with the event. So at last we all pelted through the driving rain to board the bus that would take us to the Hôtel Le Plaza, where we'd have a few minutes to dress before our first public evening banquet. I climbed into the bus and then panicked about having to sit next to someone who might be a murderer. I stood sodden and dripping in the narrow aisle, scanning the seats, trying feverishly to remember which of the racers had landed after me and couldn't possibly have caused the accident.

There in the second-to-last row were the Greek and Polish pilots, Philippos Gekas and Stefan Chudek, sitting in a cloud of cigarette smoke and carrying on a conversation they'd begun back in the flight school clubhouse. Philippos had landed last, flying a trainer called an Avro Tutor, much like my Avro Cadet but a little bigger and not as fast; Stefan had overtaken him in the air, in his modest RWD-8 bearing the proud red-and-white chequerboard flag of the Polish Air Force on its tail. Either of them could have sabotaged somebody else's plane on the ground, but they'd both been so far behind me in the sky that there was no way they could have been responsible for the attack I'd witnessed.

Behind them, in the corner at the back, sat Tony Roberts.

I thought I could deal with Tony. After Lady Frith had hung up with Capitano Ranza, she'd called the airfield in England where Tony had made his emergency landing, and his story seemed to be true. The timing made it very unlikely that Tony could have been ahead of me over the English Channel, even though he was such an astonishing flier that by the time I'd reached Brussels he'd managed to catch up with me. *Better the devil you know than the devil you don't.* I headed to the back of the bus to sit next to Tony, behind Philippos and Stefan.

When I got there, I found that the last bench was a row of seats that went across the whole width of the vehicle. Tony Roberts sat slumped against one of the side windows with his

66

legs across the seats, one boot propped up on a pile of flight bags at the other end. For a moment I thought he was asleep. Then I thought he was ignoring me on purpose.

And then there was a very odd moment when I realized he was neither asleep nor ignoring me, but so lost in his own trouble and anxiety that he hadn't noticed I was there.

He had his head half turned away, toward the back window, as if he were trying to see out. The window was a gray waterfall of rain, turning the aeroplanes and factory buildings on the other side into a smeary blur of shapes like an Impressionist painting. Tony's lips were pressed tightly together, his jaw taut, his dark brows lowered, and I couldn't tell if his frown was one of fear or anger or physical pain.

Suddenly he became aware of my shadow, or maybe just my closeness. He turned his head to look at me. The thick brows stayed down in sullen hostility, but the look of desperation vanished.

"Do you mind if I sit back here?" I asked.

He shrugged. "Suit yourself."

"Could you move your feet?"

He didn't answer, but after another second he swung his legs down to the floor and made room for me on the bench, though he kept one leg stuck out at an angle in the aisle. I gave his foot an accidental kick as I climbed over it.

"Oh! Sorry."

He scraped his heel a hair's breadth further out of my way, his lips pressed together, and still didn't answer.

"I *am* sorry," I repeated icily. His flying boots were so stiff my own toes felt like I'd accidentally kicked a brick doorstop. It couldn't possibly have hurt him.

He shrugged again, as prickly as if he were wrapped in barbed wire. Presumably he still suspected me of trying to sabotage his plane, though he surely realized by now that it could have been anybody.

I sat down next to the pile of flight bags. But then I didn't have any place to put my own feet, because Tony's were in the way. I curled my legs beneath me. Lady Frith was the last to climb on board, and after doing a grim headcount, she seated herself near the front of the bus. The engine grumbled, and we slowly began to move away from the flight school and out to the road that would take us to Brussels. In front of me and the flight bags, Philippos and Stefan were smoking and talking quietly to each other in broken Russian.

Russian was my first language. Like French, I can speak it fluently, though I can't read it. I leaned forward a little so I could more easily hear the conversation, hoping I'd find out how much these boys guessed or knew about what had really happened that afternoon.

But they weren't talking about the missing pilot. Philippos was complaining about having come last in that day's race; Stefan pointed out that he, too, was flying one of the slower planes. "The handicaps are there to make it fair," Stefan reminded Philippos.

"You flew well, though," Philippos returned. "You took off after everybody else and landed before me."

It was the most ordinary of racing conversations. As I sat listening to their innocent postmortem of the day's flying, Tony unexpectedly moved his legs fully out of my way and straightened his back like a ramrod, as if he'd suddenly remembered he was in the presence of a lady.

"Done much racing?" he asked me.

His mild, curious tone caught me off guard. He didn't sound friendly, exactly, but he had a nice voice—a husky baritone, with a sort of boyish eagerness about the way he talked that made him seem younger than he was. The American drawl had something in it of freedom and wide-open spaces that was wildly alien to my lifetime of tidy English fields and cluttered city gardens.

It was a straightforward question and, wary of getting into an argument with him, I gave him an honest answer.

"This is my first long-distance race. I did a closed course race last spring—the 'Junior King's Cup.' You had to be under eighteen to take part."

"How'd you do?"

I bit my lip, remembering. My plane in that race, not the Cadet I was flying now, had been hopelessly outclassed, and I had been far too cautious about the steep turns. Oh, well—it wasn't a secret. "I came eighteenth out of twenty-one. And two of the planes I beat had engine trouble and didn't finish. So really I came second to last."

"How'd you qualify for this race, then?"

"Sent in an application, as it said to do in the papers," I answered defensively. "I got a recommendation from my instructor, and put down the number of hours I've flown and the three languages I speak, and drummed up sponsorship, and wrote an essay: Why this would be a good experience for me. Why I want to succeed in a personal achievement that will also be a British achievement. Why peace and cooperation in Europe matter to me."

I didn't mention my passport. I didn't mention my Russian

aunt and uncle and how I'd had to fight them, how I'd had to *move out* and sleep on Jean's settee because Aunt Marie kept tearing up my letters from the Race Committee, how she and Uncle Max hadn't even turned up to wave goodbye to me as I set off.

"How did *you* qualify?" I challenged him.

"Keep your shirt on, sister," he said in that pleasant, mild drawl. "I was just asking. Since we both know there are a pile of other things we've been warned we *can't* talk about."

I met his eyes for a moment, our gazes mirroring each other's fear and distrust.

The hatred was gone from his look. He was still edgy and suspicious, but it was no longer directed at me in particular.

"Major Rosengart told us not to gossip with the other race contestants," I said. "That doesn't mean we can't talk to each other."

Tony looked away first. "Maybe I don't want to talk about it at all."

"Well then, tell me how *you* qualified for the race!" I retorted levelly. "Have *you* raced before?"

"I've raced all right," he said. "But not in any bourgeois political propaganda contest like this one."

There was contempt in the way he strung those words together.

And although I thoroughly agreed with him that it was political propaganda, those particular words struck me harder than they should, harder than he no doubt meant them to strike. *Bourgeois*—what did he think that word meant?

My cheeks were suddenly hot. I said sharply, "Well, I *am* bourgeois, if by that you mean educated. Or if you mean middle class, or cultured, I suppose I am those things too. Or do you mean rich? Or *royal?*"

For my parents, being connected to aristocracy during the tumultuous years of the Russian Revolution meant they were thrown out of their own house and told to live in one room in the cellar with their new baby. It meant they had to change their name to try to avoid being arrested. It meant they could not get papers that would let them work or buy food.

My parents were killed because they were bourgeois.

I wasn't going to tell Tony Roberts *that.*

But he saw that he'd annoyed me. "Sorry," he said quickly, and earnestly. "I guess I'm a little jealous. You being 'Britain's own North Star' and 'our Flying English Rose' in the *Daily Comet.* It seems like everyone else in the race belongs here, and I'm the one who doesn't fit the mold."

I stole a glance at Tony in wonder. He'd been chosen to represent France, and barely spoke French; perhaps he really did feel the way I did about representing Britain.

"Well, you *aren't* the only one," I said. "How do you think it feels to be the only woman? You don't know anything about me."

"Nor anyone else," he agreed grimly. "I wonder what the others think, though. I was in Spain last year when the civil war started, and I don't buy this baloney about being able to promote peace in Europe. Old Lady Frith's speech before we took off this morning, telling us to keep quiet about the war in Spain because the Great Powers want to stay out of it, doesn't change what's going on there..."

For a moment he seemed lost for words, and in passionate anger I filled in for him: "Did you see the news this morning?

71

The Fascist rebels are closing in on Santander. They're taking more towns every day, using German weapons—the Spanish government's about to lose its grip on the whole of the north! It's a disaster—"

"Yes—*yes!*"

For half a minute, he forgot about sabotage and I forgot about murder. We were suddenly both in furious agreement.

"Peace in Europe is a pipe dream," Tony exclaimed. "I feel like a fraud trying to pretend I believe in it. And having to dress up in a penguin suit every night, and the press interviews—I guess when I entered the race I didn't think about how much I'd hate everyone looking at me and judging what I'm wearing. I just thought about the flying."

He finished plaintively, "I really just wanted to have fun flying."

I nodded, breathless with anger and disappointment. I knew.

For a moment neither one of us said anything. Then Tony winced and said ruefully, "Maybe it doesn't bother you. You seemed to know how to talk to the reporters this morning. And you looked nice all dressed up last night. I feel ridiculous in evening clothes."

He wasn't trying to flatter me; I could see that. He was just speaking with straightforward honesty, saying what he thought.

"No, you look just the same as all the others," I assured him. "It's only the little details that are a bit off. You need a haircut."

He tossed the hair out of his eyes defiantly. "But you notice," he said. "The press will notice too. And that's what they'll report—*French Racer's Hair Is Too Long.*"

"That's usually how they report on girls," I said drily. "'Miss North was ravishing in a petrol-blue evening frock.' You can go ahead and smash any record to smithereens, fly higher or faster or further than anyone's ever done, and all they'll put in the papers is how you weren't wearing lipstick when you got out of the plane."

He gave a bark of mirthless laughter. "Well, that's too bad," he said. "I guess you're right."

We both fell silent. I wasn't sure I liked him, and I definitely didn't trust him. But he was easy to talk to, and whatever else was going on, there was no doubt we stood firmly together on the war in Spain.

The bus was traveling at speed toward Brussels now, but still we couldn't see a thing out of the streaming windows. I went back to listening to Philippos and Stefan in the row ahead of me. Now they were talking about the chaperones and their wartime flight achievements again.

"*Three* air aces of the Great War!" said Philippos. "Dozens of kills between them! Flying with these pilots is a dream come true."

"Not all of them fought on the same side," said Stefan.

"I want to see them fly together. Maybe they can join us and perform at the air show we are to give in Paris. I want to see them dogfight."

Stefan waved that aside. "You know the race is to promote peace among nations. You will not get them to fight each other, even for sport. But they are going to give a flight demonstration in Geneva."

Tony leaned forward a little, concentrating his clear, direct gaze on the back of their heads.

"I think that Major Rosengart is secretly a vain man," considered Stefan, smoking furiously, holding his cigarette between yellow-tipped fingers. "All those medals he wore to the banquet last night? And why else would he fly a training aircraft from the last decade? He could be flying one of those fast new German designs, but instead he chose to bring his own plane to show off his flight skills."

"The French chaperone, Capitaine Bazille—he isn't vain, but he is a showman too," said Philippos. "It comes of being the only Black man in his squadron."

Tony leaned back again and looked at me. He twisted his mouth and shook his head.

"Those fellows are looking forward to the chaperones flying together," he said in English, his voice pitched low. "It'll be pretty hot with all three of the Great War aces in the air at once! But I bet Capitano Ranza won't participate unless the Italian contestant turns up."

I stared at him. "You understand what they're saying?"

"I can figure it out. I had to work with a bunch of Soviet pilots last year, and I picked up their aviation lingo."

"Why don't you join that conversation, then?" I challenged.

"I'd like to," he admitted. "But I'm terrible at speaking it. My Russian's worse than my French. That's why I'm talking to you in English."

I shook my head in confusion, thinking that he'd somehow guessed I spoke Russian too. It took me a couple of seconds to realize all he meant was that he couldn't talk with Philippos and Stefan, so he was talking to me.

"Is comparing veterans' combat scores really so fascinating?" I asked. "You boys all seem obsessed."

"Oh come on, you know it'll be amazing to watch them in the air all at once. It'll be a real circus! And it might teach us something."

"How to fight back in an air attack?" I challenged.

Tony barely heard me; he was eavesdropping on the conversation again. Or if he did hear me, he didn't show any sign he knew what I was talking about.

Unless he'd made the attack himself, he didn't know about it. He thought only that his plane, and maybe another, had been sabotaged.

I didn't get to find out anything else. The bus pulled up at the Hôtel Le Plaza.

Pigeons on the Palace Steps

Less than an hour later, I stood on the terraced entrance of the Royal Palace of Brussels, wearing my "ravishing" evening gown and rubbing at the gooseflesh beneath the gauzy silk wrap I'd draped over my bare arms. Everywhere I went I seemed to make a scene, without even opening my mouth, just because I was Stella North, the Flying English Rose. When I'd checked in at our hotel, the forgotten flag had fallen out of my jacket; I'd panicked for a moment, thinking it was my passport, and as I scrabbled to pick it up, somebody started snapping pictures of me. It had been easy to save face just by waving the flag, but it was *so hard* to keep the false smile plastered on.

It seemed weeks ago that I'd been at Old Sarum Airfield having my photograph taken with Jean and Lady Frith; then the takeoff and heading straight into the sun, the flight over the water and the clouds moving in, and then...

It wasn't weeks ago. It had only been that morning.

I'd been awake since five thirty a.m., flown three hundred miles, and witnessed the death of another pilot.

I longed to be alone in my hotel room in my pajamas.

Above me now, in the stone arches that roofed the entryway, I could hear pigeons cooing and fluttering their wings. I looked up. There were swallows' nests there too, and dark holes in the stonework that might have housed swifts earlier in the summer. No one was home now but the pigeons. I envied the swifts, on their way to Africa already, eating and sleeping in the air, never touching down. If one of their companions fell, they'd just keep flying and forget about it.

I shivered, and looked back down at the taxi that was parked at the bottom of the terrace stairs. We'd all come in taxis from the hotel, and the moment ours had pulled up, Lady Frith had gone bounding into the palace ahead of me to supervise the reception that was going on there. But I'd paused, reluctant to face the other racers and the royalty inside. Now I stood watching Capitaine Dupont, the Belgian race contestant's father, arrive in the last taxi.

The double-amputee war veteran was only in his forties, a strong man whose hair and mustache were coppery ginger, barely touched with silver. He sat waiting patiently with the door open as his driver assembled his wheelchair, which had been stashed somehow in the back of the automobile.

I couldn't see any way that this man was going to be able to get up the wide stone staircase leading to the palace entrance.

I turned and went after Lady Frith into the grand reception hall, where serene waiters were serving champagne to a crowd of important-looking guests, and the racing pilots were nursing crystal flutes of sparkling mineral water. I remembered the Belgian contestant's name.

"Gaby? Gaby Dupont?" I called out randomly.

All the young men wore boiled shirt fronts, starched collars, white ties, and black tailcoats, and Gaby Dupont was no exception. I recognized him as the one all the Belgian reporters had been haranguing at the airfield earlier that afternoon. He had the same gingery hair as his father, shining like new pennies.

"Your father's here," I told him. "He needs help getting up the stairs."

Capitaine Marcel Bazille also turned around and put down his glass. He was the only Black man in the hall, and stood out against the crowd. He, too, was elegant in evening clothes. He leaned over toward Tony Roberts, lounging indolently against one of the drinks tables; Tony looked like he was desperate to be somewhere else.

Bazille said quietly, "Monsieur Robert, your assistance is needed."

Tony appeared not to hear him. Instead of raising his voice, Capitaine Bazille gripped him by the shoulder with a strong hand to get his attention.

I saw Tony freeze like a rabbit beneath the shadow of an owl. His hands tensed so suddenly he knocked over an empty glass on the white-clothed table next to his thigh. He stood there for a split second, staring, with feral, irrational fear in his face.

After a moment he tilted his head slowly to look down at the dark fingers gripping the black wool of his evening jacket.

The scowl descended again as Tony came back to earth. His thick eyebrows came together, and he asked in French, "What?"

"Go help carry Capitaine Dupont up the stairs."

Tony gave a curt nod and wrenched himself free of the older man's grip. He loped off across the gallery behind Gaby Dupont.

Capitaine Bazille followed them, and so did I. Outside the palace, all three clattered down to the taxi waiting in the rain. Another boy dashed past me to offer his help as well. But when he caught up with the rest, Capitaine Bazille took this one aside, said a cool word in his ear, and the boy reluctantly turned around and climbed the stairs again.

For a moment I was confused. As he came toward me, bedraggled with rain and choking in the stiff uniform of men's formal wear, for a second I thought it was Tony Roberts again— he looked so much like Tony. But it was the young officer from Germany, Sebastian Rainer: the cool-headed race contestant who was a pilot in the Luftwaffe, the new German air force.

Germany. I didn't trust anything about Germany; no one did. Sebastian and the Swiss pilot, Theodor Vogt, couldn't have been far ahead of me in the air that afternoon. Maybe Sebastian had fallen behind Theodor on purpose to lie in wait for another pilot—for *me* even, as I would have been over the same spot only a minute or two later.

Now the German boy stopped alongside me in the cover of the grand stone terrace to watch as the others helped Capitaine Dupont out of the car and into his wheelchair.

I edged away from Sebastian, who was silent as a block of wood. Or—not wood exactly. Something warmer and more alert; a still cat watching birds through a window, perhaps, and twitching its tail. One of the pigeons above me suddenly fluttered and flapped its wings in alarm, and I glanced up, startled. But it had grown too dark to see them anymore. I stole a look at the German.

His resemblance to Tony was superficial but striking. They were both fair-haired, clean-shaven, and square-jawed, and they were exactly the same height, though Tony was more sturdily built. Sebastian's hair was close-cropped, like the new military recruit that he was, while Tony's was so long in the back that it brushed against his collar.

I glanced down at Tony to compare them. As he whipped off his dinner jacket to use it as a makeshift umbrella for Capitaine Dupont, I saw that the real similarity was in their *eyebrows*, equally heavy and square, and a shade darker than their hair. It gave them both the same look of wearing a perpetual faint frown.

I could stand there next to the German pilot and ignore him, or I could try to find out more about him.

Better the devil you know than the devil you don't.

"Herr Rainer? I'm sorry, I've forgotten your officer rank," I said. "I'm Stella North. Northie."

"It is Leutnant Rainer," he answered, with a stiff, formal little bow, exactly the way Tony had bowed earlier that afternoon. "Second Lieutenant Rainer in English. But it is all right to call me Sebastian."

"Don't they need your help with Capitaine Dupont?" I asked.

Sebastian shook his head and corrected carefully, "They do not *want* my help."

80

"Whyever not?"

"Ach—" He shook his head again, as if to clear it, and said levelly, "Capitaine Dupont lost his legs in combat with a German air force pilot. I am to stay away from him—as is Major Rosengart. No Germans allowed." Sebastian gave a neat little sigh, like a cat, breathing a short puff of air out through his nose. "In this race we fly in the name of peace, do we not? So when the great Capitaine Marcel Bazille gives me an order, I do not disobey."

It was impossible to tell if he was hiding resentment, or guilt, or even cutthroat cold blood, beneath his stiff formality. He saw me looking at him and gave me an enigmatic smile. It wasn't reassuring.

"I admire Capitaine Bazille perhaps more deeply than the other chaperones," Sebastian said. "What courage he must have! He is from Martinique, where his grandmother was enslaved. He was the only Black man in his squadron during the Great War. Yet of all our chaperones, he was in combat the longest. Capitano Ernesto Ranza has the larger score, for Bazille only shot down six enemy aircraft. But he damaged thirty-seven others. I feel he is the greater hero."

"Gosh. That is impressive," I said drily. Good God, was every boy in the world *obsessed* with tallying damaged aircraft? I couldn't even pin it on a thirst for blood. It was genuine admiration.

The taxi driver, assisted by Tony and Gaby and Capitaine Bazille, had settled Gaby's father in his seat. Now each of them took a corner of the wheelchair and raced up the stairs with it, in an exuberant triumph of brute force over gravity and weather. Sebastian stepped back into the vast shadows of the terrace's columns as they stamped into the entrance hall, and I paused politely to wait for him.

As he stepped forward again, Sebastian reached into the breast pocket of his evening jacket and, with a twirl and a flourish, produced a silver cigarette case. He held it on the palm of one hand for a moment before flipping it open.

It had square edges and a black enamel rim. In a rectangle engraved in the middle was the monogram A.R.

It exactly matched the lighter that Tony Roberts said he had found tangled in his rudder cables.

Leutnant Sebastian Rainer offered politely, "Would you like a cigarette?"

———◇———

I sucked in a sharp breath.

"No, thank you, not just now," I managed to say.

And then, swallowing the accusations on the tip of my tongue, I choked out the most mundane of statements: "Sebastian does not begin with the letter A."

He looked blank for a moment, then down at the cigarette case in his palm. His face lit with understanding, and he shut the lid.

"It belonged to my father," he said.

He put the case back in his pocket without taking a cigarette himself, looked out into the darkening rain, and abruptly changed the subject. "I hope the lost Italian pilot managed to find a place to land before this storm began. Perhaps we will hear from him tomorrow."

I turned away from him abruptly.

"I'm going inside now," I said.

A German in Belgium

"*Bonjour, bonjour, tous les pilotes!*" cried Capitaine Dupont when he made it inside. "I am here to wish you good luck and safe flying!"

Tony didn't seem the least bit in awe of Capitaine Dupont's severe disability. He tossed his head to get the wet hair out of his face and skillfully maneuvered the wheelchair across the crowded marble reception hall, as if he were a familiar and trained assistant to the veteran. Tony pulled the chair up abruptly at the table where the drinks were, and Gaby held out a glass to his father.

"No champagne for me, thank you, boy, I am flying tomorrow morning as well, and earlier than the rest of you," Capitaine Dupont told his son. "I will take mineral water. The search for your missing plane begins again before daybreak, and I am going along as an observer."

Tony's American drawl boomed over everyone else's muted French. "Well, I'm sorry I'm racing, because I sure would like a flight with you in that swell plane someday."

I'd forgotten that those reporters at Old Sarum had said something about the Belgian's plane being specially modified. They'd asked me if I thought it was fair. I wondered briefly if Tony had asked Gaby's father about it.

But now my thoughts quickly raced away from flight controls; my mind was a whirling tempest of engraved silver smoking accessories.

Lady Frith swooped forward to welcome Capitaine Dupont, leaning down to take his hand and kiss him on both cheeks. She was magnificent in a rustling silver evening gown that was, if anything, more dazzling than her silver flight suit. I heard Sebastian Rainer's quiet, authoritative voice dropping trivia over my shoulder: "The brooch with the diamond wings that she wears was a gift from the King of England for her Azores flight, because she was a civilian and a woman and they could not give her a military decoration. You see, I have studied."

"You didn't know a thing about Guernica," I uttered coldly.

"Not until yesterday," he agreed. "But now I have learned."

I fearfully wanted to shake him off. He was sticking to my side like a stray dog—a stray dog that might be capable of tearing my throat out if I made the wrong move.

I glanced around desperately for someone I'd feel safer with. There were too many people gathered around Capitaine Dupont for me to join them without attracting attention. Then I caught sight of Erlend Pettersen, the Norwegian pilot, standing alone at the bottom of the grand marble staircase to the upper floor. He'd taken off first that morning, and I knew he'd landed in Brussels an hour before the accident I'd seen.

I approached him deliberately, with Sebastian clinging to my heels like an evil shadow.

"Hello, Mr. Pettersen," I said.

Erlend broke into a sunny smile that seemed absolutely genuine, pale blue eyes beaming at me from his round, red, baby's face. "Good evening, Miss North," he answered. "Please, call me Erlend. The arguments yesterday made me sad."

He towered over me. I stepped back so I didn't have to tilt my head up like a little girl to look at him.

He added, "I hoped the other racers would be more friendly!"

"Yesterday everybody was nervous, and today we're all worried about Vittorio," I agreed hollowly. "Call me Stella. Or Northie. Everybody does."

Sebastian gave one of his stiff little bows, and Erlend nodded in acknowledgment.

"It distressed me as well to argue," Sebastian said coolly. "I would like to begin again. You are an artist, the newspapers tell me. You are enrolled at the National Academy of Art in Oslo, where you have had an exhibit specializing in ships and airships."

"Yes, I am a painter," Erlend said cheerfully. "I am fascinated with new machines and airfields, but I have been flying for less than a year. I have much to learn."

Tony Roberts suddenly joined us, struggling back into his now-damp jacket. It didn't quite fit him: it was a little too broad in the shoulders and a little too short at the wrists, as

85

if he'd borrowed it from someone else at the last minute and hadn't had the time—or the money—to get it altered.

"That man's amazing," Tony said, gesturing over his shoulder with his thumb toward Capitaine Dupont. "Amazing! You know that jazzy new Tipsy B that Gaby Dupont flies? Well, it belongs to his dad. Capitaine Dupont flies it with no legs— he's got a sort of push bar he attaches to the rudder pedals so he can control them with his hands. He gets the mechanics to lift him in. I sure wish we were here longer—I'd love a chance to go up with him."

He sounded honestly impressed and full of interest. I didn't think anyone who'd just killed an opponent could sound so compassionate only a few hours later.

But Sebastian, too, was as cool and neutral as if nothing had happened.

The vast entrance hall felt scarcely warmer than the cold, wet summer night outside. I said to no one in particular, using small talk like a shield, "Erlend only learned to fly this year, but I've been flying for nearly two years, since I was sixteen. What about you chaps?"

"Almost as little as Erlend," Sebastian answered readily. "I trained at a gliding school in the Bavarian Alps for one year, and I have trained with the Luftwaffe, Germany's new air force, for another."

Tony shoved his hands in his pockets, glowering, no doubt thinking of those German air force bombs exploding over Spain. There was a moment of awkward silence.

"I'm not looking forward to crossing the Alps! I suppose mountain flying doesn't frighten a glider pilot," I said inanely, and immediately wished I hadn't. I *was* nervous about crossing the Alps, even before today's events, and the worst thing I could do was to lay bare my weaknesses. At best they could take it straight to the newspapers, and at worst—

But Sebastian was already giving another sober, self-confident answer: "You suppose correctly! Those foehn winds and mountain thermals are familiar friends to a glider pilot. I plan to fly directly from Geneva to Venice, and I am looking forward to seeing the Matterhorn again! But I have less experience than you in powered aircraft. Perhaps Tony has been flying longer?"

I wondered if Sebastian was hiding a challenge beneath this light question, and I half dreaded Tony's reaction.

"Seven years," said Tony Roberts, flushing with sullen pride. "Since I was twelve."

"The French start young!" Erlend exclaimed.

"No, I've only flown in France since I began working there in June," Tony admitted in a rush of straightforward honesty, as if he were pulling out his own loose tooth and wanted to get it over with. "I used to visit my grandparents in the USA in the summer, and that's where I started to fly. At one of those little flight schools on a farm where the barnstormers like to land. It was magic. My dad and I took lessons at the same time."

Sebastian said casually, "Would any of you like a cigarette?" His restless fingers flashed.

I was sure I didn't see him reach into a pocket, but suddenly he was holding his silver cigarette case, which he flipped open and offered to Erlend and Tony. "Please."

I held my breath.

"*Danke,*" Erlend said in gracious German, and took one.

Tony Roberts stood suddenly still. I knew exactly what he

was thinking, what he was wondering, as for the first time he recognized the design of the thing in Sebastian's hand.

Tony didn't fly into a rage and yell for answers. Instead, he deliberately took a cigarette himself, and waited while Sebastian took one as well.

I breathed out very slowly, lightly, aware of the grand curve of the stairs behind us, the courtly guests chattering in their silk ties and family diamonds, the bright ribbons of the veterans' Great War decorations. I felt irritatingly small and vulnerable, bare necked beneath the gauze stole, surrounded by these three tall, black-suited young men I suspected of sabotage, or worse.

Tony dropped three words coolly at Sebastian's feet.

"Got a light?"

The German pilot responded with a conjuring trick. His fluttering fingers moved quickly. There was something fascinating about watching this otherwise stiff and formal boy perform these magician's sleights of hand.

An irrational part of my brain expected him to produce the lighter that Tony had found in his rudder cables. Instead, from Erlend's collar, Sebastian pulled a single flaming match.

"Bravo!" exclaimed the Norwegian pilot, letting the German light his cigarette for him.

Tony narrowed his eyes, his square brows lowering so that it exaggerated his frown.

"I'd rather you just handed me a matchbook," he said sullenly.

With another flourish of his quick fingers, Sebastian obliged.

It was an ordinary hotel matchbook embossed with the

crest of the Hôtel Le Plaza, where we'd all changed our clothes an hour earlier.

"I have lost my lighter," Sebastian explained. "I used it to weigh down my chart at Old Sarum yesterday. I must have left it on the table there, or dropped it."

Tony took a step forward like a terrier scenting a rat, and at exactly that moment Lady Frith came sweeping in among us.

"Upstairs, upstairs!" she cried, clapping her hands. She spread her arms toward the splendid chandeliered length of the Long Gallery above us. "The Belgian Queen Mother is waiting to be introduced to the flying youth of Europe. Put out those cigarettes, if you don't mind! Come along, all of you. If you're too full of nerves to smile, please don't frown."

I knew I could construct a perfectly pleasant smile for Queen Elisabeth of Belgium. I am good at hiding my thoughts.

I wondered how good at it Tony Roberts was.

He gave me a brief glance as we went up the marble staircase together, clear gray-green eyes like a reflection of my own, transmitting to me a conspiratorial message of quiet understanding, alarm, and anger; and then he quickly looked away.

The Flying Dutchman

The hotel lobby was quiet as we boarded the bus back to the airfield at five fifteen the next morning.

But the early newspapers lined up on the shining reception desk screeched the same headlines in English, French, and German:

Air Race Contestant Mystery!

Circuit of Nations Olympics of the Air Racer Lost in Flight!

Young Italian Pilot: Missing or Dead?

And the poisonously inevitable: *Could It Be Sabotage?*

Tony and I hadn't had a chance to say a single word to each other about Sebastian Rainer's cigarette case. We weren't likely to get a chance before this morning's flight; it wasn't the sort of thing you could talk about in a crowded bus. I wasn't sure I even wanted to get tangled in a conversation with him until I had landed safely in Geneva.

I was now sixth in the departure lineup, instead of tenth. Vittorio Pavesi and Capitano Ranza weren't there, and I'd been moved up into the second echelon of racers. Tony was supposed to take off half an hour after me. I didn't think he could possibly catch up to me in the air today the way he'd done yesterday.

The one good thing about Vittorio's disappearance was that the chaperones weren't allowing any reporters airside this morning.

The late August morning was dawning fine and warm; steam rose from the concrete pavement of Mont des Bergers airfield. Juggling coffee and an open-faced tartine sandwich from the buffet breakfast provided for us, with my flying gear hanging over my shoulders, I went out to the rickety wooden tables on the flight school's handkerchief of muddy grass.

I found a place to sit by the slim, youthful Dutch racer. He had his map spread out and held in place with a fuel sample tube, a coffee cup, and his stopwatch. I didn't get out my own map, but I put my coffee and plate on the table, with my flight bag and parachute still hanging over my shoulder. I'd done all my planning the night before, and I was damned if I'd let anyone know what route I was taking.

"You're Willem van Leer, is that right?" I asked.

He looked up from the chart, which he'd been marking with a grease pencil. "Yes, I am the one your British newspaper insists on naming 'The Flying Dutchman,'" he answered, offering me a handshake with a brief flash of a smile. "But I am called Pim. I believe I am the youngest of us."

Footsteps behind us made me glance over my shoulder, and for a split second I was tricked again into thinking it was Tony. But it was Sebastian.

Unlike Tony, Sebastian had the sharp air of a well-drilled military officer, with his shining black Luftwaffe boots and short black leather jacket. He carried a carefully folded map and a windspeed calculator tucked beneath his arm, and he twirled his stopwatch between his fingers. It was a Swiss Hanhart stopwatch exactly like Pim's, exactly like mine, exactly like the one Tony said he'd lost. Sebastian's was sensibly attached to a thin chain.

"May I join you?" he asked in his cool, courteous way.

I hesitated, biting my lip, the back of my neck crawling with distrust. I wasn't sure I wanted to confront Sebastian with Pim listening. *Ugh*—it was possible I was avoiding the inevitable confrontation with him because I dreaded the thought of it.

To my surprise Pim also hesitated, his dark eyes burning. Then he spoke out in a rush. "Join us if you like, but be warned that you will be sharing a table with a Jew, Leutnant Rainer. What will your Nazi air force think of that?"

Sebastian blinked. He drew back a fraction, the spinning stopwatch suddenly falling still. He gripped it in his fist and lowered his hand.

"I myself have no quarrel with any Jew," said Sebastian slowly, "and I do not want to start one with you an hour before a race to Geneva, the home of the League of Nations and of peace. Why should the Olympics of the Air be different from the Olympic Games? Germany did not ban Jews from competition in Berlin last year."

"Only because my country and five others threatened to boycott the games if you did," said Pim.

Sebastian couldn't fall back on ignorance as an excuse as he'd done last night over Guernica. He must know perfectly well what Pim was talking about. The Nazis came to power four years ago, and Hitler had been persecuting the Jewish people ever since: firing professionals, banning people from working, all of them viciously taxed, shops shut or impounded. Vile and mocking posters plastered on public walls. It wasn't a secret.

"Perhaps there is no room for another map on this table," Sebastian said.

There wouldn't be, if I unfolded mine.

He stood still for another moment, then smoothly turned away from us and crossed to the other wooden table, where he neatly began to lay his things.

Pim watched him with dark eyes that seemed to be aflame with hatred.

But at last he swore softly to himself under his breath in Dutch, and bent over his flight plan.

I looked out over the steaming concrete of the airfield. The edges of the wings on Erlend Pettersen's red-and-blue Breda 25 were fluttering up and down like a bullfinch ruffling and settling its feathers. Erlend was testing his flight controls, getting ready to take off ahead of the rest of us. Further down the row of parked aircraft, Tony Roberts was running his hands up and down the wires of his own plane, his heavy eyebrows lowered in a grim frown.

My plane was right next to his. With a shock, I saw the Cadet's wings fluttering just like those of Erlend's Breda.

Those shouldn't be moving, not on their own, not without someone controlling them.

Someone was in my plane. I stared in alarm and saw the rudder on the tail move back and forth. Someone was testing the controls—or making adjustments to the cables beneath the seat. Or—

"Oh, you *wouldn't!*" I exclaimed aloud, scrambling to my feet. *"The very next day?"*

I couldn't tell who was in the pilot's seat. All I could see was the back of a flight helmet. Pim, alarmed, followed my gaze.

I grabbed all my things: flight bag, parachute, flying helmet, leather jacket that was too warm to put on just yet. I wasn't going to leave my gear anywhere near Sebastian Rainer at the next table, with his restless fingers doing tricks with matches and cigarettes. I didn't know how that fire started in the 1929 women's air race in America, but it was rumored to have been a hot cigarette butt dropped in a flight bag. That wasn't going to happen to me.

Pim van Leer leaped to his feet and followed as I stormed across the muddy grass.

"What is the matter?" he called.

"There's someone in my plane."

Pim caught up with me and grabbed hold of my sleeve. I whirled around.

"Why—" He broke off suddenly, and I turned to look at him. I saw a boy sixteen years old, slightly built, only taller than me by a whisper, and with a face so smooth he probably hadn't started shaving yet. His dark eyes were clouded with worry in his pale face, and he hung on to me with the unthinking, fierce, fighting intensity of a wren or robin defending its territory.

"What is wrong? The others say you saw the Italian's accident. What do you know?"

His face was drained of color, apart from two livid spots of red flushed high on his cheeks.

"Go look over your own plane," I said to Pim. "Make sure your controls work and there's nothing loose on the floor, and check your fuel."

"Damned Nazis," Pim swore, as if I were referring to a specific incident that we both knew about. "They will stop at nothing to come out ahead of the rest of us."

I glanced back at Sebastian, bent over the wooden table and absorbed in his map. I didn't trust him, either, but I had a reason for it; as far as I knew, Pim's distrust was founded on nothing but a hatred of Nazis.

I pulled my arm away from Pim and sprinted toward my plane.

If I were Jewish, I would be just as worried as Pim, I thought. If I were Czech, or Polish, or a Communist, I would be worried about what the Nazi pilot Sebastian Rainer thinks of me... He thinks I'm English. But perhaps I should be worried just because I'm a girl.

Tony was French. There wasn't any good reason for a Nazi to go after a Frenchman. And Vittorio Pavesi had been Italian, a Fascist like the Nazis. The Italians and the Germans had bombed Guernica *together*. None of it made any sense.

Erlend Pettersen was sitting in his red-and-blue Breda 25, waiting for the mechanics to start his engine. He was in the same type of plane that Vittorio Pavesi had been flying. I wondered if I should warn Erlend to look out for trouble, as well.

I reached my Cadet, breathless, just as the mysterious interfering pilot climbed out.

The moment he turned I recognized him immediately:

95

it was Capitaine Marcel Bazille, the French chaperone. I attacked him in French, in his own language.

"Why are you in my plane?"

He stepped down lightly from the Cadet's lower wing, his long legs taking the height with a calm lack of fuss, like a crane or heron stalking fish in a still pond. He answered me courteously, smiling, obviously delighted to be communicating in his own language. "Miss North! Of course I am here for your safety. Major Rosengart has commanded that each plane be checked by two chaperones. He has scoured this one already, and now it is my turn."

"You didn't do this yesterday morning!" I said.

"Exactly why we must do it today," Bazille agreed. "Miss North, I'm interested: did you encounter any trouble in the air yourself, on your flight yesterday? Any trouble with your own plane?"

After yesterday's brush-off from the German chaperone, I was surprised.

"No," I said. "No, my plane was fine."

"You'll be all right today as well," he assured me. "All is in order here. You have a nice little machine."

I foundered a bit, wondering what he'd expected to find, or what kind of *trouble in the air* he thought I might have had.

"The Hanriots you fly aren't bad," is the bland comment I came up with, and added, "The young man who's flying for France, Monsieur Robert, you must be proud of him. I don't know how he made up so much time after the fright he said he had."

"Ah, yes, Antoine Robert, the natural pilot. He is capable of winning this race, if he keeps a cool head, I assure you."

96

Capitaine Bazille's tone wasn't enthusiastic. I wondered if I was kicking a wasp's nest, and prodded a bit further.

"You've known him a long time?" I asked.

"I have known him since June, when he joined the club where I fly," Bazille said. "If I'm not mistaken, he has considerably more flight experience than all you others, even within the two hundred and fifty flight-hour limit set by the Race Committee. And I fear that he is too angry to fly well. I disapproved of him as a competitor, but the English Lady Frith sees only how he will broaden the range of participating nations. In Monsieur Robert we have an immigrant from Spain who speaks English and German better than he speaks French. The German flying ace Rosengart admires genius, and the gutless Italian chaperone always votes with the German flying ace. So I was outvoted, and Antoine Robert was approved."

I was rather taken aback by Bazille's frankness. He saw my expression and laughed, which brought out the fine lines of age in his young-looking face.

"I beg your pardon, Miss North, perhaps your very fluent French makes me speak frankly," he said. "Please excuse me — I must move on to the next machine, as there are three more I've agreed to look at. We want no more accidents."

"No, certainly we do not," I agreed.

I threw my gear into the front cockpit of my plane and began feverishly to check everything Capitaine Bazille and Major Rosengart had already checked.

I wanted to be doing something now. Not planning, not making polite conversation with people I didn't trust; not agonizing over what did or didn't happen to Vittorio Pavesi, or how Sebastian Rainer came to have a silver cigarette case that matched the lighter Tony Roberts said he'd found on the floor of his plane, or if the German pilots would dare to try to eliminate anyone who was Jewish.

Now I wanted to be flying.

I wanted to be in the air. I wanted to be up there following the swifts on their journey southward, alone in the sky.

Flying.

PART TWO

EUROPE IS
THE LESS

Monday, 23 August–
Wednesday, 25 August, 1937

The Western Front
Geneva, Switzerland

I'd reached three thousand feet above the ground and I planned to go higher. I wanted smooth air and a good height over the Jura Mountains. But not just yet—I was still getting used to the unfamiliar French map.

With the wind in my face and my hand lightly on the Cadet's controls, tension seemed to seep away from my entire body. For a few hours I wouldn't have to think about anything but flying.

Though I was heading steadily south, I crisscrossed the border between Belgium and France three times, and then actually laughed aloud at how snaky it was. The national boundary seemed so *arbitrary*. The country below me looked much like England—fields and woodland, roads spooling out like Ariadne's golden thread, neat avenues of poplar trees like orderly strings of dark green beads. Unless I checked my position on the map, there was absolutely no way to tell from above which of it was French and which was Belgian.

But at last I was solidly in France, approaching Reims, and it stopped looking like England. The fields were enormous, a patchwork of long rectangles, and in those open fields, I began to notice the trench scars.

I was flying over the old Marne front line: the line along which the terrible battles of 1914 and 1918 were fought in the Great War twenty years earlier, day after day in blood and mud. You could still see the trenches, unnatural zigzag scars rucking through the green fields.

In the air, looking down at them, I suddenly understood why Lady Frith wanted to encourage peace among Europe's nations. I suddenly understood why the Great Powers worked so doggedly against stirring up trouble with the Fascists—why Britain and France turned a deaf ear when places like Ethiopia and Spain complained of the Italians and the Germans dropping bombs on them.

No one wanted to see these trenches opened up again.

No one who fought here twenty years ago and survived wanted to see their sons come of age and go straight out to fight another war.

I gently tilted the Cadet so I could stare down out of the cockpit.

Why, it would be us! I thought, and a shudder went through me as I looked down at the broken and healed fields. *Our generation will have to fight the next war—these boys I'm racing against, these boys I'm flying with—we'll be the ones fighting this time. They'll be dropping bombs or firing guns and I'll be mending ambulances like Lady Frith, or sneaking messages across enemy lines like Mata Hari. We'll all lose loved ones or our legs or our sight or our minds. We'll be killed in battle or in front of firing squads. It will all happen again.*

The murderous pilot, too, would have to go to war.

I found myself gasping aloud in outrage: "Oh, why would you *kill* if you didn't have to? This race—*no* race is that important!"

I couldn't hear my own words over the roar of the engine.

I straightened the Cadet's wings, but still I flew over the ragged lines of the old battlegrounds, a belt of scarred land that stretched from Reims to Verdun as far as I could see. I longed to hurry away, but that would burn fuel I couldn't afford to waste.

The other pilots would have to fly over it, too, even if they took a more direct route than me.

They couldn't miss this. They might be treacherous, but they weren't oblivious. Sensitive Pim van Leer and good-natured Erlend Pettersen would notice. Philippos Gekas, Stefan Chudek, Jiri Jindra, and Theodor Vogt all had the Great War on their minds; they, too, would surely notice. Gaby Dupont's father had lost his legs here. Tony Roberts and Sebastian Rainer—even if they were already killers, I didn't have a doubt they'd understand this damaged landscape.

I wondered if Lady Frith had made us begin the race over Belgium and France on purpose, if this was why she had planned the route this way round. This was our lesson, right from the start, that the race was all about peace in Europe.

This broken landscape, these thousands upon thousands of ghosts, were our vivid reminder of what happens when there is no peace.

The route I'd planned to Geneva took me right to the limit of the Cadet's fuel capacity. But I stayed high, where my engine was more efficient, and I used the wind.

The flight seemed to be over in no time at all. The Jura Mountains were gentler than I'd imagined, carpeted with forest. Over the top of the Juras appeared Lake Geneva, stretching blue and glittering ahead of me with the Alps gleaming beyond it. I used the lakeshore to guide me to the brand-new concrete runway at Cointrin Airfield, just outside the city.

It had been a relief to be in the air, away from everyone; now relief washed over me again as I realized I'd completed an uneventful flight.

There was no more being alone on the ground, though. The swarm of reporters knew I'd made fantastic time, and Major Rosengart congratulated me in front of them before I'd even climbed out of my plane.

"Well done Britannia! A very respectable performance for such a sensitive young lady."

The patronizing compliment irritated me, but the crowd cheered. There wasn't anything to do but shower them with bland smiles and wave my British flag. Lady Frith was talking rapidly to the interviewer from the *Daily Comet*, and by the time I'd jumped down from the Cadet's wing and taken off my flying helmet, I was surrounded by photographers and people with notebooks.

"Splendid work, Miss North! Lady Frith says your flight time has been excellent both yesterday and today."

"You'd be in first place if you hadn't stopped to hunt for

the missing race contestant—have you always been willing to sacrifice your own success for the well-being of others?"

"Do you think you'll be able to make up the lost time?"

"Are you feeling stronger today after last night's spell, and will two nights in Geneva give you a rest? Or do you think that the social engagements and sightseeing might take the edge off your focus?"

"Are you still worried about crossing the Alps?"

Last night's spell—what was that supposed to mean? Had Rosengart told them he thought I was hysterical?

"Which of the other pilots are you most afraid of?"

I stared, my mouth falling open.

"Goodness, Northie, do go on *smiling*," Lady Frith hissed at me under her breath.

Sense came back to me. The question meant, Which of the other pilots did I think was my closest competitor? I shook my head and insisted grimly, "Of course I'm not afraid of any of them!"

The reporters laughed and scribbled down my defiance.

Which of the other pilots are you most afraid of, Northie? I asked myself. Answer honestly.

If I continued to come in first place or close to it, there would be a plausible reason for every single one of the other racers to resent me.

Perhaps it was true I wasn't afraid of any of them.

I was afraid of them all.

———◇———

Major Florian Rosengart caught me by the arm as I came out of the lift at the Hôtel de la Paix in Geneva. It wasn't five minutes since I'd checked in. I had my flight bag in one hand and my room key in the other, and I hadn't even had a chance to notice which direction my room was in before the German chaperone swooped down on me. The lift door clanged shut behind us, and I turned to face Rosengart, my heart galloping in my chest for no good reason.

He'd already changed into his evening clothes. I don't know how he'd managed to be so fast, unless perhaps he'd been flying in his dress shirt and trousers and only had to put on his dinner jacket and a different tie.

"Miss North, I would like to congratulate you once more. The handicaps have not yet been applied, but I can see from the initial results that you have come close today to making up the time you lost on yesterday's flight." He paused a moment, then added, "You said you chose not to route through Lorraine, but why? You might have been first this afternoon if you had flown directly to Geneva. Inexperience in flight planning, perhaps?"

"Oh! I—" I felt myself reddening. "I was a little nervous about going straight over the forest of Ardennes. I planned to stop at Dijon if I didn't manage my fuel as well as I'd hoped." I took a careful breath. "Thank you for the congratulations."

"May we enjoy a drink together before dinner when you have changed your clothes?" Rosengart asked politely.

"Shall I come down in an hour?" I suggested.

I'd been hoping for a few minutes to myself before the challenge of the next gala dinner. I wanted to write things down in a sensible order, to make a list of all the contestants and what I knew about each one—Pim's fearful hatred of

106

Nazis, Tony being able to understand Russian, when exactly Sebastian lost his father's cigarette lighter—before these details went straight out of my head with more flight planning.

But Rosengart said, "Surely you are able to refresh yourself in half an hour? I would like to keep this interview informal, for your sake. But as time goes on, the matter of Vittorio Pavesi's disappearance grows desperate. I am interested in what you believe you saw."

Anger rose and faded in me as I realized that the growing certainty of Vittorio's death was forcing Major Rosengart to take me seriously.

He must have thought I looked stricken, because he smiled and apologized reassuringly. "There is no need for alarm. If you were not mistaken, you may have been the last to see Vittorio Pavesi's aircraft. I would like to ask you the details of your flight—in confidence, of course. Half an hour, please? I will wait for you in the public vestibule at the passage's end, by the window."

Rosengart pointed. There was a desk, a bookshelf, and a comfortable chair arranged in a nook overlooking the lake. He began to fill his pipe with tobacco in a leisurely way, as if to show he didn't mind waiting.

He'd be in view of my door, halfway down the passage according to the numbered arrows on the wall ahead of me. He wasn't going to let me slip off someplace else without him. I pressed my lips together.

"Yes, all right."

Of course this tight vigilance was what the chaperones were here for.

I left Major Rosengart in the cozy little public lounge and let myself into what would be my room for the next two nights.

Wide French windows looked out on a magnificent view over Lake Geneva from the no-expenses-spared lodgings, three stories above ground level in the Hôtel de la Paix. Beyond a vista of bridges, pleasure boats, and clipped trees, in the distance behind the nearby hills soared the majestic Mont Blanc, its summit veiled in snow.

A couple of weeks' training in the Scottish Highlands earlier that summer was all I'd had to prepare me for crossing the French Alps, three times as high. It was true that I was apprehensive about my next flight. But until yesterday, that had been a pilot's sensible and healthy respect for unfamiliar terrain and wind. Now I faced the ominous possibility that the same thing that sent Vittorio plunging into the English Channel might send me hurtling toward jagged rock below the peaks of the Alps.

I thumped my flight gear down on the bed. My other luggage had already been brought up. Each flying day, Lady Frith transported the bulk of our gear in her twin-engined Dragon Rapide, which was a great deal bigger than anything anyone else was flying. There was a private bathroom attached to my room, and I stripped off my flight suit and bent over the shining porcelain basin to splash cold water on my hot face.

On Wednesday I'll fly to the other end of Lake Geneva and follow the road through the passes between Chamonix and Zermatt, I told myself. *I'll refuel in Milan. I won't let any of the others know my route. I made good time on today's flight, and I'll lose a little on the next one. But I'll be safe, and the hardest part of all the flying will be done with.*

The thought of purposefully losing more time again made me bitterly angry. Somewhere in the sky on the way to Geneva, earlier today, Tony Roberts had managed to overtake the Swedish pilot. He'd landed twenty minutes ahead of schedule. He'd been helped along by the same stiff northwest tailwind that had buoyed me over the Jura Mountains, but there was no denying that he flew unbelievably fast. I knew that if I kept following longer routes, I risked being unable ever to catch up with him.

I slipped into the mallard-blue evening gown and stood for a moment staring at the unfamiliarly elegant girl in the tall mirror. The deep blue made my eyes look like storm clouds. *My hair is like a Shetland pony's mane*, I thought in annoyance; even pulling it back didn't make it any less thick and black and shaggy. *Perhaps if I cut it off like Amelia Earhart...*

But no, I didn't want to think about Amelia Earhart, lost at sea less than two months ago.

I didn't have time to fuss with my hair. I brushed it quickly and clipped it back from my face. Major Rosengart was waiting to interview me. Perhaps the French coast guard had found something he wanted to ask me about. Perhaps someone else had reported seeing the crash; someone on the ground might have seen the same thing I'd seen, one plane forcing another plane down. A fisherman might have seen me searching the area and wondered what I was doing. Or perhaps he was wondering if I—

I shivered. My bare arms broke out in gooseflesh again.

Perhaps someone thought I'd been the pilot who caused the crash.

Perhaps Major Rosengart thought so too.

13

A Professional Investigator

"I assume we would both prefer coffee to an aperitif," said Major Florian Rosengart. "No doubt you are tired."

We'd gone downstairs, and now we were sitting in a discreet corner of the reception lounge with a low table between us. On it, Rosengart spread out a notebook, a ruler and pencils, and a flight map showing the south of England and the Low Countries of Europe. His eyes were vivid, matched by the blue topaz pinned to his lapel, and the enamel of the Blue Max medallion on a black ribbon around his neck. Over his heart he wore a bar of miniature military decorations, including an Iron Cross. Everything else, from his gray hair to his black-and-white clothes to his pale skin, gave him the faded dullness of a photograph in a magazine.

"The *thinking* is more tiring than the flying," I said.

"Yes, you must have worked hard to manage your fuel

today," Major Rosengart said. "Some of the other pilots have planes that can cover the same distance with greater endurance, and I apologize that it is not taken into account in the handicaps. It is one reason I fly the Albatros L-75—the Albatros Ace, as we call it in Germany."

He smiled warmly, color coming into his gray face, as he glanced up from the things he was laying on the table. "Not because I am an ace myself, but because it has an excellent range. It is ten years older than your own aircraft, but it can travel three times as far on a single tank of fuel. The Race Committee agreed it might be useful to take with us a machine that could be used for search and rescue."

The smile disappeared like the sun behind cloud cover. A waiter arrived with the coffee and found places to position cups and cream and a sugar bowl around the spread-out map.

"You are no doubt aware that Capitano Ranza has joined us again this afternoon," Rosengart said. "He has discovered where Vittorio Pavesi flew after leaving Salisbury, and it is very likely that you and Vittorio crossed paths at the moment of a fatal accident. We are moving increasingly far from the site of that crash, so we must supply the search party there with as much information as we can. You were in shock yesterday when you told us your story. But I would like to hear it from you again under a calmer circumstance." He held open his hand briefly to gesture at the splendid hotel lobby surrounding us.

"I am a police inspector in Königsberg," he went on, and met my eyes frankly. "You may remember my name in connection with the unpleasantness that came out of Spain last spring."

For a moment I thought he meant the war in general.

Then I thought he meant Guernica. At last I realized what he was actually talking about.

"The Rocketman Affair?" I said.

"Aha." It was a quiet affirmation of agreement. "Although it is more correctly named the Santa Agnès de Marañosa Investigation."

I wondered if he expected me to say something else about it.

Good for you.

I'd joined this race to prove my flight capability and my British patriotism, and now here I was, being interrogated by an international police inspector investigating a murder.

I hunched my shoulders, cold again. In the awkward pause, Florian Rosengart reached across and clasped my arm in a reassuring grip. I was startled by the human warmth and sympathy in his long-fingered, bony hand.

"Be courageous, Miss North! You can help now."

He let go of my arm and poured coffee for me. I dropped three spoonfuls of sugar into it very quickly.

"Black and sweet!" Rosengart said wryly. "That is how I also take my coffee. You are all right?"

"*I'm fine,*" I said sharply. If he'd wanted to baby me, he could have given me the extra half an hour I'd asked for.

Rosengart was silent for a moment. There was desolation and intensity in that pause.

All he wants is my help, I reminded myself. *I haven't done anything wrong and he hasn't accused me of anything.*

He took a deep breath and leaned over the map. "We'll begin, then. Let me tell you what we've learned since last night."

He pointed to a spot marked on the chart.

"Capitano Ranza never caught up with Vittorio Pavesi. But the boy stopped to refuel in Amiens. He landed there just past ten yesterday morning, after he realized he was heading in the wrong direction. The landing delayed him, as he was not expected and spoke no French, but he took off again just before eleven. And—" Rosengart drew another long breath. "And tragically, this would have brought him to Calais at exactly the time you were—at exactly the time you say that you witnessed an accident."

Florian Rosengart's voice was taut with carefully controlled anguish. "This is a terrible thing, Miss North."

Talking about the missing boy was making this cool, formal policeman quiver with emotion.

"But why—why would he have flown to Calais from Amiens, instead of straight to Brussels?" I asked.

The German chaperone rubbed at his forehead. "Why indeed? Why did he mistake Winchester for Salisbury? Why did he aim for Paris when he should have aimed for Brussels?" Major Rosengart sounded as if he were reining in frustration. "He was a poor navigator—worse than we were aware. I believe he was attempting to pick up his planned track."

Rosengart drew a line with his finger from Old Sarum to the coast of France, pausing just short of Calais. "This was your course, and you flew straight here, making notes of your time?"

I nodded.

"And it was here, at eleven thirty-five, that you say you saw another aircraft, is that correct?"

"Yes, exactly there."

113

Rosengart raised his eyes from the map to meet mine again. "Describe to me again what you saw."

Increasingly, I couldn't remember exactly what I'd seen. I'd thought the image was burned into my brain, but it wasn't. I was sure I'd seen two planes, but now I couldn't remember what they'd looked like. The second or two of the attack itself had been clouded and overcast by the long, sickening quarter hour I'd spent circling over the waves staring at the debris of the wrecked plane.

I'd already told Major Rosengart I'd seen a plane crash into the English Channel. He hadn't believed me until, a day later, he realized that one of the Circuit of Nations Olympics of the Air racers really was missing. If I gave him new details, or told him that I couldn't remember, he'd surely be even less likely to believe it; he might even assume I was lying about the whole thing.

And I was still afraid to admit all that I'd seen. I was afraid that the murderer would find out and try to attack me next.

"I saw a plane go down into the sea and break up, just off the coast south of Calais," I said. "It was utterly destroyed. I circled over the place where it happened for fifteen minutes, and there was nothing left of the plane but splinters. The pilot couldn't possibly have survived the impact."

"That is precisely what you said yesterday."

"I don't have a new story," I told Rosengart angrily.

"You are afraid of your fellow racers," he guessed. "You trust none of them. You do not want any of the others to know you suspect sabotage."

It was just as patronizing as calling me hysterical—but

this time, it was true. His reading of my mind was uncanny. I grabbed at the accusation of sabotage.

"Someone tried to foul Tony Roberts's flight controls," I said. "That cigarette lighter he found belongs to Sebastian Rainer. Sebastian says he lost it, and if he's telling the truth, anyone could have picked it up—the same person could have put something in Vittorio Pavesi's plane, too. If Sebastian isn't telling the truth..."

"Monsieur Robert could just as easily be the liar," Rosengart pointed out evenly. "Angry, bold, careless by his own admission—he may well have invented that story to cover a bad mistake, or to cover an attempt to sabotage another pilot. Had he not landed in England, he could have easily crossed paths with Vittorio Pavesi."

Then Rosengart added, "Or—you yourself could be the liar. You could have crossed paths with Vittorio Pavesi yourself."

I knew it.

I knew I looked like a suspect. Rosengart could only be guessing at the full extent of what I'd seen, and he suspected me anyway.

He'd mentioned Tony. Did he suspect anyone else—of sabotage, at least? Perhaps he was too professional to tell me whom he had in mind. He'd have to consider Sebastian. But the Nazi government wasn't going to be happy about another murderous Luftwaffe pilot smeared all over the international newspapers, barely six months after the first one.

I thought of Pim's white face and remembered the hatred and fear in his dark eyes. Wouldn't it be easy for this German policeman to use the Jewish contestant as a scapegoat, even if

Pim had nothing to do with any of it? What would happen to Pim when we got to Germany?

A wave of resentment swept over me. I hadn't realized how deeply I hated Hitler's lackeys. Major Florian Rosengart's neutrality and expertise be damned: I wasn't going to tell this Nazi anything more.

Rosengart leaned back. He said unexpectedly, "It is hard to fly alone. I learned to fly with my brother. We joined the Imperial German Flying Corps together, as our air force was then, and flew together throughout the Great War. I do not think I could have done what I did at that time and survived it, without this friend and comrade flying with me."

"I love flying alone," I said. "I love being in the sky alone."

"But you are here to represent a nation of millions." The German chaperone sat very still for a moment. "When one flies for one's country, one is never flying alone; no more in this peacetime competition than in an air force at war."

I swallowed. As a member of the Race Committee, Major Rosengart had surely seen my passport; he knew perfectly well that I didn't travel under my English name.

It didn't have anything to do with Vittorio Pavesi's disappearance. But he could use it against me if he needed to.

Rosengart picked up his coffee cup, took a sip, and put the cup back into the saucer. The pieces of china gave a quiet click as they came together.

Suddenly I was worried that the story of Rosengart's brother might not have a happy ending. Vittorio's accident, Capitaine Dupont's missing legs, the trench scars... Perhaps the entire race was tearing open old wounds.

I asked, "Did your brother survive the war?"

Rosengart didn't answer right away. He calmly tucked his notebook and pen into his breast pocket. The question had been a little awkward, but he didn't seem offended. "We both survived the war," he assured me. "It is kind of you to ask."

He began to fold up his map.

"I understand your anger," Major Rosengart said. "And your fear. But I hope you will confide in Lady Frith if you remember any other details, even if you are not comfortable confiding in me."

"Yes, of course," I said stiffly.

"I will do everything in my power to prevent another attempt at sabotage," he went on. "I will question Leutnant Rainer. And I will question Antoine Robert myself this evening." Rosengart stood up, giving a little frustrated sigh through pinched nostrils. "We need to be certain."

He sounded almost as if he were talking to himself now.

"Yes. I want to be certain."

Press Meeting

It was clear that all the other hotel guests knew which of us were the Circuit of Nations Olympics of the Air racers, and it was impossible to appear in the public areas of the Hôtel de la Paix without being stared at and whispered about.

But there wasn't enough time to go back up to my room before the formal dinner. I ducked down the nearest passage and found a minute's sanctuary in a newsstand at the back of the hotel, invisible from the lobby. Newspapers! I'd seen those awful headlines earlier but hadn't had a chance to take a closer look.

My own face smiled out at me from the cover of that morning's *Daily Comet*, prominently displayed, my hair caught flying every which way as if I were standing in the wake of a spinning propeller. On the rack below me was a picture of three dashing pilots in flight jackets and silk scarves.

I recognized the Norwegian, Erlend Pettersen, and the pock-marked Swiss competitor, Theodor Vogt; but who was the young man with the mustache?

I picked up the paper and let out a quick little gasp as I realized who I was looking at.

"Oh!"

Vittorio Pavesi, alive yesterday morning, gazed at me from the photograph.

The newspaper promised profiles of each of the contestants within its pages.

It struck me that I might have stumbled on a gold mine. Here, in the tabloids in five different languages, was a rich vein of cheap gossip that might tell me something revealing about my fellow contestants.

"I want one of each of the English language papers," I told the cashier. "This one, and this one—and the French language ones as well. Can you charge them to my room and send them up? The weeklies as well as the dailies—"

"You might as well have this month's *Voici Paris*, too," drawled an American voice at my back. I glanced over my shoulder and saw Tony Roberts behind me.

I steeled myself for a confrontation.

"Why *Voici Paris*?"

He was wearing his obviously borrowed evening clothes. They showed too much wrist, and his shirt cuffs were held together with loops of white cotton string—*string!* I could scarcely believe it. His trousers had been inexpertly let down and dragged at his heels. His hair was still wet from a quick bath, the honey-blond gone mouse-brown with damp.

"You look nice again," he said to me.

"*French Racer's Hair Is Still Wet*," I said.

He rolled his eyes and tossed the French magazine on top of my pile.

"There's an interview in this one with my old flight instructor, Rosario Carreras. She'll tell you all about me. Anyway, you'll like her story even if you don't like mine. I'm not sure what all she said—I don't read French so well. Say, did you see what the *Daily Comet* said about *you* this morning? Here—"

He snatched it off the rack, held it up, and pointed. It was Lady Frith's account from yesterday, when she'd canceled my interview.

"It says here, 'Miss Stella North declined to speak, feeling faint with an attack of nerves after an exhausting flight battling deteriorating weather—'" He stopped, tongue in cheek, and let me read the rest myself.

"*Blast and drat!*" I exclaimed. "Why in heaven's name would she tell them that? Exactly what she *doesn't* want people to think about women flying aeroplanes! She couldn't be more frustrating! Oh—" I gave a wild bark of laughter. "That explains what that reporter meant about my 'spell' earlier."

Tony picked up another copy of the *Comet* and dropped it on a stack already on the counter. I saw that he was collecting exactly the same pile of international newspapers I was, only in German and Spanish instead of French.

"Look at that," he said. "Both of us digging up dirt on the other racers."

"I'm staying informed," I said primly.

"Sure you are. Nobody sabotaged *you*, did they? What are you worried about?" His voice was quiet.

"No, nobody has, but I bet somebody wants to," I hissed. "And I bet they'll try again."

———◇———

It was the newspapers that made me sure he hadn't tried to kill anyone.

He was scouring the tabloids for criminal motives in the other racers, exactly as I was.

Such a simple, straightforward declaration of innocence: a pile of newspapers to comb through in three languages.

———◇———

We waited while the cashier wrote up our receipts. We stood a little apart from each other, not speaking or looking at each other, but we left the newsstand together.

I made up my mind. In the passage I said in a low voice, "Vittorio's plane wasn't sabotaged. Another plane came so close to him that it startled him into a spin. I saw it happen."

Tony missed a step and stood still for a moment.

"*Phew.*"

It wasn't spoken; it was a low whistle of outrage and understanding.

He didn't say anything else about it. "C'mon, we'd better go. They must be starting to sit down in the dining room."

We turned out of the passage and crossed the hotel lobby, but we'd forgotten about the reporters. It was like an ambush. Suddenly we were surrounded.

"Miss Stella North! Please, a few words for readers of *Crosswire?*"

"Miss North, do you think your fellow contestants are envious of the attention you've been getting? Of your remarkable performance today?"

"Did you have a chance to speak to the Italian contestant before the race began?"

"I really haven't anything to say about the other racers," I told them coldly.

The pushiest of them were with photographers, and they used their flashbulbs to disorient us. I'm sure they did it on purpose. Tony teetered on one foot in midstep and grabbed instinctively at my arm for balance. Almost immediately he let go of me again, and rubbed his eyes in flustered embarrassment.

"Oh! Leutnant Rainer—" someone cried out, in another stunning error of mistaken identity. "Our English readers are so keen to know what it's like flying with the new German air force—"

"Get your dirty cameras out of here before I toss them into that lake out there!" Tony growled. "Can't you leave us kids alone for *five darn minutes?*"

Lights popped all around and Tony winced, squeezing his eyes shut and hunching his shoulders. He stood frozen, his fists clenched at his sides as if he were willing them to behave, and uttered: "I am not Sebastian Rainer and I swear I will plant my foot right in the seat of the pants of the next guy who takes a picture."

Astonished, I realized he needed rescuing.

I deliberately wound my arm through his. It is easier to barge your way brazenly through a crowd when you are attached to another person. I lowered my head, shaking the

122

Shetland pony's mane forward around my face so the photographers couldn't possibly get a decent picture of the two of us together. I could just imagine the headlines: *Romance Blossoming in the Circuit of Nations Olympics of the Air!*

I dragged Tony through to the grand dining room that had been set aside for the racers and their guests, and the reporters were barred from following us in. I dropped Tony's arm and pushed my hair back, adjusting the clips. We stood for a moment catching our breath.

The large room was splendid with crystal and white linen, the tables heaped with bronze chrysanthemums in silver bowls. There was a small five-piece orchestra tucked into a recess at the other end of the room, playing very softly while people found their places. We had to sit in a different order each night, to mix us up and give us a chance to talk to local dignitaries. Tony found his name card on the corner of a long table, several places down from mine; he pulled back his chair abruptly, then seated himself with a surprising amount of caution, one hand bracing himself on the table and the other on the chair rail.

Bother these seating arrangements, I thought.

I swapped my card with the one at the place next to his, then waited for a soft-footed staff member to help me into that chair.

"Huh. You really are fearless," Tony said appreciatively after I sat down beside him.

"*Fearless!*" I almost laughed, and bit my lip instead. "I am not fearless."

"Yes you are. You get on with things. You don't let anything stop you. I saw you nail down your landing yesterday, when your plane started to bunny-hop. It didn't bother you a bit."

"That's just flying. I'm not scared of *flying*."

"That wasn't flying, that was landing. I'm always scared of landing. Especially as an instructor!"

"Are you really?" I turned to look at him. He seemed more relaxed now that he was off his feet, though his natural scowl made it hard to tell. I already knew he was a superb pilot.

"It's the rough landings that get you in trouble," he said, leaning back in his chair and returning my gaze steadily. "When I couldn't get out of that spin..."

He trailed off.

He'd said his brush with death at Lympne had made him physically sick. It wasn't really something anyone would admit to if it wasn't true.

"But don't you think learning to fly is all about learning to cope calmly with an emergency?" I said. "You know how in your early training your instructor keeps badgering and quizzing you about what to do if your engine stops in flight—I expect you do it to your own students! I hit a bird the very first time I soloed; the propeller broke and my engine quit. I assumed that hitting birds was something I'd have to get used to if I wanted to fly. It surprised me, but it didn't scare me— I knew just what to do, and I landed in the field below me. And—"

Tony listened with his head tilted, watching me, frowning and intense, interested.

"It was honestly the softest, quietest landing imaginable," I said. "The gentlest landing I've ever made. It was the beginning of August last year; the field was golden with wheat, all

124

dotted with poppies and cornflowers, unbelievably beautiful. My engine was dead, so the plane was completely silent except for the wind in the wires. And all around me were skylarks, leaping up from the wheat in alarm—the sky above me was suddenly full of larks singing. It was a lark that I'd hit. You know how they sound in the air, trilling and trilling?"

"Yes," he said, still listening. "The fields around the flight school where I worked this summer are full of 'em. They stay out of our way, though."

"Well, this one was unlucky. I was so sorry. Sorry for *all* of them! What was this giant monster of a Tiger Moth aeroplane doing in their field, crushing their nests, filling their blue sky with exhaust fumes before the engine conked out? It made me think hard about sharing the sky with the flying things that live there naturally."

"Birds, bugs," Tony said lightly. "On the airfield in New York State where I learned to fly, we had to start the day firing shotguns into the trees at the end of the runway to get the turkey buzzards to leave. And just before sunset the mosquitoes would descend on us in clouds. We burned piles of grass at the edge of the field to make smoke so they'd stay away, but nothing worked. We'd always have to scrape hundreds of dead mosquitoes off the wing surfaces when it got light again. I've never hit a bird, though."

It was such an unexpected pleasure talking with someone who wasn't my instructor about learning to fly that I suddenly wanted to make it last a little longer.

"How did you end up working at the same flying club as Capitaine Bazille?" I asked.

"He's a friend of Rosario. My Spanish flight instructor.

She spent a summer in France before the war in Spain started last year, and flew from the same airfield as Bazille. When I needed work, she got me the job there. She's the one who pushed me into this race, too."

"My instructor did exactly the same thing," I said. "But you're lucky to get paid to fly!"

"I didn't always," he said defensively.

"I couldn't have learned to fly if I hadn't already had a proper job," I told him. "My aunt and uncle only let me do it because I paid for every lesson myself and I'm too big for them to stop me without locking me up."

"You said you work at the Natural History Museum in London, right?"

"I've been there since the moment I turned sixteen and left school."

"How'd you get there?"

"I had an egg collection when I was younger," I said. "A good one! I stopped adding to it when I joined the Society for the Protection of Birds, but I didn't want to waste the collection, so I tried to donate it to the Natural History Museum—"

"Kind of ambitious, aren't you?" he interjected.

I grimaced. "Obviously, or I wouldn't be here, would I! At any rate, they suggested very politely that my collection wasn't quite of national importance, and my school might be grateful if I donated it to them instead."

"And did you?"

"Yes, and I thought that was the end of it, but then the museum wrote to me very soon after and asked me if I would like to work with them on their own collection. It changed my life; in about a month I was able to pay for my first flying lesson. It all felt like magic happening, but honestly I'd never have had such a marvelous job offer out of the blue if I hadn't been bold enough to approach them in the first place."

"'Miss North is fond of birds' is what the *Daily Comet* said. And that you paid for your own lessons. You are much more interesting than they give you credit for," said Tony.

"I expect so are you. They know all that and haven't bothered to print it."

He leaned closer to me across the table. Being on the corner meant we could talk to each other almost intimately without having to turn our heads or raise our voices.

"I bet those newspapers waiting upstairs won't tell us anything," he murmured. "They tried to make it sound like that Belgian kid has an advantage 'cause he's flying a modified plane, and it turns out it's just got a special rudder bar so his dad can handle it with no legs. But one of us might already know something that the papers don't. I guess you have a list of potential crooks?"

"Don't you?" I said. "Well—"

"Well, I'll share if you will," he finished quietly.

An Ordinary Dinner
Conversation

No one was seated on my other side yet. Tony tilted his head toward me and whispered quickly, "Could you tell whose plane it was? The attacker?"

"No, I wasn't close enough to see color or markings," I answered. "I can't even be sure the one that crashed was Vittorio, except that he hasn't turned up and the timing is right. They were definitely both bi-planes. One of them dived out of the clouds as if it were going to ram the other, but they didn't quite touch. Then the other went into a spiral."

What a difference it made when someone took you seriously! I took a breath, inwardly astonished at how easy and natural it had been to say all this to Tony, when I'd struggled with doubt while Major Rosengart was questioning me.

I added, "Anyone could have thrown Sebastian's lighter

in your cockpit, but only someone in a bi-plane could have attacked Vittorio."

"Who flies a monoplane?" Tony asked. "Besides Gaby Dupont. That Tipsy B he flies is a low-wing monoplane so that his dad can be lifted in."

"The Czech boy is in that sporty new machine—the Bibi, I think it's called—and that only has one low wing. And Stefan Chudek, the Polish pilot—his is an RWD-8, their basic trainer. It's a parasol, it's only got one high wing. So that leaves three people with bi-planes—besides me and you."

Tony listened intently. He'd already worked it out. "So it could be Torsten Stromberg—that's the shortsighted Swedish guy who broke his fiancée's nose. He took off right behind you, and that Tigerswallow of his can really zip along at top speed."

"Yes." I didn't dare nod; I didn't want anyone watching us to think we might be agreeing on something. "He could have just about had time to pass me, make the attack, and still arrive on schedule. But also it could have been one of the Jungmanns. They're terrifically powerful—either one of them could have been there at the right time if they'd waited in that spot, then sped on to Brussels. So Theodor Vogt—the Swiss pilot—or—"

"—the German." Tony finished the sentence for me.

"Sebastian Rainer," I said. "Yes."

I glanced around to see where Sebastian was sitting, and he was right at the other end of the long table, spinning his fork nervously. Light winked between his fingers.

"He's number one on my list," Tony growled.

"On mine as well."

"But you've forgotten the chaperones," he muttered at my ear.

I shook my head. "No, I haven't. Major Rosengart landed long before I did, and Capitaine Bazille took off last, so I don't see how it could have been either of them. And Capitano Ranza also flies a monoplane, so it definitely wasn't him. But I thought Lady Frith could have done it to try to fix a win for Britain."

"I don't think it could have been Lady Frith," Tony said. "That Dragon Rapide is enormous. It's nearly twice as big as the other planes. And it's the only one with two engines. You'd have seen the silhouette."

"Oh—" It was like light dawning. "Of course I'd have noticed that!"

That was when someone sat down next to me, a Swiss woman who was a delegate to the League of Nations. Tony straightened and gave one of his surprisingly formal nods as we introduced ourselves, and we shut up about sabotage and murder.

Between courses we had to listen to speeches from French and Swiss dignitaries earnestly sharing ideas about peace. The other racers sat quiet and well-behaved, sober with the events of the past two days. Then, just before coffee was brought, the president of the League of Nations got up to talk.

"You have all come here in the name of peace," he began, and went on in confidential tones, "I want to talk to you about why the League refuses involvement with the civil war that has been raging in Spain for over a year now."

I pressed my lips together in bottled anger. I didn't want war in Europe. But Spain was being destroyed. And Germany just grew stronger while everyone else tried not to provoke

130

Hitler, fearful of starting a real fight with his modern military and its horrendous arsenal.

"It is a terrible thing to watch the devastation in Spain's beautiful, vibrant nation," the president continued. "But the consequences of an international military intervention would be more terrible—"

Suddenly Tony couldn't keep still.

His face twisted with contradiction and rage as he listened. He twitched and fiddled with his napkin and the tablecloth, like Sebastian Rainer doing his magician's tricks, but without Sebastian's skill or direction.

I could no longer listen. I was angry, too, and now I was distracted by Tony, fidgeting beside me. I sat stiffly, trying not to look at him as Tony tried and failed to contain himself.

After a couple of minutes he accidentally snapped the stem of his empty wine glass in half.

Florian Rosengart stood up, frowning faintly, with turmoil in his striking blue eyes. He paced over to Tony's chair, with a hand held out ready to lay on Tony's shoulder. I thought again of the warmth and strength I'd felt in that hand, of the emotion and compassion that Rosengart hid so well with cool reserve.

But as Rosengart's hand came unexpectedly from behind him, Tony reacted even more dramatically than he'd reacted to Bazille's touch on his shoulder the night before.

He started half out of his seat as if he'd received an electric shock, knocking the broken wine glass into his plate. Then he spun around with his fist clenched and took a blind swing at Rosengart.

Lightning-quick, the German chaperone gripped Tony's wrist with his free hand and held him down, pressing him back into his chair.

It all happened in silence, apart from the faint tinkle of glass on china, and was over in seconds.

I stared at Tony in astonishment.

After a moment he seemed to recover. He sat back, looking up at Rosengart in fury.

The chaperone leaned down to whisper something in Tony's ear. I couldn't hear what he said. I knew he wanted to talk to Tony anyway, and this was the perfect excuse—removing an unruly and impolite dinner guest, helping an overwrought race contestant to calm down.

But Tony's reaction tied another anxious knot in my stomach. Rosengart's touch had sent Tony into an irrational panic; he seemed to be constantly expecting an assault from behind. I felt sure now that he hadn't attacked Vittorio, but if his nerves didn't stem from guilt, then what was he afraid of? An after-dinner speech shouldn't make you fall apart like that, even if you disagreed with it.

I found myself shivering again, realizing that the Swedish Torsten Stromberg might not be the only contestant who reacted to stress with violence.

Tony did as he was told now, though. He pushed his chair back from the table and stood up, and Major Rosengart let go of him, holding one palm open with a gesture toward the door. Tony held on to the back of his chair for a moment, as if he were catching his balance. He half turned his head to look at the older man, scowling, and then set off ahead of Major Rosengart.

But he limped visibly for the first couple of steps.

I realized I'd noticed Tony's uneven gait several times before. He didn't normally limp, though, more sort of a light canter when he was moving quickly. I'd never noticed it when he walked.

This looked like it hurt him to be on his feet.

He stopped suddenly, stock-still beneath the sparkling chandeliers of the dining room, oblivious to the rest of the dinner party. He didn't look back at me. I saw him square his shoulders and pull himself together.

Rosengart bent to whisper something else close to his ear, and Tony nodded. Then, courteously and cautiously, Rosengart took him by the elbow to support him as they left the room. When Tony started off again, he didn't limp.

———◆———

Tony was right. I liked the story of Rosario Carreras, the woman who'd been his flight instructor.

Finally alone in my bedroom, I locked my door and wedged the desk chair under the handle so it couldn't be pushed open. But I didn't want to turn out my light without first skimming the interview in *Voici Paris*. Rosario said she'd spent the past year flying for the Spanish Republican Air Force, dropping leaflets and making ambulance flights, in the same kind of plane that Tony was now flying in the race. There weren't many women in Europe with the experience and the certificate to be flight instructors, and I realized, as I read, that I thought more highly of Tony because he seemed to think so highly of this one. It made me think well of Capitaine Bazille, too, because Rosario and Bazille were friends.

As Tony had promised, the interview with Rosario also told me a little more about him than he'd told any of the rest of us himself. I knew he'd trained at a flight school in Madrid after moving to Spain with his mother; I didn't know his mother had been killed in one of the air attacks on Madrid last year.

I didn't know he'd been injured himself, in a different one.

He'd been in the hospital for quite some time after he was hurt, a converted convent called Santa Agnès de Marañosa. Rosario Carreras said she flew him over the Pyrenees herself, in the Hanriot 436 she used for ambulance flights, to get him out of Spain.

My tired eyes stumbled over the musical name of the hospital, the Spanish words glaringly foreign in the French article I was reading. I read the name twice, then three and four times over, without taking in what it meant anymore.

Santa Agnès de Marañosa, Santa Agnès de Marañosa... Why did that sound familiar?

When had I heard someone say that? It was recently— earlier today—

I sat up in bed with a start when I realized what it was.

The Santa Agnès de Marañosa Investigation was what Major Rosengart had called the Rocketman Affair.

Tony had been in the same hospital as those terrible murders, when the German airman went berserk and killed everyone on the ward.

"Was he there when it happened?" I exclaimed aloud.

I smacked the page of the article as if I could shock it into telling me more.

He couldn't possibly have been. I knew the Rocketman murders had been back in February or March, because it had been before Guernica in April. And Rosario Carreras said she'd taken him to France very recently, only in June of this year.

It must be a random coincidence—as random as Vittorio Pavesi crossing paths with me at the moment of his death.

I was too tired to make any sense of it tonight. I tossed the magazine on the floor and turned out the light.

———◇———

I dreamed I was flying. At first it was a monotonous dream of being constantly lost, of resetting my heading, resetting my stopwatch, timings that didn't come out, landmarks that never turned up. I was trying to get to Amiens, and that made no sense. Every time I looked at my map I discovered I was still in England.

Then suddenly I was landing at a strange airfield, and just as I was about to touch down, the grass below me turned to rolling gray water.

I panicked, shoved on power, tried to take off again; but the controls would not move and my wheels were caught in the waves, and the Cadet began sinking, sinking, sucked down by a relentless sea.

Formation Flying

I woke with a gasp before I went under.

It was just before dawn; Mont Blanc, the highest peak of the Alps, was blue in the distance outside my window, and the hotel room was warm and quiet. But I could not go back to sleep. I lay there thinking about Santa Agnès de Marañosa and Tony. If it wasn't a coincidence, the only connection I could think of was that German-speaking Antoine Robert must be the Rocketman himself, the German airman who'd gone berserk.

Don't be ridiculous, Northie, I scolded. *I thought you trusted him now.*

I sat up and threw back the covers. I was too restless to lie in bed anymore; I decided to order coffee and work on tomorrow's flight plan. Whatever was going on, I couldn't convince myself that Tony Roberts had murdered fourteen Spanish

Republican soldiers and medics, and he still had the friendship and support of a woman like Rosario Carreras.

There must be another connection that I didn't know about, or couldn't see.

The morning passed in a blur, with a boat trip on Lake Geneva and a tour of the new Palace of Nations where the League of Nations held its meetings. It was impossible to enjoy any of it. In the afternoon we were taken back to the airfield at Cointrin to check our planes before the next day's flight. There we had to shake hands with dozens of Swiss Scouts and Girl Guides, as well as several hundred other people who all seemed either to be related to or former schoolmates of Theodor Vogt.

The tall, pockmarked racer was a national aerobatics champion in Switzerland, and now he gave a solo performance to thunderous applause. I watched Theodor's loops and spins in the heady blue sky, against the backdrop of the Jura Mountains, and found myself longing almost desperately to be back in that golden afternoon over Stonehenge before the race started, soaring over the English fields with the effortless exuberance of a lark. Oh, to be alone in the sky again, away from the other racers!

I bit my lip, realizing wryly that I hadn't been *alone* in the sky over Stonehenge.

When Theodor landed, the spectators' buzz moved to the German and French chaperones. Tony had been right about this demonstration: Capitano Ranza decided to drop out of the show. But Capitaine Marcel Bazille and Major Florian Rosengart shook hands and then ran for their planes as if they were rushing off to defend their respective nations. The crowd cheered wildly.

137

A couple of mechanics were there to start their engines almost before they'd scrambled into their seats. Then Major Rosengart's German Albatros Ace and Capitaine Bazille's French Hanriot 436 raced over the concrete toward the point where they'd lift off together. Even on the ground they were going too fast to be quite safe, weaving like hares so they could see ahead around the high noses of their planes.

I glanced over at the young men lined up next to me, standing in a row with their eyes all locked on the horizon. They looked like untidy soldiers waiting for the order to charge over the brow of a trench.

Which one of you is a murderer? I wondered.

Furthest in the line from me, the volatile Swedish law student, Torsten Stromberg, peered through his spectacles at the machines rattling off into the distance, as if he couldn't possibly see well enough to read a map, let alone fly.

Tall Erlend Pettersen stood next to him, fair and sunburned, his sky-blue artist's eyes no doubt admiring the symmetry and shape of the moving planes. Even taller, on Erlend's other hand, stood the lanky Swiss pilot Theodor Vogt, his scarred face glistening with sweat, flushed and triumphant after twenty minutes of throwing his plane around in the air in front of an excited audience.

Pim van Leer stood a little forward of the line, slight and dark, childishly short next to Theodor. There was a faint frown on his intense smooth face, the fresh breeze gently lifting the hair off his forehead like floating silk. Redheaded Gaby Dupont stood next to him with his hands on his hips, looking more relaxed now that he was out of Belgium and no longer the center of attention.

138

Then there was the square-shouldered Greek pilot Philip-pos Gekas, and the Polish pilot Stefan Chudek, who was smoking like a factory chimney as usual. I could hear them making comments to each other in broken Russian again, with Jiri Jindra, the big Czech with a bear's mop of curly brown hair, listening over their shoulders. I wasn't quite close enough to be able to catch what they were saying.

Sebastian Rainer stood on my right, flipping his stopwatch like a magician's coin dazzlingly back and forth between his nervous fingers.

And a little apart from the lineup, on my left, Tony Roberts gazed across the airfield, his thick brows lowered in his increasingly familiar faint frown, the wind stirring his too-long honey-brown hair. It was impossible to guess at his thoughts.

I looked up at the planes now soaring over the airfield. Rosengart's was gray, dull against the sky, with only its front cowling his signature sapphire blue. Bazille's plane was painted silver, the wing surfaces flashing as they caught the light.

The first thing the chaperones did after taking off was to fly at top speed around the airfield. The German plane was so much faster than the French one that Rosengart literally flew rings around Bazille as he lapped him. Next, they spun steeply around each other, terrifyingly close, winking blue and silver as they turned. Bazille set the pace, and Rosengart never once came unglued from his tail.

It was impossible for me not to think of Vittorio Pavesi's last moments alive. After a few minutes my whole body tingled with worry. As the dancing aircraft came tumbling earthward again, I couldn't bear to watch.

I turned my head, and Tony was standing beside me, and he wasn't watching either.

Everyone else had their necks craned back and the sun on their faces as they stared up at the breakneck performance going on in the sky. But Tony was gazing stonily across the airfield toward the Jura Mountains. The expression on his face was identical to the one he'd worn on the bus two days ago: as if he were enduring some nagging, relentless pain, like a backache or a migraine.

Suddenly I simply couldn't bear that look.

Small talk. Safe.

"What do you think of Bazille's flying?" I asked abruptly.

Tony wasn't listening. He was away somewhere else.

"Hey, *Tony!*"

He gave a jump.

For a moment he seemed confused. I saw him reconstruct his face. When he looked at me his expression was calm and blank.

"You're not watching the show," he accused me.

"I am. I want to know what you think of it."

"They're a couple of crackerjacks, aren't they?"

He sounded like he really thought so.

"Yes, it's wonderful."

I caught my breath and steeled myself to look up again. Bazille was descending with Rosengart still hot on his tail, a couple of seconds behind him.

"They're just playing around," said Tony. "That Ace is faster than the Hanriot, so it would be an unfair fight if they really went at it. But if they did—"

140

He paused, and glanced up for a moment, narrowing his eyes at the bright sky. Then he looked away quickly.

"What if they did?" I asked in a low voice.

"I don't know."

He turned to me again, and our eyes met. I wondered if he, too, thought our eyes were alike, cool and gray-green. We gazed at each other, the only two people on that airfield who weren't focused on the sky.

"Bazille is the better pilot," Tony said seriously. "And when I say 'the better pilot,' I don't mean he's the best of twelve kids trying to beat each other for a bucketful of cash. I mean that Bazille flew reconnaissance and combat missions for a year and a half in the Great War and landed his machine in one piece *every single time*, and never once was wounded. I don't know what Rosengart's war record is, but I know he's not remotely in the same league as Bazille, or I'd have heard of him before—" He paused for air, and took a deep breath. "Before he got involved in that mess in Spain. In a dogfight, it's all about maneuvering. It doesn't matter that the Ace is a little faster; neither of those planes is a modern fighter. If Marcel Bazille wanted to knock Florian Rosengart out of the sky right now, he could do it. He could do it in *that plane*."

I almost felt as if Tony was thinking he could do it *himself*.

"One of those new German Messerschmitt 109s would make mincemeat of any of our kites in combat," he went on. "They can do over three hundred miles an hour. But someone like Bazille might be able to outfly one."

"Could he really?"

"Sure. Reconnaissance pilots have to do that all the time. I mean, they don't always *succeed*. But when you get chased by a pursuit plane, you have to have a few tricks up your sleeve. Turn fast and head the opposite direction. Fly slow so the other guy can't match your speed. Get the sun behind your back and blind him, or fly straight at him like you're going to ram him."

I wasn't looking at the sky, but in my head I saw two bi-planes hovering side by side, one a little higher than the other.

"Or just hide," Tony finished. "Get down, fly as low as you can, skim the treetops. It's called 'hedgehopping.' It makes you really hard to see from above, and if the pursuit plane doesn't slow down fast enough, he'll overshoot and never find you again."

Both planes roared past us, barely over the runway, and climbed into the sky again. Tony watched them this time, his face calmer. The corner of his mouth twitched into a quirk that was nearly a smile.

"The Hanriot 436 is all right. It's not fast, but it's an update on a solid little machine. Mine's brand-new and Bazille's isn't much older."

I realized that not once had I ever seen him really smile, not even a mug for the cameras.

"Yeah, Bazille could fly the pants off that German if he wanted to," Tony said.

I was *sure* he was thinking he could do it himself.

Hedgehopping
The French Alps

We returned to Cointrin Airfield at sunrise on Wednesday morning. The public's obsessive fascination with us, as they waited for more public details of Vittorio Pavesi's disappearance, was beginning to feel ghoulish. Even this early in the day, there was already a fresh crowd gathered, anxious to watch the Olympics of the Air get started again.

It felt to me as if they'd never left. Surely they'd just stood around drinking coffee all night? Reporters asked spectators for their opinions; people pointed and gossiped, matching newspaper photographs to our faces. But Lady Frith bravely pretended everything was going according to plan. She made a show of handing out our daily flurry of telegrams, sent by wire transfer from all over the world, wishing us good luck and safe flying.

Nothing of course came from my aunt and uncle. The little girl in me was hurt, but the independent grown-up knew it didn't matter. Jean Pemberton sent one, containing only three flippantly cheerful words:

MOUNTAINS WHAT MOUNTAINS!

It was actually the defiant encouragement I needed.

I sat in the cockpit of the Cadet and checked over all my equipment. Everything was secure and accessible, map folded and clipped to my kneeboard, kneeboard buckled onto my thigh, grease pencil in my pocket, stopwatch on its chain attached to a buttonhole of my flying jacket.

I thought of Sebastian Rainer, spinning his stopwatch between restless fingers, and Tony Roberts, snapping the stem of his wine glass in two. All our nerves were jangling.

I rested my forehead against the Cadet's control column for a moment, waiting for the mechanic who would start my engine at exactly 9:25 a.m. so that I could take off at exactly 9:30.

I counted slowly to one thousand and forty-three before he turned up.

The Alps! Mont Blanc! They stood majestic in the distance, daring me to get closer.

It was another beautiful day, with a northwest wind that would help speed everyone directly to Venice. It was a perfect day for flying.

I wished I did not feel such constant dread in the pit of my stomach.

———◆———

I took off and flew along the southern shore of Lake Geneva. It meant I had to struggle against a crosswind, but it also meant that

144

no one else knew where I was. I followed the Rhône River to the pass between the towering peaks of Mont Blanc and the Matterhorn, then followed the narrow road over the Alps as it made its way toward the Italian town of Saint-Vincent in the Aosta Valley.

On either side of me, the sunny, snow-capped crags loomed higher than I was flying. I was sure the other racers would take a straight line over the mountains; Sebastian had told me that's what he planned to do. I even saw another plane cross ahead of me about a minute before I got to Saint-Vincent. It vanished among the peaks around Zermatt.

I hadn't thought about this when I planned my route. There was a point where I could cross paths with anyone taking off after me who planned to fly directly to Venice—Torsten Stromberg from Sweden or Tony Roberts were the most likely. The plane ahead was one less to worry about, at any rate.

I didn't see the plane behind until it was right on top of me.

———◇———

The pilot swooped down from high above, exactly the way he'd swooped down on Vittorio.

I saw the wings out of the corner of my eye. The turbulence made by their passing buffeted me so hard it was like being hit with something, even though the other plane didn't touch mine.

And then my attacker swooped away again.

Gasping, I looked back over my shoulder, and couldn't see anything. For a moment I couldn't believe I hadn't been physically struck. But the Cadet was still flying steadily, perfectly balanced, just the way I'd set it up for flight. The first attack only jarred *me*, not my plane.

Spooked, I glanced around wildly. At last I spotted it: above and behind, against the sun, a black shape speeding down toward me out of the heavens. Dazzled, I couldn't tell what color it was.

"Oh God—"

It was like watching a gloved hand aim a pistol at my heart—not that such a thing had ever happened to me.

The other pilot dived beneath my plane from behind. I yanked the nose up instinctively to avoid a collision. The entire aircraft shuddered for a moment, jarring my teeth—

Then the Cadet stalled.

The nose pitched violently forward, and the dipping left wings dragged the machine sideways. My stomach swooped as I went down with the plane, pinned in place by my safety harness. Suddenly I was out of control over the Alps, falling into a spin.

My head and my heart were in a numb shock of panic, living the nightmare of plummeting down toward mountains of rock.

But my hands and feet reacted automatically.

Jean Pemberton's relentless badgering came to my rescue. She'd thrown me into a spin like this more times than I could count, and now the repetitive drills paid off: I cut the engine, bore down on the rudder, and pushed the control column forward, all without thinking about it. When my thinking brain began to function again, I straightened the rudder and leveled my wings.

The Cadet was climbing again, I was in control of my plane, and the plane was all right: nothing had hit me and I hadn't hit anything.

But as I pulled the nose up and pushed the power back on, the reality of what was happening hit me like a sleety waterfall, like ice being poured down my back. The other pilot must be coming back, circling for a third attack. I craned my neck wildly, not knowing where in the sky to look. I imagined the other plane hurtling toward me again from above—

—And a low, serious voice in my head echoed, *Just hide.*

I didn't think about where I'd heard that voice. But I knew I had to listen to it.

Get down low, fly as low as you can, skim the treetops.

I pushed full power on and shoved the nose of the Cadet forward. I forced the plane into another screaming dive toward the earth's surface.

But this time I wasn't out of control—this time I was doing it on purpose.

I wasn't afraid of *flying*.

The larches of the steep slopes around Saint-Vincent came rushing up to meet me. I straightened the controls and raised the Cadet's nose before the plane got too low. Still descending, but no longer slipping and diving, I followed a swathe of forest up a narrow valley.

I turned my head to left and right, frantically trying to see above and behind. The larches below me were dark green, just beginning to be tinged with autumnal fawn higher up the slopes.

I thought suddenly, *My plane is painted green! I'm camouflaged! Thank God my plane is painted green!*

I wasn't quite at treetop level, but I was getting fearfully near as the ground rose beneath me. I coaxed the Cadet to climb a little, fifty feet or so, desperately trying to keep my green wings close to the sweet, concealing green forest of larches without hitting them.

It makes you really hard to see from above, said the echo in my head. *And if the pursuit plane doesn't slow down fast enough, he'll overshoot and never find you again.*

That low, serious voice in my head had an American accent.

I gasped aloud as I realized where I'd heard it and why it was so fresh.

He'll overshoot.

I was looking for my attacker in the wrong place. If he overshot, he would be ahead of me, not behind or above.

I lowered the Cadet's nose a little more and adjusted the power so I wouldn't descend any further. I forced myself to throttle back a bit, making tiny adjustments, trying to stay with the trees. If I went shooting out over bare rock, I'd be a visible target again.

And then I saw the other plane.

It was another trainer, a single-engined bi-plane like my own. Tony was right about that: the other plane definitely wasn't Lady Frith's Dragon Rapide, even though I couldn't tell what color it was. It was climbing in a slow spiral against the mountain slope ahead of me, like a hawk riding a thermal. As long as I stayed hidden, low against the tops of the trees, I might stay safe.

I'd have landed if I could, and the race be damned.

But there wasn't any place to land. The road behind me was narrow and winding and didn't run flat, and everything around it was trees and slopes of rock.

There was nothing to do but keep flying.

PART THREE

ANY MAN'S
DEATH
DIMINISHES ME

Wednesday, 25 August–
Friday, 27 August, 1937

Refugee

Milan, Italy

I'd shaken him.

It was like diving into icy water to make myself climb back to a safe height and set a new track.

But I did it. I couldn't stay circling over the larches until I ran out of fuel.

The attack had come just as I passed Saint-Vincent. In fact I was already most of the way across the French Alps, though any edge I might have had in the race was gone. The sky seemed empty, but I didn't dare stay with the road now. I headed almost due east. The other pilot wouldn't be likely to guess my route to Milan without knowing where I'd started from.

The lower slopes of the southern Alps felt like gentle and forgiving meadows after what I'd just been through, soft swathes of woodland with no sign of habitation.

I landed in Milan forty minutes later. I was expected there, because it was my planned refueling stop. I climbed out of my plane and fumbled for my passport, but the ground crew who greeted me weren't immigration officials and waved it aside. My hands shook so much I couldn't get the passport back into my flight bag.

I laid it momentarily on the Cadet's lower wing, while they found a mechanic in greasy overalls who spoke French. When he saw how badly I was shaking, he offered me a cigarette, and I couldn't hold that, either.

They took me into the shelter of one of the hangars and gave me a cup of strong coffee that I couldn't drink—I couldn't hold it steady enough to get it to my mouth without spilling it everywhere. They made me sit on the lower rung of a stepladder and set the coffee beside me on the floor while it cooled.

"What happened?" the French speaker asked.

"I ran into—"

I stopped sharply.

I was in a foreign country I'd never landed in before. I didn't know any of these people and I didn't dare tell them what had actually happened.

"I ran into...into turbulence," I said at last, finding that I could speak as usual even if my hands weren't working. "Mountain wave wind. I...my plane got thrown about quite hard."

A few others were gathered around me now, concerned and interested as mother ducks. They all knew who I was.

Blast and drat, I thought. *I have got to pull myself together or they'll never let another girl into a European air race.*

"We will give your machine a thorough check!" the French-speaking mechanic told me soothingly. "Our money is on you now, Miss North. If the tragic Vittorio Pavesi cannot

152

finish the race for Italy, we are going to back the prettiest contestant!"

I grimaced, trying to smile. One of them had his hand comfortingly on my knee, but I couldn't feel it through the thickness of my flight suit. Another handed me the coffee again, as the shaking eased off a little, and I warmed my hands by folding them around the thick, cracked enamel of the well-worn cup.

"Do you have a map you need to look at, wind calculations to make for Venice?" the translator asked me. "We will find you a desk. Sit here while we arrange a place for you to work."

I didn't want to stay. Whoever my attacker was, he'd guessed what my flight plans were from Geneva. He might also guess that I'd landed in Milan, because I was supposed to refuel there, and he might try to meet me in the air again on my way to Venice. Perhaps he'd even been watching as I landed—

"I've already planned the onward flight," I said, speaking as calmly as I could. "I'll go as soon as the refueling is finished. I'll be all right in a moment."

They left me alone for a few minutes.

I sat staring out of the dimness of the hangar and into the brightness of the day outside, trying to breathe steadily.

When I first began to fly, I read everything I could find about aviation: the fictional adventures of Biggles, Antoine de Saint-Exupéry's novels and memoirs, Amelia Earhart's *The Fun of It*. Now I vividly remembered a passage from a book called *War Birds*, a diary kept in between combat missions by an American Great War pilot while he was in France in 1918.

Over and over he described what a wreck of nerves he

became on the ground between flights, going completely to pieces the moment he shut down his engine: not being able to button his overcoat or light a match, having to use both hands to hold a mug or he couldn't drink—exactly as I felt now. And the dread of going up again, the leaden way his feet felt as he dragged himself out to his plane for his next mission.

But then in the sky, he said, in the sky, as soon as he took off, his hands on the flight controls would be steady as bedrock, his aim through the gunsights unerring. In the air he became a bird of prey, calm, focused, fearless.

I tensed my hands into fists.

I will take off again in ten minutes and I will be as fearless as a bird of prey.

I tried to relax my fingers. I raised the warm mug to my lips with both hands and managed to take a sip through clenched teeth. But I didn't dare finish the strong Italian coffee. I was as awake and alert as I could possibly be, and the last thing I needed was to give my nerves another jolt.

I put down the coffee and got up and walked to the hangar door, blinking as I stepped back into the sunlight. There were the Alps in the distance, the mountains I'd been so apprehensive about, which had ended up protecting me.

The French-speaking mechanic came back, giving me a friendly wave.

"Your aircraft is fine, not at all damaged. But you left this on the wing—you are lucky one of the boys picked it up."

He held out my passport.

"*Hell's bells,*" I gasped aloud in English. I reached out to take it from him, and he saw clearly how my hand still trembled.

Blast and drat and damnation! I lashed myself with a

silent string of curses. I *wasn't* careless, I didn't lose things like Tony Roberts. But this was *exactly* the kind of thing everyone expected a girl to do—leave her passport sitting on the wing of her plane while she wandered off to drink a cup of coffee. CARELESS, I lashed myself. *Thank GOD it happened here where there are no reporters—*

I shoved the passport into the breast pocket of my flight suit and said aloud, "Thank you, thank you! You have saved me so much trouble—"

"You have a Nansen passport?" the mechanic asked curiously. "Refugee? But you are Northie, Britain's North Star!"

Had he talked about it with the rest of the ground crew? Did they all know?

"Yes, I am English, I speak English, I grew up in England, but I don't have an English passport," I babbled furiously, realizing as the words tumbled out that I sounded exactly like Tony defending his claim to being French.

———◇———

My arms and legs seemed to be filled with concrete as I climbed back into the pilot's cockpit of my Cadet. I felt exactly like the flier who'd written the combat diary.

What would Jean tell me to do? *Stick to routine, do all the checks carefully, make sure everything works.*

One of the mechanics had pushed my seat back as far as it would go to accommodate his longer legs as he'd looked over my plane. I reached down to pull the seat forward again. In between the metal supports I touched a smooth, round object, cool beneath my fingertips, wedged firmly in the braces that held up the seat.

I felt around the edges of the unfamiliar piece of metal, trying to figure out if it was part of the plane. I realized that if I pushed it upward, it got looser. The space between the support bars was wider at the top than the bottom.

My hand was just narrow enough to slide it down between the seat and the side of the plane, and after a minute I managed to work the thing loose and lift it out.

"Ouch!"

A pinprick of pain stabbed into the tip of my finger.

I opened my hand. There on my palm lay a Swiss Hanhart stopwatch, its metal rim scratched and battered, its face webbed with cracks.

A tiny drop of blood appeared on the tip of my finger, where I'd caught it on an invisible sliver of glass.

My heart turned over, thinking grimly of the lighter that had jammed Tony's rudder. Dropping my stopwatch in flight could have done the same thing.

It must have fallen off and slipped into the seat support when I'd stalled, or perhaps when I'd pushed the Cadet into a dive. The watch looked as if it had taken a beating. I was unbelievably lucky that it had wedged itself into the seat braces. If it had fouled any of the cables during that spin over the mountains, I didn't think I'd have been able to recover.

I glanced down to look for my watch chain, and thought suddenly, *But I was checking my times the whole way to Milan— when did I lose the watch? After I landed?*

The chain was still attached to the buttonhole of my flying jacket, disappearing into my pocket.

I reached into the pocket and there was my own stopwatch, secure, exactly where it was supposed to be.

156

The one I'd just found beneath the seat of my plane didn't belong to me.

———◆———

Almost everyone's Hanhart stopwatch looked alike, in a plain steel alloy case. I examined the broken one I held now, and saw that it was an earlier model than my own. The face had probably cracked when the seat of my plane got moved, but I thought the battered metal rim looked worn with ordinary use. There were lines and loops around the edge that seemed deliberate. Tony Roberts had lost a stopwatch with his father's name scratched on it. Could this possibly say *pogopob*? The design looked decorative, but not like lettering.

Suddenly I was angry. Yes, of course I was competing for money and fame like all the other racers. But none of us should be desperate enough to *kill* for it, trying to ram each other's planes and planting loose objects in open cockpits again and again.

The anger steadied me, and I stopped panicking. The stopwatch in my seat had been securely wedged and might have been dropped accidentally, perhaps by one of the mechanics who'd just checked my plane. I didn't want to squander more time finding out; I was only allowed twenty minutes to refuel, and anything over that would add to my racing time. And the watch could belong to *anyone*. Whoever lost it was likely to have bigger hands than mine, and hadn't been able to free it. Perhaps it had been caught there since before I'd started flying this plane, which I'd borrowed from a friend of Jean's for the race.

I wrapped my handkerchief carefully around the mysterious cracked stopwatch and put it in my pocket with my own.

If that Great War diarist could get back in his plane, *every day*, and fly out to combat again determined not to die, so could I.

Birds of prey did it without fear.

So could I.

———◆———

I flew like a demon from Milan to Venice. With a full load of fuel and only a hundred and fifty miles to go, there wasn't any reason to hold back. Focusing on the plane, on speed and on keeping the engine cool, kept me from looking constantly over my shoulders to try to see above and behind me.

This must be how those combat pilots managed it, how they managed to keep taking off again day after day—just focusing on flying.

This must be how Tony Roberts manages it, too, I thought suddenly, as the Cadet tore through the sky. *This is why he's so incredibly fast. He has to make a refueling stop on every leg, but that means overall he doesn't ever risk running out of fuel. He doesn't have to think about it in flight. He just burns it all and flies as fast as he can.*

In just under an hour and a half I touched down at the busy Nicelli Aerodrome on the northern tip of the island of Lido, across the lagoon from Venice, as close as we could get to Venice by air without floats for a water landing. There was another small bi-plane coming in to land when I got there; I taxied after it to the parking area, and as I pulled up next to it I recognized Tony Roberts's green Hanriot 436.

He'd obviously flown another ridiculously fast course.

How could he *possibly* have beaten me to Venice? He'd taken off half an hour behind me.

Of course, he probably hadn't lost time hiding from a murderer in the Alps.

Hell's teeth. I was sweating and breathless. As I attempted to climb out of my cockpit with dignity, I discovered that my hands were still shaking.

Enthusiastic aerodrome personnel were standing ready to greet me, including a well-dressed young woman who held out an enormous welcoming bouquet. There was an impressive-looking streamlined modern passenger terminal at Nicelli, and Tony and I were escorted into the building together; he'd also been given a bouquet. The Italian hostess led us to an immigration desk, chattering excitedly to us in broken French all the way. With our arms full of flowers and flight gear, and our grim expressions, I thought we must look exactly like a newlywed couple on a honeymoon gone wrong.

The immigration official behind the desk turned to me first, of course, because I was the girl, and it was the polite thing to do. I passed the armful of flowers back to the Italian woman and dug in my flight bag for my passport.

It wasn't there.

I panicked for a moment, thinking I'd left it on the Cadet's wing back in Milan.

All in a flash, I remembered how the mechanic had found it and that I'd put it in my pocket. Tony was close behind me; I was delaying us both, and, blast and drat, I couldn't stop the shaking. My hand quivered as I held out my passport to the man behind the desk.

Everyone was watching. I couldn't keep my hand still enough to let the immigration official take the document from me without us both looking silly. I slapped the passport down on the desktop and stepped back.

The official beckoned to Tony, asking for his passport as well. Tony was ready with his. He stepped forward to lay it next to mine without a second's hesitation.

Then he suddenly froze, staring down at our two passports, side by side on the desk in the Italian aerodrome.

I stared too.

Our passports were identical: two tattered gray paper documents that didn't bear the name of any country.

Tony Roberts was traveling abroad on a Nansen passport just like mine.

He lived and worked in France. Before that, he'd lived in Spain with his mother, who was from America. I'd assumed that he felt at home in at least one of those three places, maybe all of them; regardless of which he valued the most, proud to belong to some proud nation.

My passport, issued by the Nansen International Office for Refugees, says that I am "a person of Russian origin not having acquired another nationality." But it is not considered a valid passport in the Soviet Union, the place that used to be Russia, and I am not considered a Soviet citizen.

A Nansen passport—it meant that Tony, like me, was stateless.

Tony stepped back, turned his head to catch my eye, and gave me one of his long, cool, direct glances through clear gray-green eyes. He asked in his slang-laden American English, "What's the matter with your hands, sister?"

160

"Shut up," I hissed. "Not here."

"How about I buy you a drink when we get to the hotel, then?"

"You and the other boys are staying at a pensione, not a big hotel with a bar, and I can't anyway because Lady Frith's got a friend who lives here and we're both staying with her. You know I'll never get a moment to myself until we get to Prague in Czechoslovakia."

I shoved my hands into the pockets of my flying jacket. A chill crawled across my shoulders as my fingers met the pair of stopwatches hidden there.

It was rude, and risky, talking to each other in English while we were being held captive at the Italian immigration desk.

"What about tomorrow morning, just before the memorial service for Vittorio Pavesi?" Tony suggested. "Old Lady Frith can't object to coffee in St. Mark's Square. You could play at wanting a date. She'll eat that up, just like the reporters. She can sit across the café keeping an eye on us and fending off the press, and everyone will be happy." He took a deep breath. "We need to talk, Northie."

I knew we did.

"All right. Coffee in St. Mark's Square," I agreed. "I'll tell her we want to discuss performing together in her air show in Paris."

"Couldn't be better," Tony said. "Make it for nine thirty, and I'll wait for you in the square."

The immigration official stamped my passport and handed it back to me.

Tony and I walked through the passenger terminal

161

together to join the other racers who had already arrived. I knew I'd have to give my *Comet* interview in a moment, and I needed to compose myself for that—if anything, I was in a far worse state than I'd been on the first day. I was damned if I'd try to report an attempt on my own life and be brushed off as hysterical.

But—what if I said something about it to the reporters?

What if I made it sound like something the press had come up with, or their readers, perhaps, but made it serious enough that the chaperones would have to do something about it?

Think carefully, Northie. Don't let the killer know you're going behind his back...Don't let Lady Frith hear, either.

I looked around quickly for the hats and cameras. The French newspapermen were descending on Tony, and I grabbed one of them by the sleeve.

"*Bonjour! Mademoiselle Stella North, c'est moi,*" I told him. "Please don't take my photograph or I won't speak to you. I think one of the other racers is a murderer."

He stared at me and we quietly stepped aside together.

"I'm really not supposed to be speaking to you," I said. "You mustn't make it look as if I reported what I'm about to tell you. You'll have to pretend that you or one of your colleagues was on the ground in the Alps near Saint-Vincent this morning, and that you saw it yourself. I'll tell you exactly what happened."

Coffee in St. Mark's Square
Venice, Italy

Ten minutes later, I joined the other contestants amid piles of flowers, in a room that had been set aside for us while we waited for the water taxi from Lido to Venice. Our baggage was stacked in a corner, and I dug out the day-old newspapers I hadn't yet read. I sat down next to Tony and, breathing hard, opened a paper with shaking hands. I started to read about Torsten Stromberg, the studious-looking Swedish pilot who flew the Tigerswallow.

Those journalists had all said he'd broken his fiancée's nose. The real story was more complicated. Torsten had taken his fiancée flying last spring, and she'd panicked and grabbed at the controls while they were landing. The plane did a ground loop and ran into another aircraft, and the girl broke her nose against the dash and had to have stitches in her forehead. Torsten was so cut up about it that he failed his law exams—and then went on a bender and got arrested after trying to beat someone up in a barroom brawl!

I sat for a moment letting this wealth of information sink in. Torsten Stromberg could be both thoughtless and violent when he was angry. But he hadn't attacked his fiancée.

Commenting on the incident, Lady Frith confessed to having a soft spot for unhappy people, the news story ran. *She is an activist for several causes supporting children and women's rights, and of course her own childhood was lived in the shadow of a violent father.*

"Gosh," I said aloud.

I wondered if this was why Lady Frith had taken such an interest in *me*. All I saw in her was the brazen, attention-seeking, twice-divorced adventurer who liberally spent piles of her ex-husbands' money on clothes and expensive toys.

But she'd spent the Great War fixing ambulances. She supported children's charities. And this race, in the name of peace—maybe Lady Frith really did believe she could somehow make a difference.

Tony, sitting next to me, frowned as he watched the other racers. I folded the newspaper and tapped his knee with it to get his attention and show him.

"*Shh.*" He brushed it aside with one hand and raised a brief finger to point across the room.

Major Florian Rosengart was having a quiet word with Sebastian Rainer. Sebastian listened with wintry politeness, white-faced beneath his cropped barley-fair hair; he looked as if he wanted the ground to open up and swallow him.

"He was late getting in," Tony informed me in a low voice, close to my ear. "He got here fifteen minutes before us, and Rosengart was still reading him the riot act when we landed. You should have heard that old German ace going on about punctuality! Apparently Major Florian Rosengart always times his own landings to the exact minute he estimates. He said he'd been waiting for Sebastian for an *hour.* Boy, I wouldn't want to be in that kid's shoes—thank God I'm not German. Imagine being the Luftwaffe pilot who loses the Olympics of the Air for Hitler."

Sebastian had somehow ended the day's flying *a whole hour late.*

So there'd been plenty of time for him to attack me over the French Alps.

It would be two days before we had to fly again. There was also plenty of time for those European newspapers to come to my rescue.

———◇———

That night's banquet was held in the Doge's Palace in Venice, where we were brought in a parade of gondolas, encouraged by a cheering audience who waved flags and blew horns from the banks and bridges. It was a miracle I did not fall into St. Mark's Basin getting out of the boat with the photographers' flashes going off all around, and the reporters shouting questions at us in five different languages.

I thought of the Great War pilot being unable to button his overcoat or light a match. At least in the trenches between dogfights he did not have to put on long white gloves and an evening gown and smile at the tabloid press; not to mention curtseying to Bruno Mussolini, the Italian dictator's own pilot son, who was our guest of honor that night.

He was nineteen, the same age as three of the Olympics of the Air racers. He'd been Italy's youngest pilot when he took his license, and was already a veteran of the wars in both Ethiopia and Spain.

We were introduced to the celebrity pilot in the order in which we took off in the morning. I waited my turn feeling as if I were in a cage full of tame lions. Standing right behind Sebastian, I could see his hands locked behind his back, his fingers hooked together. He was nervously scratching the back of one thumb with the nail of the other. But he was controlling himself; everyone was under control here, and I was protected by the crowd.

Sebastian's turn came. He bowed and shook hands seriously, and for once didn't pull any magician's tricks. He said a few words in German, which Capitano Ranza translated into Italian. I heard the word "Jungmann," the name of the plane Sebastian was flying, but nothing that wasn't purely ordinary and formal.

"Miss Stella North, of the United Kingdom of Great Britain and Northern Ireland, flying an Avro Cadet," Capitano Ranza announced as Sebastian moved away.

I stepped forward and made my curtsy. I hadn't been educated at an elite English girls' school for nothing. Then I straightened and held out my hand in its long white evening glove, trying not to grimace as I desperately attempted to steady my trembling fingers.

But when the dictator's son took my hand, instead of shaking it, he raised it to his lips for a chivalrous kiss.

He held my gloved fingers there for a moment, letting cameras flash. He suddenly reminded me very much of Vittorio Pavesi, and I knew that, under the circumstances, I had to be polite.

I held myself together, beating down anxiety. This would

be on the front page of a dozen newspapers tomorrow morning: Britain's North Star being wooed by the son of the Fascist dictator of Italy. I tried to jerk my hand away, but he had it fast. After a moment he lowered our hands. He looked down consideringly at my unsteady fingers in their smooth white kid, then let me go.

"I'm sorry about Vittorio," I murmured in French. "I know he was your friend."

"You are distressed by his death," he answered. "I can see this. As I am. You must take care that it does not affect your flying."

"I will," I said through my teeth. "Thank you."

Tony was next in line.

"Antoine Robert, of the French Republic, flying a Hanriot 436."

Bruno Mussolini held out his hand again. Tony stood for a moment looking bleakly into the young Italian's face. I watched, expecting Tony to make that neat, sharp, unexpectedly formal bow of his.

Instead, he put both hands behind his back and stepped away.

It wasn't dramatic. His passionate hatred of Fascism, or maybe his loyalty to Spain, his adopted nation that was crumbling under a Fascist-supported civil war—or maybe both— just took over all his rational brain. Tony refused to shake hands with the Italian dictator's son.

This time it was Capitaine Bazille, not Major Rosengart, who calmly escorted Tony out of the reception hall.

It was the highlight of the evening for the other Circuit of Nations contestants.

"Phenomenal! Lady Frith will add half an hour to his flight time as a penalty," Jiri Jindra, the irrepressible burly Czech, reported to the rest of us as we filed in to dinner after the reception.

"I wish I had done it," said Pim darkly. "But all of Europe is watching and I have not the nerve."

"Very wise too," Erlend told him. "He is lucky he did not get arrested."

Was that lucky? Wouldn't he be *safer* in an Italian prison cell?

Would I?

———◆———

I was, in fact, probably safer than Tony for two nights. I was as safe as I could possibly be under the circumstances, because I was staying with Lady Frith in Casa Rossa, her friend Aida Benedetti's house on the Grand Canal.

Aida Benedetti was a tall, cool-looking woman who wore floating Bohemian silks and spoke finishing-school-perfect English just like mine. She was a welcoming and gracious hostess, full of friendly kisses and interested questions about aviation. From my bedroom in her house I could see lights on the Rialto Bridge, and I could hear the lap of briny water, the hoot of late taxi boats, and the voices of gondoliers. I should have felt safe in Casa Rossa, behind private walls, with a butler turning away the curious from the door. It should have been like coming in out of the cold to a warm fire in a cozy room. But I couldn't feel safe. I might be fine for the next two days, but after that I'd be back in the air again.

God! *My hands.* Before going to bed, I asked Aida for

buttons and needle and thread; I thought that doing a little domestic work might help to steady me. I was going to make sure that Tony Roberts did not shame Lady Frith with his slovenly clothes held together with bits of string, when the racers and chaperones were all lined up in a row beneath the golden mosaic dome of St. Mark's Basilica the next morning to remember Vittorio Pavesi.

———◆———

Thursday dawned overcast and sultry. I dressed in the plain navy skirt Lady Frith had advised me to bring, as neither evening clothes nor flying trousers nor my summer cotton frock for touring felt appropriate for a vigil in St. Mark's Basilica. I had only a plain white cotton blouse to wear with the skirt—I tried to make it pretty with one of my dotted Swiss silk flying scarves, limp from being used to wipe sweat and dead bugs from my goggles. I'd brought along a small handbag for when I wasn't racing, which Jean had given me as a good-luck present; but even so, I ended up with the uneasy feeling that I must look as if I were wearing a school uniform. I hadn't expected to have to make a public appearance in a church during the race.

At least I was neat and sober, appropriate for the Flying English Rose, and at the same time I wasn't going to give the photographers much glamour to work with.

Tony was even less appropriately kitted out for a church service than I was, in his usual khaki flannel flying shirt and a brown wool jacket with patched elbows. Like me, though, he'd knotted a silk pilot's scarf around his neck for a sort of cravat. Lady Frith, who'd agreed to Tony's suggestion of sitting protectively on the other side of the café during our meeting, spotted him right in the middle of St. Mark's Square, hands in pockets, pacing slowly to and fro as he waited for my arrival.

He wasn't looking out for us. He was lost in his own world, whatever that was, anonymous without his flying gear, alternately staring up at the wonderful starry blue-and-gold panels of the St. Mark's Clock Tower and aiming kicks at pigeons to get them out of his way.

"You have half an hour," Lady Frith reminded me. "Enjoy yourself." She squeezed me around the waist confidentially, suddenly calling to my mind the unpleasant Wonderland Duchess trying to make a bosom companion of the reluctant Alice. "I do like your idea of flying with Tony. There's no denying he can be unpleasant company when he's in a sullen mood, but he's a very good pilot. And your machines are well matched in size and speed. They'll look appealing in flight together, both being green."

We crossed St. Mark's Square to meet Tony, and found the café Aida Benedetti had recommended, in the arcade on the north side of the piazza. It had high, ornately plastered ceilings and white-painted gossamer wrought-iron tables; topped off with Venetian glass chandeliers shaped like hanging fruit, it was almost like walking into a room made of cake decorations. Tony seemed such a fish out of water in this frothy confection of glass and sugar that for a moment, as we waited for tables, I worried they'd ask him to leave.

But Lady Frith was always like a force of nature. She arranged a discreet corner table for me and Tony while she installed herself in the best seat in the house, in the great plate glass window looking out through the arcade and into the square beyond. There she'd be able to keep an eye on us and everything else at the same time.

A wide-eyed young waitress, who looked even younger than Pim van Leer, handed Tony a menu. He then surprised her, and me too, by ordering coffee and macarons for both of us in perfectly polite and adequate Italian.

The moment the waitress turned her back, Tony quietly handed me his passport over the table, laying it flat on the white cloth.

I opened it and read: *"Anton Vasilievich Roborovski, d'origine russe, n'ayant acquis aucune autre nationalité"* — Anton Vasilievich Roborovski, of Russian origin, not having acquired any other nationality.

He was traveling under a Russian name.

He was *exactly like me.*

"Is that your real name?" I asked.

"It's my real name," he admitted grimly.

The English Rose

"'Tony,'" I said, and couldn't keep the sarcastic disbelief from my voice.

"My mother called me Tony." The familiar scowl briefly shadowed his face. "My flight instructor suggested I get a Nansen passport in 1936, when the war started in Spain, since I didn't have any other official papers and my father originally came from Russia. Antoine Robert is just an easy French translation."

He let his expression go neutral again as the waitress came back. She set down a coffee pot and a mouth-watering pile of macarons on a glass plate.

"*Grazie.*" Tony nodded coolly to her and waited until she'd retreated before he continued. "Dad left Russia in 1905. He was a language teacher—both my parents were language teachers. He lived in Hamburg, in Germany, until the Great

War broke out, and then he went to Spain in 1915 because he didn't want to fight for Germany *or* Russia; Spain was neutral. That's where he met my mother."

He poured coffee for himself, and went on.

"They worked at the same school in Madrid, teaching English and German and Italian. Probably also a few other languages they didn't speak at home. When I was a baby they used to read to me from *The Odyssey* in ancient Greek to put me to sleep—every bit as good as a lullaby! After the war they went back to Hamburg, and that's where I grew up. You know how we had to put down a list of our languages on the race application? I think that's how I squeaked in as a contestant. I'm pretty fluent in five languages."

"I wouldn't be here either, if the Race Committee were strict about citizenship," I agreed.

"I'll admit I'm a dark horse as a French national," Tony said. "My ma spoke French but my dad didn't, so I didn't hear it at home and I didn't pick it up as easily. Same with Russian, but the other way round. Would you believe I don't even know what my first language was? I guess it could have been German. But I was born in Spain."

"How do you speak such American English?" I asked. "Your English sounds like you just stepped out of a Western moving picture."

He snorted. "It does not. I've never been west of Lake Erie! Until I was fifteen I spent every summer with my ma's parents near Buffalo, in New York State. That's where my dad and I had our first flying lessons."

"It still sounds like something in a film."

"Fair enough," he agreed. "It doesn't feel real to me

anymore, either. Those Yankee barnstormers, they *loved* my dad—they'd tease him about his Russian accent, they'd make us race each other. Nobody ever had any money at that airfield: we had to work on the planes ourselves, and they let us help out with the maintenance or the crop-dusting instead of paying for lessons. I used to sweep up after air shows. I even got to fly in a show with them once—'New York State's Youngest Aviator'!"

"That's super!" I was envious.

"It was wonderful. Every summer for six weeks it was like being in a little corner of heaven. Then in 1933 when the Nazis came to power in Germany, my mother tried to renew her American passport in Hamburg, but she couldn't get me put on again because I wasn't born in the USA, and my father was known as a Russian Communist. So we stayed in Germany that year. And then—well—"

He looked up at me, his clear eyes cool and honest. "I guess you haven't heard of Dachau," he said.

I shook my head.

"It's a concentration camp. A sort of prison. The Nazis put you there for speaking your mind, or for saying or doing anything that goes against their system, or sometimes they just make up a reason. Then they work you to death, or maybe starve you to death. No one really knows what happens. They take you away without a trial, and no one ever comes back." He drew a sharp breath. "Kids whisper about it as if they were talking about trolls. *Dear Lord God, make me dumb, to Dachau may I never come—*"

"Yes, the Bolsheviks take people away like that too," I said. "I know."

Tony narrowed his eyes. "I guess you'd call my father a

Bolshevik. A multilingual Bolshevik with an American pilot's license. The Nazis didn't like him either; they lock up all their political enemies, mainly Communists. My dad had refused to fight in the war *and* he was a Communist. They sent him to Dachau and he never came back."

Tony didn't try to ply me with coffee and sweets the way Rosengart had—he looked past them at me as if the table were completely empty. "When they got my father, my mother ran away with me back to Spain," he said. "I was fifteen. It was all right in Spain in 1934, for a couple of years before the civil war started."

I said quietly, "I read your instructor's interview in *Voici Paris*. I'm sorry about your mother."

He shrugged and looked away. He said, "Madrid was bombed."

"Is that how you cope with it?" I asked. "Just shrug and pretend it didn't happen?"

"Not everybody grows up in an English rose garden," he said, not looking at me, the habitual frown thunderous. "You *have* to cope with things."

"You don't know a damn thing about my English rose garden," I told him.

I didn't remember Petrograd in Russia, and those awful years of violence during the Russian civil war. I didn't remember my real parents.

But I remembered how desperately I missed their hugs and cuddles when I was very little. Aunt Marie and Uncle Max were frosty and formal, proud of the fact that they'd only been allowed to enter the United Kingdom because they were relatives of the czar, an aristocratic couple who weren't going to be a burden on the British state. Our arrival in England was entirely based on the contents of Aunt Marie's jewel case.

And until they sent me off to Cheltenham Ladies' College at the age of eleven, we did nothing but battle. Aunt Marie would throw away any library book she didn't like the look of, and I'd have to work off the fines by running secret errands for the postmistress at the corner of our road. I had to keep my egg collection in a neighbor's shed. They pulled me out of riding lessons when they discovered I wasn't being taught to ride sidesaddle. It is true my long summer holidays were spent pruning roses, but only because I was never allowed to do anything else. I'd work in the garden alongside Aunt Marie, counting the minutes till I could go back to school, listening to her endless inventories of china and jewelry she'd left behind in Russia.

I was still battling them, but now I had a bit more ammunition.

"Your father was killed for being a Communist," I said. "Well, that makes us natural enemies. My parents were killed by the Communists."

Tony responded sullenly and quickly, "What was all that malarkey about birds' eggs and the English countryside, then?"

I clenched my fists on the table. "It didn't happen last year like it did to you," I hissed. "I was three. The Bolsheviks arrested my parents in the middle of the night, so quietly it didn't even wake me up. I was stuck in our room in the cellar by myself for four days, and would have died of thirst if there hadn't been water standing in the wash basin."

Subdued, Tony asked, "Do you know what happened to your parents?"

I answered through gritted teeth. "They shot them and left their bodies by the waste bins behind the house."

He took a deep breath. "I'm sorry." And another. "I didn't know."

"I didn't know that, either, till I was older. My father's brother, my Uncle Max, was sure he and his wife would be next, because Aunt Marie was a cousin of the murdered czar. So they took me with them and left Russia—Aunt Marie sold her grandmother's diamonds to pay for our passage to London. I'm sure you think that sounds very ritzy, doesn't it?"

Tony shook his head, tight-lipped, his natural frown ferocious. "Just go on."

"The only reason we weren't deported straightaway was because they'd already got in and there wasn't any place to send them back to," I finished flatly. "They had nothing when they got to England, nothing but *me*, and I wasn't even theirs. Max's first job there was sweeping up litter in Paddington Station. So don't talk to me about being *bourgeois*, you with your free flight lessons on a farm in New York State and your lullabies in ancient Greek!"

"All right, cool down, I—" He cut himself short, and repeated, "I'm sorry. I didn't have any idea."

"We have twenty minutes left," I reminded him. "Are we going to talk about the race?"

He asked abruptly, "Why were you such a bundle of nerves after you landed yesterday?"

I scowled at him. "Why do you think?"

"If it wasn't so far-fetched, I'd say you'd spent the afternoon in combat. Okay, I know you weren't looking forward to crossing the Alps, but you're a pretty solid pilot. That landing

177

at Mont des Bergers didn't bother you. You made fantastic time over France on the second day, and pretty good time yesterday, too. If someone's trying to win the race by picking off the likely competition, the fast planes and the good pilots, well, you're an obvious choice. Whoever put Vittorio Pavesi's plane out of action has already had a stab at me, and he might take another. So I want to know what's going on, and I think you know more than I do."

My hands had started to shake again just because I was thinking about it.

I moved my clenched fists from the table to my lap.

"You think I know more than you?" I challenged. "I guess I do. I seem to be caught right in the thick of it, Comrade Roborovski or Monsieur Robert or Mister Roberts, whatever your name is."

I reached into my handbag for the stopwatch that I'd found in my plane in Milan. I pressed it firmly onto the table between us, and unfolded the handkerchief so he could see it.

"This doesn't belong to me," I said. "But I think someone might have dropped it in my plane just the way they tossed that cigarette lighter into yours. I think you're right—someone's try-ing to kill me."

Tony picked it up gingerly, mindful of the shattered watch face.

Then he turned it over and gave a gasp of shock.

"But this is *mine!*" he said.

He stared at me in astonished outrage, as if he thought I'd stolen it.

"Yours?" I exclaimed. "You said yours has your father's name on it!"

"Well, look!"

He held the watch across the table so I could see the scratched loops and lines around the edge.

I hadn't recognized them because they were Cyrillic letters rather than Roman.

The name they spelled out was in Russian.

ВАСИЛИЙ РОБОРОВСКИЙ

Not "pogopob" but "roborov"—Vasily Roborovski.

Tony and I spoke together: *"But—"*

Now he was looking at me, eyebrows raised in anger, his clear eyes open and wide.

"I didn't put that in your plane!" he gasped.

"I didn't say you did!" I gasped in return. "I didn't *think* you did! So *how* did it get there?"

We both stared down at the stopwatch for another moment. Then he sat back with a childish huff that wordlessly repeated, *Mine!* He put the watch in his pocket, heedless of the cracked glass, gazing at me with a questioning frown of fury and alarm.

I locked my hands together in my lap, my fingernails digging into my palms. I believed him; I didn't think Tony would have been so quick to snatch the stopwatch back if he'd actually planted it himself. He could have easily pretended he'd never seen it before, and surely he wouldn't have dared to tell me his real name if he thought I'd recognize it on the watch I found in my plane.

I sucked in a breath, placed my hands carefully on the table again, and continued with determination: "I don't know *when* it was put in my plane, any more than I know *how.* It might have been before yesterday."

"That Nazi Sebastian Rainer is always doing fancy tricks with his gear," Tony said. "Flipping things between his fingers like Houdini—"

"He does it when he's nervous," I agreed.

"Yeah, I get that. I have trouble keeping my hands still too, especially when I get mad, and I've been watching him— having a trick to do looks better than tearing up paper and breaking glasses. He's got something hot going on in that cool head."

"If he did it, why does he keep showing off his cigarette case?" I demanded.

"I don't know," Tony admitted slowly. "But tossing other people's belongings into random aircraft is a really simple way to mess things up for everybody. If we *don't* find it, it might kill us. If we do, we'll be at each other's throats with accusations of sabotage. Maybe someone from one of the papers did it on the first day, just to keep things sensational."

I thought of the swaggering shirtless journalist who'd jumped up on my wing and knew about my passport. I suddenly sank my face in my hands, leaning my elbows on the table.

"Hey, don't do that, sister, you'll attract the old lady's attention."

Tony reached across the table and pulled one of my hands gently away from my face.

"*You've got combat nerves,*" he whispered knowingly, holding my trembling hand between us for a moment as evidence.

He was hiding something. I was sure he was hiding something; not just his name. I had no idea what it was.

180

But I didn't believe he was a murderer.

"All right. Listen." I leaned forward over the untouched plate of sweets.

Tony said with impatience, "I've been listening for fifteen minutes."

I told him about the attack in the Alps.

Ordinary Tourists

The words came more easily once I started. Tony paid quiet and serious attention. The scowl never left his face, but his eyes were alight with anger and disbelief as I spoke.

"So you're right about me having a sort of combat neurosis," I ended bitterly. "And that little thing you said when we were watching the air show, about getting down low to hide, probably saved my life."

Tony leaned across the table again and asked quickly, in a low voice, "Who do you think it was? You must have some idea."

"*Possibly* Theodor Vogt, the Swiss—he's such an adept pilot," I said. "But he took off half an hour ahead of me and he landed on time. Or Torsten Stromberg, the Swedish law student—he took off after you. That Tigerswallow cruises at about the same speed as us, but at full throttle he can fly about five miles an hour faster, and he didn't have to refuel. If he'd flown at his top speed to Saint-Vincent, he would have got there at the same time as me. You can probably guess the other one I think it might be."

"Sebastian Rainer. Our representative Nazi."

"Yes. He learned to fly on gliders—I'll bet he could stay in one place over Zermatt without using any power, waiting, like a hawk hovering without moving its wings."

Tony gave his low, expressive whistle. "*Phew!* That would explain why he was an hour late when he got here yesterday. He sure was beating himself up about it last night in the pensione where we're all staying—said he got lost in the mountains."

"*He got lost!*" I exclaimed in disbelief. "He told me he learned to fly in the Bavarian Alps!"

"He was pretty embarrassed about it, or he pretended to be," said Tony. "And Rosengart was livid about him losing so much time. '*You should be ashamed to be in Luftwaffe uniform, your commander will hear about this, you're a national failure.*'" Tony pointed to the macarons. "Eat up," he said irrelevantly. "The vigil starts in half an hour."

"It's only across the square. I'm not hungry, anyway—and—"

I thought suddenly of what an expensive place we were sitting in, and the patches on Tony's jacket. He'd have to pay, unless I made a fuss, and then it would be embarrassing for both of us. I ought not to waste the food.

I nibbled at a macaron. "Gosh, they're super. I've never been to Italy before."

"Me neither. If you'd told me six months ago that I'd be eating cookies in an Italian café right before going to church in St. Mark's Basilica, I'd—I'd have been *rude* about it. About how unlikely that was."

"You don't like the Italians much, do you?"

"I don't like Fascism."

We both nibbled macarons in silence for a minute, and then I suddenly remembered my excuse for this meeting. I reminded him in a low voice, "We're also supposed to be planning a formation flight performance for Paris."

"Fine. Let's plan one. You do a couple of steep turns above the airfield, and I'll follow ten feet behind you."

I gave a snort of disbelief. "You couldn't! Not without hours of practice! I've only tried it twice, with my instructor just after I took my license, and she made us keep the length of the airfield between us!"

"I sure can, and it'll look like we *have* had hours of practice. Planning done."

His passport was still sitting by my plate. I dug in my skirt pocket for the cuff buttons I'd made, palmed them, and pushed the passport back across to him with the buttons lying on top.

"What's this?"

"I saw you were using string in your shirt cuffs. These'll be a bit more respectable. I thought you'd be wearing a dress shirt to the service."

He reddened, but he took them. "I decided not to. I don't have anything sensible to wear with a dress shirt other than my dinner clothes, and those are all wrong for morning, and I reckon wrong for church, too. I thought I'd be better off in something that didn't make me conspicuous..."

He looked up anxiously.

"Or is this worse? I thought—"

He blushed again, and turned to look at Lady Frith, who was paying her own bill.

184

"No, you look fine," I said quickly. "You look like an ordinary tourist. I'm no better, am I? We're both wearing flight gear." I flicked at the end of my scarf.

He realized what it was, and the corner of his mouth twitched in a small smile.

"Well, thanks," he said, pocketing the homemade cuff links. "These'll be easier to attach than string the next time we have to dress up, that's for sure."

I wanted to know what he was hiding; and I wanted him to trust me enough that he'd tell me himself, just as he'd told me his real name and all about his family. I wanted to shake him out of his eternal sulk. I wanted to see him smile.

I wanted it so badly that as we were getting up to leave I told him quietly, "The name in my passport is Stella Valeryevna Severova."

It nearly worked. He gave me a conspiratorial nod of understanding, his green eyes dancing.

"Not Stella North?" he teased.

"Severov means North. It's much easier in English."

He looked me straight in the eye and asked solemnly, "Does your Uncle Max still sweep up litter?"

"No, he's the stationmaster at Maidenhead now," I said. "And Aunt Marie wears very pretty paste jewels instead of diamonds. But I'm not like them. I don't want to wait for the Soviet Union to take back its Russian exiles. And even if they did, I'd *never* want to be part of the Soviet Union. I want British citizenship."

"Roberts is easier in English than Roborovski, too," he agreed. "But I don't give a hoot about British citizenship. Or French. Or even American! My passport's just a piece of paper."

"Really?"

"It makes my life easier, I guess," he said, and shrugged. "But it doesn't tell you anything about *me*, does it?"

———◇———

The wide, paved plaza of St. Mark's Square was crowded with tourists, reporters, and pigeons. Beyond the bell tower, a barge was unloading. As we pushed our way through the crowd toward St. Mark's Basilica, Pim van Leer untangled himself from the knot of Olympics of the Air pilots and marched up to Lady Frith with his fists clenched.

"I am not able to go inside," he said, his voice low and his face white. "Not without telling my parents. I have not been in a church before today. I do not want to cause trouble—I am sorry about Vittorio—but I will wait in the square for the service to be over."

Lady Frith gazed at him in bafflement, then said soothingly, "Don't worry! It isn't a proper funeral, just a vigil, to show our respect and join in a prayer for him. Oh dear, wait, I understand. This is to do with you being Jewish, isn't it? I thought you said it wouldn't matter in Italy?"

"It does not matter in Italy," Pim said fiercely. "It matters in a church. I am not allowed in a church. It would be the same in France, or England, or even in my home in Amsterdam, if you like."

Lady Frith wrinkled her mouth in frustration. "Well, you can't possibly wait out here on your own. You'll be *mobbed* by the press, now that they've seen us gathering here." She waved a hand at the men with cameras and hats pulled low, lurking

186

none too far away. "I expect Major Rosengart can wait with you. He isn't a churchgoer either."

Pim's narrow, youthful face went quiet and sober. He pressed his lips together.

In his determined silence, I recognized real fear. I couldn't imagine Rosengart being anything other than courteous to him, but I knew Pim didn't trust any of the Germans.

"*Very well,*" said Pim forcefully. "We will talk about Hamburg, and what I can expect from the situation in Germany."

"Major Rosengart is very much aware of the situation in Germany," agreed Lady Frith evenly. "I hope he will be able to reassure you."

So Pim and Major Rosengart stayed outside on the steps, and the rest of us went into St. Mark's Basilica.

Even though Vittorio Pavesi hadn't been from Venice, there were dozens of his family and possibly hundreds of his friends there. People who knew him had come from all over Italy. Now they were all on their knees praying for the young man they loved, but I found it impossible to concentrate on prayer.

The soaring arches of St. Mark's, all gold-tiled in Byzantine splendor, ironically made me feel very English. It is true that Aunt Marie trotted me to St. Joseph's in Maidenhead every Sunday morning and to Mass on Saturday afternoons, but she never should have sent me to Cheltenham Ladies' College if she really meant me to remain a proper Catholic. In any case, no church I had ever seen was remotely as glorious as St. Mark's, and the only prayer I could think of was a blasphemously selfish one: *Thank you that I do not understand Italian and don't have to talk to any of these wildly grieving people.*

The service lasted longer than I expected. I stared for a long time at each of the race contestants in turn, looking for signs of penitence. Surely, here in the beauty and splendor of a thousand years of worship, surrounded by Vittorio's loved ones, his murderer might get a little twitchy. But Sebastian's restless hands were still; he looked like he was sitting on them. Theodor Vogt was staring up at the splendid gold-tiled dome as if he couldn't get enough of it. I scrunched around uncomfortably in my seat, looking for Torsten.

Lady Frith gave me a sharp poke in the ribs with a pointy elbow.

"*Really, Stella!*" she hissed in my ear. "Must you be so restless? People are watching. Anyone would think you couldn't *wait* for this to be over."

Hell's bells, I realized *I* was the twitchy one, the pilot with the visibly shaking hands who couldn't keep still and wasn't paying attention to the service.

I faced forward and in despair sat on my hands like Sebastian. I wondered if the most sensible thing to do was just to give up on the race entirely, rush out to the rail station, and catch the next train heading back to London.

———◇———

Vittorio's large family hosted a sober sort of luncheon in another marble hall on the St. Mark's piazza. We race contestants stuck together with an uneasy solidarity; Tony and Theodor, the Swiss pilot, were the only ones who spoke a little Italian, besides Capitano Ranza. It was miserable and awkward.

But afterward we set out for a scheduled tour of the

Murano glass factory, and the green water between Venice and Murano was a blessed relief. No one could speak on the motor launch, and we had to sit jammed together on wooden benches whether we wanted to or not. It was all noise and wind and warm salt air, the water rising in white crests on either side in the astonishing opaque green-blue of the Adriatic Sea. I sat between Erlend, who always landed an hour and a half before I did, and Stefan, the chain-smoking Polish Air Force pilot who took off dead last and flew a monoplane. The smell of stale cigarettes was a fair exchange for feeling safe. Either one of them, along with any of the others, might have tried to sabotage Tony's plane on Sunday morning, or mine whenever; but they definitely hadn't tried to force me into a spin over the Alps.

Tony sat several feet away from me on the other side of the open boat, gazing ahead toward the low red and yellow buildings of Murano.

It was so warm that most of the boys had taken off their jackets and rolled up their sleeves. Tony hadn't rolled his sleeves up, but he'd pulled off his aviator's scarf and undone the top couple of buttons of his shirt. The wind lifted his hair and ballooned his collar away from his skin.

And with his neck bared like that, I noticed for the first time that he had a long, ugly scar starting just behind his left earlobe.

Like a thick, ragged piece of string, it ran under his jaw and continued down beneath the flannel of his open collar: as if someone, not terribly long ago, had tried to cut his throat.

Evening in Casa Rossa

We didn't have to make a public appearance that night. Lady Frith collected everyone's evening clothes and sent them to be cleaned. My hands stopped shaking, at least temporarily, as I shared a meal with Lady Frith and Aida Benedetti in the rooftop garden of Casa Rossa, all hung with colorful paper lanterns and overlooking the Grand Canal. Sounds came floating up to us, of voices and of boats lapping through the water, and the far-off snatch of a violin. The noise of other people's ordinary lives felt far away and heartless.

"Northie, you seem remarkably ill at ease," Lady Frith commented. "I understand you are upset about Vittorio, but I do wonder if you are unhealthily brooding on his disappearance. You have had a terrible shock, no doubt, witnessing another aircraft fall to earth. I saw a similar accident once, as I was coming in to land at Croydon, and I don't know when I've ever been so shaken in the air!"

She turned away from me almost immediately and said to Aida, "Vittorio's mother suggested that I cancel the rest of the race. *Cancel* it! She feels that finishing here in Italy would be a fitting tribute to the poor boy, and we could use the results from our first three flights to determine a winner. And Ernesto—Capitano Ranza—who was translating for me, nodded gloomily the whole time as if he agreed with her. Honestly, Aida, I didn't know how to react. I said I would discuss it with the Race Committee, but of course that will be difficult as most of them are back in England, apart from those of us who are flying as chaperones. It has rather thrown me. The other chaperones are all coming over later for our scheduling meeting and I must decide before then one way or another."

"Of course you mustn't cancel the race!" her friend exclaimed explosively.

"Oh, thank you, Aida, but do you really think so?"

"Surely *finishing* it would be a much more fitting tribute to poor Vittorio? Persevering in adversity? Don't you think he'd have wanted the other racers to keep going?"

"No doubt he would, but it is his people who are expressing their wishes, not he."

I sat swiveling my head back and forth between them as if I were watching a tennis match.

"Also," Lady Frith went on, "the other race contestants are whispering about sabotage amongst themselves, I know. Isn't that true, Northie?"

I nodded, opening my mouth to speak; but she didn't wait

for me to answer, simply barreling on: "I worry about their morale; I worry about how it will affect their judgment. I don't want any more accidents. I wanted them to become friends with each other, not point fingers and make accusations!"

"Really, Diana, I can't believe you'd even consider backing down on this," said Aida Benedetti. "You chose your contestants for their determination and sensitivity, and it would be most unfair on them to pull them out now. Think of *us* when *we* were young! You fixing ambulances and me driving a tram with the Voluntary Aid Detachment—we didn't let the Great War prevent us from enjoying ourselves, did we?"

"That was for a very good cause," insisted Lady Frith.

"Well, we thought it was at the time, at any rate," Aida observed. "We weren't any older than these young people, and we risked death every day! You made some shocking errors of judgment on that Azores flight when you were only twenty years old—"

"—But I did get away with it. And you barely escaped with your life when you had that fall, climbing Kilimanjaro on your own in 1922."

"That's exactly my point!" cried Aida. "It was five whole years before Sheila MacDonald. I could have had the credit for being the first woman to the top, if I hadn't been so chagrined by my own recklessness that I didn't dare tell anybody! No, you must brazen this out. It isn't your fault. It would simply be weakness to give up!"

Lady Frith turned to look at me. I opened my mouth again, and again she spoke before I could breathe a single word.

"Aida, my dear, you are right, as always. To stop now would be a betrayal of all young women who want to fly."

I shut up. I wasn't going to be the one to back down and betray all young women who wanted to fly.

———◇———

Aida Benedetti came tapping on my bedroom door about an hour after supper was over.

"Good evening again, Stella, I'm sorry to bother you! I know you're at work planning tomorrow's flight," she said. "My goodness, what a busy house this is tonight! Diana and her colleagues have taken over the dining room. One of the other contestants is on the telephone asking to speak to you. No doubt Diana will be cross with me for not informing her first, but I didn't like to disturb her meeting. Are you available?"

I dropped my pencil and followed Aida downstairs. It was Tony on the phone.

"Hello?"

"Northie?"

"It's me," I said.

"Can you talk?"

"I think so." Aida Benedetti's telephone was in a small marble entrance hall and probably just as public as wherever he was speaking from, but Aida had blown me a kiss and floated off back upstairs so I could speak privately. Lady Frith and the chaperones were meeting behind the closed dining room door.

"Did you see the papers?" Tony asked.

"I'm drowning in newspapers! My room looks like a Royal Mail sorting office!"

"Today's papers. Have you seen the headline in the *Evening Herald*?"

It was obvious I hadn't.

"*Young Europe at War!*" Tony announced. "*Crosswire's* even worse—they think there needs to be a murder inquiry into Vittorio Pavesi's death. One of us is attacking others in the air, they said. How the hell did they find out about *that?*"

I hadn't even *talked* to *Crosswire*.

"I told one of the French tabloids just after we landed at Nicelli," I confessed. "It was supposed to be exclusive, so they must have printed their story this morning if the English papers have got hold of it already!"

"Well, the English papers aren't giving you the benefit of the doubt. They've done the flight time calculations and you're right up there in the list of suspects. Me too, of course." Tony gave a sort of snort—it might have been a chuckle. "What in the world made you do it?"

"I *want* them to know," I said fiercely. "The chaperones didn't take it seriously at all when we talked to them on the first day—you saw! That Nazi Rosengart thinks I'm nothing but a hysterical child. Lady Frith herself told our own newspaper that I was too faint to do an interview! If the tabloids are accusing us of murder, the chaperones will have to do something in response. Set a guard over our aircraft, or search everyone's bags—spread out our flight times so we can't possibly catch up with each other. There are plenty of things they could have done already."

"You know Old Lady Frith's going to blow her stack when she sees this," Tony said.

"Let her! Let her do something about it!"

"She'll blame you!"

"What will she do about it—disqualify me for being

attacked? Anyway, I didn't talk to any of those English papers, and I asked the French one to report as if he were an eyewitness on the ground. I don't think she'll guess I went behind her back."

We both sighed into the receiver at the same time.

"Listen, I'll send a telegram to Rosario," Tony said. "She's going to Paris this weekend so she can be there for the end of the race, and she'll be staying in our hotel. Maybe she can uncover something about the other contestants that we can't find in the newspapers."

"Rosario?"

"Yes, you know, *Voici Paris*, remember? My old instructor, Rosario Carreras."

For no obvious reason, the name made my skin prick ever so faintly, as if a chilly little wind had wandered through the hall. I frowned, wondering.

And then, the words *Santa Agnès de Marañosa* echoed in my memory.

"I've got to go," Tony said. "I could only get one telephone token and my time's about to run out."

I nodded, before I remembered that he couldn't see me. "Yes. All right. I need to go too." No point in bringing up the irrelevant Rocketman Affair. "I want to double-check my heights," I added; we were heading north to Prague over the Austrian Alps the next day. "Thanks for the warning."

I could see my hand shaking again as I hung up.

———◇———

I had another hideous flying dream.

I was over the Alps in an aeroplane constructed of cotton

wool and matchsticks and tissue paper. The air reeked of stale cigarette smoke. When I looked down, the trees beneath me were on fire.

I could hear them burning, could hear the crackling of flames eating up leaves like crumpled paper. My plane was sinking over the burning treetops; flames began to flutter at the tips of my wings.

There was fire below me, fire spreading across my wings, and there was nowhere to land.

Irregularities

Lady Frith seemed calm as a windless day as we climbed into the water taxi at the dock in front of Casa Rossa. She waved and blew kisses to Aida Benedetti while the little motorboat puttered slowly out into the Grand Canal in the cool light of a hazy dawn. I couldn't tell if she'd seen those headlines yet.

But she'd seen them, all right.

In the empty departure hall of Nicelli Aerodrome, Lady Frith assembled us for our usual flight briefing at 6:30 a.m. We stood ready for another day in the air, flying jackets hanging over our shoulders, helmets under our arms, routes drawn carefully on our maps. Tony and Sebastian somehow ended up side by side. They looked like brothers who'd been raised by different families: one reserved and well-groomed, the other ferociously frowning and untidy, both of them full of nervous energy as Sebastian twirled a cigarette back and forth between his fingers and Tony scuffed the toes of his boots back and forth against his heels.

I thought Pim looked nervous too, his face pale beneath his silky dark fringe, though he managed to keep still.

No doubt we all guessed what was coming.

Lady Frith broke the dreadful headlines to us like a storm cloud releasing a torrent of lightning and hail. She flourished a sheaf of freshly printed newsprint in each hand.

"'Young Europe at War,'" she cried out in the high, ringing tones of a newspaper boy on a street corner; and with the same aggressive energy, she began to thrust pages into the hands of the pilots standing nearest to her. When her hands were empty she raised them in the air to shut everybody up.

There was instant silence.

"I am *bitterly* disappointed," Lady Frith said crisply. "I planned and sponsored this race to encourage your generation to reach out in friendship to one another. Scathing stories, frankly *unbelievable* stories, accuse me of hypocrisy, and you young people of murder. There is allegedly an eyewitness account of one of you attacking another in the French Alps. Some of the tabloids are wildly assuming that poor Vittorio's death was no accident."

She paused and waited, allowing the other chaperones to make some quick translations for her. Then she fixed her gaze on each of the race contestants in turn.

It took her a long time to make eye contact with each one of us. When she came to me, I returned her frank stare with bleak challenge. My cheeks felt hot.

She looked away and warned us all coldly, "'Europe at War' is not a headline I ever want to see again and *certainly not* in connection with this race."

198

Capitano Ernesto Ranza stood with his arms folded, glaring and nodding. Lady Frith paused for another few moments. But this time, when she continued, her face softened, and her tone became unexpectedly reassuring.

"I don't believe a single one of you is capable of the terrible thing the tabloid press is suggesting. Surely if such an attack had happened in the Alps, the victim would have reported it by now! In any case I intend to treat each of you with as much support as if you are wholly innocent of any ill-doing. Please come and speak to me in private, or to any of your chaperones, if you would like personal reassurance. That is partly what we are here for—to support you as well as to protect you."

Nobody's face gave away a thing. All the racers looked just as anxious or bewildered as each other.

"However, to keep the hounds at bay we are going to take some precautions," Lady Frith continued. "There have been—ah—irregularities in a few of our flights, not just Vittorio Pavesi's. I'm sure you're all aware of Leutnant Rainer's late arrival on Wednesday."

Sebastian swiftly turned his head to avoid meeting anyone's eyes.

"To prevent rumors, and to show that we are protecting ourselves, I and the other chaperones have arranged for four of you who are under suspicion to be escorted in flight during the race. These four will also be shadowed on the ground throughout the rest of our time together. Miss North—"

It had worked. My desperate bid had worked. Whoever the attacker was, he wouldn't be able to ambush me in the air again without someone else seeing it.

"Miss North, I am afraid you will be most affected by the

changes, as you will now be required to take off last," Lady Frith said.

I nodded politely. I couldn't have cared less. There would always be someone who had to take off last, and it wasn't hugely unfair it should be me. It shouldn't affect my flying any more than it affected Stefan Chudek's. I wasn't sure I'd ever be able to get my edge back after losing so much time over the Alps, but I was ready to try.

"In essence, you will all still fly in order from fastest to slowest," Lady Frith told us. "But a few of you have been shifted in the lineup to avoid three or more aircraft landing at Prague, our next destination, at the same time. One chaperone will take off immediately ahead of each suspected contestant, and the escorting plane will hold above the airfield until that contestant is airborne. Then the escort will accompany the racing pilot at a visual distance. None of you should have to make alterations to your present flight plans, except to adjust your time estimates to account for a new departure."

Lady Frith swept around the room like a winter storm, collecting the newspapers again.

"Have you any other questions? Anyone? No? I do appreciate your cooperation. In a few moments I'll pass around your telegrams from family and friends; to the outside world I would very much like us to appear to be enjoying ourselves, in spite of our terrible loss. And now, these are the pilots who are going to fly with escorts from now on—"

Lady Frith fixed her gaze on Tony and Sebastian as she spoke, since they were standing together.

"Monsieur Robert from France, Leutnant Rainer from Germany, and Miss North from Britain: on the ground, each of you will be shadowed by the chaperone from your own nation." She turned to Torsten, who watched her seriously, his glasses catching the light. "Mr. Stromberg of Sweden, you will have to be looked after by Capitano Ranza. I do apologize about the language barrier, though it shouldn't matter in the air, of course."

She turned to me. "Stella, I will accompany you on the ground, but it simply won't be possible for me to fly with you myself. We have had to make some accommodation to match aircraft speeds; my Dragon Rapide is so much faster than the other racing aircraft that it can only be paired with Leutnant Rainer's Jungmann. So you will have to fly with Capitaine Bazille. He'll also accompany you during your refueling stop in Salzburg. Monsieur Robert, you will fly with Major Rosengart."

I let out a long, careful sigh.

I didn't think I could be any safer than coming in to Prague *last*, navigating the Alps a second time under the protective wings of the easygoing, elegant Capitaine Marcel Bazille.

I glanced over to look at him, lined up against the wall with the other Great War pilots like an honor guard. But my eyes were drawn to Major Rosengart, standing beside him with his pipe clamped between his teeth, leaking smoke like a dragon. His steel-blue gaze bored into Tony as if he couldn't believe they were being forced to fly together.

———◇———

I sat in the Cadet's cockpit, sweating in my flight suit, breathing in the warm, soupy, sea-scented air of the Adriatic as I waited for my start-up and my turn to take off.

Because I was last, I got to watch every one of the other racers and chaperones climb into the sky and depart. Lady

Frith was the first to go, taking off ahead of Sebastian Rainer in her Dragon Rapide. It was so much bigger than anyone else's plane that it looked clumsy and fat, a duck or goose trundling out to the smooth new concrete runway. But then, in the air, it became a swan—regal and gracious, circling two thousand feet overhead in the hazy bright sky.

As Sebastian's Jungmann left the airfield, climbing steadily to a height that would clear the Austrian Alps, the Rapide struck out after it with effortless power and speed. The two planes disappeared into the haze, their dwindling silhouettes flying together about a quarter of a mile apart. Watching them go, I knew I could never have mistaken the Rapide for anything else alongside another plane. Its wingspan was twice that of the Jungmann, its twin engines obvious.

Fifteen minutes later, Theodor Vogt set out on his own in the other Jungmann, unescorted; then Jiri Jindra lifted off in his sleek new Bibi tourer. Next was Capitano Ranza. I watched him circle above the airfield to wait for Torsten Stromberg in his Tigerswallow.

When it came Tony's turn to take off, I noticed again that his plane was exactly the same shade of green as my own.

I remembered suddenly that Vittorio's plane had also been dark green.

Two green planes attacked in flight, two green planes sabotaged on the ground: what if the attacker mistakenly thought it was the same green plane each time?

An unexplained sense of unease began to stir in my heart, not for myself but for Tony, as his Hanriot 436 soared over my head and ascended the blue like a skylark.

A PIECE OF
THE CONTINENT

Friday, 27 August–
Sunday, 29 August, 1937

PART FOUR

A PIECE OF
THE CONTINENT

Friday 27 August –
Sunday 29 August 1937

The Thief

Prague, Czechoslovakia

I forgot to do my landing checks.

When I reached the dazzling new runway at Ruzyně Aerodrome in Prague, I became completely distracted with scanning the ground below to find Tony's plane. I came in much too fast, and twenty feet above the concrete I rammed on full power so I could climb back into the air for a safer approach.

As I circled, I spotted the green Hanriot 436, dark against the brighter green of the grass where it was parked.

I pressed my lips together and focused on landing my own plane. The trembling in my hands set in briefly after I shut down the Cadet's engine; there wasn't any good reason for it this time, except that I was so relieved to see Tony's plane in one piece. I was wild to pull him aside and warn him.

The other boys were milling about at the edge of the runway in a cloud of cigarette smoke as I climbed out of the

Cadet. They'd watched me fail my first attempt at landing, and they let off steam in several languages.

"Finally Britain's dazzling North Star has lost some time!" Jiri Jindra cried.

"At last the rest of us have a chance to catch up!" said Philippos Gekas.

Stefan Chudek smiled at me. "Don't worry, the press still like you best, you are the prettiest of us for photographs—"

"Go on, smile for them—" Torsten Stromberg waved at the usual flock of vultures frantically pointing their cameras in our direction. The press was penned in a fenced-in box to keep them from running in front of taxiing aircraft.

"Oh, this will confuse them," said Pim van Leer, slinging his arms around the two pilots nearest him—Theodor Vogt, who must have been a full foot taller than Pim, and redheaded Gaby Dupont. "Why should they blame *you* for anything, Northie? You were worried about your own plane back in Brussels, were you not? And looking out for me and mine. We are not at war. Let us all smile for the camera—"

"Splendid!" agreed sunny-tempered Erlend Pettersen, beaming. "Come, we will show them young Europe is not in the least bit at war. The Olympics of the Air pilots are a united league of our own nations!"

A sudden defiant solidarity seized everyone. I wound one arm around Erlend's waist and opened the other to the boy nearest enough to pose with me, Stefan Chudek, the Pole. He held up one hand, showing me his tobacco-stained fingers, then plucked at his flight suit and held his nose.

I laughed in spite of myself.

"Tobacco, oil and fuel, sweat—we all smell the same!"

I told him in French. "Don't worry! Let's pose for the photographers."

All eleven of us huddled tightly together, arms around one another's waists and shoulders, trying to plaster determined grins on our faces. Torsten whipped off his glasses, suddenly vain in front of the cameras.

"How did you like being escorted by Capitaine Bazille?" Erlend asked me.

"It made me feel like royalty," I answered unhesitatingly. "He's the perfect diplomat; it must come of being in politics. We refueled at Salzburg and all the aerodrome mechanics kept bowing to him."

Everyone who could understand me laughed in delight.

I added, "I think they were confusing him with the Ethiopian emperor! I'm not surprised—he's absolutely regal."

Stefan dropped his arm from around my shoulder and reached into the breast pocket of his flying suit. He pulled out a paper packet of cigarettes, and I could see that he was just about to offer me one when he realized the packet was empty.

"Somebody help this chain smoker!" Erlend called. "And me—I would like a smoke too."

Sebastian Rainer produced his silver cigarette case, apparently from thin air, and gave it a flourish between his fingers so that it caught the light. He flipped it open and offered a cigarette to Stefan.

Whether or not Sebastian meant to, he'd caught Tony's attention.

"You can tell a lot about a fellow by what he smokes," Tony commented in his husky drawl. "Rosengart has a brierwood pipe, not a plain old corn cob. That's a pretty fancy case you've got there, Leutnant Rainer. Are your cigarettes special, too? Do you roll your own, or are they straight out of the pack? Are they fine Virginia shag tobacco or that awful Russian manure?"

"I bought these in Geneva," Sebastian said. "They are all right, but not expensive. I must buy some more or I will have none left for this evening. The case makes them seem special."

He flipped it shut and handed it to Tony.

Tony steadied his hand against his chest, cradling the case as he examined it. Then he glanced up at Sebastian and met his eyes deliberately. "These aren't your initials."

"It was my father's."

"He gave it to you and didn't change the monogram? Or is he dead, and you're sentimental?"

Sebastian returned Tony's gaze without flinching. "My father is very much alive," he said. "We do not see eye to eye on most things. So I took it without asking. And his fancy lighter, which I have lost."

A few gasps exploded from the racers who understood him, and Erlend gave a shout of laughter.

"You *stole* your dad's stuff?" Tony asked incredulously.

Sebastian shrugged. "Everything I do annoys him. Even being in a glider club and joining the air force—'Is the army not good enough for you? Do you think you are better than your father and your grandfather?' Now I enjoy annoying him on purpose. So I learned the sleight of hand and I take his things. There is nothing he can do about it except make everybody hunt for them."

Tony gave his low, appreciative whistle and handed the cigarette case back to Sebastian.

"All right, Leutnant Rainer, you have finally impressed me."

Jiri let out a torrent of Russian to Stefan and Philippos, gesturing toward Sebastian and Tony as he translated.

Philippos said abruptly to Jiri, "Ask the German if he also lost his stopwatch. I found one, but I do not know whose."

Tony and I both turned to stare at him. Also in Russian, Tony asked Philippos, "When?"

"The day before the race began," said Philippos. "On the English airfield just after I arrived. I could not tell whose it was, so I gave it to Major Rosengart."

"To *Rosengart?*" I burst out explosively.

Tony touched me lightly on the sleeve, the mildest of warnings.

"If that stopwatch had 'Roborovski' scratched on it, it's mine, and it belonged to *my* father," Tony said in English, letting Jiri translate. "Unlike this German Luftwaffe clown, Second Lieutenant Rainer, I didn't steal it. You could say I inherited it." He took a deep breath. "I guess Philippos doesn't read Russian."

Jiri told Philippos what Tony had said, and relayed the Greek boy's answer.

"He says it must be the very same watch," Jiri explained. "He doesn't read Russian, but of course he can read Greek, and he was able to make out most of the letters. Had the name on it been Robert, he would have known it was yours and given it to you."

Philippos added something else, and Jiri translated, "He says he is sure Major Rosengart still has the watch if you want it back. Rosengart would not throw it away without knowing whose it was."

———◆———

But Rosengart didn't still have it.

I'd found it in my plane in Milan.

My mind spun feverish excuses for the German chaperone. He must have accidentally dropped the stopwatch while he was checking my plane in Old Sarum. I remembered how he'd sat there moving the seat back and forth in the Cadet's cockpit for no obvious reason. He must have been trying to get the stopwatch out of the braces.

But... if it had been an honest error, why hadn't he said anything? Surely he would have warned me—surely he'd have at least confessed when Tony said his watch was missing!

Could he possibly have done it on purpose? *Major Florian Rosengart?*

He'd been confused when I'd landed in Tony's plane. While Tony and I were soaring over Stonehenge, there were reporters crowded all around my dark green Cadet, and Rosengart might not have been able to see the British markings on the side and the tail.

He might have mistaken my plane for Tony's.

He could have tossed the stopwatch into my cockpit as he was clearing away the reporters. After they moved off, and Tony and I landed in the French plane, the German chaperone must have realized he'd made a mistake; then he'd tried to get the watch back.

It seemed unbelievable that Major Florian Rosengart would do something so casually malicious. But there was also that cigarette lighter Tony found jamming his rudder cables.

If Rosengart had purposefully picked up the lighter, believing it was Tony's, it would have been an unhoped-for second chance. He might have dropped the stopwatch into the wrong plane, but he wouldn't have made the same mistake twice.

The stopwatch could have been a spontaneous idea for sabotage. But the lighter had been planted with cold calculation.

Inevitably, now, I wondered if Rosengart might have also made the attacks in the air.

He could have planned to cross paths with Tony—both times, over the French coast and again over the French Alps—then fly with the devil on his tail to arrive precisely on schedule after he'd knocked Tony out of the sky. But Vittorio turned up by accident the first time, and I did the second time, and both our planes looked like Tony's.

Rosengart would have had to wait in the Alps for at least an hour. Then he'd have had to go like a rocket to get to Venice on schedule. I had no idea if his Albatros Ace could carry that much extra fuel.

But maybe it could. The German chaperone had literally flown in rings around Marcel Bazille. Rosengart told me the Ace had three times the endurance of the Cadet.

Maybe it could.

Surely Florian Rosengart hadn't meant to kill Vittorio. I'd seen him quivering with emotion over Vittorio's death, and I didn't think it had been faked. Maybe he'd even let me go, after the first attacks from above, because he'd seen the markings on the Cadet's tail and realized it wasn't Tony's plane.

But what possible motivation could he have to keep trying, again and again, to destroy Tony?

"Our planes are the same color," I reminded Tony now, desperate to give him a warning. "So was Vittorio's."

"Yeah, I noticed that too."

211

I wondered if something had happened on the flight to Prague, something that Tony hadn't been able to tell me about yet. I glanced at his hands, but they were hidden in his pockets.

If they were shaking, he was being very careful not to let anyone see.

25

A Siege in Vladislav Hall

That night's banquet was held in the Old Royal Palace of Prague Castle, in Vladislav Hall. Over four hundred years old and cavernous, the hall was big enough that there was a Bibi aircraft like Jiri Jindra's assembled inside. During the reception before the dinner, Tony sat off by himself at one end of a long banquette sofa in an alcove below a tall window, typically taking up space. He stretched out his legs across the seat just as he had on the bus in Geneva, so that no one else could possibly sit down next to him.

I felt sure he'd chosen that spot because it might be a safe place to sneak in a private word, though he hadn't tried to catch my eye and seemed lost in his usual self-centered perpetual sulk.

The four of us "suspects" were under guard now, and Marcel Bazille hovered a few feet away from Tony, commiserating with one of the guests about Czechoslovakia being the only democratic state in central Europe and how terrifying it was to share a border with Nazi Germany. Lady Frith stood so close to me I could feel the older woman's breath warm against the side of my neck.

I glanced around and spotted Erlend Pettersen's canary-fluffed head moving toward the table of champagne flutes filled with mineral water specially for the pilots. I knew that Erlend would help me, and I hoped that some of the others would too.

I dodged away from Lady Frith just long enough to meet Erlend at the mineral water table. We both reached for glasses at the same time.

I whispered quickly, "Can you get everyone to distract the chaperones so Tony and I can talk?"

Erlend grinned. "Give me a few minutes to plan a siege."

I went demurely back to Lady Frith with my drink and spouted harmless gibber to distract her.

"I am absolutely ignorant about Czech politics. You should be proud of me; I saved myself by explaining Bernoulli's principle to the mayor's wife. Pavla, she's called. I used the Bibi's wing to show what an aerofoil looks like!"

I took a deep breath and a sip of the fizzing water, and scanned the hall to see how Erlend was getting on.

He was doing the work of an international ambassador. First he dragged Sebastian and Theodor into a discussion with Major Rosengart, which involved a lot of mock flying using hands and Rosengart's pipe as aeroplanes. Then he wandered away and encouraged Capitano Ranza into a similar demonstration to some guests on the other side of the enormous medieval hall. At last he led Pim and Stefan triumphantly in my direction.

"Our wonderful Lady Frith!" Erlend cried out engagingly. "You did not tell us that these two both want to fly passenger planes!"

He launched into a four-way conversation in which he stubbornly used German as the language of clarification. This meant everybody had to whisper, so as not to offend the elderly Karel Baxa, the former mayor of Greater Prague, who disliked Germans so fiercely he'd even tried to get German banned from being spoken in the city; I saw Lady Frith actually rise onto her tiptoes to look around for him. Her attention was not on Britain's well-behaved North Star standing demurely by her side.

I turned my head to look at Tony, sitting close behind me. He swung his legs down and arranged himself in the ramrod-straight formal pose he often took up just before he started fidgeting, with both feet neatly in line with each other. Erlend's German translations were getting loud enough that Lady Frith leaned in and spoke to him sharply, and I stepped back and sat down in the alcove at the other end of the long sofa, two yards away from Tony.

"Well, something's up," said Tony conversationally, staring straight across the room without catching my eye.

"*Are you all right?*" I asked.

"One old buzzard flying a bit too close isn't going to kill me," Tony said. "Florian Rosengart must think I was born yesterday."

He turned his head then, to look at me, and his gray-green eyes were cool, the line of his mouth grim.

215

"He's been after you all along," I said.

"He made that pretty clear this afternoon. He got under my wings, *dangerously* close—it was like he was trying to line up next to me to jump into my plane! I dived away the first time; I thought he'd misjudged the distance between us, but then he did it again. So I thought I'd give him a taste of his own medicine, and got behind him—well, he backed off after that, and we landed safely at Linz for me to refuel. He had the nerve to chew me out for irresponsible flying and threatened to disqualify me."

"He won't settle for that," I said quietly. "He wants you dead."

I didn't think I had time to lay all my cards on the table to back this up—I had to give Tony a direct warning and hope he'd already come to the same conclusion.

"Why would he be after *you*, Anton Vasilievich?"

Tony gave me a dirty look. "*Shut up.*"

But I could see him thinking, privately going over past events that he kept to himself, and I could also see, in his candid face, that he wasn't able to make a clear connection.

He shook his head.

Then he said in a low voice, "I flew with the Spanish Republican Air Force last winter. Lady Frith knows. She's kept it out of the press, but she might have told the Race Committee."

He stopped to take a breath, and I wondered why that had to be a secret. Sebastian and Stefan were also enlisted men, in the German and Polish air forces.

And then I realized that Tony meant he'd flown in combat.

"I was in a fighter squadron," he went on hurriedly, with

his scowl deepening to something like alarm. "It could be controversial. But it shouldn't make anyone want to kill me."

———◆———

I wasted precious seconds rearranging the inside of my head to make room for the image of Tony Roberts as a fighter pilot in the Spanish Republican Air Force.

He was hardly any older than I was—only a year or two.

But of course, he was the same age as Bruno Mussolini.

Hell's teeth, I thought, *he could have been flying in battle against Bruno Mussolini.* No wonder—

Tony must have left when he was injured last spring. He'd been hurt in an air attack, Rosario Carreras had said. I'd assumed it happened when his mother was killed in the bombing raid on Madrid. But maybe he'd actually been wounded in combat.

It took me a minute to tick off all the things it explained— Capitaine Bazille telling me how much more flight experience Tony had than the rest of us, the sure way Tony identified why my hands were shaking, and the way he'd talked about aerial strategy while he was watching the flight display with me in Geneva.

Among the smoke-wreathed lamps of Vladislav Hall, with a little chamber orchestra playing cheerful sonatas in the background and the Czech dignitaries in evening dress chattering and drinking with their glittering wives, it was hard to believe that what we were talking about was real. For another few seconds it felt as if it must all be accident and coincidence.

"Thank goodness I didn't tell Rosengart I saw a second plane on that first morning!" I exclaimed. "He was quizzing me to find out if I had, and I came close to saying something. Although I suppose it wouldn't have made a difference. Now that he's attacked me as well, he's bound to be afraid I'll work it out. But if I try to say anything about it to Lady Frith, won't she just go straight to him with it?"

"Don't say anything to *her*," Tony agreed. "She wouldn't believe you anyway."

At that moment Sebastian Rainer sidled away from the crush around Florian Rosengart and sat down in the empty space on the sofa directly between me and Tony.

"Good evening," Sebastian said in his careful, formal English. "What is going on, Stella? Do the fastest racers share their plans only with each other?"

"Aw, go fly your own kite," Tony said darkly. "You're a thief and a conjurer."

I had no idea what Sebastian knew or how he knew it. If I hadn't been so increasingly convinced of Rosengart's guilt by what Philippos and Tony had said about him, Sebastian would be the one I'd point a finger at. But I didn't know when I would get another chance to talk to Sebastian.

I looked straight ahead of me at Lady Frith and her admirers standing just a few yards away. Erlend had planted his broad, neat, black-clothed back squarely between me and Lady Frith in her glittering silver dress, but I could see that she was keeping an eye on me.

I smiled, my hands clasped primly together in my lap, as if I were listening to the music.

"Let Sebastian speak," I said to Tony, holding my head high and not looking at either one of the boys. If Sebastian knew something we didn't, I wanted to hear it.

218

Tony was silent. After a moment, Sebastian spoke quietly.

"Major Rosengart has used my navigation error in the French Alps to support the excuse to have us guarded," he said to Tony. "He does not believe I got lost, or perhaps he thinks I did it on purpose. But after seeing these news stories, he insists one of us attacked the girl as she flew through the pass over Saint-Vincent, and Vittorio Pavesi over the English Channel. I know it was not I."

"He did it himself," I swore quietly. "I'm sure he did it himself."

Sebastian's face showed nothing. I wondered, in alarm, if he might be in on Rosengart's plot, whatever it was.

"Can you prove this?" Sebastian challenged.

Tony shrugged. "Maybe in court. Probably not to Old Lady Frith in the Grand Hotel Steiner later tonight. It's a lot of smoke with no damn trace of a fire. And she and Rosengart are pretty thick."

For a moment we sat in a row like the three little maids from school, carefully not looking at one another, all of us breathing hard and staring out across the Gothic hall. It was almost pointless to hope we would be able to talk together for another five minutes without being separated.

"You both believe he killed Vittorio Pavesi?" asked Sebastian.

"You heard Northie," said Tony with grim certainty. "And after today's flight, and what he tried to do to me, I'm sure of it."

"I think so too," said Sebastian.

The Conjurer

Sebastian briefly held open a small black appointment book against the black wool of his dress trousers, just long enough for me and Tony to be able to glance at a list of calculated flight distances and times noted there.

"I was angry when Major Rosengart accused me," Sebastian said. "My God. I did not—would never—do such a thing. And also—I do not need Rosengart to tell me my navigation error will cost me the race. I know that. He threatened me with a dishonorable discharge from the Luftwaffe. He can see to it that I will never fly again—perhaps never find work again, or worse. So I thought I would try to prove myself innocent of this attack, by setting out my flight times against yours. And when I discovered that the evidence works against me, I wondered who else might have done such a thing—I wondered who else *could* have done it."

Sebastian closed the little notebook and tucked it inside the breast pocket of his evening jacket. Then he drew out his cigarette case, which he'd obviously managed to refill, and very deliberately extracted a cigarette from it. He didn't offer one to either me or Tony; he closed the case and balanced it on his knee while he struck a match from the Hôtel Le Plaza paper matchbook.

Sebastian drew on the cigarette, not looking to either side of him, as if he'd sat down there to have a quick smoke all by himself.

After a moment, still gazing serenely into the distance as if he were dreaming of being in the air, he said, "I do not have a suspicious nature. But I was angered by Rosengart's treatment of me, so I calculated his flight times also."

Sebastian raised the cigarette to his lips again and calmly drew in smoke. "He could have done it," he finished quietly. "He could have done it quite easily."

"I think this week he's attacked three of us in flight," I breathed. "Vittorio, and me, and today Tony. And since you've already blown the race for Germany, Second Lieutenant Rainer, I think he might be desperate enough to sacrifice you for whatever he's after."

"I think so too," Sebastian repeated seriously.

The long skirt of my frock was spread on the seat around me, and I found myself crushing handfuls of mallard-blue silk to try to contain my nerves, exactly like Tony tearing at his dinner napkins.

"What does Rosengart *want*?" I asked. "I don't understand why he'd want to ruin the race."

"I do not know his plan," said Sebastian. "But if I am on his

221

list of false suspects, he does not care about a win for Germany. He is Gestapo, Germany's secret state police, and I think he has a mission to foul things for Lady Frith, regardless of who takes the prize. You and Tony and I represent Europe's Great Powers, Britain and France and Germany. Vittorio Pavesi represented the fourth, Italy. We are supposed to be promoting peace and we look as if we are at war—"

Tony interrupted dryly, "Yeah, and what about Torsten Stromberg? Sweden? Isn't Sweden always neutral? Rosengart's picking on him too."

"Well—to throw the rest of us off the scent—what do you call it—" Sebastian hesitated.

"A red herring," I supplied.

"It's simpler than your theory," Tony told him. "Rosengart's trying to kill me. He went for Vittorio and Northie by mistake because our planes are all the same color."

Sebastian bit his lip. After a moment he slowly raised the cigarette again. Then he, like me, asked, "Why?"

"I think—I think it's probably because of my father. I grew up in Hamburg," Tony said. "My father was a Communist. I'd call him a German Communist, but he was originally from Russia, so two strikes against him there. He was taken to the concentration camp at Dachau when I was fifteen."

Sebastian nodded. His calm acceptance of every new shocking thing he'd been told in the past five minutes gave me chills. He never seemed to doubt that the German chaperone could have a valid reason to kill.

"Tony—" I dared to glance across at him. "Rosengart will make you fly with him again tomorrow."

Tony's ordinary scowl was now replaced with something

222

bleaker and more focused, the summer brown of his face gone white around his eyes and nostrils, and he no longer stared straight ahead across the room; now he was staring at Florian Rosengart.

"His plane isn't armed," Tony said. "He doesn't have a machine gun on that dinosaur of an Ace he flies. He can try to ram me, but that's dangerous for him, too, and now he knows I might try to ram him right back. His combat experience was all twenty years ago in obsolete planes. Mine was last winter in a brand-new Soviet fighter that can do three hundred miles an hour, and I'll bet he knows that, too. I'm not afraid of him."

"A *Soviet fighter?*" breathed Sebastian.

"Yes, I flew in Spain, against your filthy Luftwaffe Condor Legion," Tony explained briefly, brushing it aside as if it were nothing. He went on with dark confidence: "Rosengart won't try to bump me off in flight again—not this next flight, anyway."

"But that means he'll probably try something else, if he really wants you dead," I pointed out grimly. "We'll be in Germany tomorrow. He could *get* guns if he wanted to, couldn't he? He could get his plane armed before the next leg of the race—"

"Don't be ridiculous," Tony said, leaning back and rolling his eyes. He stretched his legs out ahead of him, lined up with his heels on the ground and the toes of his dress shoes pointing at the vaulted ceiling. He looked as if he couldn't wait to be lying flat on his back. "A German plane firing a machine gun at a French plane on its way from Hamburg to Amsterdam wouldn't be murder—it would be a declaration of war. A real one, not some tabloid fairy tale. And it wouldn't be very

223

secret, either, when the International Criminal Police Commission started sifting through the wreckage and discovered it was full of German bullets."

"He does not need to do that." The still sureness in Sebastian's voice gave me chills again. "He is Gestapo. The moment your passport has been stamped in Hamburg, you will no longer be protected by international law and he can arrest you."

"But I haven't done anything!" Tony exclaimed.

"It does not matter. In Germany, he is above the law—if he wants you, he will make a telephone call tonight and six policemen in civilian clothes will escort you from the airfield when you land. You will sign your own warrant asking for their protective custody, so that it does not look like an arrest; and since I am accused of attacking other racers, it will even appear that you have reason to ask for protection—"

"I wouldn't sign a thing like that!" snarled Tony.

Sebastian said quietly, "They can make you."

Tony swallowed, gazing up at the ceiling where his toes were pointing. I thought I knew exactly what he was thinking: he must be wondering if his father had been forced to sign his own arrest warrant, his own death sentence.

Sebastian persisted: "If they want you to vanish, they will do it. You know what people say: *Lieber Herr Gott, mach mich stumm—*"

Tony finished in English, his voice low. "*To Dachau may I never come.*"

"There are other camps besides Dachau now," Sebastian said. "Last year, Sachsenhausen. This summer, Buchenwald. More whose names I do not know."

Tony took his eyes off the ceiling and looked over at Florian Rosengart again.

And suddenly Rosengart turned toward us, putting his pipe in his mouth and casting his intense blue gaze on Sebastian, his ward. I realized he must have been keeping a careful eye on all three of us the whole time we had been sitting there. I arranged my face in a big, false, beamingly beautiful smile and leaned forward with my elbows on my knees, tugging the long white gloves higher up my arms to try to hide the goose bumps, and then cupped my chin in my hands as if I were listening to Erlend and his crowd.

My mind raced with possibilities for keeping Tony out of Germany, and the only thing I could come up with was for him to run out of the Old Royal Palace *right now* and head for the railway station. And that would be too dramatic to get him anywhere. If he tried to leave Prague, Lady Frith would send someone after him. If he tried to leave the race, if he tried to fly off east to Poland or Hungary, Rosengart would go after him himself.

I could see Tony running over all the same ideas in his own head.

"We're only in Hamburg one night," Tony said. "What if I stay on the airfield after I land there—never get out of my plane—never officially set foot in Germany?"

Neither Sebastian nor I answered, and I didn't think Tony even expected an answer. We all knew he'd still have to face the reporters and the ground crew.

"The other racers will help," I said. "Erlend—Pim—Jiri and Stefan. I'll tell them. I'm sure they'll help."

"But in Germany—" Sebastian began. He hesitated, then said quickly, "In Germany, you need the help of a German."

He tapped his fingernail against the cigarette case on his knee and let the tip of his finger rest beneath the monogrammed initials A.R.

"Would you let me?" he asked cautiously. "Would you trust me?"

Someone in the crowd spoke to Rosengart again, and he looked away from Sebastian for a moment. Sebastian flipped the slim silver case through his fingers and then suddenly held it out to Tony.

"I have an idea," Sebastian said. "Here, a pledge of trust from a Luftwaffe officer."

Tony took the case from him.

Small Talk

There was the usual buffet breakfast at the crack of dawn at Ruzyně Aerodrome, in a bright and spacious conference room with huge streamlined windows. We sat to eat around a long table designed for business meetings. Lady Frith clearly didn't feel she needed to help me choose my sliced ham and cheese, and sat sipping coffee and making notes of her own. Every now and then she looked up to make sure I was still in the room.

But Capitaine Bazille stuck to Tony like glue, and Rosengart wouldn't even let Sebastian up out of his seat to get another cup of coffee.

I watched Rosengart out of the corner of my eye. He didn't cast a single glance in Tony's direction; he didn't even seem to be aware Tony was in the room. All his attention was on Sebastian. I could just imagine Lady Frith's reaction to our guesswork: *Of course you have had a terrible shock, Stella; of course you want answers. But you mustn't let your imagination run wild!*

I clattered my knife against my plate, slicing down hard into the thick rye bread. Today Rosengart must feel confident of his catch, like a spider with a fly safely trapped in its web but still alive and thrashing. He must have already made whatever arrangements he needed to make, and all he had to do this morning was wait for Tony to land ahead of him in Hamburg.

Sebastian had said he had an idea. The loan of his cigarette case hadn't explained his plan, and he hadn't been able to tell us more last night. He was supposed to take off nearly two hours before Tony, and nearly two and a half hours before me; there wasn't going to be much time to find out what his idea was.

If Sebastian wasn't allowed to go freely about the room, I would have to be the one to make a move.

I went to the buffet table, picked up a silver coffee pot, and went to stand right between Sebastian Rainer and Florian Rosengart.

"Good morning!" I said brightly. "Isn't it a lovely day for flying again! Haven't we been lucky in the weather! You can't imagine how glad I am we're not crossing any more mountains."

I froze for a split second. *Goodness, Northie,* I warned myself, *don't show your hand to Rosengart by mentioning mountains.*

"Isn't it wonderful how friendly all the contestants have become with one another since Venice!" I rattled on. "It's as if those horrid headlines made us pull together and now the competitive edge has gone. I think Vittorio's vigil made us all feel closer. It's terrible that it took a tragedy to do it, but—"

Sebastian took hold of my left hand and squeezed it.

Rosengart was looking up at me, mindful of the coffee pot that I held in my right hand, close to his shoulder. He couldn't see that Sebastian and I were gripping each other's palms on my other side, just below the surface of the table.

God! I had to keep pegging away at this mindless chatter for another minute or so. I wondered if Sebastian had written a note he wanted to pass to me; I had no doubt his quick conjurer's fingers could complete the exchange without anyone noticing. I opened my hand from around his, ready to take whatever it was. I bent over Rosengart's plate, refilling his coffee cup very rudely from the wrong side of his place setting, completely blocking Sebastian from his view.

"Black and sweet, I remember," I said blithely.

"Thank you, Miss North," said Major Rosengart.

I couldn't bear to meet his tumultuous blue gaze.

Sebastian slipped a small, flat paper booklet into my hand. I thought it must be the notebook in which he'd done his flight calculations.

I closed my fingers around it as I straightened. It was about the size of my hand, too big to fully hide in my palm, so I held it against the thigh of my flight suit as I leaned over to fill Sebastian's cup too.

"*Danke*—thank you, Stella," said Sebastian with his usual stiff courtesy, as if using my first name made him uncomfortable and he had to force himself to do it.

"Why, you're both very welcome," I said.

Now I had to get away from them as quickly as possible. I glanced around the table.

"Oh, Pim! Don't get up—I have coffee right here."

I stepped behind Rosengart's back and slapped Sebastian's slim little book against the bottom of the pot, hiding it between my palm and the silver base. I carried the coffee pot around the table in two hands like that, as reverently as the Grail Maiden carrying the Sacred Chalice.

"You are better at being polite to them than I am," Pim said darkly, as I filled his cup.

"You just need to practice," I told him. "Small talk's a skill. It doesn't have to come naturally. You can learn it, like flying."

I returned the pot to the sideboard and set it down. With my back to the rest of the room, I quietly tucked Sebastian's gift into the breast pocket of my flight suit.

———◇———

It was easy to get a moment alone simply by excusing myself to the lav. Safely locked in on my own, I took the booklet out of my pocket, expecting instructions and a complicated plan. But Sebastian hadn't given me his notebook. He hadn't written down anything that would get him in trouble.

He'd given me his passport—his German passport.

———◇———

For a moment my heart plummeted. *Hell's teeth,* I thought in fury, *what am I supposed to do with someone else's German passport?*

A second later it was obvious. It was for Sebastian's rough-diamond look-alike—for Tony.

Could Tony blindside a crowd of curious German officials with a stolen passport? Maybe he could. He'd grown up in Hamburg; he'd told me German was probably his first language. And he obviously had nerves of steel when his life depended on it.

I went back to the boardroom and picked up the coffee pot again.

Tony was telling Capitaine Bazille about his flight plan. It was the most innocent and mundane conversation in the world. I stood between them and said, "I am working on my serving skills this morning."

"Sabotaging your opponents by filling them with coffee?" said Tony. "I'll need an extra stop now."

Capitaine Bazille laughed out loud. "Shame on you—that is no way to speak before a young lady."

I managed to force out an unaffected laugh as well. "Thank you, Capitaine Bazille."

I leaned over Bazille's cup, pouring with one hand, and with the other hand I dropped Sebastian Rainer's passport into Tony's lap.

———◇———

Erlend and Gaby, the first to take off that morning, got up from the table to go do the pre-flight checks on their planes. I watched them unhook their flight jackets from the coatracks just inside the door of the conference room. It took them a minute or two to sort out which ones were their own, and suddenly I was inspired.

I went over to join them, and like a demure young housemaid, I started distributing everyone's flight gear.

I hung Tony's cracked brown leather flying jacket over the back of Sebastian's chair, and dropped Sebastian's shining black Luftwaffe jacket behind Tony.

Their jackets were completely different cuts and weren't even the same color. But Sebastian picked up Tony's when he got up, as casually and naturally as if it had always been his own, and Tony picked up Sebastian's without even looking. Of course, nobody ever put on a flight jacket until right before getting into an aeroplane, because the weather was so warm, so no one else was likely to notice.

I found I was holding my breath as they each left the room under the watchful eye of a chaperone. With the caution of an explosives expert defusing a bomb, I let out the air in my lungs without making a noise that might sound like a sigh or a gasp.

———◆———

Agitatedly, Lady Frith pulled on her flying gloves and helmet an hour later, getting ready to make the changeover from keeping her eye on me on the ground to keeping her eye on Sebastian in the air.

"What's the matter?" I asked.

"Oh, it's just one thing after another. Pim is unbelievably nervous about being in Germany overnight. It's less than twenty-four hours, for heaven's sake, and the Nazis were very well-behaved about the Olympics, letting Jews compete, not allowing any brawling in the streets. I don't like to remind him that it isn't just in Germany where Jews are being attacked—it's bad in Poland and Hungary, too—even here in Czechoslovakia—and Major Rosengart has *promised* to keep a close guard on him while we're in Hamburg. Anyway, I'd just finished reassuring Pim when Sebastian announced that he is feeling poorly—he thinks it is something he ate."

I was beset for a moment with a wild notion that I had poisoned Sebastian myself when I poured the coffee for him.

Lady Frith went on in frustration: "He has spent the past twenty minutes in the lavatory, and Major Rosengart is refusing to allow him to delay his departure. Bother these Germans— you'd think the man would be more sympathetic to the flier from his own nation! I've promised Sebastian I'll allow him a diversion if he's caught short in flight. I had expected we'd manage without any injuries or illness—goodness, you're all healthy young people! I do hope it is something he ate, and not a stomach flu that will affect us all—that would be the absolute limit."

I didn't believe it.

Thief and conjurer, Tony had called him. Sebastian must be putting on a show to drag out his flight time. He was supposed to arrive in Hamburg well ahead of Tony; of course he'd never be able to avoid the reporters once he was on home soil, and it would destroy Tony's chance to use the borrowed passport if Sebastian got there first.

If Sebastian was doing it on purpose, it meant he was throwing away any shred of a chance he still had of redeeming himself in the race.

Thief and conjurer.

He was risking danger and disgrace to try to save someone else's life. Beneath the watchful surface, Sebastian Rainer must be as much of a principled hothead as Tony Roberts.

There was one more thing I could do to cover for him.

"Oh, perhaps it *is* flu," I improvised recklessly. "I've been shaking for *days,* haven't you noticed? And feeling feverish and achy ever since we left the Old Royal Palace last night. I thought it was just an attack of nerves"—I couldn't resist the jab—"but perhaps it is something contagious."

"Oh, Stella, not you too!" Lady Frith exclaimed in dismay. "Will you be all right to fly?"

"If Leutnant Rainer can do it, so can I," I said with grim assurance.

A Few Dutch Masters
Hamburg, German Reich

I was the last contestant to arrive at Hamburg Airport. Circling above it, I was horror-struck at the size of its huge green fields and sprawling new passenger terminal. Even if Tony had landed safely, there was no conceivable way he could avoid being swept up in some kind of official greeting.

I tried to count the Circuit of Nations aircraft from overhead, but I had to give up so I could concentrate on landing between two huge triple-engined Lufthansa passenger liners in the sky ahead of and behind me. Airport employees with field glasses, looking for my small plane in the air, signaled with flashing lights to give warnings to the larger aircraft as I approached. On the ground, three flagmen waved me in the right direction.

The racing planes were parked close together, and I frantically counted them as I taxied across the neatly cropped lawn. At last I let out a sigh of relief; except for Capitaine Bazille, landing now, every one of our machines was already there, and they all appeared to be in one piece.

I shut down my engine, and Lady Frith took over from Capitaine Bazille as my chaperone on the ground, unleashing a torrent of distress as she met me.

"Oh, Northie, I *am* glad to see you've made it ahead of schedule. I have had such a time with that young German boy today, you would not believe. He was ill before we left, and he landed at Altenberg to be ill again, and for a few minutes I didn't think they were going to let him in the clubhouse there because he could not locate his identification papers! Fortunately I have everybody's passport details in my traveling files…"

She trailed off, frantically digging in her flight bag, as if she were suddenly worried she'd left all her careful paperwork in Altenberg.

"Truly, Stella, at that point Sebastian seemed so confused I did not feel it was going to be safe for him to fly on," Lady Frith continued, still searching. "Before we took off again he insisted on taking a nap—can you believe it? He sat in his cockpit and slept for half an hour! The airport manager here has been very efficient in holding off the press, thank heavens. I've enough to worry about with Pim van Leer being Jewish; luckily, Florian's called on some plainclothes policemen to shadow our group and make sure there's no trouble."

Lady Frith found what she was hunting for: her own packet of cigarettes. She paused for a breathless moment to light one and, astonishingly and defiantly, offered one to me as well as I climbed out of the Cadet.

"Go on, take it, no one is looking, and quite honestly I don't care if they do look. *Young British Lady Seen Smoking on German Airfield!* Frankly I would be shouting hallelujahs if that were the worst headline they could come up with. I am heartsick."

I felt my own heart constrict a little. *Plainclothes policemen to shadow our group?*

"Is everyone else all right?" I asked cautiously. I thought it was a fair thing to ask, as they all seemed to have disappeared—Stefan and Philippos couldn't have landed very much ahead of me and Capitaine Bazille.

"There are taxis arranged to take everyone to the hotel. Ernesto is organizing it." In her careless frustration, Lady Frith stopped bothering to be formal about everyone's names. "You and Marcel are the only ones who haven't had your passports stamped—well, and Sebastian of course, but they let him in eventually as it's perfectly obvious he's German. Florian has had to take him straight to the Stadthöfe to have a new passport issued, which gives the international press a bit of Nazi scandal to speculate about, as that's also where they make all the worst kind of rules and arrests. And Tony went through the wrong queue and has managed to get himself separated from the rest of us."

I swallowed and stood silent for a moment. Lady Frith called out something in German to the marshal who'd guided me in on the ground.

"'Separated?'" I echoed numbly.

"Yes, and I wouldn't be surprised if that *bloody* boy didn't do it on purpose."

I had never heard her swear, either.

"Oh, don't look so shocked, Stella, it's enough to try the patience of a saint. Tony gave Florian as much of a devil of a time in the air as Sebastian gave me—apparently he stopped to refuel in Czechoslovakia only about twenty minutes after they left Prague! And when he got here, he didn't wait for Florian to land, he didn't even speak to anyone, he just simply *vanished.*"

"'Vanished?'" I repeated, my voice coming out as little more than a croak.

She didn't hear me, or didn't answer if she did.

This was agony. Not knowing what had happened—it was agony.

———◇———

An hour passed at the airport, and Tony was still nowhere to be found. Lady Frith paced the lofty new terminal, and finally dragged me out of the building with her, after Capitaine Bazille promised he would wait there for news.

"It's entirely possible the boy has made his own way to the hotel," Lady Frith told Bazille as she climbed with me into our waiting taxi. "I suppose there's no way he could have sent a message to me in a place as busy and big as Hamburg Airport. He's been rude to the press before."

"He dislikes the attention," said Bazille. "I'll follow up your inquiries with the airport authorities. Of course he'll reappear."

"I am stunned that your French reporters are so forgiving with him! He has until this evening—" Lady Frith held up a hand to stop Bazille interrupting. "If he attends tonight's gala I shall consider the matter closed. We needn't alert the police when we've got Florian's colleagues to assist us. I dread the moment everyone in Hamburg finds out I can't keep track of my own contestants!"

Tony had not checked in when we arrived at the hotel, and

238

of course then we had to endure a formal luncheon and a tour of the Kunsthalle art museum.

I stared up at the dark paintings by the old Dutch masters without seeing them, feeling as though I might scream with anxiety and frustration. Rembrandt and Rubens, stormy skies and the looming sails of ships and windmills, it all seemed remote and irrelevant. Perhaps Erlend was appreciating it from the point of view of a painter.

Pim touched my shoulder and I jumped.

"Is Tony safe?" he asked quietly in English.

I glanced at him, then back at the artwork I wasn't taking in.

"I don't know."

"He knows these men are hunting him, though? He knows to be careful?"

"Yes," I said briefly. "How do *you* know?"

We stood close together, not looking at each other, staring at the walls of the museum. Pim spoke quickly, nearly in a whisper, filling me in.

"There are two men in our company—you will see them as we pass into the next gallery. They are careful not to seem as if they are with us. They look like automobile merchants, expensive hats and jackets, one of them carrying an umbrella, but they are special police here to make sure there is no trouble for—ah, you know, us 'foreigners.' Major Rosengart introduced them to me but not to anyone else. But"—Pim took a breath and rushed on—"I heard these two talk of others that Major Rosengart *didn't* tell me about, and those men are looking for Tony. Not because he is missing, but because they have been told to arrest him. That is the word they used."

I, too, sucked in a sharp breath. "And have they?"

"I don't know that either."

Staring straight ahead of me, I felt, rather than saw, as Pim shrugged.

"That is why I asked you and not Lady Frith," he went on quickly. "She means well, but she trusts Major Rosengart and I do not. I am worried she will warn him if I ask her. Rosengart is in the Stadthöfe all afternoon to get Sebastian a new passport, and who knows what else he may do while he is there in the center of Nazi police operations? I think they have not found Tony yet, because they spoke of being watchful, and of communicating with their friends when we go back to the hotel."

"How on earth did you hear all this?" I hissed.

"Ah, the discretion of the Gestapo!" Pim gave a little choke of laughter. "I speak German. I didn't put it on my race application because I didn't want to have to translate for the German pilot. So Rosengart told them I understand only French and Dutch."

I glanced at the slight, pale boy next to me. He was grinning fiercely.

"They are using me," he said. "'Protect the Jewish boy'—it is an excuse for them to be here. It is Tony they want. They will accuse him of Vittorio's death. That cannot be their real reason, with no evidence, and I don't know what the real reason is. But I think I am safe, and he is not. So if you see him, tell him to stay as far away from me as possible. It will force them to divide their attention."

"Tell the others as well," I said. "Tony said that Rosengart tried to ram him in the air yesterday."

Pim gave me another friendly tap on the shoulder and walked away as if he'd grown bored looking at that wall.

My room in the Hotel Reichshof connected with Lady Frith's. She put her head through the door to give me an update as she was dressing for the evening's reception, which was to be held at the Rathaus, Hamburg's splendid city hall.

"That terrible Tony Roberts did check in while we were at the museum, but he's not in his room now; he's supposed to be next door to Gaby Dupont, adjoining Marcel—Capitaine Bazille, the French chaperone, don't look so bewildered. Anyway, Gaby hasn't seen him and neither has Marcel. Of course Marcel has only just checked in himself after waiting at the airport all afternoon. I swear, if that young man doesn't appear at the Rathaus this evening I will *disqualify him* when he does appear."

Lady Frith paused before returning to her own room and said critically, "My goodness, you are pale, Stella. How are you feeling? Were you all right in the air? Perhaps you should stay here and rest instead of going to the banquet tonight."

"Oh, I wouldn't want to miss the banquet, I am fine," I said quickly. I didn't dare fake illness so effectively that it kept me from finding out what was going on.

"You can borrow my face powder if you haven't any of your own."

I sat in front of the dressing table mirror with my face in my hands. I knew that anyone could have checked in under Tony's name. Rosengart could have arranged it to stop Lady Frith from worrying. Even if no one saw Tony all evening, Lady Frith wouldn't begin to suspect anything had happened to him until tomorrow morning.

Combat Nerves

M ost of the other racers were standing nervously in the long lobby of the Hotel Reichshof when Lady Frith and I came downstairs, ready to board a rented bus that would transport us to the Rathaus. Capitano Ranza hovered close behind Torsten; Major Rosengart was close by Sebastian, who stood stiff as a lamppost spinning an unlit cigarette between his fingers.

Lady Frith swooped down on Sebastian as well.

"I hope you are feeling better this evening, Leutnant Rainer?"

"Much better," answered Sebastian, startled. "Yes—better— I think—" He examined his cigarette tentatively, as if he thought it might be the source of his utterly faked illness.

"It's a pity your family is not here," Lady Frith said, laying a hand on his. "But I feel that it's so important for you young people to make your own way in the world, even when your loved ones seem to withhold their support. I hope you don't mind too much!"

"My mother sent me flowers," said Sebastian shortly. "My father disapproves of the attention from the press."

"You and Miss North have that in common, I am afraid," Lady Frith reassured him.

Sebastian met my eyes in silent surprise, and I nodded grimly. Aunt Marie had not sent me flowers.

Behind me, someone came clattering down the stairs between the lobby's square marble columns, and Sebastian suddenly grinned.

I looked over my shoulder. There was Tony loping toward us, perfectly dressed in his ill-fitting white tie and tails.

I felt as if my knees were filled with hot water. *Thank God.*

He looked surprisingly neat, I thought, for someone who'd either just made a getaway or else was under a death sentence—freshly washed and shaved like everybody else, his longish hair combed back from his forehead. He deliberately pulled Sebastian's cigarette case from his pocket, and as he flicked it open I could just see the mother-of-pearl cuff buttons I'd made for him, glinting at his wrist.

He didn't have a chance to light up before Lady Frith exploded in outrage: "*I hope you have a good explanation, M'sieur Robert!*"

"The best," Tony drawled. "You remember the big Luftwaffe Junkers trimotor from Berlin that was unloading when I landed? All those passengers came crowding around to watch me, and I got tangled up with them."

"I don't believe you even *tried* to find me!" Lady Frith exclaimed.

"I was going to." Tony was at his most persuasive. "But there was one old lady who'd never been in the air before; she told me she was born in 1850—this flight was a birthday present from her grandchildren! Well, I offered to carry her bag of course—"

"Of course," Lady Frith agreed grimly.

"—And then I ended up going through the air terminal and got caught up in the birthday party," Tony finished in triumph. "I didn't even have to show my passport—the folks I was with hadn't come from outside Germany, and they all thought I was a Luftwaffe recruit! I was pretty lost in that huge airport, but I know Hamburg, and I thought that the most sensible thing to do was to get myself to the hotel. Which I did."

"But you didn't check in until the rest of us had finished lunch and were already on the museum tour!" Lady Frith scolded. "What in the world were you doing all that time?"

I could see Tony fighting to control his perpetual scowl.

"Well, I walked, of course," he said. "I haven't any German money. It must be about six miles—it took me nearly three hours—"

"*Tony!*" Lady Frith interrupted explosively. The shock and concern in her voice were genuine, and puzzling.

"I took a couple of breaks," he said defensively. "Or I'd have been quicker. Walking's good for me."

"It is like running an *infants' school*," Lady Frith complained to no one in particular. "We're already ten minutes late." She looked around and exclaimed in irritation, "Where is that van Leer boy? It's not like him to hold us up—"

She didn't need to finish. Pim, his face white as chalk, came hurrying over from the lifts. He wore a devilish smirk in

244

the corner of his mouth, apologized quickly to Lady Frith, and then started speaking to Stefan in rapid French about commercial airlines.

The bus was ready, and we all climbed in.

Florian Rosengart didn't get on board with Sebastian, though. He stood outside the bus finishing his pipe while the rest of us sat down. Another hotel guest in evening dress, a man about Rosengart's age with thinning blond hair, glanced at the bus and then gave Rosengart a stiff Nazi salute.

He wasn't one of the men that Pim had pointed out to me in the museum.

Rosengart nodded coolly to him and raised a hand in acknowledgment, and the other man climbed into a private car, which pulled away.

I desperately wanted it to be coincidence. Some coworker perhaps, some dignitary, even a friend. But it seemed more likely that Sebastian and Pim were exactly right about what Rosengart hoped to accomplish in Hamburg, and this man was part of a planned arrest.

Erlend threw himself down next to me in the bus, forcing Lady Frith to take the seat across the aisle from us. "How does it go with you, Northie? And what are you up to?"

I wondered how much detail Pim had shared with him. I didn't dare give much away with Lady Frith so close by.

"Everybody's trying to avoid their chaperones," I said.

"Not Torsten. Look at him, studying his map through those thick spectacles. He works hard. He is a very good boy."

"Well, none of the rest of us are being good."

Erlend spoke softly into my ear: "Tony asked me to keep his luggage and flight bag in my room. He is moving about to keep them guessing. He had a short sleep on the floor in Stefan's room, and then he took a bath in Philippos's room and dressed in Theodor's. His own room key he has given to Gaby so that he can—how do you say it—Gaby will cover Tony's tracks for him! Pim *rode the lifts* for half an hour to distract those policemen, can you believe it? Up and down from the top floor to the lobby fifteen times, with two Gestapo agents! He told them it helps condition his inner ear for the pressure changes in flight."

I spluttered with astonished laughter. "That's *super*."

I'd taken Pim for a bit of a coward. I'd clearly underestimated him.

I'd underestimated all of them.

I squirmed around in my seat on the bus to try to catch a glimpse of Tony. There he was in the back again, his legs up across the length of the last seat, apparently sound asleep. I imagined him stretched out on the floor of Stefan's smoke-filled hotel room, perhaps alongside the bed where he'd be out of the way and invisible to anyone who stepped in looking for him. He'd woken up at five-thirty this morning, flown three hundred miles, walked another six, and taken a twenty-minute nap on the floor; now he was desperate enough to snatch another five minutes' sleep in the back of an omnibus.

I wondered uneasily how he was going to manage to fly out of Germany tomorrow morning.

———◆———

It was an absolutely perfect evening of late summer, as if the Nazi government managed to have the weather under its iron regulations like everything else. Drinks and a military band were set up in the courtyard of the Rathaus around the fountain of Hygieia, so that the trumpeted melodies of traditional folk tunes drowned the noise of bubbling water flowing from the bowl in the statue's raised bronze hand. The courtyard was open to the sky. Between stately windows, the walls of the Hamburg city hall were hung with the bloodred banners of the German Reich, each stamped with a black swastika against a white background, stark as a brand against skin.

After only a little while there, I began to feel as if I were inhabiting some terrifying future world in a novel by Jules Verne or H. G. Wells. After the Circuit of Nations Olympics of the Air racers filed in, joined by the usual collection of official dignitaries and their wives, the stone walls seemed to begin rumbling as if they were about to collapse. All around me, people's heads suddenly tilted abruptly up to the sky. Then a zeppelin in the livery of the Luftwaffe began to pass overhead, so low it must have been level with the top of the city hall clock tower.

I watched in riveted amazement. I couldn't believe the brazen arrogance of such a display, especially after the terrible fire outside New York only three months ago, when the German airship *Hindenburg* exploded.

But it was a compelling show of strength. Everybody stared up, faces toward the sky. As the airship passed over, gleaming dark gold in the low light of the setting sun, I thought the noise would die away. Instead, it changed—growing louder and more frantic, an angrier sound, more of a roar than a rumble.

Then the first planes went over.

There were three, flying like a skein of geese in a V: two aircraft following a leader, black, knife-blade shapes against

247

the white-and-blue-streaked evening sky. They were single-cockpit fighter planes, deadly and diabolically fast. I *felt* their passing almost more intensely than I heard or saw it. The noise of their engines drowned out the sound of the band. It was so furious it shook my entire body.

But the noise didn't stop as the first three planes went over. Behind them came more, wave after wave of them. I lost count at twenty-seven. As they passed above the Rathaus, each echelon began a climbing turn, spiraled up, and came around again higher up, until they were layer upon layer overhead, and the higher they flew, the more of them you could see.

I did not know what they were, but I could guess. Tony had told me that a Messerschmitt 109 could fly over three hundred miles an hour, nearly twice as fast as the Hawker Hectors at Old Sarum. Major Rosengart and Sebastian Rainer must have been holding back laughter when they landed there. These new Messerschmitts were the sleekest, fastest, most dangerous aeroplanes I had ever seen. I hated them and at the same time I wanted so badly to be able to fly one myself that I thought I would choke with longing. What could it possibly feel like to hold all that power between your thumb and forefinger?

Tony must have some idea, I thought. He'd flown a Soviet fighter. I dragged my gaze from the thundering sky and looked around for him.

As before, he was the only one not looking at the planes.

He was sitting on the edge of the fountain, bent over with his head in his hands. After a moment I realized he was holding his ears, pressing the balls of his palms so hard against the sides of his head it must have hurt, and plucking at his hair with tense fingertips.

Is this what it's like, I wondered, *when the planes come and come and you try to hide, waiting for the fire and the explosions? What it was like in Madrid? In Guernica?*

But of course there were no explosions here; it was *nothing* like Guernica. It was just the Germans showing off their splendid new air force, the Luftwaffe saluting their Circuit of Nations Olympics of the Air contestant, who was one of their pilots too.

I dodged away from Lady Frith, still gazing at the sky with everyone else. I crossed the courtyard and sat down next to Tony. I remembered not to surprise him from behind by touching his shoulder; I put my hand on his arm.

You've got combat nerves, his husky voice echoed in my head.

He didn't uncover his ears. But he didn't pull away from me, either.

This is awful, I thought. I could see that it was torture for him. I tugged him by the elbow.

He turned his head to look at me resentfully, not taking his hands from his ears.

There were two arched gateways to the street in the courtyard, but uniformed guards stood attentively on either side of each gate. I didn't want to attract their interest. I stood up and pointed to the nearest open door leading back into the city hall. I mouthed, *Come on.*

Everyone else was still looking at the sky. Bazille and Rosengart were side by side, staring up, one of them wearing an expression of horror and the other of rapture.

Tony stood, never lowering his arms, clutching the sides of his head as if he were trying to stop it from flying into pieces.

But he came with me, limping, his odd, irregular gait more pronounced as it always was at the end of the day. I remembered that he'd walked six miles from the aerodrome to the hotel.

It was a little quieter in the Rathausdiele, the long vaulted entrance hall of the building. Everyone else was outside watching the planes, so the cool and lamplit hall was empty. Tony, blushing, smoothed his hair back from his forehead and wiped his palms on the black wool of his trousers. He blinked himself back to reality as if he'd been stuck in a dark cellar and was just coming out into daylight.

I sat down with him on one of the polished benches that circled the hall's huge sandstone pillars.

"Were you at Guernica?" I asked.

"No, Jarama. In February, when the Fascists tried to cut off the road from Valencia to Madrid."

I remembered a battle: news stories throughout the month describing bodies lying in olive groves, falling rain, flooding rivers. There'd been conflicting reports from the leaders of both sides. It had been hard to put faces to the numbers of the dead.

"It wasn't as much of a story as Guernica," Tony added bitterly, as if he knew exactly why I didn't remember the details. Then he said hastily, "I mean—everything else looks like a picnic when you compare it to Guernica, doesn't it? All those bombs and airborne machine guns ripping into shops and churches and bedrooms for three hours. A whole town destroyed in a single afternoon! Jarama was an ordinary battle, day after day for weeks in the mud like the Marne, thirty thousand soldiers lying dead when it was done. They wouldn't have sent me near Guernica anyway; there isn't really any organized air defense except around Madrid. My escuadrilla—my squadron—was close enough that we could go to the bars and hotels there when we weren't flying. Anyway I—well—I—"

"Were you shot down?" I prompted, so he wouldn't have to say it himself or give me elaborate details.

"Yes," he said gratefully. "More or less. About two months before Guernica. And I couldn't go back—I tried and they wouldn't take me. *Didn't want me.* So I left. That's when I went to France."

We sat together listening, waiting for the sound of the engines to fade.

Finally it seemed like it was over. I could hear spontaneous applause breaking out in the courtyard. A dozen people came running through the hall past me and Tony, the women clattering on their high heels and hanging on the arms of their escorts for support. They all disappeared through the huge wrought-iron front gate out to the Rathaus market square to catch a last glimpse of the vanishing planes.

Sebastian came with them, looking around him. He spun on his heel when he spotted Tony and me.

"Come," he urged, pointing at the gate to the street.

Tony shook his head.

"No one is watching," said Sebastian. "I told Lady Frith I was returning to the hotel because I am ill again; I did not tell Major Rosengart anything, and in a moment he will notice I am gone. Right now it will appear natural for us to follow the rest out. You saw the uniforms."

There were intimidating armed police sentries at this door, too, standing at attention like soldiers. They hadn't paid the faintest notice to the guests when we'd first gone in, but Sebastian was right—now was the only chance to get out past them without anybody asking questions.

Sebastian offered me his arm. I took it, and held out my other arm for Tony.

Then, with our elbows linked, in our evening clothes, the three of us stepped unnoticed out of the Hamburg Rathaus and into the darkening night.

A Few Automobile Merchants

We crossed the very open market square in front of the city hall. On the other side of the tram tracks was a set of wide, curving stone steps leading to Kleine Alster, the canal made by the dammed river Alster. Rising from the water level and soaring heavenward stood a tall stone war memorial to Hamburg's Great War dead, close against the bridge where the city street crossed the canal. I led Tony and Sebastian down the steps to the canal so we could get away from the street.

"What are we going to do?" I said.

It was Saturday night, and there were plenty of other people about, some of them as dressed up as we were. But I had only a flimsy silk stole for a wrap, and the back of my shoulders prickled with chill and the awareness of armed policemen who might come after us at any moment.

"I do not know Hamburg," Sebastian said.

"I know it pretty well," said Tony. He sat down on one of the stone steps that led down to the water, his back to the bridge and the trams. "But I was only a kid when I left. My dad's friends were all German Communists, and if they're even here anymore I don't think we'd be safe tracking them down. I don't know any place we can go except back to the hotel."

"You will not be safe in that hotel now," said Sebastian. "Major Rosengart will have no choice but to go there first to look for me. It might gain some time for you. But Rosengart will certainly make sure that all the doors are watched, and all our rooms—he had men there already this afternoon."

I knew he had men there. Pim had pointed out two of them. The blond Nazi with the thinning hair and the aggressive salute might be a third. Maybe there were others.

"We cannot stay here," Sebastian urged. "Rosengart will come looking for *me*, if not you, Tony, the second he notices I am gone."

"Lady Frith said she would disqualify you if you didn't turn up at tonight's gala," I told Tony.

He laughed wildly. "Will she do that if I'm dead?"

I caught my breath.

"Anyway, I did turn up," he said defensively. "I just left early."

Sebastian did not laugh. "What will happen to you, Stella?"

I hadn't thought. I sat down next to Tony, turning my back defiantly on the Rathaus.

"Lady Frith might assume I also went back to the hotel. She thinks I'm not feeling well either," I said. "Maybe she'll disqualify me, too."

254

"You go back inside," Sebastian said. "I am already in disgrace; it will not matter what happens to me."

"It will if they catch you with me," Tony said.

I couldn't shake the feeling that none of this could possibly be real. The beautiful modern city, busy with its trams and canal boats and well-dressed people heading to restaurant suppers and concerts—it couldn't be possible for everything to hold such slinking menace.

But the armed policemen and bloodred banners were real, too.

I said, "What about a nightclub?"

They both turned to look at me.

"Well, if we're going to be disqualified anyway..." I said. "If we just keep moving, perhaps an hour in one and an hour in another, we could make it through most of the night. And then we could head back to the hotel and get on the bus with everyone else tomorrow morning, do our flight planning at the airfield—they can't pluck you out and kill you while everyone's watching, can they, if they don't have a real reason for it? There's not a shred of evidence against either of you for Vittorio's disappearance—why, there's more evidence against me than there is against you! The danger is when you're alone, or going in and out of some place, or when you stop moving and give them a chance to catch up with you—"

"They are on the bridge over the canal lock," said Sebastian quietly. "They cannot see you and Tony—the memorial is in the way. But they can see me."

"Is Rosengart with them?" I gasped.

"No."

Sebastian reached into his breast pocket and took out a

paper packet of cigarettes. He selected one, twirled it between his fingers, then lit it with the last match in his Hôtel Le Plaza souvenir matchbook, as if he'd only stepped outside to look at the water and get away from the crowd.

I stood up, very deliberately, and let the stole slide down my arms into the crooks of my elbows so that my back was bare. I placed my gloved hands against Sebastian's shoulders and stood close against his chest, raising my face to his.

He tossed his cigarette into the canal. I heard it hiss as it hit the water. Then a tram thundered by on the far side of the street above us and rattled across the market square.

Sebastian held me lightly with his palms against the bare skin of my upper arms, between the tops of my long gloves and the bottom of the floaty dark-blue silk sleeves of my first really grown-up evening frock. He bent his face close to mine so that our lips were just touching, and it looked like a kiss.

When Sebastian spoke, I could feel his lips moving against mine. He said to Tony in the same quiet voice, "Stand over by the wall. Go quickly."

Tony scrambled up the steps on hands and knees, keeping low, and stood silently in shadow with his back flat against the embankment where the steps met the bridge. If anyone leaned over the bridge railing and looked down from above, Tony wouldn't be hidden at all, but he was in darkness now. Sebastian and I were in the open, a beautiful young couple in evening dress, necking in the starlight by the still waters of Kleine Alster; and maybe we would distract Tony's hunters.

I couldn't tell how long we all stood there like that. Another tram rumbled past. It felt like time had stopped.

"What are they *doing*?" I gasped at last, in a whisper.

"Shh. They are smoking and dropping ash in the water. They are watching people crossing the bridge."

"Are they watching us?"

"No, but they know that we are here."

"Who are they?"

Sebastian turned around slowly with me in his arms, his head bent close to mine still, so that I could get a better view.

There were three of them, all in white tie and black tails like Tony and Sebastian. It wasn't obvious they'd stepped out of the reception at the Rathaus, but it was likely; they didn't seem to be on their way anywhere, and they wouldn't have been all dressed up like that without hats and cloaks unless they'd come from someplace nearby.

"I do not know who they are," said Sebastian quietly. "The short one with the mustache I saw at the Stadthöfe while I awaited the new passport this afternoon. So it is strange to see him again here."

"That one with the thin fair hair combed over the top of his head, the older one—he was at our hotel earlier," I said. "He waved at Rosengart." I swallowed. "Perhaps they're just dinner guests."

"That may be," said Sebastian.

Another endless time passed, while Sebastian and I brushed our lips tentatively across each other's cheeks and hair, at once fearfully intimate and ridiculously, howlingly prudish. Neither one of us quite dared a real kiss. I began to think I would freeze to death before the hunters left. Maybe they *wouldn't* leave. Maybe they were voyeuristically enjoying our show, waiting to pounce on their prey when we tried to get away from them. Maybe their job was to stand on that bridge all night in case anyone they were looking for tried to cross it.

Sebastian swallowed. "The one you saw at the hotel has a pistol. He has taken out the magazine and seems to be counting the rounds—he is using the railing of the bridge to hide what he does."

"Maybe they all have guns," I breathed.

God—it would be easy enough for them to come down off the bridge, slam Tony against the embankment wall, and wait for a tram to pass overhead; the screech of the rails and thunder of the wheels would muffle the sound of a shot, and they could dump his limp body in the canal.

But they didn't. Two of them set off across the bridge at last, walking briskly away from the Rathaus. The third, the one I had recognized, headed back across the square.

Maybe they hadn't realized they were looking at a pair of air race contestants. Maybe they'd thought Sebastian and I were just a sophisticated young Hamburg couple out together for the evening. Maybe they weren't infallible; their colleagues had made the mistake of allowing Pim to overhear their conversation, and Rosengart had made far too many quick assumptions about green planes and engraved accessories.

"We could go walk along the canal," I pointed out. A long promenade led away from the bridge.

"Do not move," Sebastian warned. "They may come back. We would be in the open that way, and they could see us the whole length of the bank."

"Then couldn't we get on a tram? They go by right at the top of these steps!"

258

Sebastian shook his head. "You know they will watch the trams."

"My God—are we *trapped* here?" I exclaimed.

Tony's low voice came huskily out of the dark. "We can get over the lock gates," he said. "Under the bridge."

He was talking about the barriers that allowed boats to move between the upper and lower stretches of the canal. But all I could see beneath the bridge was inky blackness.

I sat down on the steps again and pulled Sebastian down beside me by the hand. He held a protective arm around my waist, as if we really were that romantic young Hamburg couple watching the city lights come out on the waters of Kleine Alster. I angled myself so that I could see Tony, still flattened against the wall of the embankment.

The white of his cuffs and the white bib of his shirtfront glowed among the shadows, as if he were a large cat prowling in the dark. He stood on the edge of the platform by the tall stone memorial, assessing the lock gates, also like a cat—a cat about to leap off into the night.

"You can reach the lock by a walkway under the bridge," he said. "This memorial wasn't here when I was a boy. They put it up just before the Nazis took over—there used to be a kiosk under the bridge that sold ice cream and boat rides, and the access is still here. Look, the lock's closed on this side, and the gates are plenty wide enough to walk across—or you could crawl, if your tightrope dancing's rusty."

"Where will it get us when we cross the lock?" Sebastian asked.

"That restaurant terrace on the other side of the canal," Tony said. "Then out—anywhere. They won't notice us going that way. We're only about a kilometer from Saint Pauli. We could try the nightclub idea. The men who went that way must think we're ahead of them; they won't expect us to follow them." He paused. "Maybe you *should* go back, Northie. You'll be all right. This is a silly thing to do in an evening gown. And I don't have any money."

"I have money," said Sebastian.

"I'd better get rid of my heels for the tightrope dancing," I said fiercely. "But I'm coming with you."

---◇---

I took off my T-strap evening shoes with their Cuban heels and buckled the straps together, and Sebastian carried them around his neck. It was easy crossing the lock gates beneath the bridge. The three of us waited a bit before invading the restaurant on the other side; when a couple got up and left the candlelit table nearest us, Tony vaulted lightly over the terrace railing and offered a gallant hand to help me. Sebastian handed me back my shoes, and Tony and I sat down at the table while I put them on. Then Sebastian followed us quietly over the railing and stood guard, watchful.

"Look, there is another party leaving," he said. "Come—if we stay behind them, no one will notice us."

Waiters held open the doors as we all trooped through the building, and then the three of us were on the street and no one had paid any attention.

We trailed after the people from the restaurant, who were chattering and laughing together. We tried to make it look as if we were all in the same big party.

"We can cut through the park by the museum," said Tony.

Sebastian said, "They will think of that."

"Oh, come off it," Tony growled. "I can't be important enough for them to guard the whole darn city park. They don't have a clue where I'll go next. I don't even know why they want me. *Goddammit to hell!*"

One of the women ahead of us turned her head to eye him with cold curiosity. He'd spoken in English, and the explosive curse was obvious.

The attention made us all shut up, chagrined. We didn't want to be alone and equally we didn't want anyone to notice us. The small group ahead of us weren't walking along the tram route, which meant this way was less public; without their company we'd be riskily exposed. So now, instead of discussing what we ought to do next or where to go, we paced along behind the German strangers without saying anything, letting them do the talking.

The Germans were heading more or less north, and before long we arrived at Inner Alster, the smaller of Hamburg's lakes made by the dammed Alster River. Out in the dark a pair of late sailboats moved quietly under the dim stars; for a moment my heart twisted with envy, thinking of the lucky people alone on the open water, enjoying the night without having to worry about being silenced by the secret police.

The road here was busy with trams again, traveling alongside the lake. Yellow light outlined the hatted heads of passengers sitting in the carriages. We had to decide whether to get away from this very public roadway, or to stay with our protective escort.

The Germans stopped to wait for a tram. For a breathless moment we stood there too, a little apart from the others.

Then Tony said under his breath, "Say, that's the Hotel Vier Jahreszeiten, the Four Seasons, just past the wharf. What if we went in there for a while? There's bound to be some overgrown ferns in the lobby we can hide behind. They're not going to watch every hotel in Germany, are they?"

"All right," Sebastian agreed. "And they may be looking for one man only—they may not yet realize that we are with you."

"You'd better go in on someone's arm, Northie," said Tony, without offering his. "You've already made it pretty clear which of us you prefer—"

"We were doing all that fake romantic petting to save your skin!" I exclaimed. "We didn't even kiss! None of that was real!"

"It wasn't real?" Sebastian repeated in surprise.

It was impossible to tell if he was serious or making a joke.

"Typical German, no sense of irony," Tony uttered kindly. He stepped aside. "Better not hurt his feelings, Northie."

I gasped in annoyance and let Sebastian link his arm through mine. He led me along the pavement and into the lobby of the grand building, and Tony followed us.

Wedding Cake and Scissors

We stood assessing the grandeur of the Four Seasons. There were chandeliers, an ornate staircase, and a roaring fire in an absolutely enormous fireplace, as if it were the great hall of a castle. Without realizing it, we'd all become at ease in expensive hotels. We watched elegantly dressed couples and threesomes, some old, some young, coming and going.

"We do not have a booking," Sebastian commented seriously, and again I could not tell if he was worrying or joking.

"Too bad," said Tony. "If no one's expecting us, that means the press won't be here. We'll be safe! Come on."

Following a family with three darling girls in matching pink satin, all wearing rosebud wreaths in their hair, Tony led me and Sebastian up the stairs to a mirrored ballroom overlooking the lake.

And there we were, in the middle of a wedding reception.

The guests had already finished eating and the tables were in disarray. There was a shining black grand piano in a corner, where a bored-looking pianist in white tie was playing perky Mozart sonatas like an automaton. The rosebud children grabbed one another's hands and began swinging around in circles, watching themselves in the mirrors.

"Tony! We can't stay here—" I hissed, but he ignored me and moved artlessly toward one of the mostly abandoned tables, where, absolutely without shame, he attached himself to another old woman.

He bowed and spoke to this elderly wedding guest in polite German. She smiled in surprise and pleasure, and gestured to the empty chair beside her. Tony flipped his coattails out of the way with a flourish and sat down.

I watched him in astonishment. He was always so blunt and straightforward, and I'd assumed that meant he'd be a poor liar. But he wasn't lying now, exactly; he was *pretending*. I hadn't realized what a capable actor he could be and how dangerously he enjoyed it.

Tony beckoned to me and Sebastian and pointed to the chairs next to his. He explained to me in his villainous French, "This is Frau Grunwald, grandmother of the—the marriage woman. We are the friends of the marriage man, he and me"—he waved toward Sebastian—"I am little brother—you French girl will marry him. Also Frau Grunwald says I need haircut."

I burst out laughing. *"C'est vrai, bien sûr!"*

The servers had not yet cleared our table of the remains of wedding cake, and when Tony scavenged plates for us,

Sebastian produced three small silver dessert forks from out of his sleeve. The old woman laughed in delight and exclaimed, "Bravo!" Within five minutes of sitting down, using the grandmother of the bride as a go-between, Tony spoke to a waiter and managed to acquire fresh coffee for everyone.

I sat between Tony and my pretend fiancé, Sebastian—who, for all his bravado, was so tense and stiff with anxiety I thought he might truly be sick. Tony chattered easily with Frau Grunwald, turning to me with a translation every now and then. Not once did he break into English.

"She asks, you like Hamburg city?"

"*C'est ma ville préférée,*" I said snidely. "*Cet hôtel est magnifique.*" I would have gone on to say that this was the most exciting evening of my life, but Tony was already busy relaying my answer in German.

Sebastian, ignored, began to nibble at his cake, and watching him made me suddenly realize I was starving. There was chocolate and fruit on the table as well. We helped ourselves like sneak thieves. I wondered if Sebastian was quietly and secretively filling his pockets with nuts, and found myself giggling nervously.

"Now there is dance," Tony translated from perfectly good German into diabolical French. "A band comes."

We had to leave Frau Grunwald before long. It didn't feel safe sitting in the same place for any length of time, and we didn't want to risk an encounter with the wedding couple. Someone who knew the "marriage man" was bound to come along eventually, perhaps even the bride or groom themselves, and ask us who we were and realize we were impostors.

We moved to an empty table and then, when the dancing

started, we shifted to chairs lined up in the open windows overlooking the Inner Alster lake. The lovely bride danced with her rosy bridesmaids, and the increasingly tipsy groom went from friend to friend, handing out cigars.

"We go now," Tony said in French, his voice low, before the groom reached us.

Sebastian held out his arm to me and we slipped from the crowded ballroom, hesitating at the top of the stairs to the lobby. I thought of Cinderella running away at midnight and finding herself on a lonely country road, shoeless, dressed in rags. Sounds of people enjoying themselves seemed to come from every part of the hotel; I felt like an angry ghost, longing to be part of ordinary human life and at the same time so filled with envy that I almost hated everyone I saw, including the dancing children.

Sebastian said in English, "I think the old woman is right, Tony. You need a haircut. It will disguise you."

"Northie, rustle us up a pair of shears," Tony drawled.

"Don't be ridiculous!"

"Ask at the front desk. Or the concierge. Say you want a nail scissors to trim your hem or whatever it is girls have on their dresses—say it's for one of the bridesmaids. They'll buy that, coming from a girl, and they'll give you something properly sharp."

"A razor would be better," put in Sebastian.

"They won't give a girl a razor without a lot of questions, and it's too risky for you or me to talk to anyone who's actually working here," said Tony. "Northie won't be able to come into the men's room with us. So you're going to have to be the barber, pal, and you're going to have to put those fast hands

266

of yours to work with a scissors, and she's going to have to get hold of some."

"I don't speak German!" I exclaimed.

"Oh. Blast it. Well—just ask in French. I bet they'll be able to find someone who speaks French. Don't let on you're British."

I didn't bother to retort that I wasn't British. I just went and got the damned scissors and sat by the fire in the lobby to wait nervously for them to get the job done. And it helped waste another half an hour.

When they emerged from the men's cloakroom after having done their impromptu barbering, my mouth dropped open in astonishment at the simplicity and completeness of the transformation.

"What's wrong?" Tony asked gruffly. "We worked very hard to keep it neat. It shouldn't have taken such a long time, but people kept coming in and we didn't want to attract attention."

"You really do look alike!" I said. "Or—not really *alike*—not like twins, exactly—you couldn't take each other's place at the guillotine. But you look as if you're related."

It was in their thick square brows, of course, but also in the clean lines of their jaws and the shape of their hairlines, and because they were so evenly matched in height and build. Their noses weren't the same, nor the color of their hair exactly, nor their eyes—neither in color nor in shape—and the more I looked, searching for similarities, the more different they seemed to me. But at first glance, or if you didn't know them, you'd take them for brothers. From behind or separately, you'd mix them up.

"It's weird, but it's like I'm seeing *two* changed people

267

instead of one," I tried to explain. "You match now, and it disguises you *both*. It's perfect. No one's looking for a pair of brothers! Listen, I've been thinking while I waited for you, and we might be able to sleep here—not overnight, I mean, but we could stay for an hour or so while there are still people coming and going, and we could take turns napping for twenty minutes each while the other two stand guard. This chair faces away from everything and it's so big that you don't really notice anyone is in it until you're close by."

Tony's mouth quirked a little, half a grin. He looked older and harder with his new military haircut. I suddenly wondered if he'd grown out his hair on purpose to try to hide the scar below his ear.

"You'd make a fine soldier, sister."

"Maybe I would," I flashed at him. "But we're here in the name of peace. You're sleeping first."

I thought, if we had to leave suddenly, he needed the break more than the rest of us.

So Tony dozed for twenty minutes in the big leather armchair by the blazing fire that warmed the Hotel Vier Jahreszeiten lobby. No one noticed. Sebastian stood silently with his back to the flames, watching the entryway and fiddling with coins and cigarettes; I perched on the wide arm of the chair and found myself studying Tony's sleeping face.

He was asleep, really sound asleep, from the moment he arranged himself in the chair and closed his eyes. I wasn't sure I'd be able to wind myself down so quickly, and I gazed at him, wondering how he did it.

Ugh, that livid scar along his throat. It was so much more apparent in stillness, without the subtle curtain of tawny hair brushing the top of his shirt collar to conceal it. I couldn't imagine how he'd survived whatever it was that made that scar. Yet it had taken me days and days to first notice it was there. Perhaps it had happened innocently, in a bicycle accident during one of his childhood summers in New York State. But perhaps it happened in hand-to-hand combat during the Battle of Jarama. I wondered if it was something he didn't need to think about, or something he didn't *want* to think about.

"Twenty minutes," said Sebastian, stepping to my side so suddenly it made me jump. "Do you want to wake him?"

To my horror I felt my face heating up—as if Sebastian had caught me in some shady act of intrusion.

"You do it," I said, and stood to get out of his way.

Tony and Sebastian both insisted that I nap next. I'd worried I wouldn't be able to; but I hadn't realized how absolutely shattered I was until I closed my eyes, just as I hadn't realized I was hungry until there was food in front of me. Twenty minutes—it felt like twenty seconds—and then Tony was lightly tapping me on the shoulder so Sebastian could take his turn.

Tony and I managed to perch side by side on the arm of the chair while Sebastian slept.

"This was a good idea of yours to come in here," I said to him.

"Yes, and a good idea of yours to get a bit of rest," he answered. "I think we need to leave soon—it's a lot less busy than it was, and we can't stay in this lobby all night. Maybe try your nightclub idea next."

It felt less attractive now than it had earlier in the evening. I wanted to go back to sleep.

"You've got goose bumps," Tony said.

"I've got bare arms." I tugged my long gloves higher. "Nobody ever takes that into consideration when they tell you to dress for dinner. Or notices, really."

"I noticed on the first night," Tony said. "When we were all having our picture taken in front of Salisbury Cathedral and they made you take off your gloves. We were standing right up against each other, and I could see—"

He stopped, and I looked at him. He went crimson as he realized what he sounded like—and also, we were close enough that he must know I couldn't miss the scar snaking down his throat. He gave his collar a little jerk, self-consciously pulling it higher. But he went on talking, dogged and defensive.

"Well, I *did* notice you were cold. Because it made me think. There is this fine downy hair along your forearm, but later, when you took off your gloves to eat and you were across the table from me, your skin seemed smooth again. And I thought: You don't see these little secrets about a person until you come close. I wouldn't have seen the hair on your arm if I hadn't been standing right next to you."

He wasn't flirting with me. He was very serious, trying to explain something.

He went on, "I thought—it isn't a flaw, like a bad haircut. It isn't something you have to learn to live with. It was there from the beginning, part of your whole self."

But of course, I *did* think about the dark hair on my arms, and tried to bleach it with peroxide, and was glad of the gloves that covered it up. Part of me was outraged that he'd noticed.

And part of me was secretly thrilled.

"Your haircut isn't bad," I said cautiously. "It's fine."

"I'm not really talking about the haircut." He folded his arms and looked away. "Never mind. I'm just embarrassing us both."

"Maybe when you learn to live with whatever it is, you'll stop thinking of it as a flaw," I said.

Silk Stockings

Hoping for safety in numbers, we left the hotel with a flurry of merry wedding guests.

"Do you really think they'll watch the park entrances?" Tony asked Sebastian in a low voice as we hurried away from the tramlines. "We've been gone for hours now, and it's a long way around to get to Saint Pauli if we don't cut through the park. I think the new fountains in there are illuminated at night, and there will be people coming to see it."

"All right," Sebastian agreed. "But let us not stop in one place."

My pretty shoes with their little heels and narrow straps were not designed for prolonged walking over cobbled streets. By the time we'd reached the public park built over the medieval city fortifications, I very much regretted the choices I'd made in the past five or six hours. It was no good gritting my teeth; if I didn't sit down and do something about the developing blisters, I wasn't going to be able to walk.

Gas lamps lit the park's larger drives beneath sprawling trees, but there were narrower, darker paths among the fountains and well-kept flower beds. The nearest bench wasn't particularly hidden; it stood in a pool of lamplight illuminating an ornamental brick archway.

"I've got to fix my shoes," I said grimly, sitting down. "Women's shoes are so silly, my God! Have either of you a handkerchief I can use to pad them? My heels are being worn to shreds. I'll be quick as I can. Or you can just go on without me."

Tony sat down next to me with a small grunt. He always seemed relieved to get off his feet. He didn't say anything, just leaned down and, quickly and efficiently, untied the laces of his left shoe. With another small grunt and a bit of effort, he crossed his left ankle over his right knee and pulled the shoe off. Then he rolled up the leg of his trousers and began to peel off his sock.

"You can have this," he said. "It's pretty clean, I wash 'em each night, and it's not like I've been flying in them. Purest silk—and I paid for them myself, because you can't really borrow socks, can you?"

"You'll get blisters too!" I protested.

"Not on this foot. This sock doesn't even smell."

As if to prove how clean it was, he stretched the sock between his hands and bit into the middle of it; then in one efficient yank, he ripped it in half where he'd nipped a small tear in the fabric.

Sebastian and I both stared at Tony's bare leg where his ankle still rested on his knee. His shin gleamed coldly in the lamplight.

273

Extending below his rolled-up trouser leg was a prosthesis of beaten aluminum, as sleekly machine-smooth as the airship's belly passing over in the twilight earlier. It was attached by a mechanical joint to a toeless foot of some dull, darker material, wood or rubber.

"I don't really need this sock," Tony said, as if that explained what we were looking at. He held out the two ripped tubes of black silk. "But it looks weird without matching socks, and these shoes don't fit very well unless you use a bit of padding. This is a pretty cheap shoe on a very expensive foot."

Sebastian let out an explosive snort of nervous laughter.

Tony slipped his shoe back on. I couldn't help watching. The artificial foot bent at the ankle just like flesh and bone.

"Get a move on, Northie," said Tony, with irritation in his voice. "We can't stay here."

I got to work unbuckling my own shoes.

"That is why you keep your shoes on when you are in your nightclothes in the passage?" Sebastian asked with frank curiosity. "So we do not see this artificial limb?"

"It is a Desoutter aluminum leg with an articulated bumper foot," Tony informed us loftily, tying his shoe. "I have had it for four months."

"Where did you get it?"

Tony glanced up at him with fury on his face.

"I mean *how*," Sebastian corrected in haste.

I guessed how. He'd been shot down, and then—*I couldn't go back*, he'd said. *I tried and they wouldn't take me. Didn't want me.*

I knew he didn't want to talk about it, and at the same time I thought he probably *did* want to talk about it. He liked showing off his combat experience without ever really admitting that it was *his*. And something nagged at me, something I thought I ought to be quicker about digging out—that thing he was really hiding, the thing that felt like it must be the connection between his straightforward loss of a limb in action and the strange, serpentine maze of intrigue that led Tony to be the target of a Nazi secret police hunt. I didn't believe it was just because of his father being a Communist. Tony had left Germany three years ago; they couldn't possibly be organizing an international assassination attempt to get rid of the teenage son of a dead Communist.

I slipped my feet into the soft silk pieces of his sock, wadding the cloth over the straps of my evening shoes and behind my heels. It wasn't classy, but it was a thousand times more comfortable. I stood up.

"Come on," I said, holding out an arm to each of them once again.

We set off through the shadowed park toward Saint Pauli and its clubs and beer halls, still pretending to be ordinary young people on a Saturday night.

———◆———

"This music is illegal," Sebastian told us in his serious way, as he paid for our drinks. He did it with conservative caution, placing payment firmly on the counter, taking care not to attract attention with spinning coins. "There is no law against a live band, but this music has been banned from the radio. This dance, the foxtrot, it is considered degenerate. I will be removed from the Luftwaffe for spending money in this place."

"Only if anyone finds out," I said reassuringly. "Isn't that why we're here—so no one finds us?"

"You're going to be removed from the Luftwaffe anyway, pal," Tony reminded him.

Sebastian shrugged, his face pale, his mouth set in a hard, thin line. I thought he must be in despair over his future, unable to think beyond the next five minutes.

This place went by the mixed-up English and German name of Neuer Hot Club, and it was loud and dark and crowded, featuring a live jazz band on a tiny stage above an even tinier dance floor. None of the three of us was drinking anything stronger than Coca-Cola, as we hoped against the odds that we'd be in the air the next morning. Of all places we might have ended up, this was perhaps not the safest, a stone cellar accessed by a single dark staircase, noisy with American swing music. But it was an even less likely refuge than the Hotel Vier Jahreszeiten, so perhaps we would be overlooked.

Sebastian found an unoccupied spot against a stone wall hung with silver cloth. The table he'd grabbed was still littered with the empty glasses and filled ashtrays left behind by some previous merrymaking group, as well as a pool of wax from a guttering and dripping candle in a round wine bottle. But there were three chairs, and we huddled close together in the tight space.

"You are correct about me being removed from the Luftwaffe," Sebastian considered morosely. "Major Rosengart has made that clear. He threatens me with a dishonorable discharge, but that is no longer my greatest fear. When he discovers how I have aided you, I too will be on the Gestapo's list of degenerates. Dear God—make me dumb—"

"What will you do?" I breathed.

"Finish—finish the race," he faltered, attempting to smile. "Should that not be the goal for us all? To finish. If I can fly out of Hamburg with the rest of you tomorrow..."

He let the sentence hang, and neither I nor Tony tried to complete it for him. I wondered if Sebastian might leave Germany and not come back—if he could possibly do such a thing. It hadn't dawned on me how enormous the consequences of helping Tony would be for Sebastian himself.

I remembered Lady Frith's hand on Sebastian's, sympathetic because none of his family had come to see him land in Germany. He'd taught himself magic tricks to annoy his father, stolen his father's cigarette set on purpose to nettle him. But turning your back on your family, I knew, wasn't nearly as terrifying as turning your back on an entire nation. If Sebastian left Germany he'd be utterly on his own.

"After the race is finished, I will think of other things," Sebastian said, frowning faintly. "For now I have a question—"

"I'll tell you," Tony interrupted. "That way you don't need to ask. I flew with the Ninth Hunter Group of the Spanish Republican Air Force in the defense of Madrid. So I'm not exactly the ideal representative for 'peace in Europe.' It's not a secret, but Lady Frith is trying darned hard to keep it quiet because she doesn't want it to get into the papers. Just like she works hard at keeping it quiet that Pim is Jewish."

He dug Sebastian's silver cigarette case from his pocket and laid it on the table along with Sebastian's passport.

"Thanks for these," Tony said. "It was pretty big of you to take that risk for me."

Sebastian took back the cigarette case, but not the passport.

277

"Keep it," he said. "I have a new one."

He opened the case and set it on the table next to the ash-tray. "Please," he said, waving a hand as an invitation.

Tony took a cigarette and, after a moment's hesitation, so did I. Finally Sebastian did too, and we all took turns lighting them in the candle flame, like some new form of Holy Communion.

Tony tucked away the passport and drew on his cigarette, nervously tapping the fingers of the other hand in syncopation with the music. From where we sat we could see the nearby door behind a curtain of smoke, and we perched on the edges of our seats, poised for flight, our heads close together so we didn't have to raise our voices.

"Listen, I'll tell you the whole story," Tony said.

New York State's Youngest Aviator

"I joined the air force after my mother was killed."

Tony's husky voice was steady as he began, though he'd narrowed his eyes as if he didn't trust us to believe him. It was too dim in the low light to see any emotion in their clear depth; all I could see was the reflection of the candle flame dancing on the surface of his irises.

"There wasn't really anything else for me to do. Madrid was home. I couldn't go back to Germany, and I couldn't bear the thought of turning up on my grandparents' doorstep in New York State with the news that Ma was dead—not when I knew I could be fighting with the International Brigades for Spain's freedom. This was last November. I was already a pretty good flier, and because my passport has a Russian name in it, some pencil pusher assigned me to an operational squadron full of Soviet pilots who were supporting the Republican forces."

"What did you fly?" Sebastian asked.

"Polikarpov I-16s," Tony said, eager to talk about them and a little peacockish about having flown them. "First-rate Soviet fighters, brand-new low-wing monoplanes, top speed about five hundred and twenty-five kilometers an hour. For two years they were the only fighters out there with an enclosed cockpit and retractable landing gear—all speed, no drag. They could outfly anything in the sky until your damn Messerschmitt 109s came along. We call 'em Moscas—Houseflies—"

"I heard that your enemies call them Rats," said Sebastian.

They looked at each other eye to eye, and Tony laughed.

"Yeah, I know what they call 'em."

Tony raised his cigarette to his lips, and the burning end glowed for a moment; then he picked up his story again. "I was totally out of my league at first. I was younger than everyone in my escuadrilla by at least five years, and my Russian was pretty rusty. But they treated me like a kid brother, teased me and babied me and dragged me along into the bars in Madrid as their translator, and for sure they didn't waste any time training me. I flew my first combat mission in early January."

"You were shot down?" Sebastian asked.

"I *went* down," Tony corrected. "More than once. The first time I was able to glide in to our field, and while they were fixing up that machine they gave me a new one and I was back in the air the next day. Those Moscas always needed fixing up after a few days in the air anyway. The second time—that was over the Jarama valley, when the Fascists crossed the river and we were defending Madrid. I got in a fight with a couple of Heinkel 51 pursuit planes—this was before I'd even seen a Messerschmitt 109. Those Heinkels weren't any kind of match for the Soviet fighters, but there were two of 'em, and I ran out of ammunition. So I did what all the Soviet pilots do when they're out of ammo—you know what a *taran* is?"

Sebastian and I shook our heads.

"It's the Russian word for aerial ramming. Just what Rosengart tried to do to me."

"And me," I added.

"Only mine was successful," Tony said, somehow managing to sound sulking and preening both at once. "I got above one of the Heinkels and smashed his tail, but I knocked off my own propeller when I rammed him, and I went down too. I lost a lot of height making the attack, and I was too fast and too low over a pretty rough hillside, waste ground above an old olive grove, and I ended up plowing straight into a pile of rocks."

It's the rough landings that get you in trouble, he'd said to me.

His words were tumbling over one another now, as if starting to tell the story had set off a mental avalanche.

"But I couldn't get out of my plane. The whole front end of it was smashed up, the frame pressed together like an accordion, and that's where my legs were. My right leg was all right—the impact kind of pushed my knee up into my face. In fact, I broke my nose against my knee. But my left leg got sort of tangled in the rudder pedal, jammed beneath it, and I couldn't get it out. It didn't hurt at first—shock, I guess—and I was so focused on my nose and on getting the cockpit open, and worrying that the fuel tank was going to catch fire and blow up with me sitting in the plane, that I didn't even wonder if anything was wrong with my leg. So I sat there for twenty minutes trying to breathe without panicking, and when it seemed like the plane probably wasn't going to explode, I realized I couldn't feel my foot, and I reached down and—"

He paused for a couple of seconds to draw on his cigarette again, and finished, "One of my shin bones was sticking out of my boot."

The contrast between what I was imagining, as I listened to him speak, and the place where we were sitting now was so stark that my throat ached. He'd probably thought then that he was about to die. And here he was, very much alive, comfortably smoking a cigarette and sipping at a Coca-Cola and listening to a jazz band playing "St. James Infirmary," and *still* he had to wonder if he was about to die.

It made me want to fight, to fight for him and anyone like him, no matter what the consequences. There couldn't be anything more important than saving your friend's life.

There it was, I realized suddenly: the three of us were friends.

I gave a bark of inappropriate laughter, and Tony and Sebastian both stared at me.

"Look at us!" I exclaimed. "Fascist and Communist and imperial bourgeoise in perfect harmony! What a shame Lady Frith isn't here to see us! Here we are—living proof that it's possible to create peace in Europe!"

Sebastian laughed too. Tony raised his glass.

"Peace in Europe!" he exclaimed, and we all drank as if we had just signed the Treaty of Versailles.

Tony dropped the butt of his cigarette in the ashtray and took a fresh one from Sebastian's open case, lying on the table.

He leaned into the candle again to light it. He was smoking faster than me and Sebastian.

"Continue," Sebastian said. "What happened? How did you survive?"

Tony narrowed his eyes again, pulling at his cigarette and watching the band so he didn't have to meet anyone's gaze.

"Well, nothing happened," he said at last. "I sat there; I was trapped and I couldn't move my leg. After a while it started to hurt. And I was cold now, and I knew it was going to be close to freezing when night fell. I began to worry that the pilot of the second Heinkel would report my position and I'd be picked up by the Fascists and then they'd—do whatever it is you do to enemy soldiers to get information out of them."

He added levelly, "I thought so much about what they'd do to me that finally I decided to shoot myself."

Oddly, the scowl was gone while he described all this. His expression was blank, distant, as if he were telling a story about something that had happened to someone else a very long time ago, not to himself earlier that year.

"But I dropped my gun beneath the seat trying to shift around to get it out of my holster," he went on. "I couldn't get to it to pick it up again. So then I just sat there, trying to breathe through my broken nose and trying not to imagine how I was going to die. The most vivid thing I remember about waiting there is how it smelled—this awful mixture of blood and aviation fuel. And when I sniffed hard to try to clear my nose, I'd get this sharp, clean whiff of wild thyme all around me. I tried to concentrate on that—just the smell of thyme on the hillside."

He drew in a long, deep breath, as if he were remembering the smell of thyme.

"Finally the pain in my leg got to be more important than all the other things I was sweating over, and I don't remember what happened after that. I woke up in a hospital bed five days later."

Tony lifted the cigarette to his lips again. He inhaled, and blew away the smoke, and said deliberately, "I was lucky. The enemy pilot didn't come back, or couldn't find me if he did. Another pilot in my escuadrilla saw my Mosca go down and sent out a couple of scouts to hunt for me. It was nearly two days before they got to the right spot, though, and my foot was pretty well past saving. They took it off to get me out of the plane."

He tapped his foot beneath the table.

"I'm still getting used to this new one," he finished. "The hospital where they took me at first was just a converted convent, and then I was transferred to the Red Cross hospital in Valencia—before it was bombed—and after that I was in a convalescent home for a couple of months, learning to walk again."

"You seem good at it!" I said without thinking, and flushed.

"Well, they saved my knee, which makes it a lot easier," he answered readily. "I had a wooden peg leg like a pirate for a while, but when my American grandfather eventually found out what had happened, he wired me the money for the real deal. It's a pretty good leg—the Desoutter—I don't have any trouble flying with it. But it gets heavy at the end of the day, and if I walk or stand for too long, the—what's left starts to get sore, or my other leg starts to ache from all the extra work. And I have all these rules I have to follow—I'm supposed to sleep flat on my stomach so my knee and hip don't freeze up, I'm not supposed to sit with my legs crossed or with my bad

284

leg elevated, I'm not supposed to sit for more than two hours at a time—that's why my old instructor recommended I fly the Hanriot 436 in the race, because of its short endurance. It means I have to stop and refuel every day we're racing, so I have an excuse to get out and walk around."

And you still manage to land ahead of everyone in your group, I thought, and my heart swelled at his dogged pride and determination.

He paused for a moment and then added defensively, "I can walk just fine, unless I'm tired."

"Did you know—" I hesitated, then plunged ahead. I wasn't trying to get sensational gossip out of him; there was a question that nagged at me. "Did you know that you were in the same hospital as the Rocketman? That German pilot who went berserk?"

The familiar scowl closed down his face and he looked away again. He, too, hesitated. At last he said, "Of course I know that."

There was another pause, and then Sebastian asked, "When was the Battle of Jarama?"

"Last February," Tony answered shortly.

"Aha! And so you and that 'Rocketman' must have been in the same hospital at the same time!" Sebastian exclaimed. "Were you there when he made his killings?"

Tony glanced over at Sebastian, pressing his lips together. He looked as if he were determined not to say another damn thing about it, and I was sure—suddenly *sure*—that yes, he remembered, and he knew a lot more than he was letting on.

If I couldn't get what I wanted out of Tony, perhaps I could get it out of Sebastian.

"Do *you* remember when it was?" I asked. "It might have been after Tony left."

"Not to be precise. But I remember the trial of the killer," Sebastian said. "He was called Hans Rolf. They did not forget his name here as they did outside Germany. He was found guilty of those murders, and he was executed. It was an important story. Perhaps not as important to you as the bombing of Guernica... I do not know what to think about that. Though I have not yet flown in combat, so..."

He reddened. It was his turn to look away.

"We do not hear the same news reports," he finished in embarrassment. "I did not hear what happened at Guernica and I cannot believe—"

"Can't you, really?" Tony drawled. "How can I explain it for you? I didn't see Guernica; I never flew in combat against a Messerschmitt 109. But I saw plenty of the Condor Legion's other work, and—"

"*Stop it*," I hissed sharply. "People are looking."

Tony suddenly leaped to his feet. "Let 'em look." He stubbed out his cigarette, then grabbed my hand and gave my arm a gentle tug.

"What—?"

"C'mon, dance this degenerate foxtrot with me, Northie," Tony said. "Here you are, out on the tiles, alone with two young men you only just met last week, in a shady nightclub playing illegal music in a foreign country! Come on!" He pulled at my hand persuasively. "I'll bet you know how to foxtrot—the Brits are very upright, but you haven't banned jazz, have you? I'll bet you're going to be a debutante—you'll have to go to those parties and be introduced to the King of England. He's

286

probably your third cousin twice removed anyway, or something like that. Only you're *not really* very British—"

"Do *shut up*," I warned him, but I let him drag me onto the miniature dance floor in my evening shoes and makeshift silk socks.

And he turned out to be a very respectable dancer. I wondered if he'd learned to dance during those nights in the bars of Madrid between air battles. Or perhaps his American grandmother made sure he was properly schooled—maybe he'd made friends in New York State and went to summer dances there, back when he was an ordinary young person too. The "articulated bumper foot" didn't seem to bother him, though you couldn't call him light-footed. His dancing was very purposeful. But he had a good sense of rhythm and moved with easy grace.

"Doesn't it hurt?" I asked.

"I've been sitting for a while. I'm fine. I just wanted to get away from that Fascist Kraut for a moment."

"Tony, he's helping us. You, I mean."

Slow, slow, quick, quick—the band was playing "Three O'Clock in the Morning," fast, light, and melancholy, and it made me a little breathless trying to talk and dance at the same time.

It didn't stop Tony, however.

"He might be," Tony said, and leaned in a little closer, so that his lips brushed my ear, as if he were nuzzling my hair—just what Sebastian and I had been doing on the steps by the war memorial.

It didn't feel as fake, though.

"Listen," Tony whispered quickly, his breath hot against

287

my ear. "He's being nice, and maybe he's losing faith in his great nation, but it's as much as my life is worth to answer your Rocketman questions in front of him. Yes, I was there." His right hand on my shoulder steered me deftly away from another couple who'd swung too close. "Hans Rolf is the pilot whose plane I rammed."

34

Santa Agnès de Marañosa

"The folks who picked me up found him first," Tony murmured in my ear. "He didn't have to wait like I did, and he wasn't in pieces like I was. But he'd been knocked cold. He kept sliding in and out of consciousness, and he *talked*. When he realized how much, he went on his rampage; he was worried we'd heard something."

"And did you?" I breathed.

"Me? No. That's the joke of it—I was put on his ward a couple of days after he got there, and I was doped up on morphine the whole time, away on my own pink cloud. I didn't have a clue what was going on. I heard the other guys on the ward teasing him, I guess—they didn't really call him Rocketman, that was the English tabloids. They called him Rockets, Los Cohetes, and I just thought they were talking about some made-up story in the funny papers. So whatever he spilled,

I don't know what it was. Names, formulas, codes, secret air bases and factories—whatever it was, I didn't hear any of it."

"That's why he didn't kill you, too?"

"Are you kidding, sister? He cut my throat along with everybody else."

The band splashed into a new tune, and there was a smattering of applause and a change of dancers around us on the lamplit floor. Tony started talking faster, as though he expected Sebastian to cut in on the dance. He spoke quickly and breathlessly, in words that didn't even make whole sentences, as if he were reading from a telegram.

"Thirteen people. Slaughtered like—like cattle. Or hogs. Mostly in their sleep. Cold, efficient, hid a broken glass—made a blade. One shard. Thirteen bled dry, then me. I was last—"

Tony had fought him. Hans Rolf's bloodbath hadn't been entirely silent. The nurse on duty had been the first to die, and her brief cry had woken the second victim, and eventually the shuffling and gasping as the others died had woken Tony. He'd lain wondering what was going on. Then a doctor came in, wondering the same thing, and Tony heard and dimly saw the doctor being butchered, and finally understood.

He yelled a warning. The captured pilot leaped for him and, with purposeful accuracy, tried to tear open his throat.

No one heard Tony's sobbed cry for help; the nighttime staff were already dead. So Tony fought on his own, dogged and choking on blood, taking a hail of blows in his forearm at first and then, for a time, everywhere. The cutting became more desperate and less accurate as they fought. Tony was stabbed in the abdomen eleven times. As he lost consciousness, he was sure he'd never wake up.

The deadly airman vanished out into the night. A horror-stricken young nun, routinely collecting waste the next day, found Tony crumpled facedown in a pool of blood on the floor next to his bed, senseless among the bodies of thirteen slaughtered men and women, the glass blade still sticking out high in his shoulder close to the back of his neck. It had slipped out of the murderer's grip as he made one last attempt at a killing blow in the dark and missed. He made his getaway without trying to get the shard out, assuming Tony was dead too.

Most of the stab wounds Tony suffered weren't very deep. They'd been made with an improvised weapon in a desperate fight in semidarkness. But it was pretty clear that the man who'd done it didn't want to leave any witnesses. He'd set out to silence everyone who might have heard him giving out the German Reich's military secrets, and as far as he knew, he'd succeeded.

"So they hid me," Tony finished. "In case he came back, or in case someone else came back to finish up for him. They counted me in the number of deaths they reported. They even changed my name—that's when I became Antoine Robert. I'm a French pilot now. Anton Roborovski didn't have any connection with France, and it seemed safe. My old instructor Rosario Carreras knew Marcel Bazille from when she'd worked at the French flight school where she set me up for the summer, and she took me there when I was able to walk again."

"I have been racking my brain to work out why the German secret police are after you, and I believe you know perfectly well why!" I told him accusingly.

Tony shook his head. "No—I don't get it. The Rocketman Affair is over. I followed it in the German newspapers, like

Sebastian said, believe me. They chased that guy down and they convicted him and they executed him."

"But wasn't he a hero? I mean, to the Nazis? From their point of view, he'd been shot down in combat and covered his tracks when he thought he'd given away state secrets! And nobody outside Germany was watching anymore by the time they put him on trial, so they didn't need to prove anything by executing him, did they? They didn't need to make an example of him!"

"Oh yes they did," said Tony. "They needed to make sure he didn't end up running off at the mouth in front of a dozen International Brigade soldiers again, and they needed to make sure nobody else ever does it again, either. And they did it to punish him. If you know the location of experimental rocket launch sites, you have no business getting yourself carried off the battlefield with a concussion and into a Spanish Republican field hospital. He'd done his flying in the Great War—he never should have joined the Condor Legion nearly twenty years later. He was just like Florian Rosengart! What did they used to call Rosengart, the Blue Topaz? Rosengart still thinks of himself that way, you can tell. This guy was the same, leaving his grown-up job in aeronautics because he thought he was going to have a chance to relive the glory of his youth."

"No wonder they wouldn't let you rejoin your flight squadron!" I scolded. "It hadn't anything to do with your leg. You'd have just been Condor Legion bait—like an albatross around their neck—oh!" I gave a wild little laugh. "An albatross ace—like Rosengart flies!"

The music changed again.

This time it changed quite suddenly.

292

We'd been dancing to another American jazz tune, a fizzy riff on "Hot Toddy." Almost right in the middle of a saxophone trill, we found ourselves trying to foxtrot to a traditional Austrian polka. It was, if anything, even bouncier than the piece it replaced. My feet got tangled trying to keep up with Tony, and I trod on his shoes.

"Oh gosh, I'm sorry!"

He laughed. "It doesn't actually hurt when you step on my toes."

I went beet red with embarrassment; I could feel myself blushing, as fiercely hot as if I'd spent the day acquiring a sunburn.

He smiled down at me. It was the first natural smile I'd ever seen him crack.

"It's all right, sister."

And of course that was when Sebastian did cut in—or at least I thought he was cutting in—at exactly that moment, catching me by the wrist and shoulder.

"There are policemen here," he said. "Or on their way. It is why the music changed. They send inspectors to check if the band is too hot. When they suddenly change to good German music like this, it means the director has been warned. We should leave. They might not be music inspectors."

"*Music inspectors!*" Tony sneered. "What a government."

"Yes, we know you do not like it. *Come now.*"

We didn't have coats to pick up. We slipped through the crowd unnoticed and clattered up the dark stairway, and then we were outside in the cool air of long past midnight, whatever time it was. Tony started whistling "Three O'Clock in the Morning"; I thought he probably didn't know he was doing it.

"You will get us arrested," Sebastian scolded.

Tony abruptly fell silent. He glanced at me in the dark. There hadn't been a singer with the band; it was an old song and I couldn't remember the words. But I thought it was about a couple who danced all night and didn't want to stop.

It had been lovely dancing with him—treading on his toes and making him laugh and smile.

He was still watching me, his head just turned slightly in my direction, his lips parted as if he were holding in something that he thought better of speaking aloud. He wasn't being coy and he wasn't flirting.

I think he was just wondering if I knew the song.

———◇———

We set off aimlessly through the dark streets, looking for another place to lurk for a bit. But Tony was flagging.

I could see it, and I thought Sebastian could too. Tony's limp had become more pronounced, and he'd stopped working to try to hide it. Every now and then he simply paused, holding on to a lamppost or a railing for a moment, and caught his breath before he set off again.

We tried to go into a place that beckoned with blinking lights and a group of young people about our own age standing about the doorway, smoking and teasing one another. I couldn't hear any music, but there was a lot of noise coming from inside, and it seemed crowded and safe. Only about a second after Sebastian started to lead us through the door, he turned around so abruptly he crashed into me.

"Go—go—" he urged quietly, shooing me backward.

Neither I nor Tony questioned him; we turned around

also. Sebastian grabbed my arm and, rather than walking away, pulled me to the edge of the small crowd by the entrance.

"Wait for a moment," he said. "Here—"

He opened his cigarette case and held it out to me in an effort to make us seem as casual as everybody else.

"What is it?" Tony asked, reaching across me to help himself.

Sebastian took one too, but it slipped from his fingers as he gave it the automatic twirl. I could see his hand shaking as he bent to pick it up.

We were all tired.

"The man I saw at the Stadthöfe is inside," Sebastian said. "He is watching the door. If he saw me, he will come out—"

"You beat a pretty fast retreat!" Tony accused. "Of course he'll come after you!"

"No, I do not think he noticed me; I was careful to enter behind another. And also, remember? He is looking for *you*, and your hair is different now. Stella, you might wind your scarf into a turban so you look different too."

It was a good idea. I swept up my hair so that it was completely hidden in the silk, tied the stole into a big knot on top of my head, and tucked the ends under, trying not to seem as if I was doing it nervously. I was freezing. Sebastian pulled off his tie and unbuttoned the collar of his shirt. Tony gripped his cigarette in the corner of his mouth and undid his own tie.

"Oh. I am sorry," Sebastian hissed. "I am out of matches."

We waited in our flimsy disguises, nervously holding unlit cigarettes, ready to run. I thought that if it came to an open chase, Tony probably didn't have any chance of getting away. And if the man from the Stadthöfe had a gun as well...

Minutes passed and nothing happened.

"He may be waiting for us to move," Tony murmured.

"We should stay here until that car by the corner leaves," said Sebastian. "I think that man is reporting to them."

Suddenly there was an explosive scuffle at the door of the club, and four men came stumbling out over the doorstep. The young people hanging about the entrance all jumped back, scrambling out of the way, and we crowded closer to them.

The short, mustachioed man from the Stadthöfe was gripping a youth in evening dress by the back of his collar. The boy looked a lot like Tony.

There was no mistaking how similar the captive was to both Tony and Sebastian in height and coloring, a little taller than his brawny captor.

With the help of the doormen from the nightclub, the Stadthöfe man frog-marched his victim into the street. The luckless boy fought and protested wildly in German, his head down so that we couldn't see his face; the Stadthöfe man punched him viciously in the stomach to stop his struggling, and he collapsed breathless to his knees.

Herr Stadthöfe then barked an order and, kneeling beside the gasping boy, held a gun to his head while the doormen quickly went through his pockets.

My mind instantly drove this scene to its most horrific possible conclusion—blood all over the cobbles, Tony throwing himself at the murderers in fury; the inevitable flash of fire and more blood as he fell—

But nobody moved. I held my breath. The other young people watched, some in horror and some with interest, and nobody uttered a word of protest or lifted a finger to help.

Sebastian and Tony and I, frozen and quivering, tried hard *not* to watch. I stared down at the ridiculous cigarettes that we weren't able to light, terrified that in a moment they'd be knocked from our hands as our hunters noticed us.

Finally the Gestapo brute took hold of the boy's hair and yanked his head up. He examined his bewildered victim's face for a minute or so; asked him a couple of brief questions that we couldn't hear; and finally, *finally*, he let go. The boy knelt still, breathing hard, too scared or sensible to fight back anymore. The man looked over the debris they'd taken from the boy's pockets, confiscated his cash and cigarettes, and showered the rest of his possessions—handkerchief, tram tickets, a key, a pair of gloves—onto the cobblestones around him.

Then the Gestapo agent stood up and strode to the waiting car. He leaned in to have a quick word with whoever was inside, before setting out on foot down the street. The car drove off.

"Let's go back the way we came for a few blocks," Tony said quietly.

For a few moments we watched the stunned stranger picking up his scattered belongings. I felt a terrible compulsion to apologize to him, to explain the mistake—even just to replace his cigarettes.

But of course I didn't dare. He could have betrayed us.

What we did after that and where we went became a blur of darkness and anxiety and exhaustion and blistered heels. There *wasn't* any place to go. Considerably past three o'clock in the morning, we began to move reluctantly in the general direction of our hotel so we could join the Circuit of Nations racers for the early trip to the airport. But the hotel was a good distance away by now, and surely there would be guards waiting for us there, as well.

The old moon had risen in a perfect crescent, shining between rooftops. Tony and I limped along dark streets, Sebastian painfully trying to slow his own pace to wait for us.

"Shh!" I stopped suddenly. "Listen!"

There was no mistaking the sound of footsteps—the distinct, clear tap of a man's dress shoes hurrying over cobblestones, echoing down the empty street. We couldn't at first tell which direction the noise was coming from.

"Don't run," Tony whispered. "If we go the wrong way, we could bump straight into him. Quiet—there's an alley here."

We hugged the wall of the nearest building, and as we veered around the street corner, I turned my head to look back the way we'd come.

Halfway down the street behind us, a man stepped out of the dark and into a pool of lamplight. I recognized the catlike white bib and black coat of an evening suit, the white shirt-front pale in the shadows, just the way I'd seen Tony by the bridge.

The figure seemed to be looking straight at me, though I couldn't see his shadowed face.

"I think he's seen us," I hissed.

Sebastian, too, glanced over his shoulder, but we had already turned the corner, and the figure behind us was hidden.

No one asked if I was sure. We all kept walking, quickening our pace.

"We might go around the block here and double back on ourselves," Tony said breathlessly. "Or—wait, I know—the

Fischmarkt! We can go through the Sunday morning fish market! It begins at five and they'll already be setting up the stalls!"

"We'll be awfully conspicuous," I said. "Fishmongers don't wear white tie to market!"

"No, but there'll be a lot of people, a crowd, places to duck and hide if we need to. It'll be easy to get lost."

Tony was already leading the way, striding along with purpose in the dark, trying to put some impossible distance between us and the unknown prowler.

"It's not far at all, much closer than the hotel, and it'll be a lot safer than these empty streets. It doesn't matter if we're late getting to the hotel. Frith'll wait for us, you know she will."

There was a note of such childlike and desperate hope in his voice that I found myself unable to object, just because I didn't want to disappoint him.

We zigzagged through increasingly narrow cobbled lanes between tall buildings, and suddenly came out onto an enormous open plaza in front of a domed market hall on the Elbe River waterfront.

"Come on—"

Tony urged us into a maze of vendors' booths and cafés beneath canvas awnings. Market stallkeepers were unpacking vans and wagons of silver-scaled fish, spilling ice and sawdust. There was artificial light everywhere, old and new—acetylene gas and electric sodium and flaming torches—and shadows, too, wells of black between stacked crates and beneath stall tables and oilcloth. Tony was right: we'd be able to hide here.

But we kept having to wait for him. He'd stop by a mountain

of potatoes or cabbages, wincing as he steadied himself for a moment against a keg or barrel. I rubbed my arms, shivering, searching nervously for automobile merchants among the piles of boots and roses and puppets and umbrellas.

Sebastian suggested anxiously, "Perhaps we can find a taxi."

"You don't suppose they'll think of that?" Tony muttered.

"Then we must *keep moving!*"

But in the shadows behind a high-sided old apple wagon hitched to gigantic farm horses, Tony sat down on an upended empty wooden box.

"Oh, please don't stop," I begged him.

I reached out to shake him by the shoulder and remembered just in time not to spook him.

"I'm sorry," he panted. "Just give me a couple of seconds here."

Standing still made me cold again. I unwound the silk stole from my hair and pulled it over my shoulders. Sebastian stood poised on the balls of his feet like a dancer about to leap, glancing nervously up and down the rows of market stalls.

"*This isn't fair.*" The words came tumbling out of me in fury.

"It reminds me of my crash," Tony said. "The waiting, I mean. Not really knowing what's going to happen next. Kind of wishing they'd get it over with."

"*Don't you dare,*" I told him. I reached for his hands to help him up. I wasn't going to give up without a fight, not now. "That's all right when you're alone. But this time you've got me and Sebastian with you. We'll carry you if we have to!"

He gave a small snort that might have been the ghost of a laugh, and squeezed my hands. "You mean you'll drag me. I get it. All right, just give me a minute more and then I'll drag myself."

I squeezed back. "I'm counting to sixty—*Oh!*"

Every molecule of blood in my body seemed to turn to ice as a different hand, large and bony and full of strength, closed over my bare arm between the top of my glove and the silk stole.

The other man had come at me from behind. There was no escaping him now.

I froze, expecting that next I'd feel a pistol beneath my ribs—or worse, God help me, a blade. Unaccountably, I imagined broken glass.

Tony looked past me, his eyes widening with shock.

My captor spoke in French.

"I think our young chevalier can walk no farther tonight."

In horror, I dropped Tony's hands and turned my head to look behind me. I saw a regal Black man with hair glinting faintly silver in the dark, framing a deceptively youthful face.

It was Capitaine Marcel Bazille.

35

Slow, Slow, Quick, Quick

"I have an automobile," said Capitaine Bazille. "You will all come with me and there will be an end to this night."

Sebastian took a step toward me and stopped, his eyes as wide and shocked as Tony's. I shook my head, so strangled by fear and confusion that I couldn't speak.

"Who sent you?" Tony choked. He didn't attempt to get to his feet. "Rosengart or Frith?"

Bazille gazed down at him. He let go of my arm and tugged my stole over the uncovered inch of bare skin above my gloves.

"I am your chaperone, M'sieur Robert," Capitaine Bazille answered coolly. "I am supposed to watch over you at all times, partly because you are under suspicion of sabotage and possibly murder, but mostly for your own protection. A fine chase you've led me this night! But I'm glad you're together, and you may now all three come with me—"

He held wide an arm to usher us away from our hiding place.

I thought about running. But Tony hadn't even stood up yet, and there wasn't any point in running on my own.

Also, Bazille seemed to be alone.

"There are a bunch of Nazi gangsters hunting me and they have an automobile too," Tony shot at him. "Maybe it's yours. Or maybe it's Major Rosengart's?"

"I do not know where Major Rosengart is," said Bazille. "And I do not care. You ask who sent me? It was your friends."

Bazille held out a hand to help Tony to his feet, but Tony didn't move.

"The Dutchman, Willem van Leer, and the Swede, Torsten Stromberg," the French chaperone elaborated. "They saw you leave the Rathaus together. Monsieur Stromberg detests being watched at every turn, and he observed how you three evade your guardians." Bazille glanced around, checking that we were still on our own. "But Monsieur van Leer is also guarded, for different reasons, and doesn't trust those who watch over him. He remembers that Mademoiselle North warned him to check his machine for sabotage, and when he saw a stranger following you out of the Rathaus, he told me."

Bazille was still offering his hand to Tony, calmly and without moving, like someone trying to coax a feral cat to come closer.

"Of course as a chaperone I'm here for all the racers. In your case, Antoine Robert, my friend Capitana Carreras asked me personally to keep you from harm. And finally—well, finally, I am a Frenchman and I don't trust the Germans. I can see that Florian Rosengart burns with some hidden torment, and I think he's as likely to sabotage this race as anyone else. I know, too, that if he is doing it for political reasons, he has state authority to support him. And so I asked Lady Frith to telephone another friend, and she was able to borrow a car, and now I've found you."

I gasped, "But if you found us so easily—"

"Easily!" His unlined face looked merry and young for a split second, then his grim expression closed down again and he seemed decades older. "It was not easy. I, too, must avoid the Gestapo; they'd cut my throat in a dark lane without remorse, simply because they disdain the color of my skin. Indeed I have not followed you throughout this night, but them, and I can assure you they are still following. There are five men now and at least one car; there may be more. Thank God I saw you myself as you came into the Fischmarkt! Now *trust me*, and I will get you safely out of Germany if it's possible—"

Tony ignored Bazille's hand and stood up on his own, grimacing with pain as he put weight on his left leg. That absolutely awful expression flashed across his face, the one I had seen fleetingly before.

Sebastian leaped to his side and took Tony's arm over his shoulder. "Come, lean on me, imagine you are a drunkard and I am helping you home."

Tony rolled his eyes and snorted. He gave a little hop, hanging on to Sebastian, and nodded. "I'm okay. Let's go."

"Are you able to fly?" Bazille asked him.

"If they let me take off," Tony growled.

Bazille herded us like a schoolmaster, quickly and quietly. We dodged between the market stalls to an unassuming private car, newish but splattered with mud, lined up along the wharf with other cars and vans and delivery wagons.

"Get in the back, all of you, and keep your heads down," Bazille warned.

Sebastian and Tony and I climbed in obediently.

I was in the middle, with Tony folded over my lap and me folded over his back, and Sebastian slumped against me. I could actually feel the tension leaving Sebastian's body as Bazille straightened the front seat and shut the door behind us; Sebastian's breathing lengthened and grew even, and he was asleep almost before Bazille started the engine.

But Tony and I were still wide awake as the car began to creep slowly along the wharf. Tony's cheek rested against my leg, his breath warm against my knee through the silk of my frock. I could feel the rise and fall of his back beneath my own cheek and the palms of my hands.

Suddenly I heard him murmur, "It's funny what you said earlier, about me not being alone this time."

Tony's voice was muffled by my body and the noise of the engine. But his tone was ordinary, conversational, almost as if he'd grown too tired to be angry or afraid anymore.

"I didn't feel alone sitting in my plane after the crash. I knew someone would be looking for me. It was later, in the hospital, after I'd been stabbed with a broken glass a hundred times, when I was just lying there waiting to get better—and it seemed so pointless. What was I waiting for? Who was I waiting for? Dad was gone. Ma was gone. There wasn't anyone nearer than four thousand miles away who'd cry if I just died

305

there. And I couldn't move—I was *stuck* there, with my leg missing, and tubes in my arm, and more stitches than Frankenstein's monster, being alone."

For a moment I rested in quiet astonishment with my face pressed against his back, feeling him breathe.

Then I murmured in reply, "*I know!* Oh, Tony—I know. It was like that when my parents were taken away when I was three. I woke up all by myself, and all day I wandered about our one room in the cellar getting hungrier and hungrier. I couldn't get out or do anything, and no one came. I remember how frightened I was, and how it grew worse as time dragged on. Pushing a chair up to the washstand so I could reach the basin to drink, the water getting lower and more stale day after day—and how unthinkably *dreadful* it was when it got dark. I don't remember my parents. But I remember what it felt like when suddenly, like black magic, they were gone. I remember being *alone*."

We felt each other draw in a shaking breath at exactly the same time, remembering.

Then Tony said, "I wasn't really, though. Rosario came to see me when she found out, and she cried."

"I wasn't really either. My aunt and uncle found me and took me away with them to England."

He whispered roughly, "Rosengart would have got me by now if you weren't one of the racers. I'd be dead if you weren't here."

"Probably," I agreed, amazed to think that it was most likely true. "But I am here."

I knew we still had to get through Hamburg Airport, and into the air and beyond, without being caught or killed. But at rest and suddenly comfortable, in the warmth of one another's bodies packed close together, Tony and I were both soon as deeply asleep as Sebastian was already.

———◇———

I woke to the quiet sound of the driver's door opening. The engine had stopped. Sebastian sat up suddenly, and so did I; Tony slept on in my lap.

My heart lurched in horror, anticipating betrayal.

It didn't look like we had reached the airport. We were parked in a quiet suburban neighborhood, overhung with trees, next to a thickly hedged front garden. There was no street lighting, but there was a lessening of the darkness as dawn crept a little closer.

Capitaine Bazille came around the car and opened the door on the passenger side. He folded the front seat forward so we could get out. Then he went to the back of the car, quietly opened the boot, and returned with his arms full of flight suits.

"Quickly. Sebastian and Tony, you may put these on over what you are wearing if you remove your jackets. Miss North, that is not so simple for you, so I have here a blouse and your trousers and these—"

To my astonished eternal gratitude, he handed me a pair of socks and my oxfords.

"Do you have your passport?" he asked me, keeping his voice low.

"Yes." I'd been carrying it in my beaded evening bag all night, along with a lipstick and some useless French and English coins.

"And you, Leutnant Rainer?"

307

Sebastian nodded.

I glanced at the senseless Tony. He had Sebastian's old passport on him, I knew. I'd no doubt he was carrying his own as well.

"We all do," I said.

"Good. Your other things are being brought with the rest of the luggage, but I have your flight bags in the back. You will have to plan your route before takeoff. Wake your friend. Come now, my eaglets, dress quickly. We must not linger here."

There was a telephone kiosk at the end of the street. While we put on sensible clothes, using the open door of the car for a screen, Capitaine Bazille rang the hotel to let Lady Frith know her missing pilots were safe and on our way to the aerodrome.

———◇———

None of us were able to go back to sleep. It was just getting light as we pulled up in front of the streamlined new passenger terminal.

"*Mon dieu*, look at these scavengers," swore Capitaine Bazille with unguarded contempt.

Within seconds of stopping, we were surrounded by reporters. They descended on the car like seagulls at an untended platter of fish and chips. Local newspapers, national newspapers, a radio station, and—*heaven help us*, I thought—a newsreel cameraman from the Nazi state-approved film company. Everyone who'd been cheated out of the chance to celebrate Germany's young Luftwaffe hero the day before was there now.

Capitaine Bazille tried to inch the car forward, and had to stop so he didn't hit anyone.

"Get down," Tony said to Sebastian, reaching across me

to push at the back of Sebastian's head. "Don't let them see your face."

Tony leaned between the seats and said to Capitaine Bazille, "Let me out. I can handle this."

Bazille looked over his shoulder at Tony, frowning in astonishment.

Tony was again wearing Sebastian's shining black leather Luftwaffe flight jacket. I hadn't noticed him pulling it on in the half-light. He flashed open Sebastian's old passport at Capitaine Bazille, like a reporter showing his press pass.

"*What game do you think you're playing?*" Capitaine Bazille scolded. "Do you want to give them a *reason* to arrest you?"

"I don't think I'll need a passport anyway," Tony said, grinning like a fox and running one hand over the honey-gold stubble of his hair where Sebastian had cropped it close to his head last night. "I don't think they're as fussy about checking papers on the way out as on the way in, and if I can sucker this crowd, I bet no one will even bother to ask. I'll just float through the building with my adoring fans and see you at the parked aircraft. Okay with you, Rainer? *Your* adoring fans, I mean."

"I cannot allow—" began the French chaperone, but Tony interrupted him.

"Just let me out and see what happens," he bargained. "If they don't seem to buy it, you can leap in with guns blazing. So to speak."

Sebastian, with his head down and talking into his knees, said, "Let him go. The sooner it is over, the easier it will be."

Bazille got out. He came around to the curb, opened the passenger side door, and folded down the front seat. Tony climbed out, teeth glinting in a terrifyingly false smile. He threw up his arm at the press in a Nazi salute.

"Herr Rainer! Leutnant Rainer!"

A torrent of excited greetings and questions erupted, mostly in German. Tony nodded and grinned, responding with swift assurance. The cameras whirred and clicked. There was a woman in the crowd, taking notes for one of the interviewers, and Tony attached himself to her like a terrier on a rat. He pointed to her notepad, saying something close to her ear, and she looked up at him and blushed.

I leaned out the door and said blandly to Capitaine Bazille in English, "Don't you have to leave this car with a valet so its owner can collect it? Then we can meet the bus when the other racers get here."

*　◇　*

A huge audience filled the balconies of the new terminal at Hamburg Airport and crowded out over the grass, though slender velvet ropes and uniformed ushers kept everyone away from us and our planes. The airport officials had set out several long tables covered with dazzling acres of white linen and little red Nazi flags flying at the corners. There was another mouth-watering buffet breakfast waiting there, and also a gleaming row of wooden desks arrayed with inkwells and rulers and paperweights. They were expecting us to put on a busy show of flight planning.

Nobody looked at anyone's identity papers.

The other racers gave me and Sebastian curious and sympathetic glances. Tony rejoined us looking smug instead of

310

scowling, his green eyes blazing with mischief. He seemed far more awake than he had any business being.

Lady Frith hooked me by the elbow to lead me to the buffet. She hissed in my ear, "*Stella North*. You will have to give your interview to the reporter from the *Daily Comet* before you take off, but you are to say *nothing* about whatever it is you were doing last night. *Not one word*. I don't want to know, either. As far as I am concerned, you have been in your room in the Hotel Reichshof, alone, since the reception at the Rathaus finished, and I will swear to it. I refuse to let any more scandal touch this project—I simply won't allow it."

My heart rose into my throat every time I looked over at Sebastian. Major Florian Rosengart was shadowing him again—calm, courteous, aloof.

At least I didn't have to talk to Rosengart myself, and Bazille wasn't letting him anywhere near Tony.

But when the photographers gathered us up for another picture of all the contestants together, Tony and Sebastian managed to jam themselves on either side of me.

"You're home safe." Tony spoke across me to Sebastian. "I didn't even try to pretend I was you—they all just assumed it because of the jacket and me answering them in German! They figured it out when we got on the airfield and I started showing off my plane to them. My own plane, the French Hanriot. Jehoshaphat, I never thought I'd laugh so hard at a bunch of Fascist propaganda dealers—it's the best gag I've ever pulled in my life, and the cherry on top is that they'll all be too embarrassed to admit their mistake."

"But *you* are not—what did you say?—'home safe,'"

Sebastian warned. "It will be a simple thing now for them to bring in a marksman, if they truly want you dead. Stay close to me. Rosengart cannot touch you himself while he is in view of all the world, and no one will shoot at you if they think they will hit me by mistake."

Tony and Sebastian pulled chairs close together and sat down with a pile of French rolls and toast between them, Sebastian twirling spoons and pointing out which spreads and jams were local. They laid out their flight plans practically in each other's laps, leaning over to grab at each other's pencils, and compared their French and German compasses and maps like schoolboys sharing the same desk. Capitaine Bazille stood squarely behind them, occasionally bending to question their wind speed calculations. Rosengart stood a few paces away, smoking his pipe and offering curt responses to the press.

One of the reporters, from the other side of the barrier, started peppering Tony with questions about his haircut—at least I think that was what was going on—and suddenly both he and Sebastian were dragged away from their flight planning by a pair of ushers to have their photographs taken together.

Tony, previously the most sullen of us about posing for the press, hammed it up for the German cameras. He and Sebastian made a very public show of peeling off their flight jackets and trading them back in a comradely way.

I could just imagine the headlines. *Harmony Between France and Germany!*

It was going to cause the most outrageous of scandals if anyone tried to assassinate Tony now that he'd got the public's attention as a shining example of peace in Europe.

As he and Sebastian came back to the line of desks, Tony

312

threw a challenge at Lady Frith, announcing forcefully, *"I want to fly with a different chaperone."*

She looked up from a sea of paper; she was checking Sebastian's map and comparing it to her own. "You know it can't be done," she answered. "Capitano Ranza's machine and my own fly too fast to keep pace with you."

"So does Rosengart's," Tony said rebelliously. "He keeps running into me."

"Honestly, Tony, you are insupportably insolent," Lady Frith exclaimed. "Well, I suppose you and Stella could change over and he could fly with her—"

"No. No, I'm sorry I said anything. Never mind."

Tony stormed off toward his own plane, and Bazille followed him.

Pim sat down beside me with a cup of coffee.

"I hope you slept well last night," he said gravely.

"I'm all right." I glanced at him. "I can't thank you enough."

Pim flashed me his fierce, gleaming smile. "I am happy to help. I think you would do the same for me. Or for any of us."

Sebastian was supposed to leave with Lady Frith in the first group, just as they'd done the day before. He went to check his Jungmann one last time before his departure: rudder, ailerons, landing gear, engine oil. Rosengart paced at his heels like a deerhound.

Across the airfield I suddenly saw Sebastian turn to him, white-faced, with one hand raised, holding up the small glass cup of a fuel sample. With the other hand he jabbed an angry pointing finger toward the fuel tank in the front of his plane.

Rosengart reached for the cup, emptied it, and took a fresh sample from the fuel tank overflow valve. He held the gleaming liquid to the sun. His gray hair was highlighted with silver against the sky as he examined the sample thoughtfully.

Then he said something that made Sebastian go very still, as if someone had switched off an electrical heating coil inside him. He'd been incandescent with energetic rage, and now he was frozen.

Rosengart offered the filled sample back to him. He spoke again as he held out his hand.

Sebastian shook his head emphatically.

Then he snatched the glass cup away from Rosengart and emptied it with the furious abandon of despair, contemptuously tracing the air with an arc of bright drops that all vanished before they touched the grass.

36

Knight Moves

Sebastian and Rosengart stood stiffly, both of them ramrod straight as they spoke together, as if they were executing a military drill.

Lady Frith was on her feet by my desk, gathering her gear and getting ready to walk out to her own plane for her takeoff with Sebastian. Rosengart came toward her, with Sebastian treading heavily in his wake. He looked as if he were about to face a firing squad.

"Leutnant Rainer's fuel appears to be contaminated," Rosengart said calmly. "Perhaps dust from the field entered the tank as they were fueling the machine, or the nozzle may have dragged against the ground. We will discover who is responsible. It is fortunate the boy detected it."

Rosengart gave Sebastian a look of cool assessment.

"I consider his aircraft is now unsafe to fly; no doubt the

engine would fail in the air with such an amount of filth running through it."

Everyone heard.

Erlend and Gaby were supposed to leave in less than half an hour. They exchanged worried looks. Without a word, they both went off to check their own fuel tanks again.

"Oh, give me *strength!*" swore Lady Frith, throwing down her flight bag and thumping the ledger with the takeoff schedules back down on my desk. "Sebastian will have to get his fuel drained and refilled. He can take off last and I'll wait for him. Help me change the lineup, Florian. I think if Ernesto moves up to the first echelon with Torsten, and everyone else moves up a slot, Marcel can take off as planned with Stella after the slower aircraft, and I'll leave with Sebastian whenever he's ready."

Rosengart began repacking his pipe with tobacco as he bent to examine her notes.

I thought he looked tired; but he always seemed a bit weary, as if he were tired of the world. He, too, had probably been up all night—snatching twenty minutes' sleep here and there in nightclubs and taxis and hotel lobbies.

I simply did not understand him.

I glanced at Sebastian, but he didn't meet my eyes. His face was bone-white and hopeless.

In a sudden flash of passion, I hated Florian Rosengart so much I wanted to kill him myself. I wanted *revenge*. Not just for Vittorio and Tony and whatever horrible punishment he was planning for Sebastian, but for everything he'd put *me* through, for *no reason*. For Pim, being used as a pawn; for that bewildered boy who'd been beaten up in the street last night. I wanted to dive on that blasted Albatros Ace from high above

316

and knock Rosengart out of the sky in a *taran* attack, and I didn't care if I died doing it.

The moment of rage passed almost as quickly as it came, and left me feeling as if someone had thumped me in the stomach.

This was no way to prepare for a flight.

I looked around frantically for Bazille and Tony. They were leaning against the lower wing of Tony's Hanriot 436, talking seriously in private together, unaware of the drama that was unfolding over Sebastian's Jungmann. Lady Frith was distracted with Rosengart and the schedule; I leaped up, dodged around the row of desks, and dashed across to Tony's plane.

"Sebastian found flecks of dirt in his fuel," I said breathlessly. "Check yours again, Tony. And check for—" I tried to list all the suspicious things that had happened during the 1929 women's race. "Check nothing's blocking your exhaust, make sure there's no risk of carbon monoxide poisoning, check the magnetos work, check that the fuel tank is actually full of fuel and hasn't accidentally been half drained—"

Bazille didn't tell me I was being hysterical. He nodded gravely and said, "You do the same, child."

———◇———

Erlend and Gaby took off. Torsten and Capitano Ranza followed them. Then went Theodor in the other Jungmann, and Jiri in the Bibi. The mechanics hadn't finished crawling all over Sebastian's plane when the time came for Florian Rosengart and Tony to depart.

Sebastian and I stood close together to watch. He was still white as chalk.

He said, "Rosengart wants me to accuse Tony of sabotage."

"What?"

"That was what we talked about when I told him my fuel was full of specks of earth," Sebastian said. "I said I did not believe Tony would sabotage me, or anyone, and Rosengart made himself clear. I must accuse Antoine Robert of being a cheat—he would have been forbidden to fly today, held here while they tried to discover the truth—and I would continue to Amsterdam with everyone else after they have drained and refilled my fuel."

Rosengart's Ace was taxiing. Tony's engine was running, but his plane didn't move.

"I refused to cooperate with this plan," Sebastian said bleakly.

"What's going to happen, then?"

"They will take a long time to refuel my plane. They will find something else wrong with it. I will not be able to fly today. The crowd will go home, disappointed, and other consequences will follow. I do not know what those consequences will be."

Rosengart's plane lifted from the runway, and Tony's engine stopped, with his plane still on the ground.

In the sudden silence, we watched Tony climb out of his Hanriot 436 and wave to the spectators. He slung his flight bag over his shoulder and casually loped across the field to Marcel Bazille's aircraft as if this were the most ordinary of procedures, his uneven gait no more pronounced than it ever was. He said something to Bazille, then stood next to the other Hanriot 436, waving at the crowd and grinning, as if in apology for the delay.

Finally he climbed into Bazille's machine, which was identical to his own except for the paintwork.

"Aha!" Sebastian breathed. "It is like watching a game of chess."

"It is like *being in* a game of chess," I corrected.

Suddenly I saw myself clearly as one of an army of playing pieces. Sebastian and I were the knight and queen to Tony's king, and our fellow racers were the staunch and supportive soldiers protecting him: Bazille the second knight, Pim and Erlend as castles, the other racers a squadron of defensive bishops and pawns. And we were all dashing in desperate leaps and swoops around Tony on a board full of enemies, while he could move no faster than one careful step at a time.

Switching planes at the last minute was another hazardous dodge. Bazille's Hanriot was likely to be fine, and if anything was wrong with Tony's, Bazille would have a little time to get it mended.

But now Tony was going to be alone in the air with the enemy knight, the Blue Topaz, and none of the other players could move to protect him.

Check.

Rosengart was climbing to a holding point high over the airfield, waiting for Tony to take off so they could set their course for Amsterdam together. Lady Frith ran out to have a word with Tony just before he started the engine of Bazille's plane, but she too nodded and waved at the crowd, and seemed to approve the switch.

Tony guided Bazille's Hanriot 436 out to the runway. The little silver plane seemed to leap into the air. It was pure poetry in flight to watch Tony take off, ever the skylark.

Rosengart descended to meet him like a hawk.

Being aware of Florian Rosengart's treachery changed the way I saw the two planes, even though I'd seen those exact same machines racing through the sky together before.

The Ace was bigger, heavier, more powerful, and faster than the Hanriot 436, and as it sped down to meet the smaller plane, it suddenly seemed vast. I stood appalled, bracing myself for the moment when those winged silhouettes would come together.

It was happening again.

The two planes hovered side by side for a second or two, one a little higher than the other. The lark seemed to hang for a moment, still alongside the hawk, exactly like the distant wings ahead of me over the gray rolling waves of the English Channel on the first day of the race.

Then Tony's plane suddenly pitched forward, banking steeply as if to make a sharp turn.

But he didn't straighten his wings.

I watched in frozen and helpless anguish as he plummeted toward the ground in a spiral dive. The Hanriot gathered speed with every corkscrew, spinning down against the blue morning, silver light flashing against the low green wooded hills on the horizon.

And then the silhouette of those slender wings was gone.

"Oh, *what* is that appalling boy up to now?" Lady Frith cried plaintively.

My ears roared.

The roaring was real; it was the delighted clamor of the watching crowd, who hadn't expected aerobatics. The other plane, Rosengart's plane, followed Tony's descent, looking for the vanished Hanriot. Behind me, Lady Frith issued furious orders.

"Yes, Mr. van Leer, you may continue your departure according to this morning's schedule. You'll all be better off staying together, and most of the other contestants are already in the air. And you, Mr. Gekas and Sub-Lieutenant Chudek. You must rendezvous in Amsterdam as planned. I'm sure Mr. Robert is *fine*; he's the world's most dramatic show-off. He'll have pulled up at treetop level where we can't see him, and Major Rosengart will follow him at treetop level if he has to."

"*Didn't you see what he did?*" I cried. "*What Rosengart did?*"

"What Tony did, you mean? For goodness' sake, do be sensible and pull yourself together, Northie! He's clearly trying to lose Florian. A stunt like that will only add pointless seconds to his time."

Lady Frith waved at Capitaine Bazille. "Marcel! Please tell the airport manager I need two more mechanics attending to the corroded support wires on the other Hanriot; it will get the work done twice as fast. I will never forgive myself for not giving these aircraft a proper maintenance check in Nicelli or Prague!"

Corroded support wires.

I realized Tony hadn't breathed a word about it to anyone but Captain Bazille. That was why he'd switched planes at the last moment. He'd even started his engine, just to make sure Rosengart lifted off ahead of him.

But Lady Frith didn't see treachery. She didn't even seem to believe in the sabotage.

It's a lot of smoke with no damn trace of a fire.

I realized that without cold hard proof she wasn't ever going to see it, because she didn't want to.

321

Sebastian was still standing next to me. I turned to look at him, and he was staring at the sky, his hands clenched in fists at his sides.

I said to him, "Come with me."

He didn't answer aloud. He jerked his head once as if giving a brusque nod, but it might have been the formal ghost of a bow.

"I'm going to take off now," I told him. "I'm not going to wait my turn—I'm going to look for Tony, just in case he crashed. Come swing the propeller for me so I don't have to waste time getting permission from anyone."

What else can they damage? I wondered as we sprinted for the Cadet, desperately trying to construct a checklist in my head for such a thing as sabotage. I tried to remember what I'd told Tony to look for.

I quickly checked my own supporting wires and they looked fine; there was nothing blocking the pitot tube. The Cadet's fuel seemed clear and full, no dirt or water in it; there were no smoldering cigarette ends in my flight bag. I climbed into the cockpit.

"Magnetos?" Sebastian asked briefly.

He was obviously doing the same thing in his own head.

"I checked." I took a deep breath and said again, "Come with me. Don't try to fly your damaged machine; they'll make sure something else goes wrong with it. Lady Frith's given them two solid hours to turn it into a death trap. Don't wait around with her while an investigation starts, don't give them a chance to arrest you. Come with me now. Come help me find Tony's plane, and if we can't, we'll just fly straight to Amsterdam and get away from this awful place."

322

"You will be disqualified from the race if there is a second pilot in your aircraft," said Sebastian seriously.

I swallowed. I wondered if disgrace in the Olympics of the Air would ruin any chance I had of becoming a British citizen.

But in light of what the Gestapo could do to Sebastian, the thought seemed impossibly selfish. Whatever lay ahead of me, it wouldn't be as difficult as what he faced; or what Tony faced, if he survived this week; or what my parents had faced.

My passport's just a piece of paper. It doesn't tell you anything about me, does it?

"*Bother* the race!" I cried bitterly, and it came out sounding like a sob. I *needed* someone in that second cockpit; I needed a reason to take care, a reason to fly safely. I needed someone in the sky with me. "To hell with the race!"

I glanced over my shoulder. Lady Frith was shouting something in my direction; three airport officials and a man in mechanic's overalls were heading toward my plane.

"Come with me," I repeated. "Quick!"

Sebastian ran to the front of the plane and heaved at the propeller. As the engine leaped into life he scrambled up onto the Cadet's lower wing.

I held out my hand to him.

"*Come with me!*" I shouted.

And he did.

PART FIVE

INVOLVED
IN MANKIND

Sunday, 29 August–
Saturday, 4 September, 1937

A Telegram

Amsterdam, The Netherlands

I flew drenched with sweat, and, at times, dangerously blinded by tears. I had to push my goggles up and wipe the inside of them on my scarf.

For the first few miles I tried to find Tony's plane. He *couldn't* have crashed—the damage would have been obvious in this suburb of Germany's second-largest city, like bomb damage. Just above treetop height, I hugged the red and gray gables and the green lindens, flying so close to the ground I could see children on bicycles and women with prams staring up at me, waving and pointing in alarm or delight. In front of me, Sebastian leaned over the side of his cockpit, squinting into the wind without goggles or flying helmet, as he, too, hunted for some trace of Tony's trail.

We found nothing.

What would Tony do next, I wondered, if he went into that spin on purpose to get away from Rosengart?

I put on speed, wanting to be out of Hamburg. I tore across

gardens, then orchards, then open fields. The tension and precision of flying at such breakneck speed a hair's breadth from the ground was as physically exhausting as sprinting on foot. Breathing hard, I climbed higher into what now seemed to be an empty sky.

But not very high—south of the Elbe River, crossing Lower Saxony and flying southwest toward the Dutch border, the land became low and flat. There wasn't any reason to slow down, so I kept on pushing my speed. I didn't care about the wasted fuel. It was the shortest leg of the entire race and I didn't need to stop.

I didn't care about anything anymore, about *anyone*—

Yes, I did. I cared about Sebastian.

I could see him still craning his neck over the side of the cockpit, scanning the ground below us, the sky ahead of us. There wasn't a thing he could do to help Tony at this point, but he was still looking.

I was responsible for Sebastian, responsible for flying him to freedom safely, to a new life in a new country, just the way Rosario Carreras had made herself responsible for Tony when she'd flown him out of war-torn Spain with the newly healed scars of a thousand stitches, and a new leg, and a new name.

Our choices *mattered*.

———◇———

For the last twenty miles or so before I got to Schiphol Aerodrome, over the flat, shallow waters of the Zuider Zee, I could see another plane ahead of me.

It was steady in my sight directly in front of me, flying

at exactly the same height as I was. I didn't gain on it, and it didn't pull ahead.

It was also heading for Schiphol.

It landed before I did. As I passed over it in the landing pattern, I recognized those trim silver wings.

Suddenly my heart was soaring.

Tony had been flying ahead of me all along.

———◇———

By the time Sebastian and I reached the parking area at Schiphol, the racers who had already landed—everyone except for Pim, Philippos, and Stefan—came galloping across the field toward us from a striped marquee tent set out as a reception area. Sebastian jumped out of the Cadet's front cockpit and stood on the lower wing as I taxied, leaning forward like a figurehead on a ship's prow. He hung on to the nearest strut with one hand and waved at everyone with the other.

I parked next to the silver Hanriot 436, pulling up right beside Tony as I'd done on so many other racing days. He was standing up in his cockpit, waving wildly back at Sebastian.

Sebastian leaped from the wing even before I'd shut down the engine.

"Sebastian!" Erlend cried out. "Look, she has saved *Sebastian!*" He reached out to grab the German boy's hand and shook it hard. "*Sebastian Rainer!*" He didn't let go until Theodor, the Swiss aerobatic pilot, elbowed him out of the way so that he could shake Sebastian's hand as well.

Sebastian blinked, backing up against the side of the Cadet, stunned to find himself a free man in Amsterdam.

Tony also scrambled out of his plane. He shoved past the

reporters, knocking someone's camera to the ground, and stood beneath my wings with his arms open. I catapulted out of the Cadet's cockpit and he swallowed me in a fierce, tight hug, his face buried in my neck. I felt him let out a single sob, his unshaven cheek rough against my chin and his mouth and nose hot against my throat, and for a fraction of a second, nothing else mattered but that he was alive and he had his arms around me.

Gaby Dupont shouted at us in French. It was impossible to make out individual words over the clamor of the reporters' questions.

"*Buckets of blood!* Will you all *belt up!*" I bellowed at them.

Mouths snapped shut in astonishment. Erlend laughed. In the sudden brief silence, Gaby exclaimed, "Could you see each other in the air? Tony landed twenty minutes ahead of schedule— Major Rosengart isn't even here yet! What about you, Miss North? They seem to be confused about your time, because Amsterdam sets their clocks twenty minutes in advance of the rest of Europe, and you took off early and flew like the wind!"

"No, they have already worked out her time, didn't you hear?" Erlend told him. "They announced it over the speakers just as we were running from the tent. Lady Frith telephoned to say that she is going to be late, and she reported that Miss North took off exactly four and a half minutes after Monsieur Robert." Erlend suddenly turned to me and shook my hand as well. "You and Tony have set a record for the race—the fastest leg any of us have flown—and your times matched to the second. *To the second!*" He put his arm around my shoulder. "Come, there are mountains of pastries for us in the tent, and the press is not allowed in."

Theodor and Gaby flanked Sebastian and Tony, and we jostled our way back to the marquee through the excited crowd.

Erlend's words echoed in my head. *Your times matched to the second. To the second!*

We'd flown across Europe together without knowing it.

If we had been five minutes closer to each other, we would have been side by side in the air the whole way to Amsterdam: like a pair of wild geese flying, migrating without passports or even names, unaware of the arbitrary borders of nations.

Oh, the astonishing freedom of wild geese!

———◆———

I was ravenously hungry. Tony and Sebastian crowded close with me at a table full of pastries, and we heaped our plates with Dutch baked goods.

"What happened in Hamburg?" I asked Tony urgently. "Everybody thought you were showing off—but to me it looked exactly like what I saw when that other plane went down over the English Channel. *Exactly.* I thought Rosengart was trying to ram you."

"He didn't try to ram me," Tony answered under his breath, his voice low. "He tried to shoot me."

———◆———

"It must be how he killed Vittorio," I gasped. "I couldn't understand why Vittorio lost control. Rosengart must have shot him."

Something came back to me that Vittorio himself had said during that first bloodthirsty conversation in the queue for the bathroom in Maison-des-Étapes: *He could fly alongside you and shoot you with his pistol. No enemy in his sight ever escaped.*

It was how Rosengart had made his name as a Great War flying ace. Of course it was how he'd killed Vittorio.

"Did he aim at you and *miss?*" I blurted.

"He never fired. I saw the gun and dived," Tony said. "He was lining up alongside my wing. He must have suspected I'd switched planes, but he had to get pretty darn close so he could make sure it was me flying and not Bazille. I dived away from him as sharply as I could, and then I just bluffed, played dead—it's an old combat trick. I let the plane spin down like it was out of control. When I straightened up, I stayed low— hedgehopped, waved at the children."

Tony didn't seem to be as hungry as me or Sebastian; I watched him as he carefully cut an enormous apple-and-cinnamon pastry in two. His knuckles were white around the silver handle of the knife he held. "It's the only leg of the race I didn't need to drop down for more fuel. I lost the jerk and then I just kept going."

"That's exactly what I did," I told him. "I took off to try to find you, but you were five minutes ahead of me. I didn't see you until we were over the Zuider Zee, but I must have been right behind you all across the Netherlands. I was following you the whole way here."

He glanced at me with the ghost of a grin. His face was ashen beneath the panda-like sunburn of a week's flying in an open cockpit. "Like your birds," he said. "Like wild geese."

The sound of another aircraft approaching overhead drowned out anything I might have answered. Sebastian looked up in alarm, as if he expected to be crushed by the wheels and belly of a small plane crashing through the white canvas of the tent.

"That must be Rosengart," Tony said grimly.

"He'll try again," I warned.

"He won't get anywhere near me."

"*He'll try to do it again.*"

"We'd better face the music," Tony growled.

He left his pastry lying on the serving dish. He hadn't eaten a thing.

———◇———

The German chaperone was inhumanly self-possessed, as if absolutely nothing had happened in Hamburg. He shook hands coolly with the Dutch airport manager, thanking him and explaining about the aircraft breakdowns back in Germany. Then he waved to us racers and exclaimed in English and French and German, "Well flown, all of you!"—exactly as he'd done in every other city where we'd landed.

Finally, blue eyes blazing, he called across to Tony in English, "Your handling of troublesome aircraft today has been superb, Monsieur Robert. I am told that you recorded the fastest flight time of the race, in spite of the difficulties you encountered, and I congratulate you."

Tony took it on the chin. "You got told wrong. Miss North was just as fast as me."

"Miss North?" For a moment, Rosengart paused. His face didn't change; his eyes remained hard and bright, but I saw the moment of confusion.

"I took off early," I explained, with infinite poise. "I thought Monsieur Robert's plane had been damaged, and I went to look for it. I took Leutnant Rainer with me as an observer."

What an absolute pantomime! None of us acknowledged anything that had really happened back in Hamburg.

333

I expected questions, bewilderment, a lecture for kidnapping Sebastian—an official disqualification for carrying a passenger, at least. But Rosengart seemed ready to pretend that *nothing at all* had happened or changed in the past eighteen hours. He didn't even *look* at Sebastian.

Pim van Leer was soaring overhead now as he came in to land.

"I'm going back to the tent," Tony said shortly. "I need to get off my feet."

It seemed like the best thing to do: stay as far away from the enemy as possible.

And it was easy, for a little while, because Major Rosengart had so many other things to do. With Lady Frith nearly two hours behind her scheduled arrival time, and Bazille even further behind flying the slower Hanriot once it was repaired, Rosengart was in charge. He had to hold off the press interviews and make sure our hotel transportation was arranged, and give orders for the refueling of our planes; and when all the other racers had arrived, a little less than an hour after I landed, Rosengart handed out our telegrams.

Ordinarily, Lady Frith gave us our congratulatory wire messages just before the day's racing. But today there'd been so much uproar leaving Hamburg that instead of passing out our telegrams that morning, Lady Frith had entrusted them to Major Rosengart. She'd told him to distribute them when everybody else was on the ground in Amsterdam, thinking she might herself be delayed indefinitely in Hamburg.

So, still acting as if nothing had happened, surrounded by reporters in front of the festive tent on the airfield at Schiphol,

Rosengart called out our names and handed our telegrams around as usual.

There was one for Tony. He'd had them before, though I didn't know who sent them. His American grandparents, perhaps, or his French flight students. Florian Rosengart stood looking down at this one, at the printed name on the pink hotel paper, for a long moment. Then he read aloud slowly, as if he were unsure of the French pronunciation, "Monsieur Antoine Robert."

Tony stared at Rosengart as if he'd been given a challenge. He didn't move. I nudged him with my elbow.

He shouldered his way between Stefan and Pim and ungraciously twitched the piece of paper from the chaperone's hand.

"Thanks," he muttered, and retreated to where Sebastian and I were lurking behind everybody else, close to the entrance of the marquee.

Rosengart continued to pass out telegrams to the others. As Tony unfolded his own, I couldn't help peering over his shoulder.

"From Rosario Carreras!" I exclaimed, then lowered my voice in case Rosengart heard me. "From your instructor!"

Tony read the telegram, and then wordlessly let his hand fall so I could see the page.

TEN CUIDADO
EL HOMBRE DE LOS COHETES Y EL TOPACIO
AZUL SON HERMANOS

"What does 'ten cuidado' mean?" I asked.

"Have care." Tony didn't look at me. He was staring at

Florian Rosengart, and the page trembled faintly as he held it up for me. "Or—Watch out. Beware."

The message had been received and printed by the switchboard operator at the hotel in Hamburg, and Lady Frith had placed it in one of her cardboard folders along with everybody else's, and Florian Rosengart had flown to Amsterdam with it in his flight bag—could Rosengart have already read it himself? No, surely not, or he wouldn't have delivered it.

"*Los Cohetes*," I murmured. "Rockets? The man of the rockets—the *Rocketman*—"

"It says, 'Beware,'" Tony whispered. "'The Rocketman and the Blue Topaz are brothers.'"

38

The Traditional Challenge

There was a roar of aircraft engines all around us; a plane was arriving overhead.

Rosengart had finished passing around the telegrams and now stood with Capitano Ranza and an airport official wearing the livery of KLM Airlines, all of them looking up to watch the landing aircraft: it was Lady Frith's Dragon Rapide.

Meanwhile Tony stared numbly at the slip of pink paper in his hand, holding the telegram in a white-knuckled death grip as if he were clutching a handful of grass at the top of a cliff to try to stop himself slipping over the edge.

Beneath the din of engine noise, I heard him say, "I'm going to talk to him."

Sebastian grabbed him by the arm. "To Rosengart? Did you fly too high this morning, and deprive your brain of oxygen? Still there is no evidence against him—he will deny everything!"

"I'm going to talk to him about Hans Rolf." Tony shook Sebastian off. He began to push his way past the other racers again.

I also tried to stop him. "Tony—*don't*—you *know* he has a gun!"

"He won't shoot me point-blank in front of this rabble," Tony said, waving at the reporters contemptuously. "There'd be too much explaining to do afterward. He's good at hiding things, but I don't think he's much of a liar."

Tony already had the crowd's attention. His left leg dragged as he cantered across the field toward Florian Rosengart in a series of uneven hops and skips.

Tony stepped calmly forward and made a formal bow.

"Major Rosengart, I'm sorry," he said clearly. His husky voice was fervent. He sounded like he meant it.

"I know Hans Rolf was your brother," he went on. "I know I forced his plane down. We were enemies at war—you've done it yourself. *You know* how it happens, how there isn't any choice when you're in the air over the battlefield. But I'm sorry."

There was a moment of absolute quiet. Abruptly Tony began to speak in fluent German, accounting for himself with a formal intensity that *was* German.

I believe we are countrymen.

Rosengart listened, his blue eyes wintry as they rested on Tony's face. For a moment or two I didn't even notice the difference in their ages. They were two fighter pilots who'd both flown in combat with the same man, one as his comrade and the other as his enemy.

But Rosengart answered coldly in English, so that everyone could understand what he was saying.

"My brother did not die in combat. He was unjustly executed for treason."

"I know," Tony said, and repeated with force, "I know. *I'm sorry.*"

"I neither need nor want your sympathy," Rosengart said, "nor will I support any discussion of my affairs on this airfield. Good afternoon, Monsieur Robert."

But Tony wouldn't budge. In his stubborn refusal to back down, I saw an echo of the life-and-death battle he'd fought with Rosengart's brother, six months earlier.

"No, you never deal with your affairs on the *ground*," Tony challenged him. "On the ground, you get other thugs to do your dirty work for you. The only place you take action yourself is in the air, but in the sky you'll do anything—ram people, *shoot at them*—"

Rosengart struck him a cracking blow across the face, hitting Tony so hard he fell over.

A babel of astonishment erupted around us. Cameras clicked wildly. Ranza yelled at Rosengart in German; the KLM representative knelt beside Tony, who sat so stunned he didn't react for a few seconds. Suddenly, without any warning, he recovered himself and tried to go for Rosengart's throat. He hurled himself at the older man and bowled him over onto the grass before anyone else had a chance to react. Ranza, the KLM official, and Sebastian all dived in to pull them apart.

Rosengart climbed to his feet, dusted down his jacket, and checked that his pipe was still in one piece.

Tony lunged for Rosengart again, but Ranza and the airport official held him back between strong arms. Dutch newspaper reporters swarmed around Sebastian, hammering him with urgent questions, and Pim came dashing to his aid, shouting at them in Dutch.

"You think revenge is easier than forgiveness?" Tony cried. "If you want a fight, let's have one that's *just between us*. That's the old-fashioned German way, isn't it? A *duel*. Let's you and me do a number together at this air show in Paris tomorrow—a *real old-fashioned dogfight*."

They stared at each other eye to eye for a moment.

Then Rosengart nodded very slowly.

"I am sure we can fly together to finish the show," he said. "I will arrange it with Lady Frith." He drew in a deep breath and added levelly, "*I will look forward to it*."

At that moment Lady Frith also came plunging into the fray.

She'd just got out of her plane. I thought she must have seen everything, and probably heard a good deal of it, too. Like the leading lady of an opera making an entrance, she swept through the crowd in her gleaming silver flight suit, and despite the intensity of her outrage, she managed not to raise her voice.

"*In the name of PEACE!* The race is in the name of peace, *peace!* There will be no dogfighting, for show or otherwise. Tony Roberts, *pull yourself together—*"

And she slapped him across the face too, though not nearly as hard as Rosengart had done.

"We're giving a flight demonstration tomorrow," Tony said sullenly.

Lady Frith turned to Rosengart. "Goodness, Florian, I know full well what a difficult position Sebastian has placed you in by dropping out of the race. You are under tremendous pressure,

340

perhaps more even than I am, and I grant you that Tony's rudeness can be the absolute limit sometimes. But you needn't have struck him quite so hard! In such a public place, too—"

"And I deeply regret it," Rosengart said, with a curt nod to Tony. His blue gaze was tumultuous, but he had regained his control. He started packing his pipe with tobacco again. "I will not tolerate insolence. But his suggestion is sound. If Monsieur Robert would like the challenge of a flight demonstration with an expert, such as Capitaine Bazille and I flew in Geneva, I have no objection."

Tony briefly touched his face with ginger fingers, his cheek and eye socket flaming red where Rosengart's knuckles had slammed against bone. His clear eyes were wide with fury, and bloodshot with physical exhaustion.

Tony turned to Lady Frith. "A flight demonstration," he repeated deliberately. "To finish up the show. You can call it 'Youth and Old Age' or something." He gave Rosengart a sideways glance to see if this little dart had struck home, but the Blue Topaz merely returned his stare through narrowed eyes. "'Young and Old Europe in Flight,'" Tony amended with artful persuasion. "It'll be on the field in Paris and I'll be the toast of France no matter where I come in the race; stick it on at the very end, and the crowd will love it."

"No—no—" I protested, but there was no point in me saying anything—it was like whistling into the wind. Lady Frith seized on the idea. Pim and Sebastian were still being cross-examined by the press, whose attention had already been distracted from Rosengart and Tony as they argued half in German and half in English. Lady Frith's attention was distracted too.

"Eager youth and sober experience in the sky together!"

341

she exclaimed. "France and Germany at peace! And a way to iron out differences—yes, of course we'll save it for the very end. We'll schedule it to be right after your formation flight with Miss North, all right?"

She turned to me and added crisply, "And I shall do everything in my power to showcase your skill and determination during our closing ceremonies tomorrow, Stella; but you must know that you will have to be disqualified."

I swallowed. I'd known this was coming. But there was something deeply final in hearing it spoken aloud.

"I am disappointed, of course," Lady Frith went on, "disappointed that there can't possibly be a win for King and Country. But I'm not the least bit disappointed in *you*, Stella. I've earlier today had three grueling sessions with German police inspectors and Sebastian's commanding officer, and I'm well aware of what you've done for him." She cast a cool eye at Major Rosengart, but left it at that. "No matter what the papers say tomorrow, you've proved your strength as a flier perfectly well against these boys; and you've shown character and integrity above and beyond what air racing could ever call for. I'm terribly proud of you."

I didn't dare say it, but I couldn't help thinking ironically: *This is all so very, very British.*

"Thank you, Lady Frith," I said, for I knew I had to thank her for everything she'd done for me already, even if it was over. "I am so very grateful. Thank you."

◆

The headline in the *Daily Comet* the following morning shouted, "Britain's Own North Star a Guiding Light for Peace."

Lady Frith laughed and wept when she saw it.

While Tony had been ridiculously challenging the German chaperone to a duel, Sebastian and Pim had made it clear to the international press that I'd rescued Sebastian from deportation and death in Nazi Germany. He said he was going to seek refugee status when the race was over. He said he wanted to go to America. He said that *all* of us had helped him.

It changed things. Now that the headlines were trumpeting the racers' ability to work together, Lady Frith decided we didn't need to have the chaperones escorting us on our final day of racing. She told the *Comet* that she planned to take Sebastian to France with her and give him a chance at the controls of her twin-engined Dragon Rapide.

Tony wouldn't have to fly with Florian Rosengart that morning.

"It doesn't matter. He'll get his chance in the air show after we get there," Tony commented darkly, as we waited our turn to go out to our planes and start our engines for the flight from Amsterdam to Paris. His own Hanriot 436 was back in action, delivered in one piece by Capitaine Bazille late the previous afternoon. Tony was still a valid competitor, and Lady Frith thought it would look good for me to finish with everyone else, even if it didn't count.

I wanted to finish, anyway.

"Who do you think you are? Sir Gawain?" I teased, trying to make Tony smile. "You don't have to fly with him today. You don't have to fly with him *ever*. All you have to do is keep away from him until he goes home."

"Do you believe that? He'll come after me now. Anyway, I'm still a murder suspect."

"No, you aren't—don't be absurd. That was only ever the newspapers, and maybe the Gestapo; but we're not in Germany now, and they don't count. There's not even an investigation going on. It's only us who even know for sure it was a murder. The best thing to do is to stay away from him."

"He's a Nazi and a murderer and the best thing to do is to knock him out of the sky," Tony said through his teeth. "And I'll do it, or die trying."

"Don't you dare die trying!"

"I mean, I'll go down fighting," Tony amended bleakly. "You know he's not going to stop. The next time he comes after me, I'm ready for him. That's all."

"If you die trying, I'll have to knock him out of the sky myself," I swore. *"So don't die."*

————◇————

I flew the last leg of the Circuit of Nations Olympics of the Air on my own.

It seemed strange to be on my own.

The route wasn't difficult. Northern France felt familiar beneath me: ripe crops and August woodland, and the ghostly scars of trenches marking the old battlefields. I wondered if the Great War pilots noticed the trench scars as I did, and if so, how dreadfully painful it must be to pass above these gentle fields, reminded of how you fought and killed and left your comrades buried here. When Florian Rosengart crossed this scarred country, was he unable to think of anything other than that he'd once flown over this landscape wingtip to wingtip with his lost brother?

I flew through a crisp and sparkling morning with a northwest tailwind, feeling desolate in the sky by myself.

My passport didn't seem to matter as much now as it did last week. Whether I won or lost this race wouldn't have changed me.

But being in the sky with the other racers *had* changed me. I didn't want to be in the sky alone right now.

I wanted to be with Tony.

And not just for a few minutes over Paris later in the afternoon. I wanted to be with him for longer than that.

I was desperately afraid I wasn't going to get any more. He seemed to be flying on a course headed straight for destruction.

———◇———

The race ended at Le Bourget Airport just outside Paris, where Charles Lindbergh finished his famous transatlantic crossing ten years earlier. Now Le Bourget had a modern terminal so new it wasn't actually completed yet, with soaring glass terraces roped off to everyone except the painters and decorators. But there were hundreds—maybe thousands—of people crowded on the freshly dried concrete, waiting to watch as we flew in. The balconies of the new building were hung with flags of all our nations, and blue-white-and-red bunting for France.

No one in Sebastian's family had come to watch him land in Hamburg, and no one in Tony's family was here to welcome him, either. I wasn't the only one by myself. I waved my small British flag defiantly as I taxied over to the planes that had landed ahead of me, and the spectators roared. With a jolt of astonishment, I realized that there were plenty of British flags in the crowd, wildly waving back at me.

Not just welcoming the pilot representing Britain: *welcoming me.*

345

I felt I'd scarcely set foot on the ground before someone came forward and hung a horseshoe wreath of drooping peachy roses and white asters around my neck. Cameras whirred and popped. There couldn't have been a bigger fuss if I'd just won the race myself, or flown solo to Australia like Amy Johnson, or crossed the Atlantic like Amelia Earhart.

Lady Frith embraced me, her silver flight suit dazzling. She, too, was carrying a Union Jack flag. "Well done, darling, well done! As you haven't family here I thought I should welcome you myself. I wanted something starry for you specially. I could not find anything named 'North Star,' but the roses are Alister Stella Gray, and I was lucky in the asters being just a little early!"

It was so kind, and so unexpected, that childish tears sprang suddenly to my eyes.

But of course I was her protégé, the Flying English Rose. I'd spent the past week keeping so many secrets and struggling so hard to be taken seriously that I'd rather forgotten how much support and faith Lady Frith had *already* committed to me.

"They're lovely!" I bent my nose to the flowers to hide the tears. The cameras clicked furiously. "Thank you. *Thank you.*"

"Come along, the *Comet* is waiting." She took my hand and pulled me with her first to make another dutiful report, and then to be photographed with Camille Chautemps, the French prime minister. Tony had been scheduled to take off last and hadn't arrived yet; of course, he'd have to shake hands with Chautemps too, and I could just imagine what he might have to say about the French socialist government's cravenly neutral stance on the war in Spain.

Chautemps didn't talk to us about Spain, though.

After waving away the photographers, as we stood alone by a podium surrounded by enormous patriotic urns of blue hydrangeas, white lilies, and red carnations, the prime minister said to Lady Frith in grim, quiet French, "We have found the body of your lost racer."

Instinctively, Lady Frith grasped him by both hands.

"Please, tell me quickly," she murmured.

"The map and coordinates that Mademoiselle North supplied were exact," said Monsieur Chautemps. "The coast guard could not have located the spot without them. I have been waiting to tell you myself, Lady Frith, because we did not want the newspapers to speculate and perhaps destroy the case. But you should know that Vittorio Pavesi did not perish because his aircraft crashed."

He kept hold of her hands as if he thought it would help to steady her. Then the French prime minister bent forward and said quietly by her ear, to keep what he said from being overheard by anyone around us, "Vittorio Pavesi was killed by a gunshot wound. There was a nine-millimeter Parabellum cartridge behind his left ear."

We both stared at the statesman blankly, so stunned that neither of us could speak for a moment.

"He was *shot?*" Lady Frith gasped. "*Whilst flying?*"

"It appears so. That is no doubt why he lost control of his aircraft. He could not possibly have fired the shot himself—not from that angle—so it seems that another aircraft must have flown close enough to his for the assassin to be able to take aim at him in flight."

No enemy in his sight ever escaped.

Lady Frith turned to me suddenly, white-faced, and hissed, "*Did you see it happen?*"

"I saw two planes," I whispered. "I didn't know there was a gun!"

"Oh, *Stella!*"

Then she added quietly, "I do understand why you wouldn't ever have mentioned the second plane."

She turned back to Monsieur Chautemps and asked, "Is there special significance to the cartridge used? Can it help an investigation?"

"Indeed it can," Monsieur Chautemps replied grimly. "I believe it is evidence enough to open a case with the International Criminal Police Commission. It is a bullet from a military pistol such as German officers used in the Great War. It seems likely..."

His quiet words were cut off by the rumbling engine of an aircraft arriving overhead. He didn't get a chance to finish the sentence. But neither did he need to.

All three of us looked up. The now-familiar silhouette of the Albatros Ace's double wings circled over the airfield.

Florian Rosengart was just coming in to land.

The Sound of Wings
Paris, France

"Monsieur, do you suspect someone? Oh, don't tell me, I know, damn it all." Lady Frith swore in English. *"It is he.* It is Florian. I see it. Tony did say Florian tried to ram him, but I simply couldn't believe it. Damn him—damn him! And he was ready to blame *Stella* for what happened to Vittorio— *Stella,* of all people—*damn him!"* She was almost inarticulate with rage and betrayal. "But *why?"*

"Mistaken identity," said Monsieur Chautemps simply. "Revenge and passion. Antoine Robert's colleague Rosario Carreras gave us new information on Saturday, but the Italian boy's body was only found yesterday. We waited for the German to arrive in France, as the murder occurred within our waters, and it would make the arrest easier."

"We can't have him arrested *now,"* Lady Frith exclaimed. "There are still racers coming in, there is the awards ceremony and the contestants' flight exhibition—he's supposed to be flying in it himself! Please! What do you recommend we do?"

"We can see to it that he does not leave the airfield this afternoon," said the French prime minister calmly. "I have policemen here already. But I think you are right—it's best we do not alarm him until the public has departed. Certainly he must not fly in the exhibition. Let me tell you quickly what we know—Mademoiselle North, it was your own flight instructor who found the connection."

"*Jean!*" I gasped. "Jean Pemberton? How did she even know what to look for?"

The French prime minister lowered his voice even further. He didn't want anyone else to get any idea of what we were talking about.

"Rosario Carreras asked Jean Pemberton for her help," he explained. "She felt a British pilot would more quickly be able to contact wartime fliers in England than a Spanish visitor could in France. And it seems she was right. Your instructor located a Royal Flying Corps pilot in Manchester, a man who once faced the Blue Topaz in combat. He was shot down by Major Rosengart in 1918, and captured by the Germans afterward; he shared a drink with Rosengart and spoke to him, before being removed to a prisoner-of-war camp."

"Jean went to *Manchester*?" I exclaimed. "This weekend? Did she fly there?"

"She said she drove." Chautemps waved aside my exclamation. "She said the morning was too thick with fog for her to fly, and she did not wish to risk waiting for it to burn off in case she was further delayed."

My head reeled. Jean must have been ten hours on the road, and all to uncover what lay behind the secret past of Florian Rosengart and Hans Rolf.

350

Hans Rolf—

—He was the child of Florian Rosengart's mother and a stepfather who died when Florian was about fifteen. Hans was nine years younger than his brother. They were—

—Oh God, Florian was father and brother to this boy. From the time Hans Rolf was six years old, Florian Rosengart took care of him, provided for him, loved him—*loved him.* They learned to fly in the Great War. They learned to fly together. Hans was seventeen, just my age, and Florian was twenty-six, as Jean was when she taught me to fly.

I remembered what Rosengart had said to me back in Geneva: *I could not have done what I did at that time and survived it, without this friend and comrade flying with me.*

Maybe Rosengart hadn't even known who Tony was when he joined the race. The application would have come from an unknown but talented young pilot, Antoine Robert, representing France. But then Rosengart found Tony's lost stopwatch on Old Sarum Airfield, with "Roborovski" scratched on the rim. The unusual name surely leaped out at him as one of his brother's fourteen victims. He must have instantly made the connections: a young pilot recently wounded in Spain, with an unforgettable Russian name on his stopwatch, and a scar like a ragged piece of string snaking down his throat.

Rosengart was not trying to protect Germany's state secrets. He was not following orders. He was not following rules. He was not following his conscience.

His younger brother died because Tony shot him down.

Rosengart wanted revenge. That was the only thing he cared about anymore.

And I understood him now.

Tony was scheduled to arrive last in Paris.

He didn't, though; he managed to lap Stefan Chudek. With Bazille on Tony's tail, all three of them came in at exactly the same time. Tony circled over the airfield so Stefan could touch down ahead of him.

I lost Tony amid the crowd's roaring welcome, his own press interviews, and his meeting with the prime minister. Lady Frith, sticking close to me, steered me over to the buffet tables before the press had finished with Tony. But finally he found me, as I'd hoped he would, sidling up behind me as I stood waiting in the queue for lunch beneath the snapping flags and bunting.

"Hey, sister, do you know why my date with Rosengart's been canceled?" he growled ominously over my shoulder. "Bazille says I'm only supposed to fly with you this afternoon."

I glanced back at him. Tony's perpetual scowl was not improved by having to squint through his left eye, purple where Rosengart had hit him.

"How can you *see*?"

"I can see fine. Frith got a doctor to test me this morning before she'd let me fly."

I knew he could count on Lady Frith's protection now. I knew that Rosengart wouldn't be allowed in the air again. But once more, I had a hollow feeling of dread in my stomach.

"The French coast guard found Vittorio," I told Tony. "I mean, they found his body. He had—he had a bullet in his head, a German bullet from a Great War pistol..."

I couldn't go on.

352

"Are you serious? Northie?" Tony gave his low, expressive whistle. "*Phew!* Are you sure you're not making it up, just saying it to keep me from flying with Rosengart?"

"He's grounded. They think he killed Vittorio, and I told them he shot at you, too. They're going to make sure he doesn't get anywhere near you. The *prime minister* ordered it."

"Aw, c'mon, I don't believe you. Why didn't he say anything to me about it?"

"You were surrounded by dozens of people when you met him! I only heard because I was with Lady Frith when he told her. She wants to keep it quiet until after the show."

"Northie, look at me—"

I stepped out of line and looked.

We gazed into each other's faces as if we were trying to learn each other by heart, my face tilted up a little, his tilted down.

"You're still worrying about sabotage," he said. "I can tell. But nothing's happened, we're still all right, and if Rosengart's grounded, we'll be *fine* now. Jehoshaphat, we'll be the stars of Lady Frith's air circus, won't we? Flying together right at the end!" That slow, catlike grin appeared and disappeared. "The race is over," he assured me. "Cheer up! *It's over.* C'mon, let's celebrate—there's opera cake and tarte tatin!"

I shook my head, biting my lip. I had the uneasy and superstitious feeling that if I turned away I'd never get to look into his face again.

I couldn't shake off the dread.

The officials keeping an eye on Rosengart had been told to make sure he didn't get anywhere near Tony. But that didn't seem to include the rest of us. Right at this moment, Florian Rosengart was standing at the other end of the buffet, congratulating Theodor and Torsten on finishing the race, as cool as if he knew *nothing* of the events of the past week—as if he'd never been torn with guilt over Vittorio Pavesi's death, or burning with vengeance for Hans Rolf's.

"It's not over till he's been arrested," I said.

———◇———

In a flurry of tears, warmly waving both her hands to the crowd, Lady Frith called for a minute of silence to remember Vittorio Pavesi.

Then she announced the Champion of the Circuit of Nations Olympics of the Air. It was Stefan Chudek of the Polish Air Force: Stefan, in his little workhorse of a Polish RWD-8 training aircraft, the slowest of all our racing planes. Even though Tony had caught up with him so often, after the handicaps were applied, Stefan had come out ahead. Tony came second.

We cheered and hugged one another, all of us jostling shoulders to catch hold of Stefan's nicotine-stained fingers in congratulatory handshakes. The chaperones shook hands with him as well, including Major Rosengart, and Lady Frith presented him with the trophy. "Merci, merci," Stefan said into the microphone, and added in his uncertain French, "This is for the family of Vittorio Pavesi." He kissed the trophy and passed it across to Capitano Ernesto Ranza.

The crowd roared applause, and dozens of white doves were released from the terraces of the new aerodrome.

Lady Frith stared up with her mouth open and her eyes wide, watching as hundreds of white wings soared and fluttered across the airfield and over the green-and-yellow woodland in the distance.

For a moment, it made me *joyous.* I laughed aloud, remembering my first fearless solo flight—the larks, and the silence, and the sound of their trilling. *Doves!*

It was plain Lady Frith hadn't been consulted about the doves. Of course they were the perfect symbol of peace, but now her ten young pilots would have to give flight demonstrations dodging about in a sky full of pigeons.

Tony laughed because I was laughing. In another hour we'd be in the air together.

We waited. Everybody had to wait; no planes could take off or land until the doves had dispersed. For a little while it was oddly quiet, as if we'd all spontaneously embarked on another minute's silence together.

"We'll begin!" Lady Frith finally called over the loud-speakers.

Pim van Leer took off first. He flew low over the air-field and dropped a cascade of poppies over the enraptured audience.

He must have guessed he wasn't going to win the race. He'd flown that morning from Amsterdam laden with these Dutch flowers as a tribute from KLM Airlines. I watched him as he climbed out of his cockpit afterward, pale and serious, and saw the sudden gleam of his flashy smile as Camille Chautemps shook hands with him and thanked him.

Next the fast planes competed against one another in a closed course race of two laps to the Eiffel Tower and back, with an observer in the tower making reports by telephone. The small aircraft tore back and forth making heart-stopping screaming turns, the whole event being over in fifteen minutes. Gaby Dupont won, in his father's Belgian Tipsy B;

he beat Erlend's speedy Breda 25. Erlend jumped out of his plane after they landed, threw his flying helmet in the air, and pulled Gaby into an engulfing hug as if they'd been the best of friends since primary school.

The Swiss pilot, Theodor Vogt, did another aerobatics display, and Stefan showed off precision landing, and there was another race to the Eiffel Tower among the slower aircraft—the Czech Bibi and the Tigerswallow and the Avro Tutor. Philippos Gekas won that, which everybody congratulated him over, knowing how he'd struggled to make good time throughout the week.

Tony and I were the last to perform.

How many times have people checked our aircraft? I wondered. *Surely at least one thousand.*

At Schiphol, the planes had been looked at by teams of mechanics and technicians from KLM as well as from the Fokker aircraft factory. We'd all flown safely from Amsterdam. The Parisian ground crew even made sure my Cadet was full of fuel, getting it ready for the exhibition, and as far as I could tell, the fuel was perfectly as it should be.

I thought afterward that it was probably my own fault that Rosengart turned his attention on *me*.

Perhaps I gave him the final edge of fury that he needed, the inspiration for one sure, perfect way to break Tony into pieces, one last desperate play on the chessboard: taking his opponent's queen.

But I wasn't thinking about Rosengart when I did the thing that made him realize how much I mattered to Tony, just before I strapped on my flying helmet and we walked out to our planes.

Standing with Tony on the blinding, smooth, sunlit sea of fresh white concrete around Le Bourget Airport, I heard Lady Frith announce our names together over the loudspeakers: *Antoine Robert, le jeune pilote français, va voler en formation avec la petite anglaise, l'étoile polaire, Stella North—*

And in flat defiance of Lady Frith, and perhaps to show off a bit for the press, but mainly because I wanted to very much, I stood on my tiptoes and kissed him on the mouth.

It had been building in me ever since I'd felt his warm breath against my hair as we were dancing in the nightclub in Hamburg. I wanted him to know it was all right.

He kissed me back lightly, honestly, generously.

For a moment, it was bliss.

Then he stepped back. The crowd roared.

"Gee, you've done it now, Miss North," Tony said, grinning. "The world is watching."

I glanced over my shoulder at the spectators, and at the podium where Lady Frith stood at the microphone, presiding over the ceremony. She shot me a dagger-edged look that promised fearsome consequences later. I didn't care.

"I'd do it again," I told him. "Wouldn't you?"

He was still grinning. "You bet."

Then the smile faded, and he turned away from me toward the airfield. "After we land, maybe. You know what you're doing, right? I'll take off first and join you at a thousand feet. Then three times around the airfield, a low pass over the crowd, and land. I'll just follow you, but I'll be *tight* on you, and I won't be able to see you very well over my upper wing, so don't lose your nerve or change your speed suddenly."

"I absolutely won't."

"See you, Northie," he said, and walked out to his familiar green plane. He climbed in and yelled for an engine start.

I buckled my helmet and adjusted the strap on my goggles. It was a relief not to have to bother flying with maps and pocket watches and pencils for once.

Just as I reached my own plane, Florian Rosengart crossed over to me.

He put his arm around my waist and said quietly, "I understand you have little experience in this type of display. I will come with you as your safety pilot."

I went hot and cold. *Like hell you will*, I thought in outrage.

Aloud, I said with great dignity, "I don't need a safety pilot."

"You do," said Rosengart, holding me a little tighter, and that is when I realized that he was holding a pistol tight against my rib cage.

40

The Blue Topaz

I t was not a thing that had ever happened to me before.
But I understood what it was—what it felt like and what
it meant—all in a flash, exactly as I'd imagined it yesterday in
Hamburg. When it happened, I knew what it was.

I stood very still, waiting for the next play.

"Get in your aircraft," Rosengart told me quietly. "I
want you in the front cockpit, so our weight is appropriately
distributed."

Tony was already taxiing out to the runway. He couldn't
have seen Rosengart come up behind me.

I didn't move. Tony was gathering speed on the runway; as
I watched, his green-winged Hanriot 436 broke away from the
earth like a balloon let go by a child, rising as effortlessly as if
it were weightless.

In another minute or so, Tony would be circling over the

aerodrome, waiting for me to join him. There might be hope in delaying. If I dragged my feet, someone might come to my rescue; perhaps Marcel Bazille would notice Rosengart and suspect something—

"Get in," Rosengart said firmly, pressing the pistol harder against my rib cage, and I realized all at once that if he *did* shoot me, he could immediately leap into my plane and take off on his own to go after Tony. On the other hand, if Tony realized I was on board, he probably wouldn't risk my life trying to ram my plane.

The scenario in which the Blue Topaz shot me on the ground and then challenged Tony alone in my plane was by far the least attractive.

I climbed reluctantly into the front cockpit and strapped myself in. I was not going to allow Florian Rosengart to try to tip me out of my own machine in inverted flight.

"*Engine start*," Rosengart yelled in French, and a mechanic came running to swing my propeller for me, unaware this hadn't all been planned ahead of time.

"You may fly your agreed pattern," Rosengart called to me through the speaking tube, his voice ringing in my ears, and then the Cadet's small, reliable engine roared to life.

I taxied to the runway with the back of my neck prickling with a new unpleasant sensation, aware of the gun held by the man in the cockpit right behind my head.

I have to do as he tells me, I thought. *I have to stay alive long enough to let Tony know he's here.*

It was incredible how automatically my hands and feet responded to the flight controls, even when my mind was a tumultuous storm of fear and anxiety. The front cockpit of the

Cadet was a little different to the pilot's cockpit in the rear, and the only flying I'd done in the Cadet was training for the race, so I'd always been in the pilot's seat. But I'd done plenty of front-seat flying in other planes as Jean's student, and I automatically noted the shift in weight, the extra power I needed, the different way the upper wing blocked my view of the sky. I took off and climbed, watching the altimeter spin through three hundred, six hundred, eight hundred feet.

My mind hummed frantically: *What is Rosengart planning to do after he kills Tony? Is he going to let me go? He can't fly off to Berlin in my plane; it doesn't have the range.*

But maybe he didn't need to fly all the way to Berlin. He only needed to make it as far as the German border. Yes, I decided in horror, he could easily fly to Germany, maybe even to Frankfurt. I imagined the nightmare of that flight: I'd be a hostage until he decided to shoot me. He could land in a field and get rid of my lifeless body on the way. Who knows how he'd explain the stolen British plane, but by then he'd be safe inside the fortress of his own national boundaries, a Gestapo inspector above the law...

I reached a thousand feet. There wasn't anything I could do but level out as I was supposed to and turn to orbit the airfield.

Suddenly the Hanriot 436 joined me in the air, buffeting the wind beneath my wings. Tony was a shadow and a roar and the scream of wires as he closed in behind me, a presence I could feel through my entire body.

My blood turned to ice as my hands on the stick and my feet on the rudder pedals felt Rosengart wrenching the Cadet out of my control.

"You Nazi snake, it's *my* plane!" I yelled in fury.

I fought him, throwing all my weight against the stick and shoving on power to dive away from the Hanriot. It was a desperate and dangerous thing to do at only a thousand feet. I didn't have the strength to hold out against Rosengart, but I stubbornly refused to let go.

I heard the gunshot over the noise of the engine.

For a fraction of a second, I thought it was the engine misfiring. Then my windscreen shattered as the bullet went through it. Wind and the wash from the propeller swept the shards straight into my face in a storm of glass, and I let go of the control stick instinctively to protect myself. He'd fired his pistol at me.

My goggles saved me from being blinded. Gasping, spitting glass and blood, I cringed as low as I could in the cockpit, picking splinters of glass out of my cheek and lip. Hell's teeth: *broken glass!*

I knew it must have only been a warning shot. If he'd wanted to kill me, he'd have simply reached forward and put a bullet through the back of my head. He wanted me alive, at least until the moment when Tony realized what was going on.

I was completely disoriented now that I wasn't in control of the Cadet, and I craned my neck to peek at the instrument panel. Rosengart was climbing again, at speed, using the absolute limit of the engine's power. I twisted around, trying to see out of the plane without turning myself into a target, but I couldn't do it; I'd have had to raise my head to see outside.

Tony was right on me, exactly as he'd promised, the nose of the Hanriot only a few feet away from the Cadet's lower wing. It was hard for me to see the other plane from the front cockpit; my own wings blocked the view. But Rosengart must be lined up almost directly above Tony. I glanced at the instrument panel again; the Cadet was losing speed ever so slightly. But it was flying perfectly level next to the Hanriot—

No enemy in his sight ever escaped.

Rosengart leaned out and fired.

I heard the shot like another crack above the engine, and this time there was no mistaking the noise of Rosengart's gun. I wrenched at the control stick and slammed on the rudder, putting the plane into a steep turn. For those few seconds, I didn't care if I flew straight into the ground, as long as Florian Rosengart couldn't get another clear shot.

My own wings swept so close to Tony's that the wind between them buffeted both planes. As the nose of the Cadet tipped down, the nose of the Hanriot tipped up. For one terrible second, I could see Tony, his head back and his lips parted as if he were suddenly frozen in a gasp of surprise or agony, his face tilted straight up toward the sky.

He'd been hit.

"Oh please *no!*" I sobbed aloud, and behind me there came another crack of gunfire.

The uncontrolled Hanriot went into a stall.

Then the sky turned over.

The Cadet was diving and Rosengart wasn't trying to stop it. He was jamming the rudder and gripping the control stick, but he wasn't doing anything to correct the descent.

So now I fought, fought with all my strength against the locked rudder and the sluggish flight controls.

Using power, I managed to level out just before I risked hitting the treetops. I tried to gain a little height so I could

363

turn safely to get back to the runway, and I saw Tony's plane slipping out of the sky steeply and much too fast, facing dangerously downwind. It wasn't stalled now, though—it looked like the plane had righted itself and was coming down in a speeding glide like a paper aeroplane.

The Hanriot smashed into the ground nose-first and the front end folded together like an accordion.

I didn't bother lining up with the runway. I was already into wind, and I landed as close as I dared alongside the crumpled Hanriot.

As I scrambled out of my safety harness and jumped from the Cadet's front cockpit and off the lower wing, I saw why Florian Rosengart hadn't interfered with my landing. He was slumped forward into the controls, blood oozing from beneath his flying helmet.

The last crack of gunfire I'd heard over the sound of the engine hadn't been aimed at Tony. Florian Rosengart had shot his enemy and then he'd shot himself.

There were small orange flames licking at the crushed nose of the Hanriot. If the engine was on fire, it might be only a few seconds before the fuel tank blew up.

But Tony was alive.

I could see him frantically struggling to get himself out of his plane. He *had* been controlling that Hanriot 436 as it came down—sort of. He'd managed to get himself onto the ground in one piece, saved from the impact by the pilot's seat being in the rear.

I ran stumbling across to the Hanriot and leaped onto its wing. Tony's left arm hung useless, drenched with blood; he'd been shot through the shoulder. With his right arm he was wrenching awkwardly at his left leg.

"Can't get out—stuck—broken—" he sobbed desperately. *"Take it off—"*

His leg wasn't broken. It wasn't even stuck. He couldn't get out of the plane because he hadn't released the catch on his safety harness. I leaned in and unlatched it for him.

"Come on," I gasped.

He reached up with his uninjured right arm and got it around my neck. With a strength I never could make sense of afterward, I managed to pull him toppling out over the edge of the cockpit.

Tony clung to me with his sound arm around my shoulders. I dragged him to his feet and made him run with me as fast as we could from the burning plane.

We weren't quite fast enough. The blast of the Hanriot's exploding fuel tank swept us both flat on our faces on the new concrete.

Peace
Salisbury, England

I wasn't hurt. I was on my feet again seconds later, frantically shouting in French as the fire engines and ambulances came screaming out to meet us.

"Don't let the press know! Major Rosengart is in my plane—please take him away—Monsieur Robert and I came too close in the air, he lost control as our wings touched—"

There were two medics bent over Tony's arm, and one of them looked up at me sharply.

"But this is a gunshot wound!"

"Please keep it out of the press!" I roared, dreading what would happen when they discovered how the Blue Topaz had died.

I could hear them conferring around me quickly and quietly. The firefighters held back the crowd as the medics parked an ambulance in front of my plane. They loaded Florian Rosengart into it, careful to cover him up and not allow the spectators to see what they were doing.

I realized I was still wearing my goggles. I pulled them off, and someone took me by the shoulders and stared at me in horror.

"But my poor Mam'selle North, your lovely face! *Mon Dieu*—I need tweezers and iodine here—quickly. Are your eyes damaged? Let me see your hands—"

They bundled Tony into a second ambulance and I began to argue furiously about going with him.

They let me, in the end.

I crouched next to him as the ambulance tore away from the aerodrome and began to weave through the Parisian suburbs. Tony lay conscious but with his eyes closed, his face ghastly white beneath the tan and the bruising of yesterday's fight.

They'd cut away the sleeve of his battered leather jacket and flight suit to get at his shoulder. His bare arm was gory with blood, and I saw for the first time the web of ragged scars that clung to his forearm, where he'd had to use it as a shield against Hans Rolf's glass blade.

I couldn't see the new wound because they'd padded it with gauze. But I'd heard them talking, and I knew that Rosengart's bullet had wedged itself between the bone of Tony's upper arm and the socket of his shoulder; they thought his shoulder would have to be dislocated to free the bullet, and hadn't dared to try the procedure there on the airfield.

I felt every cobbled paving stone we rattled over and could not imagine the agony he must be enduring. I watched his face, all his being lost behind his closed eyes and that familiar, haunting, private mask of unfathomable suffering that could not be shared, the agony of being alone.

I slipped my shaking fingers alongside his and curled them gently around his limp hand.

He didn't try to talk or turn his head. But the anguish in his expression softened. His forehead smoothed; the thick, dark brows drew apart a fraction; his jaw relaxed. It was as if he'd been given a shot of morphine.

Then—oh, then—the tips of his fingers responded to my touch. He answered me with the faintest of pressure around my trembling hand, and gradually my own shaking fingers began to fall still.

No—not like morphine. It wasn't like morphine at all. It wasn't just a dulling of pain.

In our clasped hands there was the beginning of strength, and healing.

For both of us.

———◇———

Who am I?

Stella Valeryevna Severova—

Stella North, Britain's North Star. Northie.

The Flying English Rose.

A refugee. A daughter of dead parents. A niece of a living aunt and uncle. An egg collector. A schoolgirl.

A bird lover. A cataloger for the British Museum. A pilot.

A woman and a pilot.

A woman. A friend.

How many lives besides mine, I wondered, have actually been changed forever in the last two weeks of that August?

Stefan Chudek's, no doubt; the prizes for the race would make him rich and give him his own plane. He was a hero and an advocate for the Polish Air Force, a true national celebrity in a way I never could have been had I won for Britain.

And the changes in Sebastian Rainer's life dizzied me—he'd gone from a promising young Luftwaffe officer to a penniless refugee. The mistake he made over the Alps started it off, perhaps, but after that he had made all his own choices.

He was surprisingly buoyant about it. He bought us all extravagant gifts with what little cash he had on him while Lady Frith and I were preoccupied with Tony in the hospital in Paris: for Tony, an engraved silver cigarette case of his own and a French book of sleight-of-hand magic tricks; for me, a silver bracelet with three charms dangling from it, an aeroplane and a compass and a star. And for Lady Frith, a great bouquet of white lilies, for peace. He was determined to go to America; Tony suggested Sebastian stay with his grandparents in New York State. He could undoubtedly find work for a while at the airfield where Tony first learned to fly. Tony sent his people a wire the moment he was out of the hospital and back in the hotel, even before we left Paris, and they said yes within hours.

America! It seemed to me like a dream world.

But I knew it was as real as my own world, full of people to whom it was ordinary, to whom it was home.

I thought and thought about Florian Rosengart, and why he took me along on that last flight when he could have simply shot me on the ground and taken my plane.

I think—I feel in my heart that it's true—that it was a trace of the humane man he'd been throughout most of his life, the man who loved his young brother and who was eaten with guilt over Vittorio Pavesi's death. At the end, he must have believed this was the only way he could get to Tony without killing me. Grounded, he must have known, as surely as I do now, that there was no way out for him; that he'd played himself into a corner, that the International Criminal Police Commission was about to begin an investigation in which he'd be the prime suspect, that this was a final desperate move. By taking me along on that flight, he gave me the chance to land my plane in one piece when he'd finished the dreadful game he'd become so obsessed with finishing.

I thought of Vittorio Pavesi—annoying, blameless, doomed Vittorio Pavesi—the pawn who never made it beyond the opening gambit.

And I thought of Tony.

Who was he?

Anton Vasilievich Roborovski—

Antoine Robert, Tony Roberts.

Tony.

I could only think of him as Tony.

Tony: sullen, scarred, vulnerable, and slow to smile. An endless reel of paradoxes, simple honesty in an inspired con artist: swift to charm old women with the earnest friendliness of a puppy, then panicked at the sound of a Messerschmitt engine. Quick-footed in a foxtrot and slowly limping at the end of the day. A seasoned soldier who somehow remained naive enough to believe that a straightforward apology might stop a war. Clear mild eyes exactly the same gray-green as my own, full of the memory of pain, but gazing with excitement and wonder at the horizon where tomorrow might hold some kind of hope.

A fallen Icarus who still flew with the natural exuberance of a skylark.

For me, Stella North, the race ended nearly where it had begun, in the sprawling old Tudor house Maison-des-Étapes, in the close of Salisbury Cathedral—where, when most of the other racers had flown back home to their various European nations, Lady Frith invited me to spend the following weekend after Tony was let out of the hospital in Paris. She invited Tony there too, for his recuperation, and Sebastian for as long as he needed a place to stop before he began his new life.

If it weren't for poor Vittorio, I almost felt that the terror and exhaustion of the past two weeks were worth it, just for the pleasure of the afternoon spent in Lady Frith's Elizabethan drawing room the day after our return to England. For two precious hours, I sat drinking tea and eating scones with Lady Frith, Jean Pemberton, Rosario Carreras, Sebastian Rainer, and Tony Roberts—*Tony*—all of us rested and recovering in front of the roaring fire in the great hearth with its half-timbered chimney; while outside, thick mist heralding an English autumn hung in the silence of the Salisbury Cathedral Close, hiding the cathedral spire.

August was done. It was September.

If I was still stateless, was there any reason to stay in England, just because it was the only place I knew? I could try anywhere. I didn't quite have the astonishing freedom of wild geese, but I knew now that the arbitrary borders of nations didn't need to dictate where I belonged.

I had spent Thursday morning talking to three professors in the biology department of the Sorbonne, the University of Paris. I was too late to enroll that term, but after describing my cataloging position in London, one of the men I spoke to thought he might be able to arrange a similar place for me with the new zoological park at the Bois de Vincennes in Paris, and then I could apply to begin a degree course in biology the following term. Tony couldn't go back to work until his shoulder had properly healed; I thought we might be able to travel back to France together on the boat train.

I didn't know if I would be able to make any of it happen the way I planned it. But I was as full of excitement and ambition as I'd been when I took my first flying lesson. I'd got here *myself.* I didn't have the least idea what would come next, but I was looking forward to finding out.

Oh, there was such peace in Lady Frith's house! It was the most astonishing contrast to the past two weeks that it made me wonder if her grand scheme of promoting peace in Europe was dreamily thought up while she sat at her quiet writing table, in her beautiful old drawing room, gazing out at the serene spire of Salisbury Cathedral soaring against the blue sky. She must have heard the wireless reports on Nazi aggression and Italian Fascism and the horrors of the civil war in Spain, and thought to herself: *If only people could share the peace in the sky that I see every day, they'd all become friends!*

Of course, she did not account for people bringing their own ancient grudges and secret longings and hidden war wounds and memories of murdered loved ones into her peaceful sky with them.

But some of us did become friends.

What would happen in Spain in the next year? I wondered. *In the next five years? In Europe? In the world?*

I didn't know.

But I knew that I didn't want to be sitting alone at a writing desk surrounded by comfortable fog in the Salisbury Cathedral

372

Close while it was happening—not for longer than a weekend, at any rate. I would far, far rather be out in it, over it, part of it. Flying over the English Channel with Tony in the front cockpit as my passenger, as we had been two days earlier, battered and buoyant: over the sea and under the sky, with Tony's arm in a sling, the Cadet's broken windscreen held together with surgical tape, and my hand steady again on the control stick. Me, gently rocking the wings; Tony, singing "Three O'Clock in the Morning" over the speaking tube.

Whatever happened next, we would both be part of it, in the same sky like a pair of wild geese.

We would fly together.

AUTHOR'S NOTE

(written in a terrifying present and addressed to an unknown future)

Stateless is a story about people desperately hoping that Europe was not about to be plunged into war.

The novel unfolds in August 1937, before the horrific Kristallnacht attacks on German Jews, before the German Reich took over Austria and Czechoslovakia while the other Great Powers of Europe watched and did nothing, before the invasion of Poland by the German Reich and the Soviet Union in 1939. It was impossible, as I was writing, to ignore that the 1937 setting was on the brink of events that would alter civilization forever. During the two years that I worked on the novel, between May 2020 and March 2022, it felt rather as if I were writing a book set in the autumn of 2019, before the COVID-19 pandemic and the Russian invasion of Ukraine.

It's astonishing to think how much the world in general, and Europe in particular, changed between 1937 and 1947: the devastation of World War II followed by the Cold War setting in, Germany divided, the Iron Curtain descending, Spain becoming a fascist state for forty years. But though the years before and after World War II were transformative, Europe hasn't stopped evolving. The Berlin Wall came down in 1989, and the two parts of a broken Germany were reunited as one exemplary forward-thinking state. The Iron Curtain lifted and the Soviet satellite states became independent. As I write, another horrific war is unfolding in Ukraine that is again affecting the entire world.

Some years ago, one of my editors begged me to write a "golden-age-of-flying novel." I promised I would do that when I finished the Code Name Verity cycle with *The Pearl Thief* and *The Enigma Game*, and *Stateless* is my delivery of that promise. But it is also a tribute to Europe, of which I am an adopted citizen, using the 1930s as a dark mirror for the time of my writing: a Europe poised in denial and disbelief on the edge of an unthinkably ugly future, but clinging to the idea of peace even while war is already raging within its borders. Europe in the 1930s, as now, was also a place of innovation and energy and hope. I've tried to capture that heady atmosphere, and what better way to celebrate youthful exuberance than with an air race?

Air racing in the first half of the twentieth century was a natural result of the development of the aircraft industry. From the moment of the Wright Brothers' first powered flight on 17 December 1903, there began a never-ending competition to design faster, bigger, more efficient planes, and to prove their capabilities. Much of the first thirty years of flight was caught up in record setting and record breaking, and racing was a natural outlet for new planes to set speed records. By the 1930s, women were beginning to compete alongside men in these races.

In researching *Stateless*, I struggled to find solid accounts and descriptions of any air race other than the 1929 Women's Air Derby in the USA. This was the first all-women's long-distance air race, often referred to as the Powder Puff Derby—because women wear makeup, get it? I ended up reading several books about this race, notably Steve Sheinkin's excellent *Born to Fly*, and certain aspects of the 1929 Women's Air Derby are reflected in *Stateless*: the daily race leg filled with mishap, the endlessly repeated banquet at the end of an exhausting day in the air, the harassment of the press, the battle for women to be taken as seriously as men—and the tragedy.

One thing about the 1930s that I struggle to get my head around is that it was much more ordinary then for a woman to fly than it is now. In Britain and the USA, to be sure, she would usually have had to be a wealthy woman—often the daughter of rich parents who could afford to buy her a plane, or at least pay for her flying lessons. Women competed against men in air races in Europe and America; Winifred Brown won the British King's Cup Race in 1930, and in 1936 Louise Thaden and Blanche Noyes, flying together, won the American Bendix Trophy in the first year it was opened to women. Lady Heath, the celebrated Irish aviator on whom Lady Frith is very loosely based (Lady Heath is *much* more interesting than Lady Frith), sponsored flying scholarships for girls. The British aviation writer Stella Murray encouraged women to take to the air in any way possible (at that time, flying as a passenger was almost as exotic as flying as a pilot; as a passenger in 1928, Amelia Earhart became celebrated for being the first woman to make a nonstop flight across the Atlantic, but it wasn't until 1932 that she became the first woman to make that same flight as a solo pilot).

In the Soviet Union, teenage girls could get state-sponsored flying lessons, and by the end of the 1930s, about a third of Soviet licensed pilots were women. For a western girl, it was just about possible for someone who was hardworking and very determined to put herself in the sky without parental support or independent income. Amy Johnson, Britain's answer to Amelia Earhart, got her start in aviation by working as a secretary and paying for her own lessons. But *staying* in the sky was another matter. For that you needed sponsorship, mechanical skills, and if possible, an instructor's license. For a young, single woman like Stella North in *Stateless*, the support of established and successful pilots like Lady Frith and Jean Pemberton was invaluable.

———◇———

I kept a list of rabbit holes down which I plummeted while researching this book, and I would like to share a few.

Italian telephone tokens, Swiss and Belgian and German breakfast food, the history of streetlights, how cigarette lighters work, *Robo dwarf hamsters*. No, seriously, that's what you get when you google the name Roborovski (go try it). But also: Coca-Cola! It was hugely popular in Nazi Germany—Coke sponsored the 1936 Berlin Olympics. Swing culture! American jazz was banned in Nazi Germany, but of course that didn't actually stop people from listening to it. When World War II began, banned music became a symbol of resistance; arrests and imprisonment followed. The music scene that Stella, Tony, and Sebastian encounter in Hamburg is typical of the time.

And then there's the Nansen passport.

I discovered the Nansen passport through the great

twentieth-century writer Vladimir Nabokov. On a trip to St. Petersburg in 2016, I visited the house where Nabokov grew up. A beloved son in a wealthy, aristocratic Russian family, he was trilingual (he could read and write in English before he could read and write in Russian) and a published poet at seventeen. The events of the revolution drove his family to flee their home country before Nabokov was twenty, and his father was murdered at a political conference in Berlin when Nabokov was twenty-one. I knew all this as I began to write *Stateless*, and I had Vladimir Nabokov in mind as I invented Stella North. Then, when I went to check the details of his background, I found that he had held a Nansen passport after leaving Russia.

In 1922, in the wake of World War I and the Russian famine brought about by revolution and civil war, the Norwegian explorer Fridtjof Nansen, being at that time the High Commissioner for Refugees for the League of Nations, convened an international conference to discuss identity certificates for Russian refugees. He subsequently devised a passport that would allow stateless people to cross national boundaries, a document that eventually became known by his name. The Nansen passport was, at first, chiefly intended to help people who had fled the dying Russia and yet would never be considered citizens of the new Soviet Union, refugees whom politics had inadvertently stripped of citizenship of any nation. Later, people fleeing other nations, such as Armenia, were able to take advantage of it, too. It was a stopgap, heavily restricted, but it was deeply needed. In 1922 Nansen was awarded a Nobel prize for his refugee work, and in 1930, after his death, the League of Nations honored him by giving his name to the newly formed Nansen International Office for Refugees.

I often get asked what it is that draws me to historical fiction, and I keep answering: I'm not drawn to history; I'm drawn to *people*. I'm irresistibly intrigued by extraordinary personalities. (Did I hear you say...Volodymyr Zelenskyy?) Real people feed my frenzy for heroism and villainy, whether I'm looking for something inspirational or something devious, present or past. For instance, in 1898, nineteen-year-old Dorothea Bate walked into the Natural History Museum in London and demanded to be given a job, and *they gave her one*, sorting bird skins in their collection; it was the first step on her life's journey to become a world expert on fossil mammals. It also makes Stella North's first job entirely plausible.

I took my inspiration for Capitaine Marcel Bazille partly from the Black French World War I pilot Pierre Réjon, but mostly from a Frenchman named Raphaël Élizé (who wasn't an aviator). Élizé, like Bazille, was born in Martinique, the grandson of a woman who'd been enslaved, but emigrated to France as he was about to begin high school. He went on to graduate from veterinary school in Lyon—the only Black man enrolled at the time—and served in the French infantry during World War I, receiving the Croix de Guerre. He was a Socialist, and as mayor of Sablé-sur-Sarthe, where he and his wife and daughter were the only Black residents, he became the first Black man to hold political office in modern France. His time as mayor, during the Depression, was invested in community service, and he led the town to form its first kindergarten and community center, as well as build a soccer field and a beautiful public outdoor swimming pool.

I discovered Élizé because I was looking for a prototype for Bazille, someone who would justify my resolution to include a Black aviation hero who'd been a veteran of the First World War in a story taking place in 1937. Everything I learned about Élizé delighted me. But, I thought—goodness, what happened to him when the Nazis invaded France?

You'd think I'd learn to stop crushing on people whose predictably inevitable demise is going to break my heart. When the Nazis occupied France, Élizé joined the French Resistance. He was arrested for subversive activity in 1943 and sent to the concentration camp at Buchenwald. He was killed there, ironically by an Allied bomb attack, in February 1945.

Although I wrote *Stateless* knowing full well that my characters were all going to be plunged into war two years down the line, nothing brought it home to me quite as hard as finding out what happened to Raphaël Élizé. Writing this book, and knowing of the war that lies ahead for them, I sometimes found it difficult to think of my youthful heroes as anything but doomed. A dozen young aviators, all destined to be in their early twenties as World War II begins? Stella's fear that they will all go to war one way or another is prophetic. I like to imagine rosy futures for my characters, but realistically there is little chance of all these fliers making it out alive.

I did not set out to write a book about refugees. This *isn't* a book about refugees; it's a book about belonging, about belonging to no place and every place. If there's one consistent theme running through everything I've ever written, every character I've ever invented, it's that of TCKs—Third Culture Kids. You can loosely define this as people who are raised in cultures other than that of their parents or their nominal nationalities. Many TCKs hold more than one passport; many speak more than one language. Their nationality is their first culture, the place where they're raised is their second, and the "third" is the nebulous one that they share with *others like them*, the cosmopolitan nowhere of not belonging and yet being completely adaptable. The term has been around since the 1950s, coined to describe the children of American citizens working abroad (me! my children!). I have never been a refugee. But more than once I have been an immigrant, a stranger in a strange land, and I know how hard it is to find your place in the world when you don't think you fit in anywhere.

I am writing this author's note in March 2022 for a publication that is scheduled in 2023, and I don't know where to go with my comparisons. The crisis of European refugees that exploded this month, triggered by the war in Ukraine, is of a magnitude not seen since World War II. The same goes for the war being waged there. I don't know what's going to happen to Europe—or to our global community.

But I do know that, like Stella, I want to be an active participant in whatever happens. I want to help. I want to inspire people with my stories, and to work on the ground in our times of crisis with any practical aid that I can afford to give. I want to be part of my world.

No one is an island.

Elizabeth Wein
Sandwick, Shetland
16 March 2022

A FEW RANDOM BOOKS THAT INSPIRED *STATELESS*

FICTION

Dorothy Carter. *Mistress of the Air.* London & Glasgow: The Children's Press, 1953 (1939).

Timothée de Fombelle. *Vango: Between Sky and Earth* (Vango 1). London: Walker Books, 2013 (originally published in French in 2010).

Régis Hautière. Illustrated by Romain Hugault. *Au-delà des nuages [Above the Clouds] 1: Duels.* Veyrier, Switzerland: Paquet, 2006.

———. *Au-delà des nuages [Above the Clouds] 2: Combats.* Veyrier, Switzerland: Paquet, 2007.

Ernest Hemingway. *For Whom the Bell Tolls.* London: Vintage Classics, 2005 (1940).

NONFICTION

Association Passé Simple. *Raphaël Élizé, premier maire de couleur de la France métropolitaine [Raphaël Élizé, first mayor of color in metropolitan France].* St.-Jean-des-Mauvrets, France: Petit Pavé, 2010.

Don Berliner. *History's Most Important Racing Aircraft.* Barnsley, England: Pen and Sword Aviation, 2013.

Lady Heath and Stella Wolfe Murray. *Woman and Flying*. London: John Long, 1929.

Liz Millward. *Women in British Imperial Airspace, 1922–1937*. Montreal: McGill-Queen's University Press, 2008.

George Orwell. *Homage to Catalonia*. London: Penguin Modern Classics, 2000 (1938).

Steve Sheinkin. *Born to Fly: The First Women's Air Race Across America*. New York: Macmillan, 2019.

David Ho

ELIZABETH WEIN

is the holder of a private pilot's license and the
owner of about a thousand maps. She is best
known for her historical fiction about young
women flying in World War II, including the
New York Times bestselling *Code Name Verity*
and *Rose Under Fire*. Elizabeth is also the author
of *A Thousand Sisters: The Heroic Airwomen of
the Soviet Union in World War II*, which was a
finalist for YALSA's 2020 Excellence in Nonfic-
tion for Young Adults Award, and *Cobalt Squadron*, a middle-grade novel set in the Star Wars
universe and connected to the 2017 film *The Last
Jedi*. Elizabeth lives in Scotland and holds both
British and American citizenship. She invites you
to visit her online at elizabethwein.com.